WHEN THERE,S NO MORE ROOM IN HELL II

Luke Duffy

Copyright © 2012 by Luke Duffy
Copyright © 2012 by Severed Press
www.severedpress.com
Cover design: TCO - www.indie-inside.com
All rights reserved. No part of this book may be reproduced or transmitted in any form or by any electronic or mechanical means, including photocopying, recording or by any information and retrieval system, without the written permission of the publisher and author, except where permitted by law.
This novel is a work of fiction. Names, characters, places and incidents are the product of the author's imagination, or are used fictitiously. Any resemblance to actual events, locales or persons, living or dead, is purely coincidental.
ISBN: 978-1480041721

All rights reserved.

1

The waves of the choppy North Sea crashed against the flimsy hull of the small fishing boat. Its faded lime green and blue paintwork contrasted harshly against the mottled brown of the water in the English Channel.

The old engines coughed and sputtered as the boat fought against the never-ending tide that tried to force it back towards the French coast. The boat battled to maintain the forward momentum, ploughing headlong into the waves that threatened to capsize its rickety superstructure. The bow of the vessel dipped and crested as it rode out the heavy seas. One moment it plunged headlong into the bubbling troughs of the rough Channel waters, and the next it would ride high on the white-tipped waves that never ceased to threaten to topple the decrepit craft as its delicate fibreglass and wooden hull toiled to stay afloat.

Stu stood at the helm, straining hard with the wheel, trying to keep the bow aiming in the direction of the English coast. His forearms screamed at him for a release as he clutched tighter to maintain heading as another breaker crashed against the hull, trying to force them off course.

Marcus crouched beside him, attempting to keep his balance as he thumbed the handset of the fishing boat's radio with one hand and adjusted the frequency dials with the other.

"For fuck sake, Stu, try to keep this tub steady will you?" he shouted over the sound of the roaring engines and the howling wind.

"Marcus," Stu screamed in reply, "it's a bag of shit, mate. I'm surprised we've made it this far. This dinghy wasn't cut out for the rough seas of the Channel. I'm almost breaking my arms trying to keep her on course. Any luck with the radio?"

"I'm not sure." Marcus shook his head as he looked at the handset. "If there was anyone answering, I wouldn't be able to hear them anyway. I've tuned it as best I can, but I'm not sure my messages are getting through, or if it's even working."

Stu shook his head, bracing himself at the wheel as another wave struck the hull side on. "Marcus, whether we get comms or not, it doesn't matter. We're in the shit and there's no one to pull us out of it at the other end if we make it. We're on our own. How's Ian doing?"

Marcus looked toward the stern of the boat at the limp figure of his friend, laid out on the wooden deck. Sandra and Sini crouched over him, applying dressings and doing their best to stem the flow of blood from the wounds that he had sustained during the battle in France.

Marcus could see the look of frustration on Sini's face as he tried in vain to stabilise him. Ian lay slumped against the side of the boat, the colour drained from his face. Multiple injuries forced his life sustaining blood from his body, causing a large pool of dark claret to form around him, which swished and bubbled as it mixed with the seawater that spewed in over the side. His lungs and liver were perforated as well as the numerous other injuries he had received to his limbs. He coughed, his head lolling onto his chest as the boat swayed beneath him. Frothy and bright red bloody spittle seeped from his lips as he fought to hang on to life.

Sini, the combat-hardened Serbian who wore battle-scars like medals, turned to Marcus, shaking his head gravely as he realised there was nothing they could do. Dropping the handset to the floor, Marcus scrambled to Ian's side, wincing with his own pain from the injuries caused by the blast that had thrown him through the air during the fight through near the French coast.

"Hey, buddy," he said, staring down into the glazed eyes of Ian, "you made it this far, don't be jacking on me now."

Ian managed a half smile. "Sorry, mate, but I'm done." He reached out and gripped Marcus' sleeve and, with all his effort, he managed to focus on Marcus' eyes. "Listen to me, there's nothing you can do for me. I'm fucked and I'm not going to see dry land." His voice was weak and strained. "Do me one favour, bury me in England? Don't be throwing me overboard; I was never in the Marines." He forced another weak smile.

Marcus could feel the tears flooding his eyes, but still he tried to smile in return. "Don't be daft, you stupid shit. We'll get you sorted soon enough. Just hang on, mate. Once we...."

Ian sputtered what sounded between a cough and a laugh. "Don't try and sugar-coat it, dick-head. Just look after me when I'm done. That's all I ask from you. I don't want to be walking around like that when I'm gone, Marcus." He glanced in disgust over Marcus' shoulder, at an image that only he seemed able to see as he said it, as though an apparition of a walking corpse stood before him.

Bowing his head, Marcus nodded slowly, trying hard not to allow the floodgates to open on the wall of emotion that threatened to burst forth.

With a crack in his voice, he replied, "No worries, mate. I'll see to it that that doesn't happen, Ian. I'll take care of it myself."

"Good good." Ian nodded with a strained smile in appreciation, knowing that he would be dealt with when the time came.

"I know I asked just one favour, Marcus, but there's another. You need to make it home, mate. You have to make it home to your family. Take what's left of this fucked up world and live. We've all come too far to fail at the last hurdle, mate. I'll be dead soon, but you can live for me." His eyes were watery with tears as he spoke. "I'm not scared of dying, Marcus. I'm actually looking forward to the peace and quiet. I think," his breath became shallow and rapid, his grip weakened and his eyes lost focus, "I think it's been a long time coming, mate."

"Ian…Ian stay with me." Marcus' throat tightened and a knot twisted inside his stomach as he saw the change in his friend. From being the robust hard man that he had always known, he could see that Ian was losing his battle by the second. It was like watching an opaque/grey blanket being pulled across Ian's face as his clutch on life became weaker and death grasped him even harder, dragging him away from this world.

Ian's breath gave out and his grip on Marcus' arm was lost as the life ebbed from his body. His eyes glazed over and slowly closed, and his body slumped as Ian, the stocky little tyrant who had never backed down from anything in his life, lost his fight to survive.

Marcus slowly raised himself to his feet and looked around at the expectant faces around him. His eyes met each of theirs, and then he looked back down at the lifeless body of Ian. The howling wind seemed to subside at that moment, and the noise of the sea and the engines of the boat became distant. As the reality of Ian's death settled over him, Marcus felt detached from the world around him. It was as though he had walked through a door. Memories of Ian and their experiences together flitted through his mind at a thousand miles per hour. Images of them both, and the places they had been, vividly sprang up in front of him as though he was leafing through an old photo album. Everything came back to him in an instant: even the sounds and the smells of the places, both good and bad, that they had known together.

Suddenly, the air around him came to life again. The wind screamed in his ears and the boat pitched below his feet. The ocean's spray hit his face and its coldness seemed to snap him back to reality.

Another good friend was gone.

There was no need for an announcement; the boat was small and the look on Marcus' face was plain enough to tell them that Ian was gone.

Sini placed a canvas sheet over the body and nodded to Marcus. "We can wait till we hit the mainland, then we can take care of him."

Marcus nodded in return. The idea of doing what needed to be done with Ian aboard the boat did not seem dignified to him.

The fight on the French mainland had cost them three of their friends. Yan and Ahmed had both been killed during the battle, and Marcus regretted that he could not take care of them in the same way that he could with Ian. Yan had been shot through the head, and Ahmed had been killed in the truck when it was riddled with holes in the ambush. Marcus silently hoped that one of those bullets had hit the ex-Islamic Jihadist in the head, leaving him dead for good. As brutal as it seemed to him, he knew it would be a mercy in the new order of things.

It had been their aggression and complete resignation at an imminent death that had carried them through the battle. They were trapped in a fearsome ambush and none of them had expected to make it out. The team had turned and faced the enemy and charged the positions, screaming and roaring as they ran, encouraging each other and pouring all their firepower onto their ambushers.

Sini, Jim, Hussein, Stu and even Sandra had all fought through, killing as they went and surprisingly, winning the day as their attackers had abandoned their positions and fled.

Marcus had been caught in the blast wave of what he suspected was an RPG or even a mortar round. It sent him hurtling through the air, knocking him out cold as he hit the ground hard. The rest of the team had taken the first positions and Stu ordered Marcus and Ian to be recovered as the enemy fire ebbed and became sporadic. From there, the remaining members of the team had pushed through into dead ground and made their way toward the coast as quickly as possible before the enemy regained their confidence. They grabbed the first thing they thought would stay afloat, which was the decaying hulk of an old fishing boat, and headed for home.

Marcus stood and turned away from the body of Ian. Grimacing with pain as he felt a sharp stab run up his ribs, he fought even harder to control his emotions. He picked up his weapon and began checking it over. He was down to his last magazine.

"I'm in the same boat, Marcus. Excuse the pun, of course," Jim said as he stepped across to him on uneasy legs while the boat took another side on beating from the sea. "I think we're all pretty much out of ammo."

"Yeah, me too, I had to ditch the machine gun at the embankment when it ran dry. All I have is this piece of shit and half a magazine." Sini was clutching a French made sub-machine gun. "I picked it up off one of them bastards as he lay dying and finished him off with it." It was small consolation for the deaths of three of his friends, but Sini always gained some form of satisfaction from killing someone he felt was even remotely responsible for any wrongdoing towards him.

"What are we going to do, boss?" Jim was hoping that Marcus had formed some sort of plan, or at the very least, knew where to head.

Marcus stood, staring out into the Channel as he chewed his lower lip. He struggled to focus his thoughts and he feared that his composure was slipping away from him. The men needed him to lead them now more than ever. His head hurt. His body ached and all the time, he could not stop thinking of the men he had lost. Ian had been as close to him as anyone else had. The loss pulled at him and clouded his thoughts.

He glanced back over his shoulder. Everyone stood watching him expectantly. He looked to the bow of the boat as they crested another wave and recognised the distinct white cliffs of the Southern English coast.

"Marcus..." Stu began to speak, but he was cut off.

"Head to the east of the main harbour," Marcus ordered as he turned to face them. "We need to avoid any trouble from the town." He nodded to Sini who had taken over the helm from Stu. "Jim, get me a full ammunition count and redistribute if necessary. We need as many guns firing as possible in case we have any trouble when we get ashore."

Jim grunted, and busied himself with checking everybody's ammunition and making a tally of their overall strength.

"Once we hit land, what then?" Stu was standing beside Marcus, watching him intently. As always, he saw that the team leader was putting the immediate tactical considerations to the forefront of his mind, leaving all other matters such as grief and fear to be dealt with later. He knew that his friend would be hurting, as they all were, but Stu also knew that Marcus was a born soldier.

Marcus snorted and spat into the bubbling sea swirling around the hull of the boat. "We'll deal with Ian on the beach once we know we're out of immediate danger. After that, I say we should head up the hill toward the army barracks. Do you know it?"

Stu shrugged, "Can't say I do, mate. I didn't even know there were troops based in Dover."

"Yeah, I was based here for a couple of years. It's a complete shit hole and probably a lot worse now, but we're short on options. We'll have a look anyway and see if we can get into the armoury. We won't be able to find more ammunition for the AK's so we'll have to ditch them for British rifles, and maybe even snatch some vehicles and food. If it's still secure, we could even get some rest."

Stu looked concerned. "If it's still secure, then that'll mean that there are probably people still there. You think it's wise going there in that case? There could be trouble, Marcus."

"You mean like France?"

"Well," Stu shifted his feet and looked Marcus in the eye, "well yeah. We don't have the ammunition even to take on the dead, never mind a barracks full of soldiers. People don't seem very hospitable these days and they want to hold onto what they have, even if it means killing for it. Plus, I don't like the idea of fighting my own countrymen anyway."

Marcus bit his lip again and hummed as he considered Stu's point. "Then we had better be on our best behaviour, hadn't we? We will have a look all the same, Stu, but we'll keep our distance to start with. I'll leave the recce to you even, and then you can give me your judgment on it."

"Fair enough," Stu replied.

Land was approaching fast now. Everyone had prepared himself and was ready to launch on to the beach. Marcus couldn't help but feel as though he was about to go into one hell of a fucked up D-Day as they watched the cliffs tower above them and the shingle of the beach draw near.

"Looks pretty clear up ahead," Sini called over his shoulder from behind the wheel. "I can't see any movement on the beach."

"Roger that," Marcus replied and turned to the rest of the team. Jim, Hussein and Sandra stood by the body of Ian, ready to carry him ashore once that the rest had checked to make sure they were clear.

Hussein gave a faint smile, concern in his eyes. "Be careful, Mr. Marcus."

Sini forced the throttle forward, straining the engines and gaining as much power as possible in order to drive the bow of the boat on and up the beach. The sound seemed deafening in Marcus' ears and he involuntarily ducked his head into his shoulders as he imagined someone on the cliff top hearing them and taking an interest.

They were vulnerable on the beach and open to attack from both the dead and the living. For all they knew, Dover might have been turned into a fortress. With the castle and barracks on the high ground, the large harbour at the seafront and the natural lay of the land; it would not have been hard to do for an experienced commander with tactical thinking and enough men and assets.

A jolt and the sound of crunching pebbles beneath the hull as the craft beached itself and came to a shuddering halt, informed them that they had arrived in England.

Sini cut the engine and a moment later, an eerie silence fell over them. All they could hear was the slapping of the waves and the screech of the odd seagull overhead. The shore party stepped onto the bow and the three of them sprang forward and on to the gravel.

Marcus felt the shift of the beach pebbles below his heavy boots as he landed and regained his balance. Bringing his weapon up to his shoulder, he peered over the sight and along the length of the weapon as he moved forward. Everywhere his eyes went, his weapon pointed in the same place. Sini and Stu were doing the exact same thing as they fanned out to cover the immediate area.

Five minutes later, Marcus had the thumbs up from his left and right, as Stu and Sini informed him that the beach was clear.

"Okay, Jim, bring the others in," Marcus hissed into his radio and waved for them to move from the boat. Soon they were all in the shadow of the high cliffs, providing them with a degree of protection.

They remained silent and still for a few minutes as they tuned into their new surroundings. A blur to their left, followed by a thud and loud crunch, accompanied by the sound of pebbles being scattered into the air and clattering against each other as they landed again, forced them all to turn, their weapons raised and ready for the attack.

Just a few metres away, a bulky form lay embedded in a shallow crater in the disturbed sand and pebbles. It moved very slightly and the faint sound of groans and grunts drifted to the team on the wind.

"What the fuck was that?" Stu whispered and he tentatively took a step closer.

Marcus was on his left, also creeping forward. "Careful, Stu,"

It lay there. Its limbs mangled and twisted with the bones protruding and grotesquely pointing out at impossible angles. Its stomach burst open, spilling its contents that now filled the impact crater around it. Its fingers continued to twitch and a hoarse murmur escaped from its shattered face as the one remaining eye focused on Stu.

"Where did it come from?" Jim asked, as he stepped up and peered down at the pitiful sight.

Stu craned his neck and peered up at the cliff top before answering, "Must've taken a nose dive from up there."

Marcus also looked up, squinting at the contrast in light as the sun strained to penetrate the blanket of grey clouds above them. "I didn't see anything up there when we came ashore."

Stu shook his head. "Me neither, but I think this bag of pus certainly saw us and decided to try an overhead assault. Poor bugger. It must've pretty much exploded on impact."

Marcus felt a shudder run down his back at the thought of the thing having a better aim and landing on top of one of them instead of smashing into the shingle. He wiped his face on the back of his sleeve and took a step back.

"Finish it off will you, Stu?"

Stu drew the machete from his assault vest and stepped over the shattered remains of the once human being. A moment later and it was over. He stepped away, wiping the blade of his machete against the moss that clung to a rock, considering how indifferent he had become to the whole thing and some of the things they had seen and done.

They all gathered around the body of Ian, wrapped in the canvas sheet.

Marcus took the shovel off Hussein that they had brought from the boat and began to dig. He did not want to ponder his actions or even really consider what he was doing. He just moved automatically, wanting to get the job over and done with.

They took turns in digging, and within thirty minutes Ian's final resting place was ready.

Jim stabbed the digging tool into the sand and shingle, wiping his brow with the back of his sleeve. He looked up at Marcus. "You ready, brother?" he asked in a solemn voice.

Marcus nodded. "Yeah, let's get it done."

Moving off to one side towards the body of Ian, Marcus drew his pistol. He removed the canvas sheet from the body and gazed down at the pale face of his tough and reliable friend. He sensed the others close up around him. Ian was a friend to them all and they all saw it as their duty to help Marcus in what needed to be done; as much for Ian as for Marcus.

Stu placed his hand on Marcus' shoulder. "You were a great soldier and an even greater friend, Ian. You'll be missed, buddy."

"Sleep well, Ian," Jim added.

Hussein bowed his head, "Rahmat Allah Alayk."

Everyone said his or her farewells. Once Sini had said goodbye, Marcus cleared his throat and began.

"Ian, never once did you let anyone down, either as a friend or as a soldier. You were always there in whatever way we needed you. With a gun, or with a bottle, you were always ready to do your bit; sometimes you had both in your hands." There was a hushed laugh from the group, acknowledging the truth in the comment, and then Marcus continued. "I've always said, 'I have many mates, but only a few friends.' I count you amongst the greatest of friends. Even with all that is going on, the world is a lesser place without you, Ian. I'll miss you, old friend." Marcus leaned forward and patted the cold skin of Ian's cheek. "I'll see you again, mate."

He placed the barrel of the pistol against the side of Ian's head and slowly squeezed the trigger. The crack of the gun echoed around them as the report bounced off the cliffs and then out to sea. Marcus felt the weapon jerk in his hand as the recoil kicked the top slide of the pistol backward. Quickly, he replaced the canvas and the group stood silent for a moment, heads bowed and in their own thoughts.

Without anyone needing to speak, they acted as one and gently lifted Ian between them and carried him the short distance to the grave. Once carefully placed inside, they began to push the sand and pebbles in on top of him. Jim quickly scratched Ian's details, name, age and the letters 'R.I.P', into the blade of the shovel and placed it at the head of the grave, sticking out from the sand as a makeshift gravestone. After a brief moment, they turned and walked away, back toward the cliff face.

They climbed the old worn out wooden steps, partially built into the rock face. At the top, a cool summer breeze that swept toward them from the grasslands and open countryside seemed to regenerate them, as though the journey from Iraq had happened in another lifetime. They walked onto a track and turned west, headed in the direction that Marcus knew the barracks and the castle to be. Soon, they could see the top turrets of Dover Castle nestled in the distance amongst a clump of trees and hills.

Marcus called a halt and the team watched from a distance for any sign of movement up in the battlements of the castle. A road ran from the track they were on to the low ground, alongside the ancient building. If they had approached any closer, they might have been spotted and overlooked from the battlements, a perfect position to spring an ambush.

"I've not seen a soul, Marcus," Stu said as he sat beside him, staring through the binoculars. "What do you think?"

"We've been here for an hour. If anybody was up there, we would've seen some sign by now," Sini suggested.

"Yeah, true," Marcus agreed. "What do you reckon, Jim-Bob?"

Jim shrugged his shoulders and huffed. "I told you, I've always wanted to see Europe, and Britain is famous for its castles. All we have in the States that's even close to it is the Alamo, and that's not much more than a wall now."

Stu turned on him and winked. "Jim, I don't think the fucking gift shop is going to be open today, so you may as well get the idea of sightseeing and souvenirs out of your head."

Jim spat on the ground and then turned to Stu. "I was actually thinking more along the lines of swashbuckling my way like Errol Flynn along the battlements."

"I don't understand what any of you are talking about. Who is Errol Flynn and what is, 'wash-butting' did you say?" Sini looked confused, his eyebrows knitted together.

"Swashbuckling, Sini, you thick communist bastard. It means fighting with swords, or something like that. And Errol Flynn had a mighty sword, or so rumour had it," Stu offered by way of explanation.

"Ah, you mean he was hung like an Arabian Stallion, like you used to say about Nicky back in Baghdad?"

"Apparently so,"

"You British make conversations so difficult at times."

Marcus was grateful that the men of his team could still find a release in their humour and banter after all they had been through; now was a time when a sense of humour would be most in need. The old world was gone and if people were to survive the new one, they would need to have a light heart on occasion.

"So what do you think, Stu, is it a go or no-go for the recce?"

Stu eyed the castle. "Where are the barracks then?"

Marcus pointed to the right of the old medieval building, "Just past it, beyond those trees and on the opposite side of the road. You can't miss it."

"Roger that. I'll take Jim and Hussein with me."

They gave a radio check to one another, and Marcus was happy to hear the sound of Stu's voice through his earpiece. The batteries were low, but they hoped to find new radios soon.

Stu, Jim and Hussein moved off down the hill and along the track until the trees that lined the road obscured them from the view of Marcus and the others. Marcus felt a shiver run the length of his spine and he prayed to the Gods that he had not just sent three more of his men into a trap.

The time dragged on the hilltop as they waited for Stu's return. Marcus knew that they were out of communication's range with their personal radios. On flat open ground, at best, they had a basic planning range of a maximum of one and a half kilometres.

Anticipation grew in their stomachs as they expected to hear the sounds of guns firing and men screaming, but they heard nothing. Two hours later, Marcus heard his radio crackle in his ear.

"Marcus, are you getting me? That's us on our way back to you."

"Roger that, mate."

A while later, Stu stumbled up the hill and crouched at the side of Marcus, panting from the exertion.

"Looks clear to me, mate. We didn't see or hear anything, either from the castle or the barracks. I think they're deserted but we couldn't get as close as we would've liked without exposing ourselves. From what we could tell though, it looks like there's been a fight at some point. A lot of the buildings look dinged up from where we stood. I still think we need to be careful."

Marcus nodded, looking out in the direction of the barracks and forming a picture in his mind of what Stu was telling him. "What about the dead? The walking type that is."

"Yeah, we saw a few knocking about. We dispatched a few stragglers along the way but we didn't see any large crowds of them. But like I said, we couldn't see all that much of the barracks so we can't be sure."

"Okay. We'll just have to be on our toes then."

They huddled around a crude model that Marcus and Stu made in the sand and gave the lay of the land and roads to the others. Marcus worked from memory and Stu confirmed that the model was accurate. After ten minutes, they were ready to move. The plan was to head straight to the main gate, get eyes on the guardhouse and gain an idea of the situation within the compound.

Thirty minutes later, they were crouching amongst the trees at the roadside, and watching the gate. The windows to the guardhouse were broken, doors hung from their hinges and the telltale black marks left from fire discoloured the walls around the window frames. The gate itself, though it had obviously been reinforced and barricaded at some point, now lay across the entrance having been smashed inward.

"Looks like some sort of raid. I don't think it was those walking bags of that did this," Jim thought aloud.

"Hmm, maybe it was a smash and grab? Maybe they took what they needed then left. Otherwise, if they intended on staying, they wouldn't have left the gate wide open, would they?" Stu offered.

Marcus weighed up the sight before them, "Looks that way. We should still have a look all the same. Sini, Jim," he nodded to the pair, "clear the guardroom. We'll use that as our jumping off point."

"What about me, Marcus?" Sandra watched him expectantly, trepidation in her eyes.

"You and Hussein stay with me. You'll cover the rear. Stu, you'll take point once Sini and Jim give the thumbs up."

Sini and Jim approached the guardroom and Marcus watched as they disappeared inside with their weapons at the ready.

"Marcus," Jim's voice came over the radio, "that's the building clear. It's pretty trashed, but secure. No sign of anything to the rear, but we've found something you're going to want to see with your own eyes."

Stu looked up and raised an eyebrow. Marcus motioned for him to lead off, following the same route that Sini and Jim had taken, Sandra and Hussein close behind.

The guardroom was a mess. Furniture was upturned everywhere. Fire damage and the smell of smoke was apparent throughout and the sound of broken glass crunching under foot echoed around the room as Marcus and the rest of his team moved in.

As they passed through the command room, Marcus saw Sini stood by the large heavy door, which he knew led to the holding cells at the rear of the building. Every army barracks has a jail; mainly used to detain drunken soldiers when the police brought them back from the local town. Marcus had personally experienced a night in the guardroom cells on more than a few occasions.

Sini followed on behind as Marcus passed him. Sandra and Hussein remained in the main room to watch for trouble. As soon as they passed into the corridor that housed the cells, the foul smell of decay hit their senses and the hum of the swarming flies could be heard all the way from the doorway.

"Fuck me!" Stu exclaimed as he covered his nose.

At the far end of the corridor, Marcus could see Jim standing at the door to a cell. He looked up at the sound of Stu's voice and shook his head in disgust. He stepped aside, allowing Marcus to see into the room through the hatch in the door.

The smell from within the room assaulted their eyes as much as the horrific vision did. The air was thick with bloated flies, thousands of them. Along the rear wall was the remains of three men. All of them had their hands bound to their feet, rendering them immobile. In the centre of the room, one hand chained to the bed that was bolted to the wall and unable to reach the door, stood two snarling reanimated bodies. They grasped at the air between them and Marcus and wrenched at their restraints. Bile and blood oozed from their gaping mouths as they gnashed their teeth at the meal they could not reach.

"Sweet fucking Jesus," Stu spoke slowly, pronouncing each syllable.

Two of the bodies at the wall were dead. Most of the flesh stripped from their bodies. Streaks of dried blood splattered the wall and created sticky, putrid pools below them. Discarded bones and scraps of clothing lay broken and shredded around them, as they had been torn apart. The third body, unable to move properly because of its bonds, twitched and grunted in its own filth. The contents of its stomach lay strewn out before it, bloated and blue from decay. Its face was little more than a snapping skull, as it too joined in with the wailing chorus of the two standing corpses in its vain attempt to get at the living forms of Marcus and Stu beyond the heavy steel door.

"They're officers," Marcus stated as he struggled to tear his eyes away.

Jim peered into the room again. "How do you know?"

"Their uniforms, that's the Commanding Officer," Marcus pointed to one of the standing reanimated dead. "He has the rank of a Colonel on his shoulder and I'm guessing the others must be his staff. Obviously, whoever did this didn't like officers all that much."

"Me neither, but still, I'd just shoot them and be done with it. Not this."

Stu looked across at Marcus. "What do you think happened?"

Marcus shrugged. "It's obvious. This lot were thrown in here. The three by the wall were tied up and the boss," he nodded to the standing body that wore the Colonel insignia, "and his second in command were shot and left to reanimate, and once they were up again there was nothing the others could do to defend themselves. Yup, I think it's safe to say that they weren't all that popular."

"We can't leave them like this." Stu pulled away from the door and Marcus grunted his agreement.

"What do you suggest? I'm not going in there," Jim retorted.

"I don't know, but we aren't leaving them like that. I'm no big fan of officers either, but they're British soldiers and they don't deserve this." Stu swept his hand toward the door as he spoke through gritted teeth.

"Hey, I hear you, brother," Jim raised his hands in front of him and took a step back. "I'm in agreement with you. I'm just not going in there is all I'm saying."

"We'll take care of it from out here," Sini said from behind.

Marcus nodded. "Yeah, but not until we've checked the rest of the place out and know we're secure. It would be nice to get some weapons and ammunition first."

They moved back towards the command room in silence. Jim sealed the door behind them. The heavy clunk of the lock being slid into place gave a dull echo around the room. Marcus felt a shudder. He remembered that sound all too well.

"It was bad enough seeing what that sick bastard 'Vlad the Impaler' did back in Serbia. Now we see it here, at home," Stu spoke with clear disgust in his voice.

"Hey, Stu, it's the end of the world, buddy. You'll be surprised what people will do to one another when they know there are no consequences. We've seen plenty of that already." Jim's words of wisdom echoed in the silence of the destroyed guardroom.

"Keys..." Marcus stood jingling a bunch in his hand that he had removed from the key press on the wall. "These are marked as the 'Armoury'. Normally, there would be a lockbox full with loaded magazines and a rack of weapons in the guardroom, but I've seen nothing of either."

"Do you think there will still be weapons there?" Sandra asked.

"Well, there's more than one set of keys to an armoury, but the easiest to find would be in the guardroom and they're still here. Anyway, the people who attacked this place must have been heavily armed already in order to be able to take on a barracks filled with soldiers. Maybe they weren't interested in weapons?"

"From the looks of the spent casings all around us, I think they could've been British soldiers also, Marcus. They're all the same calibre, NATO standard. You think it could've been a rogue unit?" Stu was studying a brass bullet case in his fingers and glancing up at the numerous holes in the walls as he spoke.

"Maybe," Marcus agreed, "or it could've also been internal. The lower ranks could've turned on the head shed and then bugged out. Doesn't matter anyway, we'll check the armoury and then the ammunition store and see what's left."

The guardroom lay at the bottom of a hill and a central road ran up through the barracks with the accommodation blocks on the right and the numerous stores and offices on the left. The six of them walked slowly towards the top end of the barracks, constantly glancing left and right as they did so, ready for an attack.

Some buildings had been burned to the ground and the remains of dozens of corpses were strewn along the roadside, festering and slowly rotting in the English summer. The skeletons of destroyed and burnt out vehicles littered the road system within the barracks and piles of used rounds lay scattered on every patch of tarmac. Whatever had happened, there had been a fearsome fight.

At the armoury, they discovered the door was already open. It was actually missing from its hinges, having been blown inward.

"Looks like they wanted weapons after all," Jim pointed out as they approached.

Inside, the room was dark but enough light filtered from the doorway to allow Marcus to identify the caged sections of the armoury that were allocated to each company's compliment of weapons. He drew his torch and began to move deeper into the gloom with his pistol raised in front of him. Stu was close behind him and holding his weapon at the ready. Nothing stirred in the darkness.

"You think there's anything left?" Stu hissed from behind in a whisper.

Marcus did not answer but continued to follow his torch beam as he scanned the cage doors of each part of the armoury. All of them seemed to have been ransacked and he began to lose heart.

The darkness seemed to envelop them. The further into the building they went, the more they had to rely on the torchlight to illuminate their immediate surroundings. The light beam was narrow and Marcus felt the icy hand of fear grasp at the hairs on the back of his neck as his mind imagined all kinds of horrors that lurked just on the peripherals of the torch beam, ready to charge at them at any moment.

A scrape, then a thud from a cage up ahead stopped them in their tracks. The torch beam seemed to become narrower still and the two of them strained their eyes and ears to identify the source of the sound. The noise came again and Marcus had to fight the urge to turn and run from the building, screaming, as he had done as a child.

Stu closed up to him and stepped to his right, his weapon raised and aiming in the direction of the unidentified noise. Together, they stepped forward, carefully placing each boot, avoiding the possibility of losing their footing and crashing to the floor.

They reached the steel gate that they suspected was the entrance to where the noise had come from.

In a low whisper, Marcus counted, "One, two, three..."

Together, they moved through the doorframe and the torch beam flashed as movement darted before them. Two rounds exploded from Stu's weapon, deafening in the confined space of the armoury. Marcus fired also, loosing off at least five rounds into the darkness, adding to the crescendo of noise.

"Shit, what was that?" Stu exclaimed, the panic rising in his voice.

"Wait," Marcus moved his light, "I thought I saw a..."

"Fucking hell, is that a man?" Stu stared at a bloodied pulp in the corner of the enclosure, slumped at the foot of a large wooden table. From the boots that remained attached to its feet, they could tell it had once been a soldier. In the corner of the room, cowering and hissing at them were two feral looking cats. Their coats were matted and greasy, their mouths smeared with blood. On the floor, in the middle of the room, lay another cat, dead and bloodied from the rounds that Marcus and Stu had fired into it.

"They were feeding on this poor bastard." Marcus shone the light back on to the unrecognisable body in the corner.

"But look," Stu's hand grabbed Marcus' forearm and guided the beam to the walls around them, "there's still a few weapons left in here." The light glinted as it hit the dull black metal of weapons still sitting in their racks.

"It looks like we've hit the jackpot, then. Go and grab Sini, tell him to bring some light. We'll grab what we can then hit the ammo store."

They all stood outside the armoury, eight British Army rifles laid out before them. Jim stood, holding one in his hands, scrutinising it with a look of disdain in his eyes.

"What in the name of John Wayne's arse are these then?" He held out the weapon in one hand, wielding it as though it was a child's toy.

"They're SA80's," Stu replied. "British Army issue rifle, same calibre as your M16."

"Yeah, but at least the M16 looks like a rifle. This looks more like a drill of some kind. It's all fucked up. The magazine is in the wrong place."

Stu shook his head as he took the weapon away from his American friend. "It's called a Bull-Pup design you dumb arse redneck. It has more or less the same length barrel and range as the M16, but the weapon is shorter because the magazine is set back from the pistol grip. Size isn't everything, Jim."

"That's not what your Mama said." Jim grinned at Stu.

Sini and Sandra were left to watch over their find while the rest went to find ammunition and magazines for the SA80's.

On their return, they began filling the magazines with the ammunition they had found. There was not much of it, but more than what they had for their old weapons.

"They pretty much cleared out the ammo stores too like they did with the armoury, but we found a couple of crates left," Stu informed Sini.

They discarded the AK47's and filled the pouches in their assault vests with the 5.56mm magazines for their new weapons.

"Got a couple of these little darlings, too," Stu beamed at Sini and presented him with two heavy satchels about the size of a couple of paperback novels.

Sini instantly recognised them and his eyes lit up like a child at Christmas. "Claymores! Oh, Stu, you shouldn't have." He took one of the packages of explosives packed with small steel balls and tucked it away in his tactical vest.

"I knew you'd like them," Stu said with a smile.

Jim checked the garage and came back with a vehicle that was still in working order and fuelled. It was a longer 110 wheelbase, stripped down British Army Land Rover. Tough and reliable, Marcus and Stu knew them well. It had a frame mounted on top and just behind where the driver and commander sat, that was fitted with a cradle for a mounted machine gun. However, with no belt fed weapons to be found in the armoury, they decided that they would resort to operating it with rifles instead. Now that they had a means to fight, and mobility, it was time to search for the finer things; food, clothing and the possibility of rest.

Marcus and his team approached the closest barrack block with caution. Their weapons held at the ready and their eyes scanning in all directions. The shattered glass of the windows and doors crunched under their feet as they travelled, hugging the wall, toward the entrance. Many of the windows had been boarded over and the remains of makeshift barricades were strewn around the entranceway. The doors were splintered and shattered.

"It was the dead that did this," Marcus whispered over his shoulder as he peered through the gaping doorway.

"How do you know?" Sini hissed in reply.

"Because living people, especially heavily armed, would've just blown holes in the walls, just like they did at the armoury. Besides, I'm staring straight at a dead fuck right now."

The upper half of a man, its bloated and fetid entrails trailing behind it, slowly dragged itself along the dark corridor and toward Marcus at the brightly sunlit entranceway. It was no more than ten metres away, and even in the gloom of the building's interior Marcus could see the terrible injuries to its body. The lower jaw was missing and the skin from its back and shoulders had been stripped to the bone. Its tongue dangled from its gaping maw and smacked against the floor with a sickening wet slapping sound as it pulled itself along.

Sini had peered in also and now, he felt the tingles along his spine as he watched the horrific vision slowly edging its way closer to them. "I say we just leave, Marcus."

"This is the closest accommodation block, Sini. It looks more intact that any of the others, and they're all probably full of the dead anyway. At least here, we can just bug out to the vehicle."

"No, I mean we just leave this whole place, Marcus."

"And go where? Right now, we have no food or supplies other than ammunition. We need to rest, too. Better to be here, at the top of the hill where we can see them coming and with an escape route. We need to clear it, floor by floor, and then rebuild the barricade."

Marcus dealt the slithering corpse a blow to the head with the butt of his rifle, putting it down for good. Stu and Jim began clearing the upper floor with Hussein, while Marcus, Sini and Sandra took care of the ground floor. Most of the rooms were empty and it seemed that most of the people that had been inside had escaped through a fire exit at the far end.

Sini reached down and turned the handle to the final door in the corridor. The door swung open and immediately, clutching hands grasped at him. The cold bony fingers reached for his face and closed around his throat. He let out a yelp as he tumbled backward. The rifle in his hands juddered as he loosed a volley of shots into the bodies that fell on top of him as he lost his balance and fell to the floor. He could smell their rotting flesh as they grappled on top of him, gnashing their teeth at his face. Sini and the four bodies became a tangle of struggling and flailing limbs. Biting teeth chomped down into rotted flesh as the corpses chewed into each other, trying to get a mouthful of Sini.

More shots followed and Sini's screams could be heard throughout the building as he struggled to squirm away from under his putrid attackers. Marcus bounded along the corridor, shouting for Sini to get clear of the bodies. He ran with his weapon in the aim and the first pressure taken off the trigger as he prepared to fire into the group. Sini was still writhing on the floor amongst them.

Marcus could not get a clear shot without hitting his friend.

Sini let out another scream as a set of incisors bit down on to his shoulder. Marcus felt his heart skip a beat at the sound and knew what a blood-curdling scream like that meant. Sini, with all the strength of an infuriated grizzly bear, began kicking and punching at the dead faces that continued to lunge at him. He rolled free and scrambled to his feet.

"You motherfuckers. I'll kill you, I'll fucking kill you," he screamed as he began kicking and stomping at the heads of the ghouls that were trying to gain their footings and continue their assault.

Sini was foaming at the mouth and Marcus could see the fire in his eyes as he stepped back and began pumping rounds into the sprawling mass of maggot-infested flesh at his feet. The bullets ripped through them, sending tatters of flesh, bone and clothing flying in all directions. Marcus joined the maelstrom and the deafening roar and smoke from their weapons filled the corridor as the four corpses were reduced to nothing more than a pile of minced meat.

Both rifles clicked empty and, as one, they dropped the magazines from their weapons and loaded full ones in their place. Marcus' ears were ringing as he watched Sini change his magazine. Sini's eyes remained fixed on the dead at his feet, as though he was in a daze.

The noise of pounding feet sounded distant and muffled as Marcus saw Jim, Stu and Hussein sprinting along the corridor from the other end of the barrack block.

"Sini, you okay?"

There was no answer.

"Sini..." Marcus began again.

Sini turned and looked up at Marcus, his eyes staring right through him. He looked back down and then to Marcus again. "The fuckers wanted to eat me!"

Marcus looked at the shoulder that Sini now began frantically uncovering, inspecting the wound. "Did they get you, Sini?" he asked, a feeling of dread creeping up his throat.

Sini was busy pulling the straps of his assault rig away from his shoulder, trying to see the damage.

"Did they bite you, Sini?" Marcus asked, slowly, pronouncing each word clearly.

Sini turned to Marcus, his eyes bulging and looking as though they were about to fall out of their sockets, then his mouth gaped.

"Fuck, Marcus, my rig saved me. They couldn't get through. They bit into the leather of the shoulder strap but didn't get the skin. It hurt but they didn't get me."

Marcus rolled his eyes and let out a breath that he had not realised he had been holding in until that moment. "Jesus, Sini, you had me flapping there."

"You were flapping? I thought I was dead."

Both men began to laugh, a laugh that rang the length of the corridor, the laugh of men that had escaped a situation that should have killed them. It was complete relief. Within seconds, Sini was crouching, his back leaning against the wall as he tried to compose himself.

Later, Marcus and Stu went back to the guardroom to deal with the dead officers. The others offered to help but Marcus insisted they stay behind and gather what equipment they could find. In truth, Marcus and Stu felt duty bound to take care of the tortured British officers personally, having once been part of the same army.

The deserted barrack block provided them with what they needed. There was a lot of clothing and equipment lying about, including more ammunition. Marcus helped to find Sandra and Hussein some suitable boots and clothes while the others loaded the vehicle with what equipment they found inside the accommodation block and parked it close to the doors and then barricaded them inside.

That night, they all slept a long and much needed sleep in one of the communal rooms on the upper floor of the accommodation block.

2

"Remind me again, Stan. Why are we doing this?"

"Because it's a laugh, Kieran, that's why." Stan leaned against the wall staring back at his friend, the wind blowing his ever-growing fringe across his face.

They had been friends for many years. Now, barely out of their teens, Kieran and Stan had first met in high school. After that, with no grades or prospects and very little interest in anything other than getting into trouble and chasing girls, they had remained close. However, what they saw as a close friendship, most other people, particularly their parents, saw as a hindrance to one another, each forever holding the other back.

"No, mate, it was a laugh the first time we did it, but we've been up here for three days now and it's getting stupid. Look at them," Kieran pointed out over the rooftop of the gym that they were standing on and at the ever-growing mass of discoloured and bloated faces below them.

Stan picked up another weight plate, held it out over the edge and like a human version of the crane game, the sort he had played so many times at the fairground, carefully aimed at his target below him.

He looked across at Kieran and grinned. "Are we going to get a big teddy this time?"

He dropped the five-kilogramme plate and watched as it plummeted toward the ground. It smashed into the face of dead woman staring back up at them and dropped her like water, caving her skull inward. "Bull's eye," he screeched with glee, "see, wasn't that funny?"

"The first couple of times, yeah, like when you made that guillotine out of that sheet of metal and chopped that big fucker's head off. That was hilarious. But this is just getting dangerous now, mate." Kieran was pleading for Stan to see logic.

Stan shrugged and huffed then turned to face the weather beaten face of his friend. "What's up, you losing your nerve?"

"To be honest, yes," Kieran took a step closer, inflating his chest and preparing himself for a confrontation. It would not be the first time that they ended up in a tussle over a disagreement. "Look at them." He looked out and motioned with his chin at the dead that filled the parking area in front of the gym. "There are fucking hundreds of them, and there's been more and more turning up by the hour. We spent a whole day lugging all these weights up the stairs from the gym and making enough noise to attract every one of them for miles. Then we made even more noise laughing, shouting and dropping weights on their heads." His voice was raised and getting louder as he fought to make his point. "Now look at it, I got bored of this after an hour but no, you wanted to stay. Well we've stayed long enough, Stan."

Stan blinked as he tried to recover from Kieran's tirade. "Well, what do you want to do?"

"I don't fucking care, mate. I just want out of here. Those smelly bastards have been kicking the shit out of the doors since they got here and if they manage to get in, where are we going to go? Nowhere, because we're stuck on this frigging roof, throwing dumbbells over the side like a couple of dicks, with no other way down."

Biting his lip and looking back over the edge at the crowd below, Stan realised that Kieran had a point. "Should we go somewhere else then?"

Kieran almost punched him in the jaw. "Fuck yeah, I think we should, there's better places than this. There's a supermarket not far from here. I say we have a look."

"Yeah, we can get all the supplies we need and then take a car from the car park."

"Neither of us knows how to drive, dickhead."

"Yes I can."

"Grand theft auto on a PS3 doesn't count, tit."

"Fuck off. Well, why can't you drive?" Stan retorted.

Kieran shrugged, "Because my mum did all the driving for me."

Kieran felt a moment of shame at the fact that he was now twenty years old and he had never made the effort to learn how to drive. Suddenly, he realised that he knew how to do very little for himself. He had been completely dependent on his parents.

They walked toward the roof exit, but not before Stan had landed one last crippling blow to one of the dead with another five-kilogramme weight, and headed down the stairs. Once back inside the gym, they realised just how close they had come to being trapped on the roof.

The doors rocked and rattled as the dead pounded against them from outside. The hinges shifted in their frames and the old plaster around them had begun to crumble. They shared a moment of terrifying realisation as they looked at each other, open mouthed, and then looked back at the old wooden doors that separated them from the horde of flesh yearning reanimated corpses.

"Right, we'll go out the back way and head towards the supermarket." Stan nodded his agreement, his eyes fixed on the steadily weakening door as they moved backward, towards the rear of the gym.

Outside, they scaled the steel fence that backed on to the builder's yard behind the gym. Large stacks of bricks and timber filled the open area, creating a maze that threatened to swallow the two of them up should they find themselves in trouble. It had not occurred to either of them to check from the rooftop of the gymnasium to see whether the coast was clear in the builder's yard. Now, at ground level, and their field of vision blocked by the high piles of building supplies, they had no idea what was around the next corner as they made their way toward, what they presumed, was the main entrance, leading them onto the street.

They passed through a door that led to the reception and pay counter. Two bodies, completely stripped of flesh and covered in tatters of blackened muscle and sinew, lay in the centre of the large room. Bloated flies buzzed angrily around them and Stan and Kieran were swarmed as they entered, the warm putrid air attacking their senses like a thousand knives.

Swatting at the flies and gagging at the stench, they fought their way toward the glass door on the far side, hesitantly stepping over the two grotesque and devoured corpses on the floor. Kieran could see that the street beyond looked clear. He wanted nothing more than to taste the fresh air that lay beyond the pane of glass. He increased his pace and slammed against the door, expecting it to swing open and feel a blast of cool clean air fill his lungs.

The door juddered and reverberated against his weight, but it held fast and Kieran rebounded and stepped back onto Stan's foot. Together, they crumpled to the floor in a heap, Stan's face landing just inches away from the nearest rotted corpse.

He felt the bile and terror rise in his throat together. His eyes widened as he stared into the empty maggot-filled eye sockets of the dead man's head.

"Shit," he screamed as he punched and kicked at the heavier-set Kieran, who lay sprawled on his back above him. "Shit, get off me." He struggled free as his friend also regained his balance and rose to his feet.

"You okay, mate?"

"I nearly landed on that thing," Stan spoke and spat bile at the same time. Wiping his mouth on the back of his sleeve, he turned his eyes away from the corpse, and looked at the door then to Kieran. "What's up with the door?"

Kieran was studying the frame. "It's locked."

"Can we kick it through?"

"We shouldn't."

"Why not, I'm not staying in here."

Kieran was straining his head at the glass door and peering left and right along the street. "If we break the glass, we'll attract more of them." He pointed up the street as he stepped back from the entrance.

"More of them, what do you mean?" Stan rushed to the door and shielding his eyes with his hands to cut out the reflection and to help him see more clearly, he saw slow shambling figures heading towards them from further up the street. "Shit. What are we going to do now?"

"Find the fucking key for a start."

Stan looked bewildered and panic was clear in his eyes. "The key, where will we find that?"

Kieran pointed at the furthest body. Stan followed the line of his finger and saw what Kieran had seen. A loop of keys was still attached at the waistband of what was left of the man's jeans.

"Maybe that's them?"

Stan recoiled with horror. "I'm not touching that thing, mate. I say fuck the noise and kick the door through."

"It's reinforced and double-glazed Stan. By the time we get through, there will have been enough noise to have a hundred of those things on the doorstep."

"Well, you had better hurry up and get the keys then, hadn't you." Stan gave him a gentle push from behind and in the direction of the two bodies.

Kieran stepped forward and over the first. Reaching down with his right hand, and pinching his nose with the thumb and forefinger of his left, he began trying to manipulate the key ring from the belt loop.

With each heave, the body jerked, disturbing the flies and other insects feasting upon it, which then took to the air and, once again, swarmed him. It made a sucking slurping sound as the body shifted in the sticky blood and bodily fluids that had collected in a pool around it. Finally, the keys came free and Kieran almost lost his balance again and came close to colliding with the second body as the momentum of his heave carried him backwards.

Scrambling to the door, and fumbling with the bunch of keys, he began trying each key in the lock. Stan stood at his back, hopping from one foot to the other and craning his neck to see over Kieran's shoulder and into the street. He could see the walkers getting closer.

"Come on. Come on, for fuck's sake, Kieran."

"None of them fit." Kieran was panicking and the keys shook and jingled in his fingers. He glanced up and could now see the faces of the dead closing in on the building they were in. "Fuck it."

He stepped back and began kicking at the lower panel of glass in the door. Grunting with each swing, he continued to pound away. The glass did nothing more than rattle in its frame on the first few attempts, then with a crack and pop, the whole pane shattered into tiny square cubes and flew out all over the floor beyond the shop doorway.

Without any hesitation, both of them ducked and scrambled through the open hole and into the street. Kieran was in the lead with Stan close on his heels. There were more bodies to the left, so they automatically turned right and zigzagged their way through the mounting walking corpses that reached out for them as they sprinted into the open street.

"Which way do we go now, Stan?" Kieran shouted over his shoulder as he managed to side step a lunging pair of hands.

Stan was running as fast as he could and sucking in all the air he could squeeze into his lungs. "Just keep going," he screamed between gulps.

They tore along the road, the houses and buildings to their left and right nothing more than a blur as they zoomed past. They made a sharp left at the bottom of the street that led them into a housing estate. The dead were pursuing them. Though most of them could only stagger along, tripping over themselves as they attempted to give chase; a few were faster and managed to keep sight of their quarry as they tried to flee.

Looking back over his shoulder, Stan saw the runners behind him and felt panic course through his body.

"Shit, they're runners, Kieran," he screamed to his friend out in front.

"Here, turn right here," Kieran replied.

He suddenly changed direction, causing him to hop on his left foot, flailing his arms as the momentum of his run tried to force his body to continue in its original direction. "Come on, Stan, over this fence."

Stan had his head thrown back as he powered forward in Kieran's wake. Kieran was now halfway up the steel mesh fence and scaling it rapidly. Stan could feel himself being left behind. He leaped forward, his hands outstretched as he flung himself toward the barrier. His fingers gripped the steel mesh and his feet began to scurry against it as he followed Kieran up and over into safety.

Stan landed on the other side in a heap and unable to raise himself to his feet. His lungs were fit to burst and he struggled to compose himself.

Kieran stood above him, bent double with his hands on his knees and panting for breath. "I tell you what, considering we've spent so much time at the gym lately, you're out of shape, Stan."

Stan's body began to shudder as he struggled to breathe and laugh at the same time. His body desperately needed air, but between what Kieran had said, and the relief of the moment, he was in convulsions.

Three of the pursuing dead had reached the fence. They slammed heavily against the wire mesh, causing it to shake and rattle under the impact. They gripped the fence and jerked at it with all their might in an attempt to pull it down. The fence did nothing more than shudder and rock in their grasps and held fast.

Stan climbed to his feet. Still panting for air, he approached the fence. He kept a safe distance, though, just in case. He looked back at the dead, staring directly into their lifeless unblinking eyes. Their grey putrid skin, filled with sores and festering with insect lava, sagged and peeled from their skulls as their discoloured and broken teeth bit and chewed at the steel mesh of the fence. They were in frenzy, growling and snarling as they tore at the barrier.

"Ugly demons, aren't they?" Stan spat. "If it wasn't for this fence, Kieran, they would've got me." He turned to his friend and nodded.

Kieran returned the gesture. Between them, that was as close as they would come to anything like a 'thank you'.

"Come on, Stan. Let's get out of here."

Still watching the three corpses at the fence, Stan slowly turned and followed on behind Kieran as he headed away.

The dead moaned and sighed as they watched their meal escape them and disappear into the maze of houses.

The fence led on to a long alleyway that ran between two rows of houses creating a corridor of just a couple of metres wide and hundreds of metres long. The brick walls to the left and right were high and many were overhanging with bushes and weeds, adding to the claustrophobic atmosphere and punctuated at regular intervals with wooden gates that led into the gardens to the rear of the houses. The ground was still old style cobblestones and had been that way since the houses had been built in the early twentieth century.

Stan and Kieran made their way along the alley. The narrowness of the passage heightened their senses and made them nervous. Every gate that they passed could burst open on them, spilling hordes of ravenous ghouls onto them and swallowing them up before they had time to react.

Stan was getting twitchy. "How long is this rat run going to go on for?" he growled from behind Kieran.

"Not far now. I can see the road at the end."

Stan glanced back in the direction they had come. The walls to his left and right seemed to continue forever, slowly narrowing and converging into one another in the distance with no breaks or turns. The alleyway reminded him of the end scene from Star Wars where the final battle takes place in the narrow corridor that travelled the circumference of the Death Star. Only there would be no quick death here. If the dead stumbled upon them, they could be trapped. A shudder ran through his body. *I would rather be fighting against the Imperial Empire right now,* he thought. He quickened his pace; he wanted to be back in the open, anywhere but here.

Kieran stopped and Stan almost stumbled into him. "What, what's up?"

"Shhh," Kieran hissed, holding his index finger to his lips. "I heard something."

Stan began to sweat even more and his eyes darted left and right as he scanned the walls and alleyway around them. "What did you hear?" Without realising it, he had moved in closer to Kieran, like a child wanting to be closer to a parent when it felt scared. He *was* scared.

"I'm not sure. I thought I heard...music."

Stan stepped back, screwing his face, suddenly regaining his masculinity and shrugging away his child like insecurities. "Music, I don't hear anything."

"It's gone now, but I'm sure I heard it." Kieran was still holding his head slightly tilted, trying to pinpoint exactly where he thought he heard the noise.

"Nah, can't be. This place is as dead as a big bag of dead things. Let's keep going. I don't like it in this tube."

Kieran straightened his neck and began to walk on. Stan moved to step off then stopped. Something was coming along the alleyway behind them. He reached forward and grabbed Kieran's arm as he turned to look along the narrow corridor.

Stan stooped as he squinted, trying to see from a better angle. There was definitely something moving. In the distance, a blur seemed to unfold as it approached them. It was approaching fast.

"Shit," Stan's eyes grew wide and he began to back up, "run Kieran." He shouted as he took off along the cobbled path, "Fucking run."

Kieran quickly turned and together, they raced along the alleyway. Both of them ran for their lives, their arms and legs pumping like pistons as they pushed themselves forward. The sounds from behind reached their ears.

The growls and snarls of their hunters became as loud as church bells in their ears. Even the noise of their pursuing footsteps, as they raced along the alley after the two young men, sounded thunderous now.

They were closing fast.

Both Kieran and Stan soon realised they could not outrun them, but they did not slow and neither did those that chased them. In fact, they were gaining ground. Terror tore at them. Their survival instincts were in full swing and their quick subconscious assessment of the situation had told them that they could not fight their way out, so flight was the only option, but even that would not save them.

Stan veered to the right and lunged for a clump of vines that hung over from a garden. He felt the roots pull taut under his weight and he quickly began to heave himself up, using his feet to power himself up the wall. Kieran was following suit alongside him and they both hauled themselves onto the narrow top of the wall, away from the immediate danger at ground level.

They raised themselves to their feet just as the first of their pursuers reached the point at the foot of the wall where they had scaled. The rest soon joined it. The angry pack snapped and growled at them from below, leaping at the rough brick in an attempt to follow Stan and Kieran up the vines.

"Where did they come from?" Kieran gasped.

Stan was catching his breath and nodded down the alley. "We must've walked past them."

Kieran watched as another of the dogs attempted to assault the wall. It forced itself up on its hind legs and catapulted itself into the air, gaining a good four feet of altitude before it crashed back down into the rest of the pack. They barked and bit at one another as they jostled for prime position at the base of the wall, all the while never taking their eyes off Kieran or Stan.

"They must be starving. Look how skinny they are," Stan pointed.

"Yeah," Kieran agreed, "they would've had a real feast with your chubby arse, Stan. Come on let's keep going. We'll follow the wall until we hit the road."

Stan was still watching the pack of hungry, feral dogs circling below them. "Then what? They'll just follow us then get us when we try to climb down. We should go through one of the houses."

Kieran looked into the garden of the house whose wall they were standing on. The windows were dark and revealed nothing of what was on the other side of them. In his mind, he pictured more horrors waiting for them within.

"I'm not getting off this wall unless I know exactly what's inside the house, Stan. Come on, we'll walk along it until we find one that we can see into."

Stan looked down at his feet. The wall was only slightly wider than his foot. "You mean we have to do this balancing act the whole way to the end?"

Kieran glanced back at him as he raised his arms out to the side and began to pin-step along the wall, one foot in front of the other. "Well, if you're going to fall, try and fall that way," he nodded at the gardens to their right, "or you'll be the next best thing to a tin of Pedigree Chum."

Progress was slow and they still had a fair distance to cover. All the while, the pack of hungry dogs kept pace with them, stalking them from the alleyway below. They snarled and growled continuously and occasionally, when Stan or Kieran wobbled and threatened to lose their balance, one would leap into the air snapping its jaws in anticipation of meeting them on their fall.

Both of the young men concentrated hard on where they placed each foot, their arms outstretched to their sides. Everything else around them went unnoticed as they focussed on their balance. The sweat poured from their foreheads and their breaths came in slow, shallow gusts.

They almost completely passed it without noticing and it was only when Stan's ears registered the music that he turned his head; it must have been the music that Kieran had heard earlier.

"Kieran, stop," Stan said urgently from behind.

In the garden to their right, a strange sight greeted them. A large man, topless and sitting in a wheelchair, stared back at them. He wore a pair of sunglasses and clutched an unlit cigar between his teeth. On the table beside him was a bottle of sunscreen, a glass of what looked like orange juice with a straw sticking out from the top and a small set of speakers playing opera music that he switched off when he realised he had been noticed. He looked as if he was on holiday or just enjoying the midday sun in days gone by.

Both Stan and Kieran had to blink a number of times before they were sure that their minds were not playing tricks on them.

The holiday image was soon shattered when their gazes fell upon what the man was holding in his lap. A sawed off double-barrelled shotgun lay across his thighs. His hand gently caressed and rested upon the dull black steel, as though it was a substitute for a cat.

"That's right, boys," the man muttered in their direction, "move along. There's nothing to see." He gave the weapon a reassuring pat.

Stan and Kieran stayed still. The hungry dogs continued to snarl at them from the alleyway below as they too stopped and waited.

Kieran glanced back down at them, and then to the man in the wheelchair. "Look, we don't want anything from you. We just want to get away from them." He nodded in the direction of his feet.

"That's not my problem, and if you don't get away from my wall, I'm going to blow you both off it." Keeping one hand on the shotgun, the man reached for his drink with his other hand and manipulated the straw into his mouth with his tongue before taking a long gulp.

"Look, mate...." Stan began, but the man cut him off.

"I'm not."

Stan became confused and looked to Kieran then back to the man in the garden below them. "You're not what?"

"I'm not your mate," the man replied with a slight smile. Obviously, he had used that one before and never ceased to get a kick out of it when it went the way he wanted it to.

"Okay then, sir," Kieran had his diplomat voice in gear, "all we want is to get away from the dogs. Can we just come down and maybe leave through your front door?"

"Not a chance." He shook his head as he placed his drink back on the table beside the speakers. "You two shit bags are probably looting everywhere in sight and there's no chance of you getting your hands on my stuff."

Stan straightened. "Stuff, what are you on about? We've no interest in anything of yours."

The man pulled a large plastic bag from beneath his wheelchair and placed it on the table. At first the bag just looked green, but Stan realised the plastic was actually transparent and it was the contents that was green.

"Holy shit, look at that for a bag of weed," Stan whistled through his teeth.

"See? My *stuff*," the man said again slowly.

Kieran held his hands out in front of him. "Look, we're not interested in your weed. You've obviously smoked plenty of it. We just want to get away from here. Right, I'm going to climb down from the wall and so is Stan here. Don't shoot us."

The crippled man stiffened in his chair and placed his hand around the handgrip of the shotgun. "Don't you dare come into my garden, I'm warning you."

Kieran and Stan climbed down, ignoring the threatening tone of the man in front of them. They stood with their backs pressed against the wall, their hands raised in front of them.

"Don't shoot. Don't shoot us, mate." Kieran was attempting a soothing tone to his diplomatic voice.

The man began to huff and shake as anger swelled inside him. He slammed his fist down with a crash on the table beside him, causing the speakers and the glass of orange to rattle. With the other hand, he raised the short weapon and pointed it at the two young men who stood before him.

"I told you not to come into my garden. I fucking told you," he ranted.

Stan jumped to his right and ducked as the man in the wheelchair let off the first round. The deafening bang of the gun popped his ears and the fragments of shot slammed into the wall behind him, shattering the outer surface of the brick as he ducked his head towards the ground. His legs continued to carry him forward and the man followed him with the barrel of the weapon, about to squeeze off the second shell.

Kieran ducked to his left as the first shot was fired and he leapt towards the man. In just two bounds, he was upon him.

"You fucking wanker," he screamed as he brought his fist down to connect with the side of the man's head. The impact sent a shock wave along the length of Kieran's arm and up to his shoulder. The man's head jerked to the side and the weight of his body forced him, and his wheelchair, to topple over, the shotgun clattering to the ground as he lost his grip on his only means of defence.

Stan was upright again and he bounded over the sprawled form of the man and his wheelchair and past Kieran, who began to turn and follow, leaving the man dazed and concussed on the floor in a heap.

They barged through the rear door to the house and charged through the kitchen and into the living room, knocking over furniture and ornaments as they went. Stan reached the front door first and wrenched it open.

Kieran followed him along the garden path and out into the street, neither of them losing pace and sprinting along the road.

"That nut-job almost killed you," Kieran huffed as he ran.

Stan was beside him, his feet pounding heavily against the tarmac. "Yeah, but I got this as compensation." He hefted the large plastic bag in front of him so that Kieran could see the marijuana he had just claimed for his troubles.

3

The light shining through the window roused him from his sleep. The shafts of early morning sunlight beamed into the room; the particles of dust that floated through the air danced and drifted through the cascading light as they floated past the window.

Steve quietly cursed himself for not remembering to close the curtains the night before. He tried to close his eyes again, but it was no use. He could still see the harsh sunlight through his eyelids. He could get up and pull the curtains across, but he knew that he would struggle to drift back off now. It was too early, but it was useless to try to go back to sleep.

Lying beside him, Helen slumbered. Steve turned and watched her for a while as she slept. Even in her sleep, she was beautiful. Her black silky hair flawlessly flowed along the curve of her neck and across her shoulders like a dark river running along the course of a pale mountainside. Her unblemished skin glowed in the morning light and gave off radiance that Steve believed he could actually feel. It had been a long time since he had felt it, but he had no doubt about it: he was madly in love with her.

The end of the world had come and Steve had found love there. It made him ask certain questions of himself. *Would he change it? Would he give up Helen for the world to be as it was and the dead to remain dead?* His answer was always the same. He believed it should have troubled him, but it did not. As far as he was concerned, the human race was destined to destroy itself, so why should he feel guilty that he had found a degree of happiness when it happened?

You've been spending too much time around Gary, he thought to himself.

He smiled and began gently stroking her face with the edge of the bed sheet, tickling her and causing her nose to twitch. He continued until her eyes opened and she instinctively rubbed her nose. Her eyes blinked in the bright morning light and then focussed on him. She smiled sleepily and stretched at the same time.

"Morning, sleepy head, you come here often?"

"Now and then," she groaned, "when there's nothing better to do."

Steve squeezed her leg beneath the sheets, making her squeal and giggle as she squirmed and struggled to break free from his grip. Steve rolled on top of her, their faces close as his weight resting upon her. Her breathing was shallow and rapid and Steve could feel the heat between them as they pushed their bodies against each other. He leaned in closer and began kissing her neck. The feel of her soft skin against his lips made his blood rush through his veins. She writhed beneath him at the touch of his gentle kiss.

A knock at the door interrupted them.

"Yeah, who is it?" Steve called out, a tone of annoyance more than evident in his voice as he rolled off from Helen and onto his back, sighing heavily.

"It's Gary." He remained outside and did not bother to open the door. "I need to speak to you, Steve. I'll go and make some coffee."

His voice didn't sound urgent, but Steve knew Gary well enough by now to tell when there was something that needed immediate attention and he knew that Gary would never disturb him this early in the morning over a trivial matter.

"Okay, mate, I'll be down in a minute."

""Right," Gary replied, his voice muffled from behind the door. "I'll see you in a bit for a brew, oh and good morning, Helen."

Helen looked at Steve, slightly embarrassed as she stifled a laugh, "Morning, Gary," called out at the door. "How does he know I'm here?" she asked in a whisper as she looked back at Steve. She had a smile on her face that reminded Steve of a child that had been caught out stealing from the cookie jar.

"You know Gary, he's as sharp as a knife; and anyway, it's a small world these days."

"I suppose, and there is always the gossip. I've heard plenty of interesting stories and conjectures floating about in the kitchen when Karen is in full swing. I think she makes half of them up out of boredom." Helen closed her eyes as she spoke, a faint smile on her face as she thought of times past with nostalgia. "She reminds me of my grandma. She used to know *all* the comings and goings of the street. And if she didn't know the complete facts and details of a particular incident or person, she would make them up to fill the gaps at her weekly tea and biscuit mornings with her neighbours."

Steve smiled and nodded to himself. "Seems that we all had a granny like that, doesn't it?"

"Yeah," Helen replied with a sigh as she pulled herself away from the familiar sights, sounds and smells of her grandmother, "it was never malicious, though. It was just their way."

Steve sat at the edge of the bed, arching and twisting his back, trying to loosen the stiffness in his muscles as he climbed into his jeans that had been discarded there, on the floor, the previous night. He coughed and a look of revulsion at the taste in his mouth crossed his face as he smacked his lips and ran his rough tongue around the inside of his cheeks in an attempt to encourage some moisture.

"You got morning breath?" Helen asked as she stretched across the bed, the sheets falling away from her naked body and giving Steve a reminding view of the reason that he could not keep his hands off her.

"Yup, I had a visit from the Bedtime Troll alright," he said with a nod.

"The, what...?" she asked him, curious to know to what he was referring.

"The Bedtime Troll, everyone has one. They live under your bed. Once you're asleep, he jumps up and brushes your teeth for you with his dick."

Helen burst into fits of laughter. The mental image that she had just created in her own head because of what Steve had said was so vivid it was ludicrous. As she lay on the bed, still laughing uncontrollably, Steve went to the bathroom to wash. She was still red-faced when he returned five minutes later.

"Bring me some coffee when you've finished chatting with Gary?" she requested, throwing him the doe eyes that she had come to realise could win Steve over every time.

"Will do, boss." He pulled a t-shirt over his head and leaned over to kiss her before disappearing out the door, headed for the kitchen.

Gary was sitting at the table with a steaming cup in his hand when Steve entered the room. As always, he looked as though he had been up for hours and probably had. His silvery hair was swept back over his scalp as always and his short white beard perfectly manicured and trimmed. Steve realised that he had never seen Gary in a dishevelled state. Even now, he still insisted on wearing his immaculate Park Ranger uniform with a sense of pride and authority. The end of the world certainly had not caused his standards and dignity to wane.

"So, what's the problem then, old timer?" Steve poured himself a cup, pulled a chair out from the table and sat across from Gary.

"Fuel, that's the problem," Gary replied, sighing and rubbing his beard against the back of his large, shovel-like hand.

Steve looked up from his coffee and squinted. "Fuel, I thought we had plenty?"

"Well, even with everyday usage, it wouldn't last forever, but when I was doing my checks this morning, I noticed a leak."

"How bad is it?"

"Bad enough. We've a fraction of what we should have and I don't think the leak has sprung naturally. Looks more like sabotage." He whispered the word *'sabotage'* and glanced about the room as he said it, double-checking that they were still alone. In a close-knit community, with danger always present, both men knew that just that simple word could cause suspicion and distrust.

A look of alarm crossed Steve's face. "Sabotage? Who would've done it and more to the point, what makes you think that?"

Gary sighed and glanced down into his cup. He spread his hands out on the table and rotated his shoulders in an attempt to release the stiffness, which he was prone to in the mornings.

"Well the knife cuts in the hose were a bit of a giveaway. Not enough to be noticeable immediately, but the diesel has now created enough of a pool around the tank that the ground is turning blue. It's been slowly seeping out for days from what I can tell, maybe longer."

"Shit, well, who?"

Gary leaned back. "Hard to say, isn't it? It could be anyone; somebody from outside or maybe even here, among us."

Steve bit his lip then sipped at his coffee. "Well we can start keeping an eye out on the quiet, but I don't want a Spanish Inquisition going on, and we need to work out what we'll do in the way of replacing the fuel. How long do you think we have left?"

"I would say a week, maybe less. I've repaired the hose as best I can, but because the tank is partially buried, I can't give it a full check over."

"We're going to have to get more then aren't we; there are plenty of stations we could use. Before that, though, I'd like to have an idea of who did it."

"We'll look into it then. Anyway, anymore word on your brother?"

Steve shook his head. He had been trying hard not to dwell on it too much. "Nothing for the last two days. The last we heard was the broken transmissions we got from him."

Over the crackling and faint signals, they had been able to recognise the voice of Marcus. It was obvious that he was not receiving their replies because he kept on repeating himself and asking if anyone could hear him. Jake took over the radio from Steve and begun trying to tune the signal, but it had been no use.

Marcus continued to transmit blind, informing them that they were on a boat and headed for the English coast. The messages were interrupted with static and hard to hear, but from what they could gather; Marcus and his men were pretty banged up. The word 'battle' and 'losses' were clear enough to understand and Steve, Helen and the rest of the people assembled in the little room were able to conclude that they had been through a rough time.

Jennifer, though clearly worried, had taken it well. She knew that they still had a long way to go, but at least Marcus had survived and the fact that he was now in the same country was somewhat of a comfort to her.

She held herself together and busied herself with chores and helping out where she could to keep her mind off it.

Gary took a sip from his coffee then placed the cup back down in front of him. "I know it is hard, Steve, but at least he's alive and he survived the crossing. Maybe he's on the hunt for a new radio. We may hear from him soon, I bet."

"Yeah, I hope so. That's a hell of a long way to have come though, Gary."

Gary nodded. "A hell of a long way and with all this going on, it's a miracle that he has made it as far as he has. It is a testament to his resilience and determination, Steve. He'll make it through and you'll see him again soon, I'm sure of it."

Steve felt comforted by Gary's words. The man never failed to put people's minds at ease around him. "Do you think about your own son?" He felt like kicking himself at the stupidity of the question.

Gary nodded slowly as he stared down at the table. Without raising his head, he replied. "All the time, Steve, all of the time," The sadness in his voice reached deep into Steve and squeezed at his soul. "The last we heard of him, he was trying to get home."

Steve could not find the words of comfort that he needed to give to Gary. What could he tell him, that *it would be all right and his son was safe?* He would not be able to bring himself to tell his friend such a flippant and blatant lie that he did not and could not believe himself.

"I'm sorry, Gary," Steve replied. It was all he could manage at that moment.

Gary nodded slowly and solemnly. "Yeah, me too, Steve." Gary shifted in his seat and took in a deep breath of air that inflated his barrel chest to almost twice its normal size. "Anyway, how's that little Sarah of yours? Is she still up and at them, good and early every morning to go and see the animals waking up?"

Steve smiled and nodded. "Aye, without fail, it's her mum's turn to take her this morning. She'll probably be back soon going on about the lions. I think they're her favourites."

Lee volunteered without any hesitation for the fuel run. "Count me in on that one, mate."

"It's not a jolly that we'll be going on, Lee," Steve reminded him.

"I know, but I'm not letting you leave me out."

The prospect of a change to the routine of daily patrols and checks around the park was a welcome distraction for Lee. He was beginning to feel cooped up and the need to be outside the walls for a while was overpowering. Even though he knew the world was different and dangerous now, he still wanted a change of scenery now and then. Secretly, he actually enjoyed the danger and the rush of the outside.

John, the amateur lumberjack, also offered his assistance. Since the killing of Tony, he had felt somewhat drawn to Steve and Lee, as though they shared a bond derived from their actions. He did not regret it for an instant, but the barbarism of the act could only be understood and completely accepted by those who had taken part. The severing of Tony's penis and it then being stuffed into his mouth was a detail they had chosen to keep from most of the other people in the house.

Steve had not mentioned the subject of suspected sabotage to anyone when he told them of the future fuel run, but Jake did give him a questioning look. He knew that they should have had more than enough fuel without a resupply being urgent but he held his tongue with the intention of pulling Steve aside at a later time and getting the full story.

"Where you got in mind?" Jake asked Steve.

"I don't know yet. I'm going to have a think over the next day or two while we have..." He was cut off mid-speech by the sound of whistle blasts and the pounding of feet and hollering as someone was racing down the stairs from the rooftop.

Jake spun and ran toward the commotion to meet Carl as he bounded down the steps, the whistle still clutched between his teeth.

"What, what's happening?" Jake had his hands in front of him trying to slow the big man down and get some sense of the situation.

By now, Steve was standing beside him at the top of the stairs and a crowd had begun to gather in the foyer below them. Hushed alarmed voices could be heard within the group as they peered up the stairs toward the panting, and clearly distressed Carl.

"They're in," he gasped, "they're inside the walls."

Steve's expression turned to horror as the realisation of what he was being told hit him. He looked down at the people gathered below, frantically searching for his daughter. She was not there.

"Where's Sarah?" he yelled as panic began rising in his voice.

He sprinted back down the stairs, taking three steps at a time as he aimed for the front door to the mansion. As he cleared the last step, the large solid wood doors to the main entrance crashed open. The morning light spilled in and for a moment, Steve saw two silhouettes staggering through the brightly lit doorframe.

It was Sarah and Claire. They threw themselves into the foyer, Claire kicking the heavy doors shut behind her then throwing her weight against them as she began sliding the large bolts into place to secure the entrance.

Sarah ran straight towards Steve, her hands outstretched. She threw herself into his arms, whimpering in his ear and clutching him tightly around his neck. "Dad, don't let them..."

Steve stood up, Sarah still wrapped around him, shaking with fear. "Shhh, it's okay, buddy, it's okay. I'm here and I won't let anything happen to you."

Sarah trembled uncontrollably in his arms and sobbed with her face pressed hard against his cheek, her eyes screwed shut. "They're here, Dad. They're..."

"I know, darling," Steve said as he rubbed her back reassuringly. "It's okay, they can't get in here."

Claire had finished securing the door with the help of John who now began frantically checking the windows, ensuring that they were secure and looking for any sign of the dead approaching the house.

Claire was breathing heavily. "They're in, Steve. I don't how many, but we were up by the monkey pen when we first heard them. Thank God they weren't quiet, we wouldn't have known otherwise." She gulped for air. "We had to run all the way back, but I don't think they saw us."

Without another word, he passed Sarah across to her mother and turned for the stairs. At the top, he turned left and sprinted along the corridor, towards the door that led to the roof. Jake followed close behind.

Steve stood, peering across the open grassland of the park, shielding his eyes from the morning sun. He turned his body through three hundred and sixty degrees as he tried to gain a panoramic view of the area. To the west and south, the wooded area containing the facilities and main gate of the park, all looked clear.

To the east, the open fields with the animal fences in the distance, nothing stirred. He turned his attention to the north. The open fields gently sloped upward until they met the horizon. Then, he saw them. Silhouetted against the skyline in the early morning haze, Steve saw a line of clumsy staggering figures, mist swirling around their legs as they slowly made their way through the dew soaked grass.

They were inside the walls, just as Carl and Claire had said.

"Fuck," Jake said at his side as he looked through the binoculars. "I count about twenty from here. There could be more though. How did they get in?"

"Doesn't matter, but we have to go and get rid of them, don't we?" Steve was already turning toward the door. He had seen what he needed, and now had an idea of the state of affairs rather than rushing straight out without a clear picture of what was happening.

Grabbing his old trusty hammer and hand axe, he headed for the door. Lee followed and so did Gary, Jake and John.

Helen had joined the others in the foyer and insisted that she come along too, but Steve explained to her that they had all the help they needed.

"Besides, you're still in your underwear beneath that robe." He glanced down at the thick towelling gown that she wore and smiled. "Who do you think you are, Xena the Warrior Princess?" He winked at her. "We'll be back soon, I promise."

The group moved toward the door as John began to slide back the bolts.

"Carl, you stay here and man the roof with the radio," Steve instructed. He turned to Sarah who stood with her arms wrapped around her mother's waist. "It's okay, buddy, we're just going to go and take care of a few things. You stay close to your mum." He kissed her forehead and turned back to Carl. "Once we're out, help barricade the main doors. Make sure Helen stays here. We don't know how many have gotten into the park and I don't want anyone running around out there."

"Be careful, Steve," Carl said as he nodded that he understood his instructions.

They took the zebra patterned Land Rover that Gary used as the Park Ranger. Though it was old, it was reliable and well maintained. Gary knew every inch of the vehicle and what it was capable of doing.

"We need to find the way they got in first and plug the gap," Gary suggested from behind the wheel. "At that end of the park, it's just fence lines and walls. The old access gate is there too, so maybe they managed to break it down?"

"Maybe," Steve agreed, "but how, and why would there have been enough of them in that area to break through anyway? There's been the odd straggler in the past, but never enough to get through. It's off the beaten track and not all that accessible, especially to these mindless pus bags."

The vehicle bounced and rocked as Gary steered it, cross-country, toward the rear gate. "Could have something to do with what we discussed earlier, Steve," he commented.

"You mean the sabotage?"

"Yeah."

John, Lee and Jake all heard Gary's words from where they sat in the back of the Land Rover and looked at each other quizzically. That one word caused a degree of discomfort amongst them. The word hinted at them being vulnerable in some way. Someone had gotten to them. In spite of their regular checks and patrols to ensure the walls were secure and the people were safe, someone either from outside or within, did not want them to stay that way.

They pulled up at a safe distance from where they knew the gate was. A clump of trees surrounded the area and the dark cavernous gap between them where the track disappeared into the gloom seemed like the mouth of a giant beast that would swallow them up. They stood and watched the track where it led up to the gate for a while.

Nothing moved.

Behind them, the dead moaned and staggered on uneasy legs as they followed them. They were still a distance away and no immediate threat. Gary had made a point of ensuring the dead saw the vehicle as they headed for the rear gate, hoping to lure them in a different direction from the house. The worst thing possible would be for some of them to ignore the Land Rover and continue into the rest of the park. There would still have to be a clearance of the whole place. They could not afford to have even one walking corpse left wandering around within the walls.

Clutching their weapons, they moved toward the trees. Steve was in front, his hammer in one hand and axe in the other. Lee was at his side, his heavy iron bar ready. Gary, John and Jake were to protect their rear and deal with any of the dead that approached from behind. The dark track was too narrow to have too many people up in front. There would be too much of a risk of them crashing into and over each other if they were suddenly attacked with overwhelming numbers and needed to withdraw.

Steve and Lee entered the shadowy trees. The gate lay open; the chain, which was used to secure it, was nowhere to be seen. A dark figure stumbled toward them from beyond the opening. The trees cast everything in gloom, including the figure, but there was no mistaking it for what it was. The slow shambling gait and the swaying arms that moved in rhythm with each unsteady step.

It stopped and looked down at something on the ground. It dropped to its knees and began to tear at it and stuff chunks of it into its mouth. The creature chewed noisily and slurped at the dark, almost black blood that dribbled from the corners of its mouth and down onto its chin. The wet blood glistened in the particles of light that managed to penetrate the thick canopy of the trees above, giving off the illusion of sparks of light emanating from the ghouls rotted mouth.

At that distance, Steve could not tell what the thing was eating, but it was clearly something that had been planted there for it. He slowly edged his way closer, treading carefully and straining to see what was on the ground. Five metres away and he recognised the torn open body of a dog. Around its neck was a length of rope that was attached to a stake driven into the ground.

Lee quickly rushed forward, raising his heavy iron bar above his head. The creature, its face covered in blood, looked up as he approached. Its lips curled back in a snarl and the claw like hands came up expectantly to meet Lee. As it tried to stand, the blow landed. The bar crunched into the top of the skull, smashing through the bone. The force of the swing caused the neck to snap and the body instantly fell back to the ground at the side of the devoured dog.

"Somebody wanted them in." It was an obvious statement, but Steve was thinking aloud. The dog had been used as live bait to entice them up the track and into the Safari Park.

Before investigating further, they needed to secure the gate and deal with the ones inside. They slid the bolt back into place and headed back towards the others. Already at their feet, a number of bodies lay with their skulls smashed in.

More were coming.

"Head for the high ground, we can see them coming better," John ordered.

Everybody turned to their left and run up the small rise, leaving the Land Rover behind on the track.

At the top of the slope, more reanimated dead stumbled toward them. The five moved as a team. Stepping forward together as if medieval knights going into battle and wielding their weapons in their hands, they met the walking human carcasses head on. Blow after blow rained down on to the heads of their opponents. Bodies lay strewn over a wide area as they fought to clear and protect the park and the people within.

Jake smashed his bat into the face of a woman as she lunged at him. The bones crunched and she collapsed at his feet. As he stepped over her, she grabbed at his legs, causing him to trip and fall to the ground. Within an instant, another reached for him from above and grabbed at his face.

Struggling to stand, Jake found himself in a battle with two of the dead. The woman on the ground continued to pull at his legs, all the while snapping her teeth at his soft flesh while the other gripped onto his hair, trying to pull Jake's face towards its gaping mouth. Jake was staring straight into its throat. The foul odour reached his nostrils as he thrashed and struggled in their grip.

He felt pressure on his toes and realised that the woman was trying to chew through his shoe. He fought to pull his foot free, but she came with him, her teeth clenched tightly around his foot. With a scream, he ripped himself free from the grasp of the hands that clutched at his head. Clods of his hair came away in its fingers as he pulled his head back. He felt the sting of the roots being plucked from his scalp, causing his eyes to water and blur.

Quickly, he forced himself upright. He raised his bat again above his head and smacked it down on the woman's skull. He felt extra pressure on his toes within the shoe for a moment as the skull caved in under the blow, and then her jaw fell slack.

Pulling his foot free, he sprang to his feet and stepped to the side as he swung the bat at the head of the second ghoul. The shot hit home and the body was sent hurtling backward. Jake took no chances and as the corpse fell to its knees, he followed up with a second blow, ensuring the creature was down and unable to get back up.

He stood, panting and sweat pouring down his forehead and into his eyes. His heart pounded at his chest wall and his knees shook. He knew how close he had been to dying. He had landed himself in trouble due to his carelessness and now, with the battle over and as the adrenalin faded from his system, exhaustion and nausea took hold of him.

Steve looked back at the sound of Jake heaving and vomiting uncontrollably. He surveyed the scene that they had created around them. The dead lay strewn all around, twisted and grotesque with their heads smashed in. Some were nothing more than rotted flesh and bone with limbs missing and deformed beyond recognition, while others still held the appearance of human beings, fresh and intact.

There were children too.

That was never a sight Steve could get used to. Though he had no hesitation in doing what needed to be done with them, or any doubt about what they were and capable of doing, it still haunted Steve and probably most other people he guessed, that they had once been young and innocent children.

"You okay, mate?" he asked, rubbing between the shoulders blades of Jake as he stood, doubled over as another bout of sickness gripped him.

"Yeah, I suppose so," he replied after a moment as he regained himself and wiped his mouth on the back of his sleeve. "I thought they had me there."

Steve patted him on the back. He understood how Jake was feeling. It was not cowardice or fear as such. It was the adrenalin followed by relief. It surged through all their veins at moments like that.

In addition, he knew that he had to contend with the fight or flight instinct that was natural to them all. Steve had felt it himself on a few occasions and he knew it was a true test of character to be able to resist the urge to turn and run for safety. If Jake had done that, the others could have been left with a serious problem.

Gary raised the radio to his mouth. "Carl, are you getting me?" He too was sweating profusely and his chest rose and fell, hard and fast. He had fought his way through three of the dead and, like Jake, had found himself having to take on two of them at once.

"Yeah, Gary, you're loud and clear. Where are you?"

Gary was still struggling to regain his breath and his words were strained. "Down by the rear gate, just over the rise. We'll secure the gate as best we can then we'll have to search the park for any we missed."

"You did miss a few, Gary. I watched a bunch of them carry on towards the central area; about five, maybe six of them."

"Shit," Gary hissed and turned to Steve. "We're going to have to be thorough on this, mate. Maybe get more people from the house to help?"

"Yeah, tell Carl to take a couple of others on a search. Tell them to use a vehicle as much as they can and to clear the south and west area. Double check the main gate too and tell them, not to take any chances. If they need our help, call us on the radio."

"You do know that Helen will insist on being part of it, don't you?"

"I know," Steve acknowledged, fixing Gary with a hard stare. "She knows what she's doing."

With the immediate area clear, the four of them decided on checking the track that led up to the rear gate for any indication of who had opened the barrier for the dead to get in. For about five hundred metres, it was nothing more than a narrow dirt path, overhung by wooded areas on either side, which cast the track into perpetual shadow.

Even to a living person, the path was obscure and remote. It wound its way down to a grassy opening about the size of a football pitch and at the far end, a wide wooden gate led out onto a minor metalled road. They were secluded for miles and it was not likely that many of the dead would be travelling that sort of road.

The gate now lay wide open.

"Well, that settles it in my mind," Gary stated as they stood on the edge of the wood, looking towards the road. "Someone definitely let the bastards in."

"How can you be so sure?" Jake asked. "I mean, someone could've neglected to secure the gate properly."

"We've all checked each and every gate ourselves and they've always been secure. We check them as part of our morning patrols, Jake. You know that. Plus, there was the dog." Steve kept his eyes on the wooden gate and road as he spoke.

"What dog?" Gary asked in surprise.

Lee turned and nodded back the way they had come. "Up at the gate, the dead fuck that I killed was lay on top of it, so you probably didn't notice it but there was a dog tied up. Whoever did this used it as bait."

Jake and John shared a glance and looked back at the gate.

"Jesus," John hissed. "This isn't good at all."

"It wasn't negligence that did this. Someone went to a lot of trouble to land us in the shit," Steve growled.

John turned to him, "Who?"

"I don't know. Could be anyone and like Gary said about the fuel, even someone amongst us."

Lee sucked in air from between his teeth and let out a long sigh. "Fucking hell, this is starting to sound like that movie, *'The Thing'*."

Steve chuckled at his reference, but understood his point. "Yeah, but Lee, we want to tread carefully on this. We don't want people being interrogated or even feel like they're under suspicion. In fact, I'd rather we didn't make this public knowledge."

"Yeah, well you lot thought that that Tony bloke was great but I knew there was something about him."

"I know, Lee, and I'm willing to trust your instincts on this. We just need to use discretion." Steve was staring straight into his eyes, trying hard to make his point clear.

"That doesn't mean sneaking under people's beds at night or listening outside their windows dressed like a Ninja, Lee," Jake grinned.

"Fuck off. I'd be scared of what I would see in your room; sweaty leather chaps and gimp masks everywhere." Lee snorted at his own joke and even Jake was trying hard not to laugh too loudly.

"Okay then, if you two don't mind, let's get that gate closed then get back for the hunt." Steve stepped out from beneath the trees and headed for the open gate.

4

For weeks, they had been pounding at the door above him. Even with three metres of earth and concrete separating him from the monsters outside on the surface, he could still hear the dull thuds as they endlessly battered at the steel door.

Simon was what could only be described as a *'survivalist'*. For most of his life, he had taken a great interest in the techniques the experts used, to live off the land and survive when all others would succumb and die. He prided himself on his skill and ability.

He could find water in even the most unlikely of places and he could start a fire from just a few dry leaves and pieces of tinder. He practiced his skills at every opportunity, never passing a chance to learn more or to improve on a technique.

He endlessly watched Ray Mears construct basic instruments and tools from what he found around him and Simon mimicked his idol, even going as far as building a canoe from a hollowed out tree after watching one particular episode.

The neighbour's laughs were ignored, even when they asked, "Hey Simon, where are you going to sail that thing, down the local canal?"

He did not care about being the butt of people's jokes. He was happy doing what he did. During the week, he worked in an office as a computer programmer, something that he had been doing for twenty years. The job bored him and he constantly longed for the great outdoors. Therefore, on weekends, he took himself off to the National Parks and as far as he was concerned, lived free and completely independent from the modern gadgets and technology that humanity found so essential for their daily existence.

No, Simon was happy as he was. He was well aware of his contradictory lifestyle of helping to bring the human race deeper into the cyber age with his computer programming by day and his utter contempt for it by night, but he saw it as unavoidable. He needed to work in order to be able to afford to do the things he liked.

Often, he did fantasise about leaving it all behind and finding an untouched and remote patch of forest somewhere and disappearing from the radar. Never again would he have to worry about paying taxes, keeping on top of bills or even following the latest fashion trends. He could just live free and off the land. It would be all too easy for him to live that way but it was something he had never gone beyond daydreaming about.

Originally, he had tried to join the army at the age of eighteen, but he was refused due to his eyesight and his asthma. It had been a devastating blow to him and he had reluctantly decided on using his natural ability with a computer to carve a career for himself. Soon, though, the deep feelings for all things natural surfaced again.

Often, even though he loved learning new skills and tricks in the wild, he did question the sense of it. *"Why am I spending so much time roughing it in the woods, wiping my arse on leaves, lighting fires with sticks and rocks and then freezing my nuts off at night when I've completely misjudged the weather?"* His answer was always simple and always the same, *"Well, you never know."* Before his brain could ask the next question about never knowing *what* exactly, he would put it out of his mind and go back to building his lean-to or setting his snare traps.

The self-scrutinizing continued until one day in 2009. In an article in one of his monthly survivor magazines, he began to read about the Mayan Calendar and the theories surrounding it. Mainly, what happens when it runs out? He cross-referenced it to all the other Doomsday predictions such as Nostradamus and the Bible. It all seemed to point to the fact that something big, he did not know what, would happen in 2012.

Simon was gripped. The idea of an apocalyptic event in his lifetime where he would have the chance to use his skills for real life survival filled him with excitement and a fresh drive to further his crafts. Though people theorised that it could be an asteroid, solar flares and other worldwide devastating events, Simon chose to believe in the less drastic and final ideas such as war and plague, or famine. He considered even alien invasion as being survivable.

That was when he began constructing his bunker.

The last thing he had expected was for the dead to start walking and attacking the living. That had come as a complete shock to him and had hit him blindside.

At the bottom of the large garden to his old Victorian detached house, he dug out an area five metres wide by seven metres long and six metres deep. He had surfed the internet for the blueprints of a number of different *'do it yourself'* nuclear fallout shelters and with his own knowledge and intelligence, came up with his own design, incorporating the different techniques he had seen.

Once again, he was back to being asked numerous questions by his neighbours. At one point, even the police were involved because someone had reported him. They soon found out that he had actually obtained planning permission for it. As it did not interfere with any land belonging to other people or water mains, gas pipes and electrical cabling, and an architect and engineer had been consulted and hired to inspect the different phases of the build, much to the annoyance and dismay of some of his neighbours, he was free to continue.

He sifted through the metal scrapyards for the steel he needed. He even managed to obtain a door that was used on the interior of a ship, the same one that was now being thumped upon by the dead outside.

It took him months to build it. He toiled and laboured on his project every weekend. Even during the week, as soon as he came home from work, he would be out there, sweating and grafting until exhaustion overcame him.

He had his own water system and reservoir tank, even a chemical toilet. He furnished the place with basic, usually second-hand and no frills stuff. There was a bed, a couple of chairs and a small kitchenette.

What he was most proud of was his supplies. The place was stacked, floor to ceiling, with tins, plastic sealed bags and glass and plastic jars and bottles. He deliberately researched and stocked the foods that would not spoil and would last for decades if need be. Underneath the floor, he had his reservoir storage tank, filled with water and a pump that would stir it every six hours to stop it becoming stagnant. Also below the floor, he had a smaller tank for diesel for the little generator and a bank of batteries that was recharged by the generator. He had everything he needed, clothing, food, water, equipment and most of all, the knowledge and skill to survive.

The pride in his accomplishment faded when the 21st December 2012 came and went and the world continued to turn as normal. The jibes and remarks from neighbours and workmates did not help. The bunker was left fully stocked and the doors sealed. Before long, Simon forgot it was even there, only remembering on occasion when he saw or read something that brought it back to his mind.

Now, sitting in his gloomy bunker, he could not help but wonder why he had bothered at all. For weeks, he had been trapped in his steel and concrete tomb. He had food and water to last him for a long time, but two things he hadn't counted on now began to affect him more than anything; boredom and more importantly, loneliness.

He had never been the most sociable of people. How could he have been? What would he have chatted to people about, his computers, his survival interests? Most people, who knew him, though always pleasant enough, never took any real interest in him. The few girlfriends he had had in his lifetime, though normally of similar interests, tired of him and moved on before the relationship actually went anywhere.

The pounding at the door continued. The dull thuds echoed continuously around in the confined spaces of the bunker, as though he was sitting inside a steel barrel with someone on the outside, banging away at it with a hammer.

"Shut the fuck up," he screamed at the ceiling.

The constant banging at the door was wearing him down. It never ceased. Not even at night. His sleep was constantly interrupted and he began to lose track of time. Without the aid of the sun and the moon, he relied solely on his watch to tell him what part of the day it was. However, even that had begun to seem false to him. It was just a bunch of numbers now, illuminated green at the press of a button on the side of the watch face. There was no natural light from the sun, the moon or the stars to reference the reading against; he feared he would lose his mind.

His thoughts drifted to food, hoping that it would take his mind off the monotony. It did not work. As he sat there, eating his second helping of tuna pasta of the day, he wondered to himself why he had not been more imaginative with his selection of supplies. It had become tasteless to him.

Amongst his provisions, he had enough vitamins and supplements, including his fibres, carbohydrates, proteins and minerals to render him as the best hope for humanity when he finally emerged after a decade underground.

He had imagined the world dying a horrible and slow death and humanity being down to the wire with sickness and a severe lack of strong sperm donors. Then, he would spring from his underground lair as the saviour of the human race, fit, healthy and ready to do his bit in the rejuvenation of his species with all the women of the world.

He let the spoon drop from his hand and it clattered loudly against the cold hard concrete of the floor. His head sagged and he looked down as the tinfoil packet of bland and dry tuna pasta in his hand.

"Would it have killed you to stock a few jars of mayonnaise?" he murmured to himself.

In the beginning, he had stayed in the house and watched as the world fell apart. At first, he watched it on television or listened to it on the radio. Then he saw it in high definition, as the people in his street were attacked, then attacked one another. He listened to the screams of the parents and children who he had known for years as they were torn to pieces and watched as they reanimated and stalked the streets in their own search for warm living flesh.

One morning, when he awoke, a crowd of the dead greeted him at the front of his house. He recognised some of them as his neighbours, even the ones who had mocked him over his interests. Now, they stood in his garden, looking up at him as he peeped from behind the curtain of his bedroom window.

Their lifeless eyes chilled him to the bone but their wails and moans froze the blood in his veins. He pitied them. He felt an overwhelming sorrow for the people that he had once known, even the ones that had made fun of him. He would never have wished that fate upon any of them.

It was then that he decided it was time to move to the bunker.

The hours he spent awake seemed endless and the time he slept always seemed too short. Time stood still for him. There was nothing to distract him. The thought of installing a television, a radio or even a computer, had not even occurred to him. He had been in raw survival mode when he built the bunker and the basic human traits such as boredom and restlessness were not considered.

Instead, he had passed what time he could with old copies of his magazines, a few books whose storylines failed to entice him and a deck of playing cards. Poker or Black Jack was out of the question, so it was the loneliest game in the world to keep him occupied, Solitaire. For days on end, he had played hand after hand of Solitaire and only managed to complete it a few times.

He needed to get out. The thought of spending the rest of his days trapped underground filled him with dread. He had literally dug his own grave. In spite of its high-tech design, it was nevertheless, a tomb.

Simon looked to the rear of the bunker, past the kitchenette and toward the rear hatch. He had built it into the structure in case of an emergency such as a cave in, or even the main door becoming eroded and sealed, not hundreds of dead people banging at it or him close to dying from boredom.

He stood up from the bed and pulled the curtain that covered the rear hatch door to one side. He pressed his ear against it, the cold steel causing the week's worth of growth on his face to stand on end. He closed his eyes and opened his mouth to help block out the sound of his own heartbeat. Attempting to ignore the thuds at the main door at the other side of the bunker, he listened intently for any indication of any of them being at his possible escape route.

He could not hear any noise from that direction. He could never be one hundred percent sure, though, and he kicked himself for not having the forethought to build some kind of periscope so that he could at least have an idea of what the surface looked like.

They had basic technology like that a hundred years ago, so why did I not think of it?

Glancing back into the bunker, he began to turn the locking mechanism. It was stiff and he had to place all his weight into it. His face contorted and his shoulders throbbed, but slowly the wheel turned and a dull clunk indicated that the door was free. He pulled it open, the hinges creaking and echoing around the tomb. He peered into the concrete walled shaft and up at the manhole cover he used to shield it.

Tiny beams of light filtered through the lifting holes in the cover and Simon could feel his body aching to feel the effects of the sun's rays upon his skin again. He could almost feel himself regenerate it the glow of the sun above him.

He gently and methodically climbed the ladder attached to the wall, one hand and one foot moving at a time. The dull clunks of his feet on the steel rungs sounded overly loud within the narrow confines of the shaft. He moved carefully and he shuddered at the thought of a clumsy move causing him to fall, leaving him crippled and at the bottom of the shaft, left to die a slow and agonising death and then reanimating and spending forever in the bunker that he had built and intended as a safe house, not a grave.

He had grown to despise the place.

At the top, he paused, his ear pressed to the damp underside of the steel cover that separated him from the world above. He squinted and strained, trying to focus his senses and gain some kind of picture of what lay beyond the manhole. He could hear nothing. Nothing close anyway. He could still hear the moans and thuds of the dead just eight or nine metres to his right and at the front of the bunker but they sounded distant.

If he was lucky and the coast was clear, he could sneak out unseen; protected by the bushes and shrubs he had deliberately planted to help conceal the bunker's escape hatch. If he kept low and remained quiet, he could be away and over the fence in no time and off into the wilderness.

Surviving in the woods or mountains is much more appealing than rotting in this stinking sewer.

Gently, he placed his fingertips against the steel plate and slowly lifted it, just a few centimetres to give him a view of the immediate area. He bit his tongue as he pushed and the sudden draft of cool fresh air hitting his pale skin was like a slap in the face to his senses. He felt almost dizzy from it. He had been sucking in the same stale fetid atmosphere for weeks and now he was breathing the best air he had ever tasted.

He risked a few more centimetres and pushed the cover a little higher. There was no sign of the dead. They were all at the main hatch.

Back inside the bunker, Simon began busying himself with his belongings. He threw what he needed into his rucksack, a few bottles of fresh water, some sachets and tins of food, his survival tools, a torch and a few pieces of warm clothing. Nothing else was necessary.

He kept his machete on the belt at his waist, something he remembered Ray Mears had always insisted on doing. In addition, he added his short crowbar to his equipment. It could be used to gain entry to places and as a weapon if need be. Already it had come in handy when he had been forced to sink it into someone's skull as he raced for the bunker all those weeks ago. He was more than aware that he will no doubt need to do it again, and he accepted it. It was how the world was now as far as he was concerned.

    Simon was a survivor.

5

Hussein had suggested that maybe they should not be in such a hurry to leave, and that as long as they were careful and discreet they could gather their strength before they moved off again.

"Not a bad idea really, Marcus," Stu had offered after Hussein presented his case. "Besides, there's probably still a lot of stuff we could use around here. We need a HF radio to try to make comms with your brother, and maybe some smaller VHF radios for personal use, to replace the ones we have. Medical supplies would be useful too."

"Fair one," Marcus agreed. "We'll dig in here for a day or two then. Radios and batteries are priority."

Jim and Sini, being unfamiliar with British Army communications equipment, were tasked with ransacking the entire accommodation block for anything they could find.

"Top of the list is the likes of sleeping bags, ponchos for shelter, gas canisters and other cooking kit. You know the score and you know what is useful and what isn't. If you think we could use it, grab it and we'll sort it all out later. Find some packs to put it all in. You never know, we could end up having to walk at some point."

"Ammunition, too," Stu added. "You know how it is; there was always someone who had his own private stash of ammo in his room for one reason or another."

Jim nodded. "Where are you going then?"

"Me, Stu and Hussein are off to the comms store. Hopefully, we'll be able to send a sit-rep to Steve by tonight," Marcus replied.

On their return, Marcus presented the rest of the team with a large, green bulky looking piece of equipment. It had dials along the side and a harness.

"What's this? Don't tell me it's a radio, Marcus," Jim asked, scratching his head.

"Sorry to disappoint you, Jim, but it is. It's the best we could find down there. It's an old model, a three twenty High Frequency radio. Heavy and cumbersome but it should do the job. That's if I can remember how to use it."

Marcus looked down at the dials and switches but nothing was springing to the front of his mind in the way of familiarity on how to work the equipment. It had been a long time since he had used it. Even then, trained and fresh in his mind, it was confusing for him.

"Good news is, though, we found a few battery packs and chargers that will fit the personal radios we already have, so there's no need to search for replacements."

"Anything else, did you get med supplies?" Sini queried.

Stu raised a small green rucksack in front of him. "Yeah, we managed to get a few useful bits but we couldn't hang around. A whole bunch of those things turned up and almost ate Hussein here. Didn't they, little man?" Stu nudged him in the ribs.

Hussein grinned and looked sheepish. "Yes, I owe you my life, Mr. Stu."

"Bollocks, mate, you would've done the same for me, and cut the 'Mister' crap, you're not a Jundhi anymore, Hussein. You're one of us."

Marcus and his team spent their time scrounging supplies and equipment from within the barracks. Forever vigilant and watching over their shoulders, they foraged through the stores of kit, searching for anything that they thought would be of use.

By now, they had assembled quite a collection. A large pile of equipment was heaped on the floor of one of the large barrack rooms. They had ransacked every locker and wardrobe in the block.

Jim and Marcus conducted a full inventory of what they had, and what they believed they still needed. They went through a complete weapons and ammunition check, ensuring that everyone had a rifle and sidearm with an equal amount of ammunition for each, including a means to carry it. Hussein and Sandra were both equipped with a set of British Army issue webbing with pouches attached in order to store their ammunition on their bodies.

Next, they broke down the boxes of rations they had found and separated them into even piles. The whole thing was a routine that Marcus and the others had gone through on so many occasions before. It all came under the heading 'Preparation for Battle' in army doctrine and was second nature to them. They knew exactly what they needed to carry and what they did not.

Immediately at hand and carried on the person would be their weapons and ammunition. Radios would also be attached. They had enough food and water to see them through the day should they become separated from their vehicle and main packs. In addition, each member would carry a small first-aid kit, containing the means to gain and maintain an airway, through both the mouth and nasal passages, and the ability to arrest bleeding with field dressings and tourniquets.

People would always include their own additions such as the Claymore mines that Stu and Sini where carrying, the mini flares that Marcus had tucked away in a pouch along with his binoculars and other items.

Jim insisted on a lifetime's ration of cigarettes that he had found in one of the rooms.

Hussein was fascinated at the amount of adult magazines that had been added to the mound. He sat in the corner, leafing through a copy of a particularly sleazy edition, his eyes fixed on the images and a film of sweat coating his face.

"Are you enjoying yourself there, Hussein?" Jim asked as he entered the room, puffing away on a cigarette.

Hussein looked up slowly, unable to tear himself away from the pictures of scantily clad and completely naked women in all manner of poses spread across the pages. "Uh, I know I should not be, but yes, it is fascinating."

Jim threw his head back and let out a howl of laughter. "Yeah, that's about right, Hussein. I always referred to it as 'fascinating' as well. Here, treat yourself," Jim said as he tossed a roll of toilet paper into his lap. He left the room, closing the door behind him, the sound of his laughter echoing along the corridor.

Hussein watched him leave, a perplexed and expectant look on his face. He looked down at the toilet paper, unsure of what he was supposed to do with it or why Jim had said what he had.

Inevitably, the movements and unavoidable noise of the team as they scavenged attracted a steady stream of the dead towards the accommodation block where they were holed up. An ever-growing pile of bodies, their skulls smashed in by clubs and rifle butts, littered the grounds around the building. Still, more came to investigate the noises or glimpses they saw of the fast moving living people.

Marcus had ordered that the dead be dispatched as quietly as possible. They were still unsure of how many there were within the inner part of the barracks, and he held no desire to find out.

On the second afternoon, after completing the final touches and additions to their equipment, they loaded the packs in the Land Rover, ready to move.

Stu noticed a look of concern on the face of Sini. "What's up, buddy, everything okay?"

"It's Sandra, she isn't too good. She complained of stomach pain last night and this morning, she seems to be getting worse. She needs a doctor, I think."

"It could be food poisoning or an infection of some sort. I'll come and have a look at her now. You okay with the radio, Marcus?"

"Uh, I think so." Marcus sat at a table staring at the radio in front of him. The look on his face was complete bewilderment. He looked up to Stu and smiled. "I'll work it out, eventually."

While Marcus and the others sifted through kit and fiddled with the radio, Stu went with Sini to examine Sandra. She lay on a bed, sweating and groaning in one of the large four man rooms. The curtains were pulled shut, leaving the room in near darkness. Only a small amount of light managed to penetrate the gaps in the material of the curtains, and Stu could see the particles of dust that drifted through the air around them as they passed through the narrow beams of sunlight.

Even from the doorway, Stu could see the beads sweat on Sandra's brow. It glistened and he could see how pale she had become. Her knees were drawn up to her chest and her hands clutched at the area of her stomach. A cold shiver ran the length of Stu's spine and he prayed it was not what he suspected. A pregnancy was the last thing they needed at that time.

He moved closer and lit the camping lamps that were placed around the room. "Sini, start heating me some water, lots of it. And bring me my med bag."

"Roger that," Sini replied, and he disappeared out of the room only to return a minute later with a large plastic bowl, a couple of camping stoves with a number of metal pots to heat the water in and the medical kit.

Stu began taking Sandra's blood pressure and heart rate. He checked her pulse in a number of different places in order to gauge the strength and health of her arteries and heart. When he tried to take the pulse in the femoral artery on the inner thigh, Sandra let out a long loud grown. It was obviously agony for her to straighten, even open her legs slightly.

Without letting Sini see what he was doing, Stu quickly checked the sheets of the bed around where Sandra lay. He then checked the seat of her clothing, expecting to see signs of haemorrhaging. There was no sign of any blood. Stu had begun to fear a miscarriage, but it was normally accompanied with bleeding.

"Sandra, can you hear me?" Stu spoke gently in her ear, stroking her forehead at the same time.

Her eyes opened and she turned her head to face him. Her face was pale and contorted with the pain. "Yes," she nodded, "I can hear you. It really hurts, Stu." She let out a whimper as another bout of pain hit her.

"What hurts, where is the pain? Can you show me exactly where it is?"

With great difficulty, she slowly attempted to straighten her legs. Her teeth were gritted and she fought hard not to allow her legs to spring back up towards her chest. "It is here," she said, stroking the area of where the pain emanated.

Stu looked at her hand. "Here, this is where the most pain is?" he asked placing his own hand in the same area.

Sini had set the water to heat and had now joined Stu at the side of the bed. He took Sandra's free hand in his own. "What is it, Stu? What is wrong with her?"

"Give me a minute, Sini. Sandra, you are going to have to let me examine you for a moment. Can you hang on just long enough for me to feel your stomach?"

Sandra nodded, her eyes shut tightly and she slowly began to straighten her legs. She groaned and squeezed hard on Sini's hand as the agony tore at her.

Stu began feeling both sides of her stomach simultaneously with both hands. If he felt something on one side with one hand, and nothing with the other hand on the opposite side, then he would know that there was something in that particular area.

Sandra clenched her teeth hard and whimpered as Stu continued to push on her stomach. Up the sides and along the front, he gently pressed down with his hands systematically. A minute later, and he pulled his hands back and helped to make her comfortable again.

"Okay, Sandra, try and rest now." He motioned for Sini to leave the room with him.

Outside, Sini looked anxious. He was as pale and sweaty as Sandra was. "What is it, Stu?"

Stu was staring at the wall and rubbing the bristles on his chin. "It's her appendix. I think they're about to burst."

"What is, 'appendix'?"

"It's something we don't need right now, in every sense of the word."

Sini gripped him by the arm. "Stu, is she going to be okay? Can you help her?"

"In theory, I can. I mean, I know all about it, even how to treat it but I have never done it, and these aren't the best conditions. Even if I managed to take it out, there's the risk of infection afterward."

"Take it out?" Sini looked more concerned than he had just a moment before.

"The appendix is an organ in our body which isn't used anymore. In Sandra, it has become inflamed and needs to be removed. I know where it is, and how to get there and take it out, but the aftercare is just as important."

Marcus was still trying to work out how to use the radio when Stu walked in to inform him of the situation.

"I think I have it, but now I need to work out what type and length of antenna to use. Fuck me it was complicated enough fifteen years ago when I did the course." Marcus was running his hands through his hair and sighing a lot as his brain refused to relinquish the information that had been stored there all those years ago.

Stu leaned over the table and informed him of Sandra's condition and what needed doing to help her.

"Shit, Marcus," Jim stated from the wall by the window where he sat with a number of antenna laid out in front of him, "that's not good. I had a friend back home who died from that. You think you can fix her, Stu?"

Stu nodded. He was not one hundred percent confident, but he knew he had to try.

Marcus sat blinking at him. "Anything we can do?"

"Not really, but we will have to stay here a little longer than planned to give her a chance to start recovering. Sini can help me with the procedure while you work on the comms."

"No problem. We'll stay here for as long as we need to." Marcus smiled at Stu, nodding his approval. "You hear that, Hussein?" he asked over his shoulder. "We're staying a while, so put those dirty magazines down for now and get the kettle on. High time you learned how to make an English brew, mate. I don't mind saying it now that we're in Blighty, but that stuff you used to give us in Iraq was worse than piss."

Hussein grinned. "Marcus, it probably *was* piss."

Sandra was lying on the two tables that Sini and Stu had put together and set up as an operating table. The room was brightly lit and as much care as possible was taken to keep the conditions sterile. It had taken a few hours of preparation, but Stu now felt that they were as ready as they would ever be.

Sandra had been given a cocktail of painkillers, including morphine. She was pretty much out cold but without the aid of an ECG, it was Sini's job to continually check her pulse rate and breathing, giving Stu updated readings on both as well as acting as the Theatre Nurse.

Stu stood at the side of the makeshift operating table. His face was covered with a surgical mask that restricted his breathing, and the rubber gloves on his hands made his palms sweat. His heart rate had increased dramatically and beads of perspiration trickled down his forehead.

Even though he had treated many injuries, from burns and broken bones, to gunshot wounds and even drowning once, he had never performed any kind of surgery more complicated than stitching somebody up or removing fragments of shrapnel and bullets.

He struggled to control his breathing through the mask. He squinted at the lamps hanging from the ceiling above him and exhaled loudly. "Okay, Sini, let's get on with it."

Taking the scalpel, he began to make the incision. He felt the iodine-swabbed skin gently pop under the sharp blade and the flesh opened up easily as he drew the knife along towards him, creating a cut roughly ten centimetres in length. There was little blood and he cautiously dabbed at the opening with a ball of cotton wool soaked in iodine and clutched between the forceps to give him a better view of the next cut he would need to make.

There were two more layers to the abdomen that he needed to get through, but he had to be careful. Rather than cutting at just any point, Stu needed to slice through carefully selected points, following the fibres of the inner abdomen walls.

"Okay, Sini, I'm in. Hold it open for me. Don't be afraid to stretch it. Skin is a lot tougher than you think and I need to be able to see exactly what I'm looking at."

Sini did as he was asked, reaching for the soft, warm flesh at either side of the incision. He grimaced and turned his head away as he placed his hands into the open wound in his girlfriend's stomach as Stu began to make the cuts.

Stu concentrated hard on every movement he made. He could feel the heat raining down upon him from the bright lamps above. It seemed to sear his neck and pools of sweat ran the length of his back between his shoulder blades.

"Right, keep your hands exactly where they are, but lean back so I can see."

Stu leaned over and with a set of forceps, began to look for the inflamed organ. A moment later, he announced that he had found it. "Sini, go back to monitoring her, I can do the rest from here."

Her pulse and blood pressure had increased, but it was nowhere near a dangerous level. Stu was confident that there was no excess bleeding and he now needed to go through the tricky procedure of dividing the appendix. After that, it would be back to what he knew best; sewing up and dressing the wound, at least that was the theory of it.

Nothing was ever that simple. The inflamed organ looked nothing like he expected; he could not tell where the appendix ended and the large intestine began. Every little move or cut had to be thought and re-thought through. He hesitated continuously and he began to fear that the drugs would wear off before the operation was complete and Sandra would wake with him still routing around inside her.

Time seemed to drag. In truth, it had only been twenty minutes since he had given her stomach the final swab of iodine before making the first incision, but it felt like hours.

Finally, he was happy that the swollen appendix was completely removed. He checked around for any more sign of the organ, something he may have missed, as well as for his own piece of mind in case he had left any swabs or instruments inside. Too many times, he had heard or read horror stories about surgeons leaving equipment and soiled dressings inside a patient then stitching them back up. An incident like that now, under the conditions and circumstances, would be fatal for Sandra.

Confident that all was okay, Stu began the process of sewing her back up.

It took him a lot longer than he knew it would take a surgeon, but he was convinced that Sandra would not die from his unsophisticated surgery. However, he could not be sure about secondary infection. That was his biggest worry.

The conditions were less than ideal and the medicines they had were as good as they could get. It would be a case of sitting tight and keeping her on painkillers, antibiotics and regular cleaning of the wound. Stu guessed that if there was no sign of infection after the first three days, then Sandra should be in the clear.

It was dark by the time he and Sini had finished working on Sandra. Stu set up the intravenous fluids then added antibiotics and more painkillers to the mix. Removing the gloves from his hands, he left Sini to watch over her while he went to inform Marcus and find out how things were with the radio.

Marcus and Jim looked worried. They turned to him as he entered the room. Stu was touched at the apparent concern for Sandra he saw etched on to their faces.

"It's okay; I think she's going to be alright."

Jim was standing by the window. "That's good to know, Stu, but we have a bigger problem going on right now."

Stu raised an eyebrow. "Is the radio working?"

Marcus shook his head. "Never mind that, have you looked out of the window lately?"

Stu looked over to the curtain beside Jim, and then he heard it. The sound of dozens of hands thumping against the doors and windows on the ground floor below them registered in his ears. The moans of the dead echoed along the corridors like wind through an open window.

Stu had been so busy and concerned with Sandra, he had not noticed them. Now, the noise sounded deafening in his ears.

"Shit, how many?"

Marcus looked up at him from his chair. "Uh, lots."

The door suddenly opened behind them. Without thinking, Stu spun, snatching the pistol up from his belt, ready to confront whatever was about to attack him, the barrel pointed straight at the intruder's forehead.

Hussein threw his hands up in front of him, his eyes bulging and alarm in his voice. "No, no it is me, Stu."

Stu released his finger from the trigger but kept the pistol in his hand by his side. The sound of the thumping at the doors and windows had unnerved him. He rushed across to the window and peered down into the darkness below.

Dozens of figures swayed and staggered around, close to the walls of the accommodation block. More could be seen in the distance, illuminated by the faint moonlight as they made their way closer to the building.

"What's going on out there? Could you see much, Hussein?" Marcus asked.

"There are many of them at each entrance. More than we can fight. I think they saw the lights from the room where Stu was helping Sandra." Hussein's eyes were wide and the beads of sweat on his forehead betrayed his fear.

"Why didn't someone say something?" Stu exclaimed in annoyance as he walked back to where Marcus was sitting.

"It doesn't matter, Stu. Sandra needed help and that meant having the lights blazing in there. They can't get in, not yet anyway, so she was the priority." Marcus was back to his cool and calm self.

"What are we going to do, boss?" Jim asked as he sneaked another peek out from behind the curtain at the crowd outside.

"Nothing we can do. Not till daylight anyway. How's Sandra?"

Stu looked at him but continued to glance at the window as he spoke. "I think she'll be okay. She needs rest and she'll be in a little pain, even with the drugs. It's the risk of infection that bothers me most."

"Well, you're the doc, Stu, so we will go with your suggestion. If we have to, we'll barricade ourselves in here until she's okay to move."

Stu blew out a long sigh. "You think that's wise? Maybe we should make a run for it at first light. We can't risk the whole team for the sake of one person."

Marcus jumped from his chair, his eyes burning with fury. With lightning speed, he reached out and gripped Stu by the collar, slamming his back onto the wall.

"For a start, she is one of us," he growled, the veins in his neck pulsing and standing out from the skin. "We would all be dead now, including you, if it wasn't for what Sini, Yan and Sandra did for us back in Serbia. She fought just as bravely as you did in France and she is the other half to Sini. Or did you forget that little lot?"

Stu hung his head in shame and immediately regretted what he had said. Marcus sighed and released his grip.

"I'm sorry, Marcus. I didn't mean it that way, and fuck me, I'm well aware of how Sandra has been a big part in our survival."

Marcus sighed as he looked down at the hand he had just used in aggression against his friend. "I know, mate."

Marcus, too, was feeling ashamed. He and Stu had known each other for a long time and never once had he felt the need to use violence towards him. In fact, there had never been a time where he disagreed with him in anything other than what they were to watch on television.

"Sorry, Stu, I didn't mean to lose my temper there. I'm just protective over my team. It is *still* my team, isn't it?" He glanced about the room, looking for the approval of his leadership from the others.

"Hell, shit boss, you're welcome to this rag-tag bunch of cowboys." Jim was trying to calm the atmosphere. He understood where both men were coming from but he did not want to see them fight over their differing views.

"It isn't a question of leadership, Marcus," Stu began. "You know we would follow you anywhere. For Christ's sake, we've followed you all the way across the Middle East and Europe. That is half the fucking world. I just meant that I didn't like the idea of us being trapped here."

Stu spoke and Marcus nodded, not replying and allowing his second in command to state his point.

"Sandra needs rest and care, but all that would be for nothing if we can't get out of here when the time comes. Even worse, if those things manage to get in."

Marcus rubbed his forehead, nodding and grunting. "Okay, this is what we do...."

6

Simon, carrying his pack in one hand and slowly lifting the manhole cover with the other, balanced himself on the rungs of the ladder. He still feared a fall that would leave him paralysed but there was no other way of doing it. He could not throw the bulky pack over his shoulder because of the narrow confines of the shaft. He had no other choice but to have both hands free of the ladder.

He scanned in a three hundred and sixty degree arc, checking for any sight or sound of the dead in the immediate area of his exit point. The area still looked clear. Heaving the steel plate to one side, he strained, gritting his teeth as he tried to make as little noise as possible. With a gentle clunk, the cover rested to one side of the opening. With a final cursory check as he swivelled his head, he was happy that the coast was still clear.

He paused for a moment, breathing deeply and allowing his lungs to fill with the cool, clean air. He stared up at the green leaves above him as they fluttering in the gentle breeze. The birds twittered as they hopped from branch to branch, unaffected by the changed world around them.

Simon brought his concentration back to the matters at hand and heaved himself up out of the entrance to the bunker. Carefully, he raised himself to a crouch, facing his body in the direction of the entrance where the dead had accumulated and screened by the gentle swaying of the thick foliage of the shrubs. Remaining crouched, he slowly sidestepped to his left, never taking his eyes away from the direction of the threat. He stopped and crouched in the bushes, taking a moment to adjust to his new surroundings and gain his bearings.

The air had never tasted so good. Though it was summer, it felt cold as he breathed and his chest inflated with the fresh air.

He almost coughed.

With his hand covering his mouth and his chest in mini convulsions, he peered around the bushes he was crouched behind. He could see the creatures now, just metres away from him at the main entrance.

Though obscured by the dozens of bushes between them, he saw the unmistakable shape of human heads as they clambered at the heavy steel door. Some were pale and pasty looking, their hair dishevelled and features gaunt, while others were almost black with decay. A cool breeze blew toward him and carried with it the fetid odour of the dead. His eyes twitched and he stifled yet another cough into the palms of his hands.

He carefully moved in the opposite direction towards the back fence of his garden, gently placing each foot on the soft soil below him. He dreaded the sound of a snapping twig under his feet and he continually glanced back over his shoulder, checking to see if any had noticed him and began to follow.

The fence was just five metres away now and he stole one final fleeting look back toward the mob of cadavers, still tussling amongst themselves as they fought for pole position at the door.

He lifted his foot for another step and it lifted only a few centimetres as something gripped him from beneath. His foot had snagged a root and as his body continued forward, leaving his foot in the grasp of the natural snare, he found himself tumbling to the floor, fast.

With a thud, he hit the ground and the pack fell from his grasp. The tin cooking pots inside rattled as they were thrown about and crashed against each other, creating an ear-splitting crescendo in Simon's mind.

For a split second, Simon lay still, cringing as the thunderous sound in the otherwise silent world abated in his ears. He began to scramble to his feet and reach for the pack. His foot stayed where it was. It remained tangled in the undergrowth as he pulled and thrashed to free himself, panic gripping him from within.

The moans of the dead became louder and more excited, drifting to him on the air and clutching at his soul with an icy hand. There were many more voices crying out now than there had been before. They had obviously heard him, and in his panic Simon found his foot more firmly lodged in the tangle of weeds. Terrified, he tugged and kicked at them in the hope of miraculously freeing himself.

Then, he saw the first of them. It staggered through the wild and jumbled bushes that had blocked their view of him, the branches and leaves swiping at its face and creating minor slashes in its skin that went unnoticed by the creature as it made its way toward Simon, still writhing on the ground.

It was the walking corpse of a woman. Her hair was missing in patches and her skin was mottled grey and sagging from her face. A large, festering black wound in her shoulder was filled with the squirming maggots that ate away at her flesh and the dark and dried blood that caked the remains of her once pretty summer blouse, now looked like dried oil encrusted for all time in the material.

Simon turned away in revulsion and fear and continued to fight against the vice-like grip of the roots around his foot. The staggering woman saw him and a long and mournful wail erupted from within her. Her hands reached out and she tried to increase her speed as she forced her way through the rest of the undergrowth and bushes, her feet shuffling and scuffing against the dirt and dried leaves on the ground.

More were following. Simon saw faces appear behind the woman and they all looked back at him. Their vacant dead eyes stared at him, never blinking, and their hands grasped at him as they approached. Everywhere he looked they were there, steadily closing in on him as he lay helpless, tethered to the ground.

He was in a panic. His breath came hard and fast. His chest felt ready to burst open from the pounding of his heart. His bladder and bowels threatened to release their content as he continued to struggle. They were just metres away now. Their shuffling steps bringing them closer by the second while he remained tied to the spot.

The woman's wasted and gaunt body was already beginning to dip at the hips as she anticipated sinking her teeth into the squirming man on the ground. Her thin, dry and cracked lips curled back, exposing the rotting gums and yellowed teeth. A growl emitted from her throat, carrying putrid bile that oozed up from within her decaying insides, seeping through her teeth in long thick strands that dripped toward the ground.

A moment of clarity and Simon remembered the machete on his belt. He pulled it free of its scabbard and quickly sat upright, reaching to his foot and hacking away at the mass of tangled weeds.

His foot came free and he scrambled backwards onto his feet. He turned, looking for the pack and was suddenly gripped from behind and pulled backward. The woman had reached him and she clutched onto his jacket, trying to drag him toward to her. Without a second thought, Simon threw his hands back and stepped forward, allowing the jacket to slip from his shoulders and down his arms.

Once he was free, he turned, raised the crowbar and swung it down onto the head of his attacker. The woman, for a split second, had a look of shock etched across her face, as though it had been the last thing she had expected. The heavy iron sunk deep into her skull, causing one of her eyes to pop as the pressure forced it outward. She dropped to the floor, the jacket still grasped firmly in her hands.

Simon turned and reached for the pack. It was too late; one of them, its teeth gnashing and a whistling moan escaping from its torn and destroyed throat, was just a metre away from it. It lurched towards him, its arms reaching out and swiping at thin air as Simon took a step to the side, narrowly avoiding its grasp.

"You fucking keep it, then," he shouted in frustration as he turned for the fence.

He vaulted at the wooden planks and gripped the top. With all his strength, fear, and adrenalin driving him on, he began to pull himself up and over. As he raised his remaining foot, he felt a cold, bony hand close around his ankle and yank down on it. He pulled hard and the grip was lost, the momentum of the heave pulling him over onto the opposite side of the fence.

Simon landed heavily on the other side amongst long grass and weeds. The wind was knocked from him as he hit the ground with his back. He shook his head and quickly looked about him, fearful of any surprises waiting for him. The crowbar was still firmly in his grasp, along with the machete, and he began to lift himself up.

The fence to his left began to rattle and vibrate as the crowd thumped and pounded against it. They wailed and moaned, some building themselves into frenzy when they glimpsed him through the narrow slats of wood. To Simon, they sounded annoyed and frustrated to have lost the opportunity to sink their teeth into the man they had waited so long for outside the bunker door. If he did not know better, he could be forgiven for believing they were upset and infuriated over the fact that they had been outfoxed.

Climbing to his feet, Simon brushed himself off and stepped back. He could see glimpses of the lumbering dead here and there, as he watched the fence rattle and judder under their weight and assaults.

The smell was overpowering. Flies swirled above as the movements of the dead disturbed them as they feasted on their rotting flesh. He could feel his stomach twitch at the stench of them.

He stepped back and turned away. Behind, he left the safety of his bunker, food, supplies, survival equipment and clothing.

"Dickhead," he mumbled.

7

The hunt was on.

The rear gate had been secured again, this time using more chains, much thicker and secured with large, heavy-duty padlocks. Steve wished beyond himself that they had CCTV coverage in the area, but there was not a thing they could do about it. The people who had designed and run the park security had not seen fit to have cameras set up in the area of the rear gate, relying on the fact that it was out of the way and that not many people would know about it.

Normally, in the past when the park had been open for visitors, there was a human guard there and Steve began to consider that maybe they should mount a guard themselves, especially at night. That would mean adding to the duties of the people living in the mansion and stretching them even thinner on the ground. It would have to be a double duty, too, with two people needing to provide the guard force. To leave one person out there, so far from the safety of the house and alone all through the night, would be out of the question.

With their rear protected, for now, they turned their attention to tracking down and killing the remaining dead within the park. Carl had seen five, maybe six of them disappear from sight toward the west of the park as he watched from the roof, but he admitted that there could have been more.

Just the thought of having them within in the walls and not knowing where they were was enough to bring people to the edge of panic. Though everyone managed to keep their heads and prepare for the job that needed to be done, terror gripped them. It was the fear of the unknown.

The park was a big place, with a lot of dark corners and shady tree lines. Hungry eyes could be watching their every move, stalking them and slowly moving in for the attack when they least expected it.

People began to amplify the ability and intelligence of the dead in their own minds. With having not been beyond the walls for a while and experiencing the dead first hand, and unsure of where they were within the park, they started to think of them as phantoms, running loose inside the walls and scheming all kinds of plans and ideas for what to do with the living people within the house.

Jake had to speak loudly and sternly at one point as they prepared for the hunt when some members of the house began to suggest that maybe the dead had developed higher intelligence, or maybe a supernatural force was driving them. To Jake, these ideas were ludicrous and did nothing but add to the panic that everyone had already began to feel bubbling up inside them.

"Look, I'm scared of them too, but they're not demons," he barked, his voice echoing around in the foyer. "They don't think, or plan. They move about on instinct and are incapable of outsmarting us. Now, shut up with the speculation and rumours."

The people around him, including Steve who had been in a hushed conversation with John about the degree of intelligence and ability of the dead, were stunned to silence as Jake dressed them down.

John hefted his pickaxe handle and tested its weight in his hands. "Jake's right, they're just bags of pus. The sooner we get this done, the sooner we can all calm down and get back to normal."

"Normal, are you serious? Good one, John," Gary joked.

Steve and the rest of the group assembled outside the house. All were dressed in thick clothing, despite the heat of the day, and all were armed. Everybody would have preferred to have something a little more formidable than clubs and hammers, but guns were a luxury none of them had. No one really knew how to use one anyway. They were going to have to be up close and personal against the dead, as always.

They had all done battle against the reanimated corpses before, but it never got any easier. The idea of carrying a weapon in hand, one that could only be used up close and not from a distance, then charging into the fray to fight with an enemy that did not have any concept of fear or self preservation, was enough to scare them half to death.

They could not even afford to become injured. A bite from the infected was fatal and they all knew that. They would die slowly from a burning fever and painful infection that would spread through their body like a wildfire before returning as one of the walking dead. An accident could also be just as deadly to them. A misplaced foot or fall during a fight could leave them at the mercy of the dead.

Everyone had the same look about them as they assembled in the foyer. Their eyes were wide and the nervous glances they all gave each other spoke a thousand words. Knees were weak, hands shook and their palms sweated while their hearts raced and pounded in their chests. Adrenalin was kicking in, coursing through their bloodstreams as they psyched themselves up for the imminent clash with the un-dead.

Steve paired everyone up. Carl and John were to search together. Carl had already found two of them earlier and dealt with them while Steve and the others had taken care of the stragglers by the rear gate. The two men nodded to each other, their eyes locked as they acknowledged one another and their shared apprehension of the task ahead. Deep down, though, there was no one else that Carl would rather have alongside him.

Steve had Helen and Gary was partnered with Sophie. Everybody had designated areas to patrol.

"Jake, Lee, you two head for the restaurant area. Check the buildings then head towards the lake and clear the north-west part of the park. Carl, John, you two also go to the restaurant area and then head south west and come around toward the main gate. Try and make a little noise while you do it, only enough to get them to stumble out into the open, not ringing a dinner bell."

"Where are you heading for, Steve?" Gary asked, standing beside Sophie.

Steve looked at Helen then at Gary. "We'll head directly west, past the Information Centre and around the south part of the lake. Gary, I want you and Sophie to move directly north from the house and through the tree line. That should give us full coverage of the whole of the western part of the park. The roof watch have a good view of everything to the east with it all being open plane so that isn't an immediate concern."

Gary nodded then raised his radio. "Claire, are you happy with what you're doing?" He looked up to the roof as he spoke and three heads leaned over the side and peered down at him, giving a thumbs up in acknowledgment.

The radio crackled and Claire's voice could be heard. "Yeah, Gary, all three of us are up here and ready."

Gary was still looking up at the rooftop. "Okay, keep sending checks over the radio once we're gone and keep your eyes peeled."

Lisa had joined Claire and Jennifer on the roof team. Up until recently, she had spent most of her time in a daze and shock, but now she had begun to come out of her shell. It was still hard for her to deal with losing her young family, but she seemed to be coming to terms with it now, and rather than just floating about the house she had become more proactive. It was a hard new world, one that could only be survived by the hard minded, and Lisa had begun to prove her worth as part of the clan.

The house had been sealed from the inside. During the preparations, the boarded windows that were within arm's reach along the ground floor were double-checked and reinforced where necessary. The rear door to the mansion was locked and barricaded and the front door would receive the same treatment once the search parties dispersed and began their clearance of the park.

Karen had fought with Gary, insisting that the house needed to be left open for them should they need to retreat there, but he had talked her down. His argument was that there were children in the house that would not be able to fight the dead off if they managed to get in.

"And besides, Karen, if we need to we can always use one of the other buildings in the park to hide. There's only a few of them anyway and we're not taking any chances. Now go inside and lock the doors. Place the large couch and table behind them like we agreed."

Karen was a little on the frantic side. "But why do you all have to go after them?"

"Karen," Gary held her gently by the shoulders and looked into her eyes, "you know why. We can't risk having any of them in here and on the loose. We'll be okay, I promise. And you can listen over the radio if it makes you feel better."

With teary eyes, Karen accepted what needed to be done and allowed Gary to guide her back to the house. Gary kissed her and hugged her for a moment.

"Hey, I tell you what, why don't you think of something nice for us all to cook for dinner? That should keep your mind off things," he said it with a smile as he leaned back. His intentions had been of a good nature but his words had the opposite effect as Karen fixed him with a stare.

Karen scowled. "Don't patronise me, you old fart." She turned and marched back in the house to where Catherine, the wife of Carl, stood waiting to help her with barricading the door.

Lee and Jake burst into fits of laughter. Jake looked up at Gary who now stood on the step to the mansion, looking at the large wooden door that had just been slammed in his face.

"I tell you what, Gary, she has some fire in her belly when she wants, doesn't she?"

Gary was walking toward them now, trying to appear casual. "Yup, that's why I love her. She'll simmer down."

"I'm not sure, mate. I think you'll be sleeping on the sofa tonight."

Gary chuckled and wagged a finger at the much younger man then turned to Steve. "Okay, let's get on with it then," he said, drawing in a deep breath.

They had decided against using cars this time. The last patrol had turned up with just two finds and the group felt that they would see and hear them much easier if they were on foot. Though more vulnerable, all believed that as long as they did not get careless, they would be more effective that way.

Each pair carried a handheld radio and Gary insisted that everyone should be giving regular reports on their whereabouts, including the group on the roof of the house. At least that way they would know that everyone was safe and which areas had been covered. Gary knew the place like the back of his hand, and just from people describing where they were over the radio waves he could draw up a mental map in his head.

"Be careful down by the lake area. There are a lot of small tracks that crisscross that area and some of the trees are so close together, it's impossible to see more than a few feet at a time," Jake informed everyone.

"Will do, Jake," Steve replied.

Lee and Jake began to walk along the gravel track that led into the dark shade of the woods and toward the Information Centre. A chill ran down Lee's spine as he recalled the night that he had followed Tony through the woods and discovered what he had done, the visions of the children and what they had endured haunted him still. He still had nights when he struggled to sleep as the images of those poor children refused to allow him to rest.

He shook the memory from his mind and spat on the ground three times. To him, the memory at that moment was a bad omen and he gripped his iron bar even tighter, gritting his teeth and growling quietly to himself.

Claire's voice hissed from the radios. "Good luck, everyone."

8

John and Carl had headed into the built-up area of the park along with Lee and Jake, as instructed. At the junction, both groups nodded their farewells to one another and went in their separate directions.

For some unknown reason, maybe from watching too many movies or even from instinct, both men found themselves crouching as they walked. Their knees were slightly bent, they leaned forward at the waist and their arms were held like pistons, waiting to go into action. They looked like coiled springs, as though they were ready to sprint for their lives, or leap into a fight.

Carl looked ahead of him, towards John who was out in front. His friend's broad shoulders were hunched forward and his thick forearms were tense as he clutched on to his club. He looked rather like Carl would have expected Neanderthal man to look like: squat and robust.

"What the fuck are we doing?" Carl suddenly asked, standing upright and allowing his hands to drop to his side.

John paused, holding his position like a hunter stalking a deer. He turned to Carl, a puzzled look on his face.

"What, what's up?"

Carl shook his head as a frown creased his brow. "We look like a right pair of dicks. We aren't in Vietnam, you know."

John looked at the way Carl was standing, his eyes travelling the length from his head to his feet. Then he looked down at himself, still poised for action, his hands gripping his club in both hands at waist level like a rifle and his knees slightly bent as though he was patrolling through thick jungle. He looked around him. The area was open, tarmac beneath their feet and buildings scattered to the left and right. They were in no immediate danger and anything coming toward them could be seen well in advance, even without the ninja walking technique.

John stood up and relaxed his arms. "Sorry, but my arse is twitching at the moment."

"Mine too." Carl smiled back at him.

Standing upright, they both moved off together. They walked cautiously between the buildings, peeping around corners before stepping in the open. Apprehension gripped them both and the longer the time dragged without seeing any sign of the rogue walking dead that had made it into the park, the more nervous they became.

"Where are they?" John hissed impatiently over his shoulder.

"Just keep moving. They're in here somewhere."

They cleared the area around the restaurants and gift shops and headed to the southwest part of the wall that ran along the front of the park, paralleling the main access road. They were in open flat country and could see for hundreds of metre to their left as they looked in the interior of the park in the direction of the information centre. They were moving east along the wall when the radio crackled.

"Stop," Carl whispered from behind. "I think it's Lee."

John turned and stepped closer to his partner, tilting his head and straining to hear what was being sent over the radio-waves.

Lee's voice was faint and broken with the distance. Carl knew that they were at least two kilometres away at the far side of the park from where they were, and at that range they were lucky to be able to hear anything at all.

"We've got one. Up by the..." Lee's voice trailed off in a hiss of static.

John looked at Carl, eager to hear more. "Did he say they got one? Where is he?"

Carl looked at the radio and thought for a moment. "They're up in the north west corner, on the far side of the lake."

"You think that's where the rest will be?"

"I don't know," Carl shrugged, "anyway, quiet, I think I heard something else."

He leaned his head closer to the speaker of the radio, trying to hear through the crackles and hisses.

"Lee, it's Carl, can you hear me, Lee?" After a few moments, Carl dropped his hand to his side. "I don't think we're getting them now."

"Did you hear anything from the others?"

"Nope," Carl shook his head, "but I think they're either in the woods or around buildings and stuff, probably hard to get a signal."

John looked up at Carl, uncertainty in his eyes. "Or maybe, well...you know."

A questioning look crossed Carl's face, then he realised what John was trying to say. "Nah, I doubt it. Lee knows what he's doing. I doubt he would come undone by a couple of those things."

"He *is* a bit of a hot head, though, and you said yourself, Carl, there's a bunch of them, not just a couple."

Carl shook off the shiver that ran the length of his spine and waved a hand. "It's just these radios; they're not cut out for this kind of range. I'm sure Lee and Jake are fine." He turned to John, hoping for confirmation that he had put his mind at rest, as well as his own.

"Aye, I suppose you're right. Come on, we'd better carry on with our sweep."

Both men continued to walk. They headed for the main gate.

The day was turning out to be a scorcher. The sky was clear blue with only the faintest hint of wispy clouds high in the atmosphere. Birds chirped and a gentle breeze blew the long grass that brushed against the fingertips of John and Carl as they continued their clearance.

They crested a small rise that gave them a view of the main entrance. They could see the trees that lined the road and the open area immediately inside of the gate. Nothing moved. There was no sign of the roaming dead that had gotten inside.

"Well, looks like our area is clear," Carl said with relief as he turned to John. "We may as well do a check of the gate while we're at it and then head back to the house."

John nodded and continued to walk.

Carl raised the radio to his mouth. "Steve, it's Carl. That's our area clear. We're down by the gate and heading back towards the house once we're finished." He paused and waited for a reply. None came. "Steve, can you hear me?"

John stopped and turned to Carl. He squinted and shielded his eyes from the bright sunlight. "Are you getting anybody on that thing?"

"Steve isn't answering." Carl was looking down at the radio, gently tapping the side against his palm in the hope of it suddenly squawking to life.

He raised it to his mouth again. "Is there anyone hearing me? It's, Carl. We're down at the gate." There was no reply.

He was starting to feel alarmed and his face showed it as he looked back at John. "Shit, you don't think they've all been attacked, do you?"

John ran a hand through his short hair. "I doubt it. We would've heard from Jen or Claire on the roof at least. Maybe it's just the radio?"

"That's the problem though; I'm not getting the rooftop bunch either." Carl looked in the direction he knew the other clearance teams to be. "Steve should only be a kilometre in that direction, at the most."

"So?"

"Well I think we should walk that way in case they need our help," Carl suggested.

John nodded. "Okay, we'll do that then."

They continued walking toward the gate with the intention of checking that final area and then following the main access road towards the mansion, then veering off toward the built up area of the park and to the lake.

At the gate, all was as they had expected. There were a few strays hanging around on the other side of the bars, but they had been ready for that and it was not a shock to them. The bodies of two men and a woman hissed and moaned as they shook the gate and tried to reach through with clutching and grasping hands. They threw themselves at the steel bars as they became more excited, or frustrated; John could not be sure which.

John turned to the camera mounted at the side of the gate on top of the wall and waved.

A sudden snap from the tree line behind them caused his head to turn rapidly. He held a hand out and snapped his fingers to gain Carl's attention. Both men stooped and squinted into the gloom of the foliage, just forty metres from where they stood.

"What? What did you see?" Carl whispered from his left. He was suddenly on high alert and he had no idea why. He had heard John click his fingers and when he turned, John was back in his stalking position, crouched and poised, and focussed completely on the bushes and trees in front of them. Not knowing made him nervous.

John kept his eyes glued to the shadowy undergrowth of the trees and held a finger up at Carl. "I heard something."

Carl frowned and thought for a moment. He watched John and followed his line of sight but saw nothing except bushes and tree bark. He shook his head and stood upright again. "You heard something? For fuck sake, John...."

John looked back at him and began to speak. "Yeah, I...."

Two figures crashed out from within the woods and headed straight for them, a third and a fourth soon followed. They broke into a sprint and reached out their arms in front them, a long screeching moan erupting from their dead mouths.

Without another word, John turned and sprinted back the way they had come. He turned right at the gate and headed for the open fields and the central area of the park.

"Oh shit, oh shit...." John panted as he turned and raced away from the gate and the dead.

For a moment, Carl had been frozen to the spot as he watched the four nightmarish creatures explode from the undergrowth and head straight for them. He had not seen any fast movers for a while, let alone four of them in the same place. It was only the blur of John as he sprinted across his path and the hard tug he gave him on the arm, encouraging him to follow, that forced Carl into action.

Without another look back, Carl followed him.

"Run, John, run," Carl was screaming from behind.

He was closing the gap, and soon he would overtake John and leave him behind. He was much faster and fitter and he knew that John would struggle to keep up, or even keep going for long. If he stayed at the same pace, the pursuing dead would catch them both, eventually. Carl glanced back over his shoulder; they were still there and they were not slowing. He looked to his left and slightly ahead at his friend.

John's arms were pumping hard and his heavy feet bounded across the grass like a stampeding wildebeest as he did his best to outpace the lifeless, yet ravenous, monsters that chased him. His lungs burned and his breath was coming in gulps as his muscles screamed out for oxygenated blood. His heart pounded in his ears and thumped in his chest. It felt like it was about to burst or seize up entirely, but he kept on going. Fear alone was pushing him forward but he knew himself, he would not be able to keep going for long.

He looked across at Carl, who was now level with him. He could see the fear burning in his eyes. He looked back at the dead. They were just thirty metres away. He still clutched the heavy iron bar in his hand and, for a fleeting moment, he considered turning and fighting them, but he knew he had no chance. Not even with Carl fighting by his side. Against four runners, they would not last long.

"Keep going, John," Carl encouraged. "Don't look back and don't slow down. I'll not leave you."

Carl had already made the decision that there was no way on earth that he would desert his friend to become an easy lunch for the dead. He, too, was struggling. He had not run in a long time and it was his muscle memory and the adrenaline that powered him forward. His lungs had long since given up on keeping pace with his heart rate and the demand of his oxygen starved muscles. His legs burned and his chest hurt, but the snarling and moaning of the creatures that slowly closed the gap between them, forced him forward.

John and Carl were starting to slow.

They had run at full pace for three hundred metres and the sprinting corpses pursuing them had shortened the gap to just fifteen metres. The fall of the footsteps behind them became more audible in their ears and they could almost feel the cold, lifeless fingertips making contact with their backs. They could see the roofs of the buildings in the distance and knew that they would have a better chance once they were in amongst the offices, restaurants and gift shops.

They would never make it. Carl knew that. He glanced to his right and at the trees. He reached over and tugged on John's arm, forcing him to change direction.

"This way, move!" he screamed.

John followed suit. He was beginning to lose his vision, the blood in his veins and muscles felt like acid as his body screamed for a halt. His steps became less sure footed and he began to stumble as he followed Carl. A bone-chilling wail from behind helped him to drain the very last of his reserves and, for a second, he felt a surge of energy run through him. He picked up his pace and raced forward.

"The trees, John, get in the trees," Carl shouted over his shoulder.

John was unable to answer, but he understood and he followed on as Carl crashed through the foliage that marked the start of the woods. The leaves and branches swiped and lashed at their faces but neither of them noticed.

Carl ran headlong through the rustling leaves below his feet and bounded over fallen stumps and folds in the ground.

"There, that one." He pointed at a tree to their front. "Fucking get up it, John, quick!" he ordered.

John saw where Carl pointed and headed straight for the large, thick tree ahead of him. As he approached it, and without slowing down, he weighed it up and automatically calculated at what point he was to leap and where to grasp with his hands in order to begin a fast ascent. He dipped his head and ran past Carl, who had now slowed in order to allow John to get ahead of him and begin climbing.

One of the dead was ahead of the pack. Carl raised his club and swung with all the strength he could muster. It collided with the side of its head and the body was thrown to the side, it smacked into another tree before hitting the ground. It began to struggle to its feet again and Carl turned toward the tree they had singled out as their safe haven.

John was scrambling up the trunk, grasping at any branch or hollow he could grip onto and desperately trying to get as far away from the ground as possible.

Carl lurched and gripped on to the bark and began to haul himself up. He reached out for a branch that would allow him to pull his legs up from ground level.

A hand gripped his foot, and for a moment he almost lost his grip as the sudden weight became a larger burden on his already exhausted body. The hand clutched tighter and pulled, dragging him down and causing his free foot to slip from the bark of the tree, leaving just his hands grasping on to the branch. He was losing strength and his grip began to slacken as he grunted with effort. The rough bark cut into his fingers as he thrashed with his legs trying to break the grasp of the corpse below him.

The others were approaching fast. They reached out and moaned loudly as they closed in on the tree and the soft flesh that hung from it, writhing in a hopeless attempt to get away from them.

Carl was now hanging on by just his fingertips and his hold was slackening. At any moment his fingers would slip and he would tumble to the ground and land in the clutching arms of the four emaciated, but deadly, bodies below him, their teeth gnashing and tearing into his flesh as their claw-like fingers gouged at his soft tissue.

Carl was terrified. He peered down past his legs and saw their faces. Their lips peeled back, giving the impression of a sneer or malicious grin. Their teeth snapped shut continually and they reached in the air above them in anticipation of the meal before them. His fingers slipped and his grip was lost.

"Shit...," he screamed.

For an instant, he felt himself tumble, then he stopped.

John gripped on for all his might. He clasped with both hands at the forearm of Carl as he braced himself with his feet wedged against a large branch of the tree. He was face down and his head was below his feet as he clung on to his friend's arm. Using his feet as a counter weight, he pushed off the underside of the branch and heaved. He grunted and growled with the strain and the effort.

Carl turned to him, his face full of shock and surprise as John continued to pull him up.

He felt the grip of the hand clutching at his foot loosen. With his free leg, he kicked and began to scramble up the tree as John heaved him upward and to safety.

Carl had been sure that he was about to fall into the group of walking dead below him, but John, his friend and saviour, had caught him and was now hauling him up with all the strength he would expect of a world class power lifter.

Carl threw his other hand up and grasped on to John's sleeve, pulling himself that little bit further from the clutching death below. With both his feet now free, he scrambled up the tree and threw himself on to the large branch on which John was sprawled.

He lay there, gasping for air.

Neither of them spoke for a moment as they lay there, dizzy with exhaustion and panting for breath.

John began to cough and splutter uncontrollably, and before long he was leaning over the thick branch and throwing the entire contents of his stomach up and onto the heads of the four bewildered and thrashing dead below them.

Carl began to vomit, too, when he saw that the dead were biting chunks out of each other's faces and eating the warm vomit that John had just thrown on to them.

The two men were done. Their legs trembled and their heads spun. Both had splitting headaches and their throats were dry as bone, but they were alive.

John knew that he would never have made it without Carl being there to help him and Carl knew that he would be a bloody pulp at the foot of the tree at that moment if John had not pulled him up.

Panting for breath, and with a voice that threatened to crack, John leaned over and spoke between gulps of air. "What…do we do…now, then?"

Carl lay on his back; his head was spinning and his chest heaved uncontrollably. "Right now, I don't care. I'm fucked. I think the wife will be mad at me, though, if I'm not back for dinner."

John and Carl were stuck. Exhausted and terrified, they were trapped in a tree with four un-dead ghouls pacing at the foot of where they were perched.

9

For weeks the body of Andy Moorcroft had roamed the countryside, bouncing from one town to the next, passing through villages and trailing the roads that linked them. He headed nowhere in particular. The tarmac beneath his feet just encouraged him to keep moving, acting as a conveyor belt and feeding him from the rural, to the urban areas and back to the rural.

The miles upon miles of shuffling and staggering along the hard tarmac roads and rocky and uneven dirt tracks began to show on the shoes that he wore. They were tattered and beaten. The tread had begun to wear thin and the leather uppers were torn and ripped, exposing the rotting skin of his feet beneath.

His clothes were no better. The jacket hung from his body, waterlogged and sagging from his bony shoulders as his muscles wasted and rotted away. It was covered in all manner of filth. Stains such as everyday dirt and grime but there was dried blood, putrefied flesh and pus, too.

His denim jeans were no longer recognisable. They had once been a stonewashed blue, but now they were a grey colour with a greasy sheen. They were ripped in places, showing the green and brown mottled flesh within and the many creatures that lived off his slowly deteriorating body.

In a way, he had developed his own ecological system. A swarm of all manner of flying insects hovered around him, their lava burrowing deep into his flesh until they matured and then repeating the cycle.

Scavenging birds flocked overhead, darting in and out with speed and stealth, plucking the flies from the air around him and the bloated grubs from his flesh, then quickly fleeing to a safe distance, always careful to keep away from his clutching hands and gnashing teeth.

His decomposition had slowed substantially. His movements were no longer hampered with fluid-filled and swollen limbs, and his skin had dried to something resembling old leather. His face had lost its plumpness and his body was nothing more than skin and bone with sinew and the remnants of muscle holding it all together.

Nevertheless, he moved much more freely than he had before, as though his body consciously kept his joints lubricated. Gone were his clumsy uncoordinated movements; now he moved with a slow-paced walk, unable to manage anything more than an uncoordinated and clumsy stagger should he feel the need.

From one day to the next, he wandered aimlessly. Now and then, something would distract him and grab his attention. Things that triggered a faint memory from his life, such as a work of art hanging in a window, or a building or street that somehow seemed familiar to him, would cause him to stop. Eventually the memory would fade and he would continue his endless walk, completely forgetting whatever it was that had encouraged him to halt in the first place.

In one quiet and seemingly deserted town, he had spent hours mesmerised by a particularly attractive car, very much like the one he had owned in life but a much more expensive model. Even after months of sitting neglected and exposed to the elements in the partially destroyed showroom, the car's beauty, even to Andy, was undeniable.

Below the light sprinkling of dust, he could see the shimmer and gleam of the highly polished gunmetal grey paintwork of the body. The sparkling silver spokes of the alloy wheels dazzled him. His reflection, distorted and obscured, stretched and curved with the shape of the wheels as he leaned in to admire them.

The sleek shape of the car, its muscular yet feminine curves, sang out to him almost soothingly through his misted mind. He moved to the front of the car and gazed down at the grill.

He heard something; a low growl. Stepping back, alarmed, Andy looked around him and about the damaged shop. Nothing stirred. Glancing back down at the grill, he heard the noise again. It was a low hoarse rumble and very close.

The noise was coming from within him. An instinct, a faint memory of him doing it in the past, something made him feel the urge to growl each time he looked at the grill. No clear picture presented itself and there was no conscious effort to piece the puzzle together. Andy just accepted that the wide silver grill that spanned the entire width of the car like a large snarling mouth full of fangs, made him want to growl and he continued to growl for a while as he admired it.

The car was unlocked, and Andy felt something surge inside him as the door opened in his hand. It was a feeling he had experienced something similar to before. He paused and looked up, his teeth clashed together and he began to gulp, as though swallowing something. He stopped and looked down at the car's interior and repeated the action of gulping something.

He had felt a similar sensation when he had last fed.

When he saw the living creature he had felt lust, desire, an engulfing want and need for it. As the blood had gushed over his cheeks, down his chin and into his mouth, he had been overcome by a feeling of excitement and euphoria. Then, as the chunks of flesh slid down his throat and his teeth gnawed on hard bone, he had felt contentment and peace.

Such was his feelings for the car.

For the better part of a day, he sat in the driving seat of the luxurious sports car and felt the wheel in his hands and the hand-stitched leather seats beneath him. The dials and the dashboard clocks hypnotised him and he growled once more as he expected to see the needle of the speedometer rise and fall and hear the roar of the engine in his ears.

The car was beautiful. Even in his deteriorated state, and with a misfiring brain, Andy still appreciated beauty. It was what he had based his previous life upon and he had carried his admonition of beauty into death.

He would have stayed there forever, but he made the mistake of adjusting the mirror. The reflection he saw revolted him. The ugliness of himself and the beauty of the interior of the car around him were in stark contrast. He looked away, repulsed. He stared down at his hands; the ragged and blackened skin of his palms and the dirty broken fingernails that had no place in handling the smooth clean surfaces of the car, was like a desecration to him.

He climbed out, slamming the door behind him, a low rasping and sorrowful moan hissing from his throat.

He continued on his long slow walk.

He never had a particular goal or destination, but he did prefer to be alone. He tried to avoid the others like him. They tended to congregate in the towns and cities in tightly packed groups, and Andy always found himself turning and heading in the opposite direction when he saw them.

If anything, he felt repulsed by them.

Andy had changed. He was self-aware. He felt things, emotions. He did not understand them fully, but he was aware of them and they were strong enough to guide him. From the appreciation of the natural beauty of the rural areas that he travelled through, to the disdain for the others like him that he constantly saw around him. He watched them as they roamed the roads in packs and swarmed the cities. They devoured anything they could get their hands on. They trampled the gardens and the flowers and left a wasteland in their wake.

Even fear was an emotion that Andy knew. He had seen fire and felt the searing heat against his skin as he had passed too close to it and he knew that it could end his existence. It had scared him, and like all animals he now kept his distance from the beautifully mesmerising, but deadly orange and yellow glow, that he saw from time to time on his travels. Others failed to hold the same respect for fire as Andy did, and he watched on a few occasions as they were engulfed in its flames, staggering around and colliding with walls and others like them as the fire consumed them.

He also knew that the emaciated and ugly forms that he saw were not how things were supposed to be. The shadowy figures he saw were supposed to be agile, beautiful and full of energy, vibrant and animated. They were supposed to be living people.

Now, they were wrong and unnatural, nothing like the people he saw all around them in the slowly decaying and fading pictures and posters hanging from the walls or on display in shop windows.

Andy felt a loathing for them, even for himself to a degree. He understood that he was one of them, but something inside him pulled away from them and encouraged him to keep his distance.

Sometimes, he would stop and watch them. They were dull and lifeless to him. They did not fascinate him and as well as loathing, he felt pity towards them. He understood that like him, they had not always been that way. They had once been like the people in the pictures as he had once been like the beautiful smiling face in the picture hanging from the wall of the shop he had once owned. Now they were vulgar and wretched, unlike the birds and the trees he saw when he was on the roads and in the country lanes.

The people that swarmed the cities and infested the towns, they were wrong, grotesque and deformed. They staggered and tripped along, continually colliding with one another and the moan they perpetually emitted was like a sadness that came from within them, as if in protest of their existence and wanting a release.

The flowers that lined the hedgerows were bright and colourful and they danced in the wind, hypnotizing him as he stood and watched them for hours at a time. The birds, though he could never get close to them, sang to him, and he could never resist watching them flutter through the air as they zipped from tree to tree. They were beautiful and warm.

There were no flowers in the cities. The only birds he saw were the ones that were brave enough to swoop down and feast on the bodies that lay motionless in the street, festering and decaying in the sun. Andy never liked being in the cities and he would stagger from building to building and street to street until he found his way out and back into the country.

Now, he was in a city again.

Everything was in shadow, or at least it seemed that way. The buildings were grey and dreary, stretching up in the sky like giant tombstones of civilisation. What windows remained were caked in filth; long smearing handprints and bodily fluids from the thousands of decaying figures that had pressed themselves against the glass barriers of the shops and buildings.

The streets were littered with the relics of days gone by. Rustling newspapers, displaying the last headlines of man, drifted along the windy streets as the tall buildings channelled the air around them; creating currents that lifted the smaller pieces of debris and made them glide through the streets.

Shop fronts were broken and smashed, doors hung from their hinges and windows were shattered, open to the elements. There were cars and trucks scattered all around, some parked and locked at the side of the road, others turned on their sides or nothing more than blackened and charred skeletons from when they had burned during the panics that had engulfed the world as the dead invaded and multiplied, attacking and ravaging all before them.

Andy continued to walk, uninterested by anything that he saw around him.

Others walked with him, automatically tagging on behind him as he passed them. With nothing else to distract them, sometimes it took little more than a body to pass in close proximity and they would wander aimlessly after them, as though they were being led to somewhere of importance or interest.

Most remained where they were, either standing still, their eyes fixed on the floor beneath them or staring up into nothingness. Some remained sitting and slouched in shop doorways. Others just roamed the street in an endless slow shuffle until their path was blocked and they would then change direction. Many were trapped within the cities due to this very reason, endlessly wandering through the maze of buildings and shops that would never allow them to leave.

Others meandered through the shops, studying the things on display and even trying to use them. Cups were lifted and pondered over before being placed against cold and brittle lips, or books were opened and the pages stared upon with dead and misty eyes as instinct reminded them of what the items were.

Some of the dead even attempted at dressing themselves in the clothes they pulled down from the shelves and hangers. Normally they would end in either a tangled heap of grey flesh and garments on the floor, or a ludicrous vision of a figure walking around, its festering skin blistered and green and falling from its body, yet wearing an extremely elegant and colourful hat, artificial flowers and all.

Andy wanted away from them. He felt a sense of urgency pass over him and he increased his slow shuffling pace to a more uncoordinated, but speedier stagger. His legs forced him forward and his arms swayed from side to side in front of him as his body jerked and settled into a rhythm.

The bodies that followed behind him did the same. They began to moan as they watched Andy move away from them, as though they would be missing something and wanted Andy to slow down and wait for them.

He suddenly felt hunted. They were following him and their wails were becoming louder as he staggered and shuffled as fast as he could from them.

More of them spilled from the buildings around him as they heard the din of the ever-increasing group. It was herd behaviour and they all began to join in with the chase and the chorus of the dead song.

Andy glanced back over his shoulder, fear gripping him.

The figures were all around him now. Thousands of eyes were focussed on him and he felt vulnerable for it. He had nothing they wanted, but still they followed. The noise of their moans was becoming louder by the minute and it was constant. There were now so many of them that the street could no longer be seen. They poured from the buildings and alleyways. They were in front of him and behind, all the while closing in.

Andy was trapped. He turned on the spot where he stood in the open street, vulnerable as the mass of bodies closed in around him. Their cries became a deafening roar as they staggered closer on their battered and tatty feet along the hard surface of the high street.

Somehow, he had become the focus of the entire city's attention. He was one of them, he knew that, but still he feared them. He knew what a crowd like that could do to his frail and delicate body. Teeth and hands could soon leave him in pieces or, at best, severely damaged and more fragile than he already was.

He stopped and looked around him. They closed in; the first grasping hands reached him and began to tug at his clothes. They gripped his arms and even clawed at his face. Andy fought back, knocking their hands away from him as he tried desperately to protect himself.

Soon, the entire swarm had enveloped him. Andy was being pulled and jostled in all directions. He heard the material of his clothing tear as the seams gave under the strain. Their fingers dug into his flesh as they pulled him in different directions. Clumps of hair were ripped from his scalp and a large gash was torn from the flesh on his neck in the melee.

The grasping hands stopped and bodies and faces being pushed up close to him replaced them. The horde was too big now, and so tightly packed that they were pressed shoulder to shoulder.

Andy became confused.

One moment they had set upon him, intent on tearing him to pieces, and then suddenly they carried him along with them. Their attention no longer focussed on him but on something else and they pushed him along in the same direction.

With so many bodies screaming and pushing against each other, and even though they were no longer interested in him, Andy knew he was still in danger. He knew his body was vulnerable and weak, especially in a crowd and he desperately wanted to protect it, to preserve it.

The crowd was surging. Arms flailed and an atmosphere of excitement rippled through the mass of bodies around him. They all pushed in the same direction and he found himself being carried along on a tide of rotting flesh and wailing voices.

Bodies fell and were trampled as they struggled to climb to their feet. Bones crunched underfoot and skulls were smashed as the crowd forged forward relentlessly.

Andy fought against the others around him, against the wave of dead. He tried desperately to get away from them, but there were too many and more and more were spilling from the doorways around them.

The entire city had become a hive of activity due to Andy's sudden increase of pace.

The cries and wails grew in intensity and bounced from the buildings as they echoed along the street. The mass of bodies that were packed on the roads was so thick that anything in their path as they moved forward would be swept up by them and carried along. That was now happening to Andy.

The entire putrid population was on the move, an exodus of the dead. Flying insects swarmed above them and birds flocked overhead and swooped in to grab the buzzing flies that were thick in the air.

Suddenly, Andy found himself close to the wall of a building. Bodies still pushed against him, but he was able to get through and into the relative safety of an empty doorway. He peered out and watched as the crowd charged by him. It was a blur of grey as they staggered past.

Broken and lifeless forms were crushed and spat out from the mass. They lay broken and smashed in the gutter where they would remain to rot away.

Eventually, the crowd lessened and Andy peered out from the cover of the shop doorway. The street seemed deserted compared to how it had been just moments before. There was still movement as those that were too slow were left behind to stagger after the throng of moving bodies. Some even crawled or dragged themselves as their broken and twisted legs trailed behind them. A sea of rancid sludge followed in the mass' wake. Internal organs had erupted from numerous orifices and limbs had been ripped from sockets, leaving a scene of revulsion behind.

Andy stepped out and watched in the distance as the last of them disappeared from sight. He looked around at the streets of the city, the filth and detritus of its new occupants disgusted him.

He turned and walked away, headed for the open country again. Then, he stopped and looked up.

10

Johnny watched, as he always did. He had made a life of watching people and their ways. Shunned by society, Johnny lived on its outer fringes. Most failed to understand him and know the real man beneath the shaggy beard, woolly hat and Wellington boots. Instead, they labelled him as just another crazy down-and-out and no one bothered to look any deeper than that.

His real name was David, but someone had once nicknamed him 'Johnny Boots' because regardless of whether it was raining or clear blue skies above, he never failed to wear his Wellington boots. He could be seen trekking about the town at the height of summer sporting his knee-high rubber boots and the name had stuck.

He was always eccentric and because of the way he dressed, people assumed him homeless. Therefore, he became the local 'celebrity' tramp as it were. Everyone knew Johnny Boots. People saw him everywhere in the town, in all the districts and boroughs. He would wander from place to place, dressed in his old Wellington boots, carrying a stack of newspapers under his arm. Just by his appearance, people could be forgiven for mistaking him as homeless.

There was much more to him than met the eye. He was an intelligent and quick-witted man who had once had a prospective career in marketing in his younger days. He had been considered as something of a prodigy. His talent was boundless and he never ceased to surprise and impress colleagues and bosses with his ability to reel in even the most difficult of sales. His future was looking bright. He was successful and set to be at the top of his game at a young age.

One Christmas, at an office party, he had met Louise, the daughter of one of the directors. As far as Johnny was concerned, it was love at first sight and a whirlwind romance had followed. They were living the highlife with parties, holidays and the best of everything with the world at their feet. For their engagement, Louise's father had bought them a penthouse apartment in the city.

It had seemed that his future was paved with golden flagstones.

However, the stresses and demands of modern day society, relationships and the constant worry of finance and the need to succeed caused him to suffer a mental break down in the process. It did not help that on the day he turned twenty-five, the woman he had loved so much and had married just a year earlier walked out on him, taking their baby son with her and cutting all contact with him. She sold the apartment and disappeared.

He never saw them again.

He crumbled and withdrew from the world. Only to emerge as a man that held very little value in personal possessions and very little love for a society that was more than happy to shower him with praise and glory when he was doing well, but at the first sign of trouble, tossed him into the gutter with all the other trash.

His house became nothing more than a solid shelter for him. He no longer owned a bed or furniture of any kind and he spent most of his time wandering about the towns and cities, greeting people in the street, calling 'hello' to anyone who looked in his direction.

He laughed all the time, too. Most believed that it was because he was insane, but it was nothing of the sort. Johnny saw things that most people did not. He watched how the population of the world scurried about, striving to better themselves by the standards that were forced upon them by their peers and the pressures of society. He found it amusing how so many of the world's population rarely paused and contemplated what they were actually struggling for, or appreciated what they had.

As far as Johnny was concerned, all he needed was air in his lungs and food in his belly and everything else was an unnecessary burden. He saw no value in wearing fancy clothes or driving expensive cars. He was at his happiest sitting in parks and talking to strangers, just appreciating life in general.

Now, once again, he watched. It was a new society that he gazed upon, very different from the old ways. Gone were the days of people chasing the promotion at work or their bank balances, these new people behaved differently but Johnny did not really feel affected by it. He still lived on the fringes, and still no one paid him much attention.

He knew that the new society was dangerous and that he had to be careful. As long as he remained silent and moved slowly, as he always had done anyway, he was able to move among them and continue in much the same way as he had done before. Only he could not speak to any of them and they were not as amusing to watch as they had been in the old days when they were more preoccupied with pettiness.

Over the recent months, Johnny had seen much happen on the streets. He saw the panic of the people as they fled and fought amongst each other. He saw the police lose control and the city burst into anarchy. He witnessed killings and torture, even rape, as people turned on one another.

He also saw the dead.

He watched as they slowly and steadily became the dominant species and packed the streets as they roamed, searching for the flesh of the living. He saw how they consumed anything alive that was unfortunate enough to fall in their path. How they multiplied and how they never gave up. He witnessed how they would quickly increase in mass as soon as they detected someone living, as if they could communicate with their moans.

Johnny knew from very early on that he had to remain on the outskirts of this new society, but at the same time he needed to blend within them from time to time.

Now, he stood on the roof of the shopping arcade. As always, he had shuffled through the town, slowly and quietly, passing the dead as they staggered by or sat decaying in the street. He did not laugh or nod to the figures he saw or feel any desire to say 'hello' to them. He just kept his eyes to the floor and slowly made his way toward the place where he normally got his food.

He knew the arcade well. He had spent much time there in the old days, greeting people and receiving strange looks from them as they scurried by about their business.

Even now, though he was the only living being amongst them, no one paid him any attention. It did amuse him how he had managed to get one up on the old society and even the new one. When the old ways, the ways that had frowned upon him and his kind, had perished, he had survived. Now, surrounded by the dead, he continued to survive and the dead were oblivious to him.

He made his way into the bargain priced supermarket and gently, without any sudden movements, collected his usual tins of beans and meatballs. He always collected two of each at a time. He could have taken more, but that would have broken his routine. He enjoyed having the chance to walk through the city centre every few days. Not because he got a thrill from it or because he gloated at the creatures around him for having become what they were; it was because he had always liked being in the arcade and he did not want that to change now because it had become more dangerous for him. It was the same with his boots; he always wore them and they were part of his routine. A sudden change in it, regardless of necessity, could cause him great upset.

For the last hour he had watched as the entire dead population of the city had been on the move. At first, while in the supermarket, the moans and wails had sent him into a panic. For a moment, he believed that he had been detected and the crowd was coming for him. Through the glass front of the shop, he witnessed the multitude of bodies as they massed, their arms flailing and their cries becoming a crescendo. Fear had gripped him and turned his blood ice cold.

He had fled through the storeroom of the shop and headed for the roof. All the time, as he bounded up the steel staircase, he muttered to himself, cursing himself for being so careless. He burst onto the rooftop and spun, expecting to see a foul smelling and hideous looking crowd following him through the door. None followed and Johnny felt perplexed for a while, all the time, the anticipation building as he expected them to appear at any moment.

The noise from the street continued and he began searching for a way off the roof, still believing that they were coming for him. The roof to the supermarket was lower than the adjacent buildings and there was no way he could have crossed onto the rooftops to his left or right. He was trapped and terror clutched at him even more.

Still watching the rooftop entrance, Johnny backed himself up to the wall. A large air conditioning unit provided him with the only cover available and he squatted behind it, trembling and sure that it was only a matter of time before they came.

After a while, curiosity ruled him and with no sign of the dead pursuing him onto the roof, he decided to investigate what was going on and why the city was so riled up. Carefully, he raised his head above the lip of the wall to the roof. Below, he saw a swarm of bobbing heads and thrashing arms as the dead ploughed through the street.

They were everywhere.

They were not interested in the building he was on top of and bodies were even spilling out from the arcade that the supermarket was part of and joining the rest of the crowd. No, they were definitely not interested in him and Johnny deduced that they probably did not even know he was there. They were headed away from him, and to Johnny it looked as though the whole city was on the move.

Something or someone must have caught their attention further along the street, he decided. Craning his neck, Johnny attempted to see further along but all he could see was the multitude of moving bodies. They covered the entire street from one side to the other and he struggled to see the pavement.

Lifting himself up, he leaned out from the rooftop and over the wall, hoping to see what the distraction was. It was no use. There were just too many of them. Hundreds, even thousands, Johnny calculated.

More were coming.

Looking down, all he could see was a filthy sea of foul, decaying bodies that trundled through the street. He watched as the birds and insects swarmed them, screeching and buzzing, adding to the unremitting whine of the dead.

The sight reminded Johnny a little of the old days. On many occasion, he had sat in a vantage point and just watched the people doing their thing. Even then, in Johnny's opinion, they were mindless husks that crowded the shopping centres and swarmed the street in their bid to consume. Only back then, they did not smell as bad and they had more colours to them. Now, from the height of the roof, all that Johnny could see were greys, browns and greens. Even their clothes had become colourless and dull. Their greasy and waterlogged clothing hung from their bodies and their hair was matted to their heads. It was as if they had all been dragged through a clay pit.

He gave up on trying to see along the street and maybe catch a glimpse of what had started the commotion. It was just too thick with them down that way and Johnny knew himself that it could have been any one of a number of things. He had witnessed them swarm at the sight of something as small as a rat, or even a dog.

He had even seen them crowd and attack each other.

Only a few days before, he had watched dozens of them tear one of their own to shreds. Johnny noticed a tall gangly looking corpse enter a small tool shop, and a few minutes later emerge carrying a hammer and wearing a hardhat. At the time, he had guessed that maybe the man had been a builder during his life and still had an interest in hardware.

The creature had then set about hammering away at any surface he came across as he staggered along the street. Brick walls, steel posts, cars, even windows that shattered with a deafening racket. Everything was hit with the heavy hammer.

Before long, a mob of the dead emerged, and whether it was because they mistook him for one of the living, or that the noise offended them in some way, Johnny could not be sure; they set about the unfortunate gangly dead builder and soon left him as a bloodied limbless pulp, squirming in its own filth on the floor.

Johnny had no idea what had set the dead city off and concluded that it was pointless to try to find out. Instead, he decided to amuse himself with his old favourite pastime, people watching, or alternatively, 'dead watching' as he now referred to it.

He still found humorous moments in his hobby. Now and then he would watch as one of the dead began acting in a way that mirrored a living person, albeit in a much more unsophisticated way, very often making a complete mess of whatever it was doing.

He watched one trying to turn on a television in one of the shop windows, even sitting back on the couch that was on display in front of it and eventually, standing up and smacking the television on the top of its casing in an attempt to get a signal. Johnny had smiled to himself as he remembered his own father doing that very same thing to the television when he was a child.

He watched another endeavour to drive a car. Sitting behind the wheel, it turned the steering wheel continually and eventually began beeping the horn. In the end, it climbed from the vehicle, mimicked what Johnny could only assume was a sigh or a huff, then it kicked the door shut and trundled off.

The mob below began to thin and Johnny was once again able to see the street below. He saw the revolting trail that they had left in their wake and a shudder ran down his spine at the thought of having to cross that same street, sidestepping the piles of stomach-churning human remains, but at the same time trying not to look too animated in his movements.

As he was about to move, something caught his eye. In a narrow doorway, across from the building that he was on top of, a body moved. This body was different from the others he had just watched swarm through the streets. It moved cautiously, aware of its surroundings and as though it was apprehensive about coming out into the open. For a moment, Johnny believed that it could be a living person, the first he had seen in over a week. He soon realised, though, it was the body of a dead man. The mottled and grey skin stretched taut across its face, the sagging dirty clothes smeared in stains and grime. Then the eyes, the dead eyes, even from that distance, they were unmistakable.

Yet it was not like the others. It moved, though less well coordinated and not as swiftly as a living person; it was more purposeful and sure-footed than the usual staggering gait of the dead that he saw on a daily basis.

Johnny frowned and twisted his beard between the thumb and forefinger of his right hand.

"You're a strange one, aren't you?" he murmured quietly to himself as he watched with gripping fascination.

He looked on as the body took a guarded step out from the safety of the doorway. It stopped and peered around, its decaying head and eyes travelling the length of the street as it watched after the mass of dead that had just passed by. It seemed to be studying, scrutinising its surroundings, checking that it was safe to be in the open before it ventured further.

To Johnny, it looked cautious, even scared. He had never seen one behave in such a way. He had watched them, through instinct, mimic the living but never move prudently and watchfully. It occurred to Johnny that this particular body in the street below him was a genius amongst its peers.

It stepped out further into open and looked left and right. It glanced back at the cover of the shop door where it had emerged from and then back in the direction that the crowd had travelled.

Turning in the opposite direction, it began to walk away.

"Clever fellow," Johnny whispered to himself as he watched the corpse.

It suddenly stopped and turned. It looked up, directly at him.

Johnny's eyes widened and he felt an icy hand crawl up his spine again, but he could not look away. The thing was staring straight at him and he could not tear his eyes from it. They stared at each other for what seemed an eternity. The body stood stock still in the street, its eyes fixed on him. It did not moan or wail. It did not raise its arms or even stagger towards him. It just stood there, staring right back at him.

He pulled away from the wall and gasped. Stepping backward and cautiously feeling his way around the air conditioning unit with his hands behind him. He turned and headed for the entrance to the staircase that led down from the rooftop. His feet involuntarily picked up speed and he found himself sprinting for the door. Panic overcame him and now that he could no longer see the body, he imagined a whole horde of them gathering in the street again and coming for him.

His old Wellington boots thumped from one steel step to the next as he pounded down toward the supermarket. He vaulted the last few steps and crashed through the door that led into the main shop. He headed for the entrance. His breath came in shallow hard snorts as his heart raced in his chest. Fear clouded his judgement and all he could think of was getting out of the supermarket and away from the city centre.

He turned left onto an aisle that he knew would lead him to the exit. He let out a yelp as he turned the corner. He reeled back and his boots let out a squeal on the tiled floor as he forced himself to come to sudden a stop.

In front of him stood the same body that he had just seen in the street. It stared directly at him, its hands hanging by its side. Johnny felt his stomach flip. His knees shook and he began to step backwards.

He knew he was dead. He had not really learned how to defend himself against the dead physically, choosing instead to use his wits in avoiding detection. He could charge the walking corpse ahead of him and hope to knock it away from him and then make a run for it or, swing the plastic bag that he carried, laden with heavy tins of food, at its head and hope to knock it to the ground, or even kill it. Johnny had never done anything like either of those things before and he knew he would mess it up.

"Oh shit, oh shit," he mumbled to himself as he began to back away.

He retraced his steps as his mind raced for a solution to his predicament. The body was blocking the only door that he knew of that would lead him back on to the street. Johnny craned his neck as he backed away and tried to see what was outside the shop door behind the body. He expected to see more of them coming, but the area looked clear.

The figure remained where it was. It had not attempted to follow him and it confused Johnny. He was used to them moaning and groaning, raising their arms and chasing after the living. This one, however, just stood and watched him.

After a while, Johnny's heart seemed to calm a little. Knowing that there was no immediate danger and only one of them, he began to think more clearly. He backed further into the shop and slowly walked along an adjacent aisle toward the doorway. Through the stacked goods on the shelves, he was still able to see glimpses of the creature in the next aisle, and it could still see him. It did not move to cut off his escape; it just slowly pivoted its feet so that it could still watch him as he headed for the exit.

Johnny reached the end of the walkway and slowed before he turned the corner. He took in a deep breath and steeled himself, letting the air out of his lungs in a long slow stream, all the time keeping an eye on the figure that was no more than two metres away from him with just a waist-high freezer unit and a few shelves separating them.

Gingerly, he stepped out from the aisle and shuffled towards the doorway, afraid of making any sudden movement that would rile the walking corpse beside him. He remained facing the threat all the time as he headed for the exit, and as he rounded the corner, though he knew he would be in the same aisle and in full view of the body, the actual act forced his heart to skip a beat.

He stopped in his tracks.

It had turned to face him and, again, it did not even attempt to take a step towards him. It just stood watching him. It did not moan. It did not gnash its teeth. It just watched.

In its eyes, Johnny saw something. Though they were unmistakably dead, there was something behind them. Thought, even intelligence Johnny believed. It stood, studying him in the same way that Johnny studied it. Its sunken and clouded eyes stared at him unblinkingly. For a while, neither of them moved. Like two gunslingers about to draw down on one another, they eyed and studied each other.

Johnny realised that his legs no longer trembled and fear had slackened its grip on him. It was now replaced with curiosity. He knew the thing in front of him was dangerous, but he did not feel threatened by it. It seemed to be just as curious about him.

Johnny wondered what was going on inside its head. From his experience, whenever the dead saw a living person it became excited and more animated and aggressive. They always charged, smashing into and through anything in their path, snarling and moaning, grasping with their hands. This one did none of those things. In fact, it did nothing but watch him. It did not look angry or hostile, but by its very appearance Johnny did not feel as though it was exactly friendly towards him.

What remained of its hair lay flattened to its head in greasy dark strands. Its skin was the colour of leather with a green hue and it was stretched taut over the skull and the bones of its face. Its nose was nothing but a sunken dried up indentation and the mouth was in a perpetual grin as the lips had rotted away, revealing its yellowed teeth.

It wore what was once a green bomber jacket that was now mostly a dull grey from exposure to the elements and grime. The shoulders sagged and the cuffs had become tattered around the wrists.

The bony hands looked abnormally long to Johnny. The soft tissue had shrunk and clung to the bones of the fingers, leaving them looking like hideous talons with long broken and dirt encrusted nails.

The t-shirt beneath the jacket, though it was supposed to be white, was now grey also and torn, exposing the torso beneath. Johnny could see that the ribs were beginning to poke through the thin, decaying green flesh of the body and, eventually, they would be completely visible with just shreds of tissue clinging to the bone.

Johnny looked down at its feet. The boots looked worn and tattered, as though they had been travelling for miles. The soles looked ready to come away from the uppers and Johnny guessed that soon after that, the body would be pretty much crippled once the toes and heels wore away on the hard ground.

When Johnny looked back up, he saw that the body in front of him had followed his line of vision with its own eyes. It was staring at its own shoes. It looked back up at Johnny, as if questioning him on his thoughts.

"Sweet Jesus," Johnny slurred. He had never seen anything like it and he did not know whether to turn and run, or attempt a handshake.

The body made the choice for him.

In a move that left Johnny speechless and in utter disbelief, it raised its hand. Its bony and withered fingers folded inward until one remained outstretched in a point toward the exit and out in the street. With a slight tilt of its head, it nodded, motioning to the door, all the while keeping its eyes fixed upon Johnny.

Johnny's mouth grew slack and it took him a moment to stop his head from spinning. Here, in front of him, was a dead man that did not attack him, did not get excited when he saw living people and seemed to be capable of intelligence and even communication.

It was telling him to leave.

Johnny was unsure whether it was because the thing was territorial and saw the arcade as its own, or whether it was doing him a favour and telling him to get out of the area before more came.

It did not matter. It was telling him to get out of there and that was a hell of a lot more than what could normally be expected from the dead as far as Johnny was concerned. He turned and walked out, pausing for a moment to glance back. It remained standing in the aisle, watching him as he left.

Outside, Johnny headed for the outskirts and the suburbs, slow and careful as he always did when travelling through the town, but feeling more vulnerable this time, as though there were more like the one in the supermarket, watching him.

Again, he stole a backward glance and saw the corpse appear at the entrance to the arcade. It watched him for a moment, then turned and headed in a different direction.

Johnny continued to shuffle, headed for home. "Christ, I need a drink."

11

Steve and Helen arrived at the house to see that Gary and Lee's groups were already back. Jake was smeared in blood and grime. It looked as though he had been in a fight.

Gary was pacing, looking uneasy as he watched Steve approach. "I was starting to get worried. You have any luck?"

"Nah, we didn't see a thing. We double-checked our area, but there was no sign of them."

"Yeah, we did a couple of trips too, but we saw nothing. You think they could've got out?" Gary asked in wonder.

Steve let his hand hang at his side, hefting the weight of his hand axe. "I doubt it. Why would they want out? We're here, so they will want to be here too."

Helen shrugged her shoulders. "You'd think so, but none of them have been anywhere near the house and it's not like there's much else around here to occupy them."

"There's something not right here. I spoke to Claire just and she's seen no sign of them either. I half expected to see them banging at the doors when we got back." Gary was rubbing his bearded chin, as he always did when pondering something. "We've dealt with them plenty of times, and they always come straight for us. I've never seen them skulk away before."

"You mean, hide?" Sophie questioned raising her eyebrows. "You guys know more about them than I do, but from what I've seen, I wouldn't have thought they'd be capable of hiding or using their wits."

Steve looked up at the house and then back down at his feet. Something had been bothering him since Gary had told him about the sabotage of the fuel. Then, the rear gate had been opened and a horde of walking dead had been led right in. He knew that someone else was involved, but now, there was no sign of the dead within the park. It did not fit together in his head.

"Shit," Steve suddenly exclaimed, "they're still here!"

"Who, you mean the dead? Of course they are. We only found one of them and there was a whole bunch of them wandering across the field," Jake answered back.

"No," Steve shook his head, "not the dead, the shit head that let them in."

Every member of the group fell silent and glanced at each other with nervous eyes. The thought of the culprit being close by, or even amongst them, immediately filled them with suspicion.

Gary was the first to break the silence. "You mean one of us?"

Steve shrugged. "That's a possibility, but it's not what I meant. I think that someone has led them in and then guided them into the central areas, probably hoping that some of us would come unstuck at some point by running into them unexpectedly."

"Fuck, that's not good," Lee stated the obvious.

They headed up the steps to the house. Karen had ensured that the doors were barricaded as ordered and it took a few minutes before they were inside again. In the foyer, most of the survivors assembled.

The roof team, Claire, Jennifer and Lisa joined them. They were anxious to know what had gone on and if the dead had been dealt with.

Steve looked over at the children. There were only four of them remaining since a number of people had left after the Tony incident, taking their children with them. Liam, David, Sarah and Tyler, Carl's son, were sitting around the large oak table with a board game and seemed completely oblivious to the situation.

Sarah caught the eye of her father and came rushing across the spacious room, arms outstretched and a grin from ear to ear.

"Hey, Dad, I'm winning." She threw her arms around her father's waist and squeezed him tightly.

Steve reached down a ruffled her hair. "Great stuff, buddy, what game are you lot playing over there?"

"Risk," she beamed, "and I'm taking over the world. Liam and David haven't got a chance, Dad."

Steve smiled and looked across to the two boys sat at the table. Both were frowning and he could see that Liam was counting the number of troops Sarah had on the board and comparing them with his own. Steve had played the game on many occasions as a child and knew exactly what they were going through. Now, he found himself playing the same game, but with real lives and against a much stronger, yet unsophisticated, enemy.

"Don't let them gang up on you, though. If they join forces, they could batter you. You should do what I always did. Defend against one of them, and keep attacking the other until they're broken and have nothing to come back at you with," he said it with a smile, and the nostalgia that flooded back to him made him think of safer and happier times from when he was a young boy with less to worry about.

"Okey dokey, I better go back over there and do some butt kicking then." She turned to Sophie as she began to walk back to the table. "Can we see the animals later?"

Sophie went to answer, but did not know what to say. She looked across at Steve, hoping he could help.

"I'm afraid we won't be able to see them today, sweetheart," Gary answered, hoping there would not be more questions from her as he always expected from children. He knew they rarely took a simple 'no' for *any* answer.

Sarah was a typical child. "Why?"

"It's still not safe, Sarah." Steve avoided trying to sugar coat it.

He knew it was a different world now, with new dangers and the sooner Sarah was used to it and understood that it was not always possible to do the things she liked, the better.

"They are still here then?" she asked. At that moment, she seemed more grown up and accepting of the situation, understanding what her father meant.

Steve nodded, his arms folded across his chest and a grave expression on his face. He watched as his daughter seemed to accept it and turned back to her board game.

"Has anyone seen Carl or John?" Steve asked, looking round at the assembled members of the group. He had only just realised that they had not returned and he kicked himself for not noticing sooner. John and Carl were hard to miss, both as broad as doorways and Carl easily towering six feet four.

No one answered but all turned and eyed each other, questioning if anyone knew where they could be. They had all assembled, as planned, back at the front of the house. Only Lee and Jake had seen anything of the dead that had managed to wander into the park. One by one, they had returned, all except Carl and John.

Steve moved to the window and peered out to the park. "Well, does anyone know where they were last?"

"I heard a broken message from them about an hour or so ago, Steve," Claire offered. "They said something about being down at the gate and heading back here. I tried talking to them, but I think they were out of range. We heard hardly anything from any of you except Gary and I think that's because he was closer."

Steve nodded, concern etched across his face. "If they were down at the gate and heading back this way, then they should've been here ages ago."

Gary stood to one side, looking through the window, back into the woods and toward the administration area of the park. Jake could see that he was working something through in his head.

"What do you reckon, Gary?"

Jake's voice pulled Gary away from his train of thought. He turned to the others and focussed on Jake. "Huh?"

"What do you think, John and Carl, where could they be?"

Gary shrugged. "Could be anywhere, but if they were down by the gate and heading back here then it would've made sense to come up along the house road. Like Steve said, they should've been here ages ago." Gary placed his hands on his hips and turned to Steve. "I think we should start with that mate, and then if we have no joy, spread out further."

Steve agreed. "Okay, but we're taking a car." He turned to Lee. "You're with me. The rest of you," he eyed everyone assembled, "stay here. I don't want too many of us running around out there. We're already two men missing and I don't want us spending the rest of eternity chasing after each other. Jake, check the CCTV footage from the gate while we're gone and let us know if there's any sign of them."

Helen was about to protest, but Steve had already turned and began walking out of the door and toward the cars. He knew he would be in the doghouse for that move, but he would rather that happen than something happen to another member of their group whilst out looking for missing people.

Steve and Lee pulled away in the car. Gary watched them leave and turned to look at the others. He was worried.

"I don't think Helen is too happy with you, buddy." Lee spoke without taking his eyes away from the road as he steered them through the wooded area and along the winding track that led towards the main gate.

"Ah, you know how women are, mate. I'll get her some flowers or something."

Both men sniggered as they watched the trees on either side of the road pass by. They travelled at a slow speed, ensuring that they missed nothing. The road ahead of them snaked its way toward the gate and within ten minutes, they were clear of the trees, the main entrance was no more than fifty metres ahead of them.

The car pulled to a stop and Steve and Lee waited a moment, eyeing the undergrowth around them before stepping from the vehicle. They both moved slowly, their weapons in hand and ready for an attack. Steve moved out in front and towards the gate. The dead that were on the other side saw them and began to attack the bars. They seemed more aggressive than normal and Steve wondered if whether it was due to them seeing Carl and John recently.

Lee pulled the radio from his belt. "Gary?"

"Loud and clear, Lee, Jake has you on camera too."

Lee turned to the mounted camera on top of the wall at the side of the gate and gave a nod. He looked across at Steve who stood just a few metres back from the gate, intensely staring at the bodies that crashed against the barrier on the other side.

"You okay, mate?"

Steve did not answer. He was too concentrated on the dead.

"Steve," Lee placed a hand on his shoulder, "you okay?"

"Yeah, sorry mate," Steve turned to face him. "Was just wondering why these things keep turning up here." He nodded toward the bodies at the gate.

"Fuck knows. They probably like the view," Lee shrugged. "Anyway, I've spoken to Gary on the radio. He can hear me perfectly and Jake has us on camera. So I don't know what could've been the problem with Carl and John, unless their radio is playing up?"

"Could be, where to now then?"

Lee glanced about. "You tell me. We could go back up the track and head off towards the Info Centre?"

"Nah, I think we would've seen them ourselves earlier if they had headed that way. I think we're on foot from here, mate."

"Why?" Lee spun on him, an anxious look on his face.

"Because the only other option is that they must've gone cross country. They're somewhere in the south-west area I reckon. We would've seen something of them otherwise."

Lee knew that Steve was better than he was at working things out in his head but he wanted to know how he had come to that conclusion. He wanted Steve to spell it out for him.

"What makes you think that then?"

"Them," Steve turned and pointed at the bodies at the gate, "they're worked up more than usual. If something had happened from any other angle, John and Carl would have headed straight to the house. I think something happened here. It came from the area of the track there and they were chased back the way they had come, back along the south wall I'd hazard a guess."

Lee looked back at the bushes where the main access road disappeared into the wood and then back at the gate. "Are you having a Columbo moment, Steve?" He grinned.

"Leave the engine running, Lee. If we need to come back this way in a hurry, I don't want to be messing about with keys. I've a feeling we'll get our answers pretty soon."

Steve was apprehensive. They had only found one body during their search and he knew that Carl had seen at least five of them. Now, with Carl and John missing, he worried that their numbers could have increased. They headed towards the gate and turned right, following the line of the wall along the southern boundary of the park.

Gary's voice suddenly sounded over the radio. "Lee, it's Gary, you getting me?"

"Yeah, Gary," Lee snapped his fingers to get Steve to stop, "what's up?"

Steve turned and came closer so that he could hear what Gary had to say. He kept an eye out around them for any sign of the dead, or Carl and John, as he focussed his hearing toward the radio.

"Jake just showed me some footage that might be of interest to you." Gary sounded troubled. Even over the radio, they could hear the tension in his voice.

Lee frowned at the radio, "Go on, Gary."

"John and Carl were in the exact spot where you are now. They were attacked by four runners, Lee."

Both Steve and Lee became all the more nervous at the very mention of 'runners'. They looked at each other in alarm, then all around them, at the gate, the trees and the open fields that spanned along the length of the southern wall, expecting to see the dead charging towards them.

Steve grabbed the radio from Lee. "What happened, Gary, where are they now?"

"They ran, Steve. That's all we can see. They were standing by the gate, then they suddenly ran out of camera shot and four of the dead went after them. We couldn't see if either of them were caught, Steve. They headed away from the gate and toward the southern wall, the way they had come."

Lee looked up at Steve, his eyes suddenly widening. "That's exactly what you said had happened."

"Okay, Gary," Steve replied into the radio. "Keep the house locked down. We're going to do a search on foot from here. Let us know if you see anything."

"Will do, be careful lads."

Steve handed the radio back to Lee and nodded. "Well then, at least we have a starting point and we're on the right track."

"Yeah," Lee huffed as he tucked the radio back into his belt loop and raised his iron bar, "straight into the hungry bastards."

12

John sat with his head resting against the trunk of the tree. Carl lay on his back beside him, eyes closed and his hands folded across his chest. John wondered how he could seem so relaxed at that moment.

He peered down at the ground. To John, they were unrecognisable as having once been human beings. Their skin was dark, almost black, and blistered as though they had been over baked in an oven. Their limbs seemed longer than was normal for a person, and their hands looked more like talons. Their heads were bare and only a thin layer of crusted dried flesh clung to their scalps with the odd strand of hair floating above them.

He could only tell the sex of one of them and that was only because it was wearing what was left of a man's business suit. The jacket was gone and the shirt was smeared with numerous stains, including what he presumed was blood. The dark patches on the shoulders and back spread out across the material and then blended into the filth that covered the rest of the garment.

He guessed that one of them could have been a woman once, due to its smaller build, but with decay and grime he could not be sure. It may have been an adolescent male. Nevertheless, they were all monsters as far as he was concerned, demons.

Their smell drifted up to him. Sickly and sweet, like diarrhoea mixed with rotten food, John thought. He was surprised at how used to the smell he had become. At the beginning, he had struggled to keep down the contents of his stomach when he was close to them. Now, it was nothing more than an extremely unpleasant odour that could be wafted away.

He watched the hordes of flies that swarmed around them. The dead never seemed to pay them any attention, even when they landed on their faces and in their eyes. He considered how living people would be swatting away for dear life if flies were constantly buzzing them, yet the dead never seemed affected by them.

The maggots, too; the four corpses below were infested with them. Even from ten feet up in the tree, John could see the light patches of squirming lava that colonised the festering skin and the open wounds of each of the walking cadavers. They were slowly being eaten to nothing.

John was confused. He knew full well that by now, under normal circumstances, a dead body that had been left in the open and exposed to weather conditions and wildlife for a couple of months would be nothing more than a skeleton. These, however, were intact with enough flesh, sinew, muscle and cartilage to keep them mobile. Their eyes could still see, their ears could still hear and they were far from being ready to drop.

Dead bodies do not normally walk about. Well at least that used to be the case, John thought to himself, *but now they do not rot as they should either.*

The ghouls below continued to circle the tree. They hovered in the area around the base, as though expecting the two men above to suddenly give up and climb down to their waiting arms. They grunted and groaned as they shuffled through the rustling leaves, endlessly watching the tree.

John looked away, a shudder running down his spine. "Carl," he whispered, "Carl."

Lying on his back, still sprawled on the thick branch, Carl rolled his head towards John. "What?" He asked without even opening his eyes.

"How long do you think we need to stay up here?"

Carl looked down at the four creatures below them. They had not lost interest and he knew they would not, not as long as they were both in clear sight.

"I don't know. I think we're in for the long haul by the looks of things."

One of the dead below them suddenly let out a high-pitched wail and attacked the trunk of the tree again. It clawed and kicked at the bark, shredding its fingers to the bone in an attempt to scale the obstacle. It did not seem to notice that it had worn the flesh from its fingers and John began to feel despair as he watched the thing continually assault the tree. He knew it would never give up. It would attack and attack until either it made it to the top, or there was nothing left of it but a bloodied rotten pulp.

"We can't stay here forever, Carl. It'll be getting dark soon. I'm dehydrated and my throat is threatening to close up."

"Me too, mate, but I'm not going down there to get you a glass of water. Get it yourself." He turned to John and grinned. The frothy white spittle at the corners of his mouth told John that he was suffering just as much as he was.

It had been a hot day. The hottest that John had witnessed for a while. "Just our luck, isn't it? We have a heatwave and get stuck in a tree."

"I know," Carl agreed. "We should've brought a barbeque and beer."

"Try the radio again."

Carl lifted the radio in his hand and spoke into the mouthpiece. "Steve, anyone, it's Carl. You hear me?" He waited a moment. "Anyone, can you hear me? It's Carl and John. We're stuck in a tree in the south west."

Nothing but a hiss came over the speaker in reply.

John hunched his shoulders. "It's fucked, isn't it?"

Carl nodded, "Looks that way. We've heard nothing from anyone so either they're all dead, or the radio is broken."

They had been out the whole day. It had turned into a fine summer's day and the heat had increased throughout the afternoon. Neither of them carried any supplies. They did not expect to need them. Now they both suffered and the thirst they felt was threatening to drive them mad. Their tongues felt like sandpaper and the insides of their mouths were sticky. Their throats were raw and tender and both had developed headaches and bordered on the verge of heat exhaustion.

The fact that they had had to sprint for hundreds of metres, flat out, had added to their predicament. They had lost vital fluids through sweat and had nothing to replace them.

John knew that if their core temperature continued to rise, then they would soon be in serious trouble. From the general heat of the day and then the exertion of sprinting for their lives, fear and lying in a tree for hours in the high heat of the afternoon, and with no water intake to replenish the fluids they sweated out, it would not be long before they both lost the ability to sweat anymore. Then they would be in a whole world of hurt. They would become incapacitated within an hour and without water, they would die.

"We're going to have to try for it at some point, Carl. We both know that they're not going to go away. I already have the shakes and my head is pounding. We wait much longer and we won't be able to even think about moving anyway."

"I know, mate. I just don't want to do it yet. Let's wait a little longer. The others probably know that we're missing by now and are probably looking for us."

John sat up on his perch, a frown creased across his face as he eyed Carl beside him.

"What and you want to just sit here and wait for them to stumble across us, what if they did? They could end up being eaten by those ugly bastards down there."

He pointed to the foot of the tree. The one that they guessed to have once been a woman clambered at the base, reaching into thin air in an attempt to close the distance between her and the living flesh she so desperately wanted.

"No, I don't mean that. I mean, it would be better for us to at least hear a car or voices somewhere close by. At least, then we have a direction to head for. As it stands at the moment," Carl looked around them and scanned the woods, "we've nowhere to go. We wouldn't make it as far as the house if we made a run for it. You said yourself that you're in shit state. So am I."

John bit his lip and fiddled with a piece of the tree bark between his fingers. "Yeah, you're right. Well, if we hear anyone, then we have to move quickly. I mean, out the tree and making like startled gazelles."

Carl nodded, "Yeah, well at least I'll be okay."

John raised an eyebrow, "How's that?"

Carl grinned, "Because I'm faster than you are."

Both men burst out in laughter. Even though their throats hurt and it felt as though they were swallowing broken glass, it did them good to laugh. It was a release of stress and even with the creatures below them working themselves into a state of frenzy as they attacked the tree en-masse, Carl and John laughed even harder.

The hours passed and they remained in the tree. They tried to rest and conserve their energy hoping that someone would be out looking for them. The dead continued to stalk them below. Moaning, wailing and now and then attacking the tree, snarling and raking at the bark with their fleshless hands, leaving long smears of blackened congealed blood and greasy skin, including fingernails.

The sun was beginning to dip towards the horizon and there was still no sign of a rescue. John was becoming more anxious by the minute but he tried hard not to show it. Not because he wanted to appear macho to his friend, but because he did not want to pressure Carl into making a half-cocked decision and moving before they were ready.

Silently, they both agreed that they needed to move before it was fully dark.

"What do you reckon then, John?"

"Well we either die from dehydration, get eaten by those dead fucks as we make a run for it, or we die of hypothermia during the night." He nodded toward the distance. "Those dark clouds over there look ready to burst and they're coming this way."

Carl looked at the weather front that approached. "Right, bollocks to it, we're going to have to try for it."

John sat upright and glanced down at the dead that circled the tree below, and then back at his tree mate.

"What do we do then?"

Carl hummed to himself, as though flicking through a catalogue of ideas in his head. He looked at John, a wry smile creasing his lips. "I'll climb out along that branch," he nodded at the thick piece of the tree that John sat upon, "and you keep them occupied here. Once I am out as far as I can go, Ill drop down and get them to follow me. Then, you get yourself down and leg it for the house."

John was shaking his head slowly. "I can't let you do that, mate. I don't need babysitting and it's too much of a risk. You can't handle them all on your own."

Carl snorted. "Who said anything about me handling them? I'm out of the tree and running for my life, mate. I've no intention of taking them on, just trying to give you a headstart and I'll soon be on your heels and past you."

John nodded, understanding that it made sense for him to have a running start.

Carl placed a hand on his shoulder, a serious and solemn expression on his face. "Don't wait for me, John. As soon as you're on the ground, head for the mansion and don't stop."

Carl began to shimmy out along the branch, slowly and carefully placing his hands, knees and feet. The tree creaked beneath him as his weight spread along the limb. It began to dip slightly, and even the smallest movement felt like it would throw him from the tree. Sweat poured from his forehead and into his eyes, despite the cool breeze that blew in from the open fields.

He crawled further and the branch seemed to bow substantially toward the ground below him. He stopped. Holding his breath and screwing his eyes shut, he waited for the movement of the branch to subside before continuing. His tongue felt swollen in his mouth and his throat tightened and became drier as he struggled to swallow.

John was leaning over from the junction of the large branches, waving his arms and taunting the lurking dead below him in an attempt to keep them distracted. He clapped his hands and threw insults at them as they lunged for him, snarling and flailing their arms into thin air. He gripped the thick branch tighter with his legs as he began smacking his hands against the bark of the tree.

"Come on you dumb shits. Come on, I'm here and waiting," he mocked as the creatures below him doubled their efforts to reach him.

They were in a rage, colliding with each other and slamming against the tree, then falling to the floor as they fought to grasp the warm fleshy hands that dangled just inches above their heads.

None of them noticed as Carl crept along the branch away from them. He was close to the point where he had decided he would drop down. By now, he was no more than six feet from the ground, the weight of his bulk on the thinning branch causing it to dip toward the ground in a long arc.

John continued his insults and jeers, whipping them up to a rage that he had never seen in them before. They were whirling and snarling, their jaws snapping shut with a force that could break bones. John just hoped that Carl could lure them away far enough to give him a fighting chance.

He looked back over his shoulder, and in the dimming light he could see the silhouette of Carl, far out along the branch. John turned back to the dead below him and began waving his arms more vigorously and hurling abuse.

He began to raise himself up on to his haunches, knowing that the time for him to leap down was close. He steadied himself against the tree and breathed deeply as he studied the ground below. He searched for a patch of earth that was even and presented less chance of a twisted ankle when he landed. Any kind of injury now would be a death sentence.

The creatures still lingered at the foot of the tree, staring back at him and snarling but he knew that when the time came, they would be off chasing Carl, leaving the immediate area clear for him to make a run for it.

Carl was in position, steeling himself for the drop. His heart pounded in his ears and his head throbbed. He run his rough tongue over his lips in an attempt to moisten them but it served no purpose. He was too dehydrated and his lips felt parched and cracked. His legs shook and his stomach lurched as he began to raise himself up.

"Okay, Carl, they're all yours, mate. I'm ready when you are!" John hollered over his shoulder, all the time keeping an eye on the four walking dead below him.

The tree suddenly swayed below him as Carl leaped from the branch. The thin branches lashed at his face as he fell, feet first, toward the ground. A moment later, and he felt the soft floor of the woods as his feet made contact in the rustling dead leaves and soil. Immediately, he sprang into action and threw himself upright.

Without another thought, he headed away from the tree at a sprint. He was not sure if any of them had heard or seen him, but he did not want to pause to find out. As he ran, he began to shout. Crashing through the undergrowth and ferns, he made enough noise to be heard throughout the wood.

The dead below John stopped at the sudden commotion. They spun in the direction that Carl had landed and took off after him.

The ground was clear.

John took in a deep breath and stepped off from the tree. He felt himself fall through the air and watched as the ground rushed up to meet him. A split second before impact, he screwed his eyes shut; his feet made contact first and then his knees, followed by his palms. His arms buckled beneath him and he landed head first amongst the fallen leaves and branches. Instinctively, he rolled to the side and came up to a crouch as he hefted his steel bar above his head, ready to swing down on to the head of anything that attacked him.

He turned and ran.

Sprinting through the trees, Carl could hear the dead behind him. They crashed through the woods with all the grace of an attacking bull elephant. They snarled, moaned and wailed as they pursued him.

Carl stole a backward glance over his shoulder. All four were chasing him. Fear gripped him and his legs pumped harder. He began to work his way around in a wide arc, hoping to double back and catch up with John, who by now should be headed for the mansion.

John's legs shook with each step. They were weak and he hoped that they would not buckle on him. He could hear Carl in the distance as he ran through the woods and he could hear the creatures that chased him. John considered slowing down and even waiting for Carl to catch him up.

No, stick to the plan.

Carl was losing his breath. It was harder than he had expected. Though fear and adrenaline was enough to get him started, it was not enough to sustain him. His body trembled and his knees threatened to give way. It was beginning to feel like he was running through ankle-deep mud as his legs struggled to continue lifting his feet at the same pace. His body felt heavy and he knew he was slowing.

There was no sign of John. He was up ahead somewhere and Carl now felt completely alone as he charged through the trees, the dead gaining on him. He wanted to call out to John, but his lungs would not allow it. They burned and each breath hurt.

Fuck, I'm going to die, he began to say to himself repeatedly in his head.

At that moment, if he had carried a gun he would have used it on himself. He was exhausted and terror gripped him as he felt the dead close the gap. Tears began to fill his eyes. John was gone and he was happy for him, but now he was to face a slow and agonising death at the hands and teeth of the ever-ravenous walking, running dead.

A shadowy figure charged at him from the front. With all his energy spent, Carl could not even change his direction to avoid the threat; it ran straight at him and from the corners of his eyes, he saw two more converging. A whimper involuntarily escaped from his lips.

Shit, there are more of them.

This was the end for him. Surrounded and worn out, he was about to die.

With blurred vision, he watched as the first of the approaching figures ran straight past him, then the second, then the third. Before he could turn, he heard the sounds of heavy bodies hitting the floor and the thump and crunch as heavy objects smashed into flesh and bone. He heard voices, too, but in his pounding and ringing ears, he could not understand them. On shaky and unsteady legs, he turned and staggered after them.

Carl rubbed his eyes. John, Steve and Lee stood over the limp bodies of the four, now permanently, dead. In the blink of an eye, and with complete surprise, they had dispatched them. They now lay in a heap, their skulls smashed in on the ground at the feet of his three saviours.

They looked back at him, their clubs and hammers hanging bloodied in their hands.

"Carl, you okay?" Steve asked as he walked towards him, holding out his hand.

John was panting hard. He bent double with his hands resting on his knees as he sucked in the air.

"I...bet...you thought...I'd...left you?" he stammered.

Carl tried to focus his vision. Stars shot in from his peripherals and bright colours danced across his eyes. His knees collapsed from beneath him and he crumpled to the floor. On his hands and knees, he felt his stomach churn and he began to vomit uncontrollably. It assaulted him in waves and there was nothing that he could do that would stop it. Instead, he let it happen.

Carl rolled on to his back, bile and snot smearing his face as he gasped for air. Above him, all he could see was the dark shapes of the three men looming over him.

He struggled to form his words, gulping oxygen and trying to regain his composure. "For a moment there, I thought I was dead."

"You very nearly were, Carl," Steve said as he reached down, holding out his hand to help him to his feet. "Come on, let's go home."

"Gary, we've got them, mate," Lee called out on his radio, a tone of relief in his voice. "Both okay and on our way back to you."

"Great stuff," Gary replied. "I'll put the kettle on."

13

"Whose great idea was this?" Stu screamed as he bounded down the corridor and past Marcus.

Marcus looked beyond him at the double doors at the far end. They shuddered and trembled with each assault against them from the horde outside. Jim and Sini were busy piling beds, chairs and anything else they could find against them and adding to the barricade that they had made. Hussein and Stu reappeared from behind carrying a large steel locker they had found in one of the rooms. They struggled with the heavy object and lugged it toward the doors.

More thuds and pounding from outside and the doors rattled again. Marcus watched as Sini and Jim jumped back.

"Jesus," Jim cried, "What have they got out there, a battering ram?"

Stu and Hussein hefted the heavy steel locker and piled it on to the barricade. It crashed against the wooden chairs and beds, snapping limbs and frames with its bulky weight. All four men turned and edged their way back from the doors and towards Marcus who stood at the foot of the stairs, his rifle held on his shoulder and aiming at the shuddering doors behind the barricade.

"How are we looking at the doors at the far end?" he asked them.

"Not good," Sini answered, "we're surrounded, boss."

"Shit." Marcus bit his lip, looking at the floor with thoughts racing through his mind. "How many do we have, would you say?"

Jim placed the stock of his rifle against his hip, the barrel pointing up at the ceiling. "Well, from my calculations, and guessing how many there could've been already inside the barracks, I'd hazard a guess at fucking hundreds, Marcus."

Stu looked across at the American and nodded. He turned back to Marcus. "Yeah, good one, I'd say that's pretty accurate."

For four days, they had remained holed up within the accommodation block. Sandra was recovering, but she was not out of the woods yet. She was able to move but slowly and with pain. Stu kept an eye on her and regularly topped her up with painkillers and antibiotics. Within just a few hours of Stu operating on her, she was insistent that she could move and that there was no reason for them to stay. Marcus, however, decided that she should remain immobile to give her the best chance of recovery.

The number of dead at the doors steadily increased, and by now they were close to being overwhelmed by them. Each day, the team had had to venture out beyond the barricade and deal with the bodies that stumbled toward the barracks. At first, it had been a couple at a time and easy enough to handle.

By the second night, the numbers of curious wandering dead had increased. There were too many for the team to take care of safely, silently and at night so they had decided on taking care of them at first light. By then, though, there were too many and more and more were coming every day.

"Okay," Marcus looked at his men, "let's put our plan in motion. I think we've waited long enough."

Stu nodded. "Thank fuck for that." He turned to Hussein, "Okay, mate, you know the drill. Come on."

Stu and Hussein took off towards the stairs at the far end of the corridor, close to where the second set of doors and barricade was. As they passed and headed for the steps, they saw that the doors at that end were also taking a beating and Stu wondered how much longer they would hold out.

"My God," Hussein uttered as he stood watching the doors shake. The noise of the moaning dead was all around them, their haunting voices echoing along the narrow corridor.

"Move it, Hussein, we don't have long. Those doors won't hold!" Stu shouted as he began to sprint up the stairs taking two steps at a time.

Jim and Sini bolted past Marcus and up the stairs toward the room where Sandra rested. Marcus followed them.

Sini leaned over the bed where his girlfriend lay. In their native tongue, he informed her that they were about to move and follow the plan he had explained to her earlier. Weakly, she forced a smile and nodded as he helped her to her feet and led her over to the makeshift stretcher.

Jim positioned himself at the head of the stretcher, ready to lead off.

"Okay, you ready?" Marcus asked them.

Both men grunted and heaved the stretcher up and adjusted their grip. They carried their weapons on slings across their chests, ready to be brought to bear quickly. Sini looked down at Sandra and began whispering words of encouragement to her. She was at the mercy of the men around her. If they fell, she would fall with them. She was helpless.

Marcus reached for the radio attached to his assault vest and spoke in the mouthpiece. "Stu, how are you getting on up there?"

"We're in position. Good to go." His voice sounded broken and as though he was shouting against the wind. "Got eyes on the vehicle and there aren't too many in that area. The doors are completely blocked with them though."

Marcus nodded to himself as he heard Stu's voice in his ear. "No worries, as long as they stay at the doors. How's our escape route look?"

There was a pause and Marcus imagined Stu and Hussein, up on the roof, conducting a count of the dead in their path.

"We'll have our hands full up here, but you should get through okay. Just don't stop for *anything*."

"Roger that, moving now,"

Stu gave a double-click on the radio in acknowledgement.

It was time to go. Marcus turned to Jim and Sini and nodded. Both men gave him the thumbs up.

"Let's do it, boss," Jim grunted.

"Okay, keep close behind me."

At a trot, they moved along the corridor and down the stairs. Twenty metres to their right on the ground floor, the doors crashed and rocked as the horde outside pounded and attempted to smash their way in.

Marcus caught the eye of Sandra, who lay strapped to the stretcher to prevent her from falling out. She looked at him with complete terror in her eyes. Marcus could understand how she felt. He was scared enough as it was and he was on foot and armed. Sandra was completely helpless and her safety was entirely in the hands of Jim and Sini.

They turned right and headed away from the doors. Marcus entered the room that they had agreed upon to use in their escape. A small annex style structure protruded out from the rear of the main block. The window was larger than the rest that were in the accommodation rooms and provided them with a better chance of getting through safely and without the stretcher becoming fouled.

Marcus stopped at the side of the window, keeping himself from view. It was dark outside and Marcus struggled to see much beyond the glass.

Jim and Sini took the opportunity to rest their arms before the breakout began. They placed Sandra on the floor, rolled their shoulders and shook their wrists. Each of them checked and adjusted their weapons. Marcus flicked off his safety catch and checked the magazine was securely in place.

"Stu, we're in position, mate. As soon as you open up, we'll move."

"Roger that. Stand by, stand by."

A moment later, Marcus and the others heard the muffled reports of Stu and Hussein's weapons as they began to pour fire into the wandering bodies below. From the window, they could see the faint flicker of light from their muzzle flashes above as they illuminated the ground below. In the instances of light, they could see the numerous bobbing heads of the dead that lurked in the darkness outside.

Marcus gripped the window in both hands and forced it open. It opened inward and he continued to push it until the frame creaked and then snapped at the hinges, leaving it incapable of closing on them again.

"Move, move," he roared as he hefted himself up on to the chair he had placed below the windowsill.

Sini and Jim heaved the stretcher up and moved toward the window, close behind Marcus.

With both feet on the window frame, Marcus raised his weapon and shot two faces that loomed up at him out of the pitch black. The recoil in his shoulder was barely noticeable with the smaller calibre round, but the noise in his ears from the blast was reassuring and the effect that the rounds had on the two corpses as they punched through their heads was all the effect he wanted. The two bodies dropped immediately and Marcus jumped from the window. His feet hit the hard concrete floor and he began to move forward with his weapon pulled tightly to his shoulder.

Outside, the sound of Stu's weapons from the roof was less muffled. Their rounds snapped the air above him and he watched as body after body fell to the floor. Behind him, he could hear the grunts and heavy breathing of Jim and Sini as they handled the stretcher and negotiated the window as best they could.

Marcus fired again as a figure staggered towards him. In the gloom of the night, he could only see the silhouette but it was unmistakable. It was another of the walking dead. Its hands reached out ahead of it and a long mournful moan emitted from its dried and rotting vocal cords.

The shot hit it in the neck, passing straight through with a spray of congealed blood and putrid tissue. Its head lulled to the side as the muscle was ripped away by the vacuum created by the bullet as it passed through its neck. It continued to approach.

Marcus aimed more carefully. It was just metres away and instead of peering through the sight, he looked over it. The weapon jerked in his shoulder again and the advancing corpse was halted. Its head snapped back as it rocked on its feet, and then collapsed to the floor. Marcus spun and fired into the heads of two more that approached from the left. They fell to the ground and he stole a glance over his shoulder to check on the progress of the others.

"Get a move on, they're all over the place!" Marcus barked over his shoulder as he raised his rifle and fired into another approaching corpse.

Jim rested the stretcher on the ledge of the window and dropped down to the floor then turned to ease Sandra out until Sini was ready to jump. All of them were now outside and together again. They began to move toward the vehicle with Stu and Hussein cutting them a clear path from the roof above them and Marcus picking off the strays.

Forging a path, Marcus moved at a slow trot. Even though his mind screamed at him to run as fast as he could, he stayed close to the others, knowing he was their only close protection as they carried the stretcher.

They could not afford to slow down and join in the fight. It was their job to plough on ahead, following in Marcus' wake.

They were only a few metres from the vehicle. It appeared before them out of the night. More of the dead were staggering towards them, their moans audible even over the noise of the weapons that were firing constantly.

Marcus rushed to the tailgate and quickly lowered it. He climbed onto the bed of the Land Rover, ready to receive the head of the stretcher. Jim passed it over to Marcus. He hefted Sandra onto the vehicle and out of immediate danger, as Sini and Jim released their weapons and began to fire into the approaching masses that came from all directions.

In the flash of the rounds as they exploded from the barrels, Marcus could see hundreds of the dead. They were surrounded and the crowd was becoming more tightly packed by the second. They needed to move, soon.

Vaulting into the driver's seat, he turned the key in the ignition. For a moment, the engine coughed and sputtered and he feared the worst. If the engine failed, they were dead. He turned it again and, slowly but surely, the starter motor turned over until the engine finally bit and roared to life.

Sini and Jim jumped on to the tailgate and took up their positions to cover the left and right flanks. They loosed off more and more rounds by the second, a clear indication of the number of dead that was approaching.

"Stu, move your arse. We're ready to move!" Marcus screamed over the radio.

He hit the headlights and the beam settled on the path ahead of them, the path that Marcus and the others had taken and the same path that Stu and Hussein would follow. It was littered with dozens of still and lifeless bodies.

The weapons behind him roared as Jim and Sini continued to provide cover as the fire from Stu and Hussein stopped, indicating that they were on the move.

Marcus craned his neck in order to see Stu's progress. On the edge of the roof, he saw a figure begin to lean back from the ledge. They were both wearing makeshift harnesses to allow them to abseil to the ground.

Marcus got to his feet in the driver's seat and began picking off the bodies that blocked them from having a clear run to the Land Rover. As he fired, he willed Stu and Hussein to descend the wall. His jaw was clenched shut and he could feel and hear his heart pounding in his ears. He wanted to run forward and grab them both, dragging them back to the vehicle.

The dead that had crowded the entrances now began to pour around the corners and head towards the vehicle. The sound of Stu and Hussein climbing down the wall attracted many of them away from the main group and Marcus had to increase his rate of fire to keep the area clear for the remaining two to escape.

"Magazine..." Sini cried from behind, informing everyone that he had to change his ammunition.

Marcus spun and began firing toward the left flank to cover Sini's position while he inserted a fresh magazine in his weapon.

Stu and Hussein were at ground level.

Marcus watched as they struggled to free themselves from the ropes. Stu was entangled. Marcus could see that. Hussein rushed over to him and began pulling at the knots around Stu's waist that had obviously tightened as he had descended.

The dead closed in.

Marcus began to climb from the seat, ready to sprint forward and help Stu and Hussein. The horde of attacking corpses was becoming too thick around them and Marcus feared that they would become trapped. He began to fire again, directly into the crowd and hoping not to hit either of his friends as they struggled to free themselves.

"Come on, Stu, move," he growled between his teeth as he fired repeatedly. He had now lost sight of them both and they were replaced by a sea of rotting bodies.

"Marcus, get back in the fucking seat," Jim cried across at him.

Marcus turned, realising that he was leaving the vehicle a sitting duck with no driver if he moved away from it. He climbed back in the driver's seat but remained standing. He strained his neck, trying to catch a glimpse of Stu or Hussein.

Shots rang out from the area that he had last seen Stu. The rate of fire increased and it was obvious that the pair were both firing their rifles on full automatic, trying to stem the tide that closed in around them. Suddenly, the firing from Stu and Hussein stopped.

"Marcus, we got to move!" Jim shouted. "There are too many."

Marcus hesitated. "Stu and Hussein are in trouble," he cried back.

"We're all in fucking trouble. We have to go."

Marcus turned in his seat. "We can't leave them behind, Jim."

"They're gone, Marcus!" Jim shouted back between bursts of fire. "The dead have swallowed them up."

Marcus saw the swarm of dead faces that enveloped them. They were just metres away from the sides of the vehicle and there was no way that they could be held back for much longer.

"Stu, where are you? Stu, Stu can you hear me?" he called out on his radio.

He pressed his hand against his ear to cut out the sound of the discharging weapons around him as he waited to hear Stu's reply through his earpiece.

"Stu, we need to move, can you hear me?" he tried again.

There was nothing. No radio signals, no movement and there was no more firing from the area where they had been struggling to free themselves from their ropes. There were shambling figures all around the area where they had been and Marcus feared that they had been overwhelmed.

As the dead approached on all sides, Marcus had to slam the vehicle in reverse. He steered it around to the left as he backed up, the tailgate making contact with a number of the dead and knocking them flat before Jim and Sini shot them.

Marcus continued to watch for Stu as he slowly began to pull away. He felt the pang in his chest, as he knew that he had lost another good friend. The darkness seemed to envelop him as he pushed his foot down harder on to the accelerator and pick up speed. He was leaving another two of his men behind for the sake of saving the rest of them.

Marcus swallowed hard and steered the vehicle away.

There were bodies in his path and he had to increase their speed to be sure of getting through them. The nearest of them bumped against the body of the vehicle with loud thuds, and then they spun away into the rest of the crowd as the force of the impact threw them backward. Some were pulled beneath the wheels and Marcus could feel them being crushed beneath as the heavy Land Rover bounded over them and spat them out to the rear.

The lights illuminated the exit point of the parking area that linked on to the main road leading through the centre of the barracks. There were far less corpses in that area and it seemed that the entire dead population of the barracks were headed towards the accommodation block.

The engine roared as Marcus shifted up a gear, increasing their speed further.

"We got movement on the left!" Sini shouted from his position.

Marcus looked across to the area where Sini had begun to fire. He saw brightly lit red tracer rounds smash into the crowd and watched as the bodies toppled as the fire thumped into them. Figures dropped to the floor, others folded and some spun as they were hit. Heads exploded and limbs disintegrated as numerous bullets ripped through their decaying flesh and out the other side.

Amongst the flurry, he saw the energetic movements of living people. Stu and Hussein were alive. They were sprinting toward the Land Rover, clubbing their way through the mass of dead, as they fought for their lives and headed towards safety.

Side by side, they fought and the bodies were knocked back from around them as they smashed away with the butts of their rifles.

Marcus slammed the vehicle in reverse and swung it around so that Stu and Hussein could vault directly onto the bed of the Land Rover as Jim and Sini increased their rate of fire and more of the dead began to pile up around them.

The path was clear for Stu and Hussein, just ten more metres. Marcus waited for the jolt as the suspension rocked when Stu and Hussein climbed aboard.

It seemed to be taking forever.

Suddenly, a scream rang out from the rear. Marcus spun in his seat.

Hussein had been pulled to the ground, a group of the attacking creatures suddenly falling on top of him. Stu stopped and turned; he crashed into the throng and began throwing and tossing the bodies aside while Hussein fought from underneath, trying to crawl to his feet.

Gripping him by the arm, Stu yanked Hussein to his feet and flung him forward and toward the waiting vehicle.

Now, Marcus felt the suspension sink and the vehicle rock slightly. Stu and Hussein were safely onboard. He slammed his foot down and crashed through the lurching figures that surrounded them. They fell to the side and underneath the wheels. The tyres gripped and the vehicle shot forward.

They headed for the gate.

14

Hiding in the woods and attempting to live off the land was not Simon's greatest of ideas. In theory, while sitting in his underground bunker and surrounded with all the supplies he needed, it seemed like a good plan. He had done it on many occasions in the past. Back then, however, he had been well equipped for it and he had slightly more than a crowbar and a Swiss Army knife to help him survive.

Now, drenched to the bone, hungry and cold, he realised that he had been much better off below ground. At least there, he was safe.

During his escape, he had pretty much lost everything he needed to survive in the wild. The backpack had been filled with the equipment he needed to make a shelter, catch food and make fire to cook the food and keep warm. It also had extra clothing in it.

It was no use. He had attempted to rough it and beat the elements for three days with nothing more than a thin jacket and a small knife. He had failed miserably. He even felt ashamed of himself for failing. With all the experience and knowledge he had, he should have been more than capable.

He could almost hear his neighbours snickering and saying, "We told you so." However, they were dead and he was still alive. At least he had managed to outlive them and he put that down to his interests.

After he had climbed the fence of his garden and narrowly escaped being eaten alive by the horde of diseased dead, he headed straight for the nature reserve. Its sprawling woods and open countryside provided the ideal location for a man to survive, away from the dangers of the built up areas.

Simon had dreamed of building himself a little cabin deep in the woods and living free and without worry. He gambled that he would rarely encounter the dead due to the remoteness of his hideout. Though there were numerous tracks that crisscrossed the reserve, he doubted that many of the walking corpses would be in the area.

He had seen enough of them to know their behaviour, and during his time barricaded within his house, he had made the effort to study them as best he could. He had noticed that they moved in packs. Whether this was actual pack mentality, he could not be sure, but he suspected it was more to do with the fact that they were always attracted to noise and movement and if one of them were to go stumbling off, wailing and throwing its arms about, a crowd would soon follow it.

He also noted that they seemed to congregate in the urban areas. With the noise and amount of movement, even from themselves, Simon concluded that many of them were probably trapped within the cities, towns and housing estates due to their curiosity at the slightest noise.

In the urban areas there was glass, concrete, steel; all made plenty of noise when knocked or broken. A bin being toppled over or a window smashed would probably attract hundreds of them, their movements and moans attracting more and creating a neverending circle of distraction as the crowds' movements and noises kept them in the same place.

On the other hand, the sounds of wildlife, birds and rats probably echoed much more loudly now without the sound of man and his machines to drown them out of their hearing. Simon pictured hordes of the dead tearing through the streets, trying to catch pigeons and vermin.

Yes, he had hoped to be free from all of that, to be safe from the neverending threat of the dead. Maybe even enjoy life to a degree. He would have been doing what he loved; living off the land, surrounded by the countryside he held so dear.

Now, after spending three long nights in a muddy ditch and his days traipsing through the trees in the hope of finding something that he could use as a starting point for his new life as a wild man, he was ready to admit defeat.

Whether he liked the idea or not he needed to head to the built-up area again.

The thought made him shudder as a knot grew and tightened in his stomach. The dead terrified him. Just the sight of one of them in the distance always caused the panic to grow within him and the hairs on the back of his neck to stand on end. His heart rate would rise and his breathing would increase, and he had to fight with himself to maintain control of his nerves. So many times, while standing at the window in his house, he had been close to panic and ready to run out the door and to the bunker, and that was before everything had crumbled.

In his lifetime, he had watched many a horror movie and read countless graphic and gory horror novels and comics. Nothing in any of them came close to this. The closest thing that he could compare them to was vampires. Vampires, even though they were dead and they fed on the blood of the living, which in turn caused their victims to rise as one of the un-dead, were nothing like the monsters he saw now. To a degree, Vampires were beautiful, romantic and he himself had on occasion, as many other people had, fantasized about what it would be like to be one of them, to live forever and have the power to come and go at will and to be able to control people under your spell.

Simon considered that maybe the hordes of dead that now engulfed the world were, in fact, true vampires, and there was nothing beautiful or romantic about the rotting corpses that now staggered about the earth.

Maybe Bram Stoker got it completely wrong, or maybe he felt that to write a story about what a true vampire was like would have been too terrifying for the times?

Sitting on a fallen tree by the edge of a wood, Simon took some time to steel himself before he headed toward the house-lined streets of the town's suburbs. It was early morning and he could still see his breath forming clouds of mist in front of him as he breathed. The log of the tree was covered in moss and damp from the morning due, but it made no difference to him; he was already wet and he sat shivering with his shoulders hunched, wishing he had never left his underground lair.

"You never appreciate what you've got until it's gone," he grumbled to himself as he twiddled a small twig between his fingers. "Okay, let's get on with it, Simon."

He stood and slowly walked to the edge of the trees. The rustle of the leaves below his feet seemed amplified as he tried his hardest to be stealthy. His heart was racing and he dreaded stepping back out into the open. He could not shake the visions of hundreds of dead, standing on the dirt track, waiting for him to reappear.

He pushed the foliage aside and after a short moment of hesitation, he stepped out into the morning sun. He squinted in its brightness and looked along the dirt path to his left and right. There was no one in sight. To his front, a river flowed and the sounds of ducks and morning birdsong were carried to him on the gentle breeze that blew in from the water. The sun felt good on his skin. Already, he could feel himself warming in its rays and the feelings of dread began to ebb from him.

He crossed the small footbridge that spanned the width of the river and once on the other side he noticed the marked difference from wilderness to civilisation. The path was now tarmac and after three days of running about on dead leaves and soft soil, the sensation of hard ground below him made him feel strong and more nimble.

He was beginning to feel confident. He knew where he was heading and what he needed to do when he got there. The retail outlet park on the edge of town was where he needed to be. He had been there on many occasions in the old days. The outdoor activities store was there. It was where he had gone for the majority of his supplies for his trips into the wilderness in the past and he had made a mental list of the things he needed. He knew where everything was in the shop, so he hoped that he would not be there for too long. He could get in and out, head off into the wild again and begin his new life, this time with everything he needed on his back.

His plan was to load up with all the kit and equipment he needed and head back for the nature reserve as quickly as possible. He had no desire to hang around, to go shopping. Shelter, food, clothing and tools were all available in the store. He just hoped the place had not been ransacked and now crawled with the dead.

Steadily, he walked along the streets, leaving the safety of the nature reserve behind him. He gripped his iron crowbar in his right hand, ready to swing at anything that came near. His body trembled slightly with each step, a mixture of nerves and fear thrown in with the effects of cold and hunger.

Within a mile he was deep in the urban area. Buildings were on all sides, from houses and shops to office blocks and fuel stations. The place seemed deserted. Nothing stirred and the light wind that gusted along the street, making its very own poignant sigh, made the place seem all the more eerie to him.

The signs of panic and struggle lay strewn all around him. Buildings burned to nothing more than blackened shells, cars crashed into walls or upturned on to their sides. Newspapers, bottles and even clothing drifted along the roads, carried on the gusts of air that was channelled along the empty streets.

There was no sign of the wandering un-dead.

Had they all moved on? Were they off chasing some unfortunate soul?

The absence of the dead unsettled him even more. The more time without sight or sound of them, the more he pictured them hiding, waiting in ambush for him.

He continually glanced at the buildings around him, their doors and windows dark and uninviting. Curtains that twitched, he imagined them being manipulated by skeletal fingers as dead eyes watched his every move. The rustle of paper as it was caught by a gust of wind became the sound of a scraping foot being dragged by a bloated and maggot-infested corpse as it stalked him.

He stopped and huddled in the shadow of a large overturned truck. He fought against his fear that continued to mount. He tried desperately to control his breathing and, in turn, his pounding heart.

"It's okay. Not far now," he whispered in an attempt to calm himself down.

After a short break, he stepped off again, still clutching his iron crowbar tightly in his hands. He made swift progress through the detritus of the streets. Bodies lay scattered about him, stripped to the bone and left to rot in the sun while flies and other insects buzzed over their remains in black clouds. Birds and stray dogs fought over the scraps as rats scurried in the gutter. One thing he did notice about the animals he saw: they all kept a watchful eye out for the dead, regardless of what they were doing.

However, Simon saw nothing of the walkers. It seemed like they had swept through the town like a swarm of locusts, consuming all before them and then carrying on to the next one.

As he travelled down an empty street in a housing estate, Simon caught a glimpse of something moving up ahead. It was a man, or woman, he could not be sure at that distance, but it was definitely human, and it looked alive.

It stepped out from a side street further along on the right and began to walk across the road. It did not stagger or shuffle like the dead did. There were no lurching movements or uncoordinated flailing arms. It walked with deliberation and purpose. It seemed to know where it was going and headed straight there, rather than just clumsily shuffling about in the street until something caught its attention like what was to be expected from one of the dead.

Simon felt his confidence surge. There was another living, breathing person. The first he had seen in what seemed forever. He picked up his pace and hastened along the street toward the figure. He wanted to get a better look at them before he made his presence known. He wanted to be sure. If there was one thing that he had learned from all of this, it was to double check and be sure of things.

The distance between them lessened as Simon walked at a brisk pace, still nervous and on guard, wary of the houses that lined the street on both sides of him. He constantly glanced about him, his eyes scrutinising every corner or doorway. He could not shake the feeling that he was being watched.

The person at the other end of the street moved at a steadier pace. They did not seem to be in a rush. Whoever it was, they did not have a care in the world and just strolled along the street, enjoying the weather.

Simon began to question why someone could be moving about so casually, so indifferent to the new environment that was filled with danger. He was fifty metres away now and he could see the person more clearly. It was a man. He had crossed to the other side of the street, walking away from Simon, and he feared that the man would be gone if he did not try to communicate with him soon.

Maybe the man was drunk, or somehow completely unaware of the things that had happened over the past few months. At the very least, Simon felt that he should at least warn him and inform him of what was going on.

Simon went to call out, but before he spoke he felt his own hand cover his mouth. He paused, turning his head in all directions, his eyes flitting from one window to the next, seeking out every dark corner, every shadowy alcove. For a long time he had been careful of the noise he made. He had spoken to no one for weeks and the only words he did speak had been to his self and always in a whisper. The idea of hollering to someone in the street was as alien to him as walking on the moon now.

He was sure there was no one and nothing around other than the man ahead of him. The adrenalin had kicked in and he could feel his stomach tighten. The hairs on his neck stood on end and his knees trembled as his heart surged the blood to his limbs, ready for flight. One more glance around him, and he was sure they were alone in the street. It was now or never and time to make contact with the man.

"Hey," he hissed from behind a car that was parked at the side of the road. "Hello?"

The man continued to walk away from him, completely oblivious to his presence.

Simon feared that he would soon be gone if he did not make himself heard. He stepped out from behind the vehicle and in plain sight in the street. He began to jog along the road, carefully placing his feet with each step in order to keep the noise to a minimum.

He was closer now and he was sure that the man would hear him. Again, he glanced about the street around him, eyeing the doorways and windows with suspicion. A warm breeze was blowing from behind him toward the man and he was sure that his voice would be carried to his ears this time. He crouched slightly in the middle of the road, keeping a number of cars between him and the man ahead.

"Hey, you, over here," he hissed again. Louder this time and more confident, but as he said the words, he bobbed back down below the roof of the car.

It was an automatic reaction and he realised that the man would not be able to see him if he stayed hidden. Slowly, he raised himself upright again and peered over the top of the vehicle.

The man had stopped in his tracks but did not turn and remained facing in the direction he had been travelling in.

"You, hello, behind you, over here," Simon hissed again.

The man's head tilted at the voice that he had heard. Slowly, the man's head looked to the right, almost cautiously. Simon straightened to his full height, making himself visible in the street.

He took a few steps closer. "Hey, mate, behind you."

The man spun on his heels and turned to face Simon.

Simon was about to speak again, but as the man turned around, his heart skipped a beat, his chin trembled, his stomach knotted and his knees threatened to give way underneath him.

"Fuck!" he stuttered.

The man glared at him. His mottled pale skin with its shiny green hue looked stretched across the bones of the skull beneath. The lips were curled back, exposing the yellowed and broken teeth that looked even longer due to the rotting and receding gums. The eyes, fixed and dilated, flat and lifeless like the eyes of a fish on a market stall, stared back at him, unblinking and focussed on him alone.

For a moment, both of them stood stock still, their feet bolted to the floor. Simon was in complete shock. The man before him was, in fact, a walking corpse. His brain screamed out to him to run, to get away from the form in front of him as fast as he could. Nevertheless, his body refused to budge. It had frozen to the spot.

His mind had already accepted the figure as a living person. It was ready to open conversation with it. He had been so convinced that it was not one of the un-dead that his brain had stalled at the sudden revelation.

The body opened its mouth, its black and bloated tongue falling to the side and sliding over its withered and cracked lips. A bone-chilling moan rasped from within it and it took a step forward, raising one of its hands, its bony claw-like fingers outstretched and reaching towards Simon.

Simon staggered backward. That horrible sound that the dead made had shaken his body out of inaction. He was still reeling from the initial shock of realising that what he thought was a man, and a possible friend, was actually another of the walking corpses that would want nothing more than to tear him limb from limb.

"Fuck," he mumbled again as he continued to step backward.

The creature let out another moan, longer and louder this time, as though calling to Simon to come to it.

"Fuck."

Simon began to turn as the corpse let out another long wail, sounding more like a demand, as though its authority would convince Simon and he would turn back towards it. It began to move faster, its feet taking steady steps as it quickened its pace.

Simon whimpered at the thought of one of the dead being so close and being completely exposed in the open terrified him. He broke into a run and began to motor away from the advancing creature. It followed.

Peering over his shoulder, Simon saw the body also break into a run. It was not a sprinter, but it was definitely running. It chased him, keeping pace with him. A feeling of dread washed over him. The thing would not tire and would follow him until it caught up with him eventually. Simon knew that. He had seen plenty of footage about the dead on the news and read much on the internet. He had also seen it for himself from the safety of his bedroom window.

Pumping his legs harder, Simon was running flat out. He gulped air into his lungs and without realising it he had began to cry. The fear of the walking dead gripped him so powerfully he had lost control of his bodily functions. A dark patch appeared at the front of his trousers, his bladder having released its contents involuntarily. If he had had the luck to find food during his stay in the woods, he no doubt would have lost control of his bowels also and would be running with more stains at the rear.

He could hear the pounding feet of his pursuer behind him. He could feel its arms reaching for him as it clawed at the air separating them. Another long screeching moan and Simon became aware of more movement within the street. All around him, dark lumbering figures appeared. They staggered from the open doorways of houses and from the abandoned and overgrown gardens. They poured from alleyways and into the street, moaning and wailing as they reached out towards him as he passed them.

The rotting bodies of men, women and children were all around, some old and some young. Fat and thin, short and tall, some were fresh and others were badly decomposed. All types now crowded the road, all of them wanting Simon's flesh and wailing loudly together as they laid eyes upon him.

The tears streamed down his cheeks as he ran. He whimpered as he pictured himself surrounded and with no way out. Now, he wished more than ever that he had stayed in the bunker. He would be bored, lonely, even depressed, but he would be safe and not out in the open and being pursued by hordes of walking corpses.

There were hundreds of them. All of them emitting that dreadful and spine chilling sorrow filled moan. They all saw him and staggered after him. Only the one immediately behind him ran and, for a split second, Simon thanked the Gods for that small mercy.

The noise of the dead carried along the street, rising in pitch and intensity. It echoed along the road, bouncing off the houses like a pinball and continuing along in front of him. More of them stepped out ahead of him. The groans and moans had reached fever pitch and Simon could no longer see a clear way out up ahead. They were everywhere he looked.

Thinking fast, he changed direction and headed to his right. He hurdled over a low wooden fence and ploughed through the front garden of a house. The running corpse was close on his heels and attempted to follow him but it floundered at the fence and tumbled to the ground. It landed face first on the concrete of the garden path, the crunch of the bone audible in Simon's ears as the face of the corpse was smashed inward.

Without slowing his pace, Simon crashed through the side gate of the house that led to the rear garden. The gate collided loudly with the wall of the house as he passed through and swung shut behind him with a crash. He headed for the rear fence that he could now see at the far end of the overgrown garden. This time, he would not be able to hurdle the obstacle as he had done in the front garden. It was much too high and he would need to scale it using his hands and feet.

He felt the rough wood in his hands and the splinters that dug into his soft skin as he climbed but he did not slow. He heard the crash of the gate as the dead continued to follow him and began to pile into the garden behind him.

At the top of the fence, as he turned to drop on to the other side, he saw the mass of bodies that followed him. Their faces, dozens of them with hundreds more that were no doubt behind them, were fixed on him as they all stumbled in his wake. They pushed and jostled one another, all wanting to be at the front and to be the first to sink their teeth into his warm living flesh.

Simon dropped into the garden that backed onto the one he had run through and was now teeming with partially rotted corpses, snarling and growling at him through the fence, some attempting to climb the barrier to get at him.

He turned and headed for the front of the house. Like the one he had just passed through, this one also had a path that led up to a side gate. He walked slowly and with caution. He could not see what was in the street ahead of him and he wanted to be sure that he was not running straight into a horde of them before he moved. He fought his instincts that screamed at him to keep running.

A creaking sound behind him made him turn to look back at the fence he had just crossed. The weight of the mass behind it was causing it to lean inward. There were hundreds of bodies pushing against it and it would soon collapse.

Simon looked at the door to the rear of the house that was just a few metres away from him. It seemed intact and undamaged. Quickly, he peered through the window into the rear room of the house. Nothing stirred. It looked empty and abandoned.

A crack from the fence and Simon saw the whole structure crash to the ground. The dead spilled forward like a tidal wave toward him. They tripped and tumbled in the fallen fence, but still they came, stepping on one another, crawling over sprawled bodies and trampling their fallen into the dirt as they advanced.

Simon grasped at the handle to the door and pushed. The door opened inward and he piled inside, falling to the floor and kicking the door shut behind him. He was in a kitchen. The place was untouched and he suspected that the house had been empty for a long time judging by the lack of furniture and appliances, even before the dead had started to rise to attack and eat the living.

The door leading out to the garden flew open behind him. A figure lunged into the doorway. Simon launched himself at it, catching it in the chest with his shoulder and sending it tumbling back into the garden. There were more of them close by, very close and Simon slammed the door shut again, this time pressing his weight against it.

The dead crowded the doorway and began to pound against the timber frame and heavy plastic. Their thumps echoed in his ears and he gritted his teeth as he forced his body against the door, his feet struggling to grip the tiled floor below him. His legs juddered with each new assault from the outside. He knew he would not be able to hold on for long.

The handle turned and the door budged. His feet slipped and a gap appeared in the doorway. He turned and pushed against it, throwing all his weight onto it and managing only to gain a couple of inches. The dead forced their arms through the gap, reaching blindly into the interior of the house and grasping for the living flesh that they knew was inside.

Their smell and sound drifted through the open door and into the kitchen, filling the room with their lament and stench. Simon was in a panic. He screamed and howled as he tried desperately to force the door shut again. More and more bodies were pressing against it from outside and he was losing ground by the second.

The gap was now large enough for a couple of the dead to force their heads and shoulders through. They growled and snarled at Simon as he kicked at their faces, their hands clawing at his legs in an attempt to grasp him and pull him to the floor and out into the feeding frenzy in the garden.

Simon was crying uncontrollably now. He felt like he was fighting a losing battle, but he could not give up. He knew all too well what would happen to him the second that the dead got in the house. It was hopeless, though, and he knew it. They would get him eventually and he was just stealing nothing more than a few more seconds of life before they consumed him.

"You bloody idiot!" an angry voice called out at him.

At first, Simon thought it had come from himself, then he realised there was someone else in the room with him.

Simon blinked. He stood, braced against the door and in complete shock staring back at a man in the doorway leading out from the kitchen. He was definitely a living human being, though bedraggled and looking not completely unlike the dead ghouls that hammered at the door behind him.

The shabby man stood, wide-eyed and looking furious. His long beard was matted and tangled and the woollen hat that he wore on his head looked like he had never removed it in his whole life. Simon recognised him, but he could not remember where from, and at that moment in time he did not care.

"Help me," he shouted, "I can't hold them for much longer."

The man disappeared from the doorway.

"Where are you going? Help me, for God's sake." Simon braced himself against another jolt, as the door was battered more ferociously at his back.

A moment later the scruffy man reappeared. He charged toward Simon, hefting an axe above his head and screaming. Simon, with the dead at his back and a mad axe murderer at his front, winced and waited for the blow to finish him off. He screwed his eyes shut and sunk his head into his shoulders. A second later and he heard a sickening thud as the axe head smashed into soft flesh and crunched through bone.

Simon opened his eyes. The crazy man was close to him, leaning over him and struggling to free the axe from the head of a body that had managed to force most of its upper torso through the doorway. He began to kick at the corpse and shove it back through the door. Arms and hands continued to snatch at the two of them through the narrow opening, but with their combined weight, they were able to force the door shut. The man reached up, slammed the bolt across at the top of the door and then did the same for the bottom, securing it for the time being. Simon slumped to the floor, panting and exhausted and shaking with fright.

The man stepped back and viewed the door as the dead continued to pound against it. Nodding to himself, he grunted. "That should give us a headstart at least."

"What?" Simon looked up at him.

"Come on. We're leaving."

The man walked out of the room and left Simon, still sitting on the kitchen floor with his back to the door. Another crash from behind forced him into action. He scrambled to his feet and chased after the strange man into the interior of the house. He found him at the front door, peering through the frosted glass of the side window and clutching a plastic bag.

"What are you doing?" Simon's voice was full of panic.

He continually checked over his shoulder, back in the direction of the kitchen. The noise of the door beginning to splinter was destroying what nerves he had left in him and threatened to turn him into a blubbering wreck.

The man calmly stood upright and peered into the eyes of Simon. He was considerably shorter but his nerves seemed to be made of steel.

"We're leaving and I'm checking to see if the street is clear. What are you doing?"

The question caught Simon on the back foot and, for a moment, he was lost for words. Here was this man, completely at ease with the situation and asking him what he was doing, as if arranging a day out and wanting to know his preference.

"I'm fucking coming with you," Simon replied finally.

"Good." The man nodded with a slight smile. "Okay then. Have you got all your belongings?" he asked, peering around and past him as though expecting to see suitcases and other luggage.

Simon looked down at his hands and the iron bar he held. "You're nuts, aren't you. This is all I have."

The sound of the kitchen door crashing open and the moan of the dead echoed through the house.

The man looked up at him, a warming smile on his face. "Okay, let's get going. I'm David, by the way, but most people know me as Johnny."

15

Jake was not happy about the situation. He eyed the building with a sense of foreboding. Something was not right as far as his gut was concerned and it was now screaming its warnings at him.

"So what is it?" John asked from the rear seat.

Jake bit his lip, his eyes fixed on the large sprawling complex of the supermarket in the distance below them. They had an elevated view of the shopping centre from the hilltop where they were and they could see much of the area around the supermarket. It looked deserted, but still, something bothered Jake.

"I don't know," he said shrugging his shoulders as he sat in the front passenger seat. "I just don't like it. I have this feeling that it's all going to go to rat shit. It's been nagging at me all day and I can't explain it."

"Nah, it's just that you've not been out for a while. You're bound to feel that way. I'd be lying if I said I didn't have any doubts about this myself."

Jake spun in his seat and glared at him. "Don't patronise me, John. It is nothing to do with being wire happy or anything like that. I just have a gut instinct that I have always followed and now, it's telling me that there's trouble ahead."

Steve opened the door and climbed out from the driver's seat. He needed to stretch his legs and the atmosphere in the car was becoming stuffy. Jake and the others got out too, congregating around the front of the vehicle. Steve pulled a pack of cigarettes from his pocket and shared them with whoever was interested.

"No thanks. I gave them up a long time ago," Jake said with a wave of his hand. He glanced back at the supermarket again. The whole thing was bothering him and it was clearly etched across his face for all to see.

"Are you planning on living forever or something?" Steve asked with a smirk as he tried to force Jake into relaxing.

"No, I just don't like smelling like an ashtray."

John reached over from where he was leaning against the front of the vehicle and gave Jake a nudge on the shoulder. "You're keeping yourself smelling good for some hot young stud, then?" he joked.

Jake smiled back at him. "Hey, you never know."

Helen refused a cigarette but John was now happily puffing away along with Lee and Steve, enjoying the great outdoors and the beautiful sunny weather. They stood at the top of a hill, in a car park to what had once been an exclusive Golf Club overlooking the city and its suburbs. It was situated on the fringes of the rural area on the very outskirts of the city. From where they stood, they could see the tall buildings of the metropolis in the distance with the residential areas sprawling out from it.

It was a heavily built-up area and all had agreed that to venture too far in would be considered too much of a risk. The streets would be crawling with the dead and driving around in an old beat up Land Rover would not be a good idea.

Lee had remembered about the supermarket and outlet complex on the outskirts. It provided good access roads and easy escape routes and everything they needed in the way of supplies. If anything should go wrong, they could see the trouble coming well in advance and make a sharp exit before they became unstuck.

Steve raised his binoculars and adjusted the focus as he concentrated them on a particular street in the distance. He could see right the way along it, from one junction to the next. Houses, their short gardens slowly growing out of control, lined the street. It was a residential area close to the hub of the city.

The place looked a mess. Doors and windows were smashed; cars lay abandoned with their doors hanging open, slowly rusting away when the city was evacuated by the living. Steve could see the makeshift barricades at the far end of the street. They had collapsed and been pushed aside during the assault of the dead, their mass overwhelming the defences that the residents had feebly constructed in their desperation.

Briefly, he pictured the streets in his mind and what they may have looked like before the plague had swept across the world. It would have been brighter, full of life and colourful; people coming and going children playing and traffic beeping their horns in frustration at the lights. Parents walking their children to school or returning home from work. Life, it would have been full of life. Now it was just dull and drab, everything seemed to have been painted in numerous shades of grey.

Then he saw them, the dead. The shadowy figures that roamed the streets, they were slow and lumbering as they shuffled along the roads and curbs. They did not seem to pay much attention to one another; they just staggered about in their own world, following their feet below them that seemed to move automatically.

He could also see a number of them just sitting slouched against the walls and static cars, as though waiting for something to rouse them from their inactivity. If Steve had not known better, he could have been forgiven for mistaking the people in the street as being a bunch of drunks.

At the far end, he could just about make out a gaggle of the dead, clustered together on the ground. They appeared to be fighting one another, struggling to gain possession of something that was on the ground. Some poor dog or cat that had accidently strayed into the street,

Steve suspected. He did not want to imagine it being of a higher form of life than that.

"You think there are people still alive down there?" Helen asked as she stood at the side of Steve, looking out on to the city.

"I'm sure there will be. There *has* to be."

"Why do you say that?" she asked, turning to him with a frown.

Steve looked at her and shrugged. "I don't know really. I just suppose there has to be someone who has managed to hide out and stay alive, for now at least. It was a big city with lots of people in its day."

"Lots of dead people now though, Steve," she murmured with a sigh.

"The place looks pretty dead to me," Lee said as he raised a pair of binoculars to his eyes and began to scan from left to right.

"Yeah, but you can't see every building and street with those things from this distance," Steve said as he flicked his cigarette butt away into the bushes, exhaling a cloud of grey blue smoke from his lungs.

Lee looked across and shook his head critically. "That's not what I'm on about. We're not here to talk about the city; we are here for the supermarket and the fuel station. The place looks dead to me, empty, no one there." He highlighted his point by raising his arm and waving his hand in the direction of their objective.

Steve saw that his friend was inpatient to get on with the job. "Okay, I want to get this over with, too. What's the plan then?"

Helen shrugged. "As we discussed, we hit the fuel station and see what we can get. Then, if it still looks good, we have a look around."

Steve nodded. "That's what we'll do then." He turned to Jake who still did not look too pleased with the plan. "Are you up for this, buddy?"

Jake turned his attention from the complex in the distance and back to Steve. "Well I'm not exactly going to sit here and leave you to it, am I?"

They piled back into the vehicle and pulled out of the car park. They travelled along the narrow country lane until it opened up on to the main ring road that encompassed the city. On the next slip road, they pulled off and onto the access ramp of the outlet complex. They followed the short curving road around until they were at the entrance to the massive sprawling car park that the multitude of shops encircled.

Most of the stores and fast food restaurants still seemed intact. From what they could tell, the place had been forgotten about in the chaos that followed in the days of the virus outbreak. The fact that it was removed from the heavily populated areas with main roads and a park separating them, probably helped to keep it unscathed and out of the forefront of people's minds during the times of panic, all those months ago.

Steve slowed the vehicle to a crawl. Everyone was on high alert. Their eyes scanned every corner, every shadow and entrance of the buildings.

The dead were there, all around, but their numbers were small and scattered.

"As long as we keep moving, we shouldn't have any trouble from them," Steve said as he watched a woman stumbling toward them, reaching out and clawing at the car as they passed.

The body of the woman still wore the shredded remains of a bright pink nightdress. It was now covered in dark dried blood and it hung open at the front, revealing her pale naked emaciated body underneath. Her lower jaw was missing and her tongue hung loose against her neck, swaying from side to side as she walked, giving the effect of a grotesque bloodied and bloated pendulum.

There were shadowy jerky figures scattered throughout the large car park of the complex. Some dragged or pushed shopping carts while others stood staring at the shop windows and the goods inside. As the vehicle approached, all of them turned and followed. Soon, the small group of survivors had a pack slowly pursuing them. Although they moved sluggish and clumsily, they would follow them for as long as they could see or hear them and never lose interest. They knew that living flesh was close.

Steve steered the Land Rover towards the fuel station on the far side, close to the exit point of the complex. As they approached, his eyes lit up.

"Fucking hell, jackpot," he exclaimed in excitement.

Ahead of them, sitting motionless at the front of the pumps was a large fuel tanker. They could not tell if it was full or not, but their plan had been to try to find something that they could use to transport a large amount of fuel in. They did not expect to find a tanker, so they had planned to scrounge fuel cans and any other container that they thought would be suitable for carrying the precious liquid.

John leaned forward from the rear seat and patted Steve on the shoulder. "Couldn't have asked for better, maybe our luck is changing?"

Helen looked across at him, a serious expression on her face. "You mean like the other day when you and Carl ended up stuck in a tree? Let's not get complacent on this." Her last statement was meant as a reminder, a warning, to them all.

John breathed deeply and nodded. Just being reminded of his traumatic time within the supposedly safe walls of the Safari Park was enough to bring him back down to earth with a bump. He had honestly expected to die that day.

Steve brought them to a halt. For a moment, they all remained in their seats, staring out the windows and watching for any sign of the dead in the immediate vicinity. The fuel point was situated to the side of the supermarket with an exit road leading off between them. No movement came from the area of the station or the large buildings around them.

Steve pulled his small axe from the foot well of the vehicle and clutched it in his hand as he reached for the door handle.

Jake was holding the heavy hammer that he had become fond of and readying himself to step out. He looked back at the others over his shoulder.

"You all know the drill. Steve and me, we go in and see what we can get and you act as the lookouts."

"No worries." Lee nodded back at him and opened his door.

Helen, John and Lee fanned out in a line in front of the fuel station, facing the way they had come and keeping a close eye on the dead that slowly approached in the distance.

"I'd say you've a good five minutes before they become a problem, guys," John called out to Steve and Jake when he had finished weighing up the situation. "Hang on," he muttered them as he stepped forward and began to bring his heavy iron bar into position for a swing, "got one here."

From behind a group of parked vehicles to the side of the fuel station car park, a lone figure approached. It lurched from side to side as its legs struggled to keep a forward momentum. The shadow of the building made it difficult for John to see it clearly until it entered into the sunlight. Its entire abdomen had been ripped open and the contents torn out. There was nothing left of its internal organs. Even the soft flesh was gone, leaving nothing more than the rib cage and spinal column visible. The thing in front of him was little more than a skeleton with a thin covering of leathery skin and dried up sinew. How it was still mobile, John could only guess.

He took a couple of careful steps forward, raising his weapon, ready to swing like a baseball player. The stench of the corpse drifted into his nostrils and he gagged slightly as he moved closer towards it, but he never took his eye off his target.

He stepped forward again and at the same time, began his swing. He threw his shoulders out, allowing the weight of the iron to carry them in a wide arc with the momentum. He timed it perfectly and judged the distance to the millimetre. The iron bar smashed into the side of the walker's head with a sickening thud. John felt the bone crunch under the impact and a loud sigh escaped from the creature as it dropped to the floor.

John stepped back, looked across to Jake and nodded. "All clear now."

Jake and Steve headed for the tanker. It did not look damaged at all and even the large plate glass windows of the fuel station shop were still intact. It looked like the place and the truck had just been abandoned and forgotten about.

Steve reached up and climbed onto the small step of the driver's door. Before opening it, he wanted to have a look inside, just in case. The cabin looked clear. A thin layer of dust coated the dashboard along with dozens of dead flies, but there was nothing moving as far as he could see. He reached down and tried the handle. The door came open a little and Steve quickly jumped back down to the ground, raising his axe in his hand and stepping back in case there was anything inside that he had missed. Nothing appeared and he gingerly approached the large truck again and pulled the door fully open.

Jake stood at his back, his hammer ready.

The sudden change of air in the cabin caused the millions of dust particles to drift into the air and dance in the sunlight, but that was all that stirred from within. Steve glanced back at Jake and stepped forward. He craned his neck, trying to see into the rear of the cabin and began to pull himself back up onto the step to get a better look into the darkness behind the driver and passenger seats. It was completely empty.

Jake climbed up behind him. "Any sign of the keys."

Steve looked back at him, his eyes lighting up and a grin spreading across his face. "They're still in the ignition."

He carefully turned the key to the first click, checking to see if there was any power left in the battery. The dashboard lit up brightly and all the needles in the gauges danced and swung across before settling to give him an accurate read out of oil pressure, temperature, fuel status and battery power.

Steve chuckled, "Looks like we're good to go, Jake, even a full tank."

"What about the storage tank on the back?"

"Full," Steve informed him, "but I don't know what with. Could be frigging orange juice for all I know."

"Only one way to find out, I suppose." Jake looked up at him. "Let's check the back and see what the labels say."

To their disbelief, the truck was full of diesel, exactly what they needed. It was time to see if the truck was willing to start. Steve and Jake climbed back into the cab of the tanker. They exchange glances at one another and Steve said a silent prayer to himself. He exhaled loudly and reached down for the keys that hung from the ignition.

The sound of the large engine roaring to life sounded like an earthquake in Lee's ears. He spun and caught the eye of Helen, who looked back in bewilderment. The tanker was belching and coughing clouds of black smoke from its exhaust as it cleared its throat and then settled into a steady rhythmic rumble as it idled on low revolutions with Steve remaining seated behind the wheel.

Jake ran toward them from the truck. "We're going to drive it back to the entrance where we came in. You follow in the Land Rover and pick us up. We will sit and wait for ten minutes and let those dead heads follow us. Then, once they are close enough to us, and far enough away from the supermarket, we head back in the Land Rover for a shopping spree. A quick one, mind you,"

"Okay, you lead and we'll follow." Helen nodded as Lee and John followed her to the Land Rover.

Steve made a point of avoiding hitting any of the dead that staggered toward them as he headed for the entrance point. He did not want to risk losing a wheel or damaging the radiator and ruining their run of good luck. He drove slow and deliberately, swaying left and right as he rounded individuals and clusters of the dead in his path.

The five of them sat in the Safari Park Land Rover, watching the slow shambling corpses approach.

"Are we just going to smash in the door of the supermarket?" John asked.

"I'm hoping that we won't have to do that," Steve replied. "Maybe they didn't lock up, just like they did at the fuel point?"

"We'll soon find out I suppose," Lee said nodding at the lead reanimated bodies that approached. They were now only fifty metres away.

Steve put the vehicle in gear and pulled forward. He weaved in and out, steering the vehicle between the groups of bodies that attempted to reach for them as they passed. They tripped and stumbled into each other as they tried to turn and follow. Even in the vehicle, and with the engine drowning out much of the noise, they could hear the moans of the dead as they passed them.

At the entrance to the supermarket, the five of them climbed out and scanned the area. It appeared that all of the dead in the vicinity had followed them to where they left the tanker. Now, they followed them again, but they were hundreds of metres away and Steve and the others had a little breathing space to see what they could scavenge.

All of the doors they tried were locked and secured. Their easy meal ticket had run out with the fuel tanker still being roadworthy and full with the fuel they needed. Now they needed to work for their pay.

Without another word, Lee launched a piece of paving slab through the main door. The glass caved in with a loud crash, leaving a large hole gaping into the gloomy interior of the store. He began chopping away at the remaining shards of glass that hung on to the frame; they shattered as they hit the floor. He looked back over his shoulder as he stepped into the darkness of the supermarket.

"We're in," he grinned.

John looked back at the approaching figures in the distance. They were still far away and moving slowly. They had time to get a quick look around and grab a few items they may need.

Steve backed the Land Rover up close to the hole that Lee had created. It was just a few centimetres too narrow to enable the vehicle to fit completely through it and he did not want to risk ramming it through and possibly causing the whole frame and even the roof to collapse on top of them. They would be stranded and at the mercy of the dead if the vehicle became stuck.

He climbed out and squeezed himself through the narrow gap between the Land Rover and the frame of the doorway. It would be hard for any of the dead to be able to force themselves through the tight space.

"Okay, folks, as quickly as possible, let's go shopping." Steve clasped his hands together and rubbed his palms, smiling at the others with glee.

"I could do with some retail therapy actually," Jake replied.

Steve and Lee headed for the tinned goods, looking to grab as much as they could before it was time to head back. John volunteered to stay close to the entrance to keep an eye on the goings on outside in the car park while Jake and Helen headed for the pharmacy.

They had already discussed the possibilities of needing antibiotics and painkillers as well as basic medicines in the future. There was also the matter of women's health and hygiene that Helen was concerned with and she wanted to be able to provide the rest of the women in the house with what they needed. To her, having Jake as her looting partner was not as embarrassing as it would have been with any of the others.

Within minutes, the cart that Lee was pushing was filled to the brim with all kinds of non-perishable foods and drinks. Lee was furiously collecting every tin of beans he could find, scooping them from the shelves and into the cart.

Steve raised an eyebrow. "You got a baked bean problem, Lee?"

Lee looked back at him as he shovelled more from the shelf, knocking the contents into the shopping cart. "I can't live without them, mate. A world with no beans isn't worth living in as far as I'm concerned."

"Whatever floats your boat, mate. I think we are done here. Let's head for the clothing section." Steve moved off toward the end of the aisle while Lee followed behind, pushing their heavy load ahead of him.

Soon they had pretty much emptied the clothes racks of everything they thought would be useful, in all different sizes. The cart was overflowing with food and clothing, threatening to spill across the floor of the aisle.

"It's the middle of summer, Steve, what do we need fleece jackets and duvets for?" Lee asked in wonder as he watched his friend drop another load in on top of the ever-growing pile that was by now, becoming hard to push.

"It's not always going to be summer though, is it? And I don't fancy having to come back out to shop for winter clothes."

"Well, in that case, we may as well get over there and grab some gear." Lee nodded in the direction of a display for camping equipment.

The tent sat pitched and pegged on a patch of imitation grass with pots and pans laid out in front as though ready for cooking. The sleeping bags were rolled out, looking inviting, as they lay sprawled on a sheet of thick foam for insulation and comfort.

It reminded Steve of the visions of camping he had always had as a child, though the reality was never the same. His trips into the wilderness always ended in disappointment, soaked to the bone and shivering uncontrollably. Lee had been present on many of his aborted camping trips in their youth.

Steve chuckled to himself as he remembered a particular event. At the age of about fifteen, he and Lee had gone in the local woods, their camping gear in their packs, intent on spending the night smoking the hemp they had collected that day and getting pleasantly stoned. It did not seem to have any effect on Steve and once his failed joint was extinguished, he began griping about the lack of results. Halfway through his complaint, as he looked up to see whether his friend was in agreement with him, he stopped.

Lee's eyes had swollen to the size of golf balls. They were bright red and streaming with tears. His nose and upper lip was covered in mucus and he wheezed as he breathed. He had had a bad reaction to the hemp because of his hayfever. Steve had rolled up laughing and now, remembering the incident, he struggled to keep his laughter stifled as he stood, staring at the camping gear.

"What you giggling about?" Lee asked as he walked towards the display.

Steve shook his head and reminded Lee of the details of the night in the woods, all the time trying hard not to allow the memory to send him into fits of laughter.

"Ah, yeah, I remember that one," Lee said with a faint smile. "I didn't know that smoking weed could set your hayfever off."

Jake and Helen had ransacked the pharmacy and had now moved on to the toiletries aisle. Shampoo and hair conditioner had become a rarity lately in the mansion and Helen was craving for a hot bubble bath with scented candles, followed by copious amounts of moisturising. She smiled to herself at the thought of Steve joining her amongst the piles of bubbles and drifting steam.

John could hear the others moving about amongst the aisles. They were taking too long and he was becoming anxious. He paced the floor along the large windows at the front of the store. Standing on his tiptoes, he attempted to see further into the shop, between the lines of shelves, hoping to catch a glimpse of their progress.

Noises outside made him turn around. To the right of their Land Rover, a lone figure stumbled into view. It worked its way toward the entrance, using the side of the vehicle to steady itself. It reached the broken glass but could go no further because of the vehicle that blocked the hole. It pushed its face against the narrow opening, its fingers attempting to widen the gap with the remaining shards of glass slicing into its hands and leaving smears of dark, coagulated blood all over the frame. It snarled and thrashed its arms through the gap at John when it noticed him standing amongst the aisles in front of it.

John stepped back. The sight of the thing unnerved him. Its skin was pale and pitted with dark holes that showed the bone underneath. Its teeth looked extra long as they gnashed at him and, as always, the lifeless haunting eyes never looked away from him. Its eyes were fixed on him, staring right into his soul with no emotion or indication of its intentions. It was its body language and John's experience with them that made him fully aware of what the thing wanted and intended.

More of its skin had started to come away from its hands. Its dried and congealed blood smeared the glass of the store window and the zebra stripes of the Land Rover in dark stains that looked more like oil.

John could not understand where it had come from. The dead that had followed them to the far side of the outlet car park were still a distance away; he could see them getting closer. The one by the vehicle had come from somewhere much closer by. John plucked up the courage to venture nearer to the window.

The corpse at the vehicle thrust its hands through the gap again, shredding the skin of its forearms on the jagged shards of glass and stripping it almost to the bone, leaving strips of clothing and flesh hanging from the spikes of glass that remained protruding from the window frame.

John fought his urge to step back and craned his neck to see past it and along the side of the building. His shoes squeaked against the waxed and polished floor as he raised himself on to his toes.

There, moving along the side of the shop front, coming from around the corner by the fuel point, hundreds of figures emerged. The grey and brown mass of tattered clothing and rotting flesh were headed straight for him, for the shattered window. Their heads bobbed and their arms flailed as they approached. The sight of the lone figure thrashing and moaning at the window by the Land Rover attracted them to that same spot.

John's eyes widened and he struggled to form the words to alert the others. His throat seized up and he felt the hair on the back of his neck stand on end. He began to step back, away from the terrifying sight before him. They would get in, he was sure of it. With their numbers pushing against the Land Rover and the glass, they would pile into the store.

He turned on his heel and began to run. He headed down an aisle in the direction he thought Steve and the others were.

"They're here. There's fucking hundreds of them," he finally managed to scream the warning to the others as he raced away from the glass front and deeper into the supermarket.

He reached the end of the first aisle, panic rising within him and still screaming for the others. He turned to the left without slowing his pace, his feet changing direction and his body swinging around with the momentum.

Something slammed into him from the right, knocking the wind out of him with a loud gasp of air as his lungs emptied, sending him tumbling to the floor. The body fell on top of him, pinning him to the cold linoleum and gasping for air.

John began to scream.

Helen was the first to run, closely followed by Jake. They sprinted through the aisles following the sounds of the high-pitched screams. She burst around the corner and saw two figures squirming at their feet.

John was on the floor, still shouting for help with the body on top of him. It grunted and thrashed about as it struggled to gain a grip of the struggling John who was lay, prostrate, below.

Helen raised the small baseball bat she had in her hands and stepped forward. She judged the distance and brought the weapon down in an arc, aiming for the body's head. A second body grabbed her, tackling her from the side, sending her falling to the ground and the baseball bat tumbling from her grip. It rolled from her hand and across the floor out of her reach. Immediately, she twisted below the weight of her attacker, kicking out at the same time and reaching for the bat.

Jake was now in the same aisle as he came sprinting around the corner. He saw the scene before him and began his own attack. He, too, raised his weapon and aimed at the closest of the figures, the one that had slammed into Helen and was now fighting to maintain a grip on her as she fought against it.

"No!" someone shouted, but Jake was in full swing with his heavy hammer. It was already on the downward arc, the weight of it carrying it through the swing and impossible to stop. It was aiming directly at the figure's head. The body on top of Helen suddenly raised itself to its knees and forced itself into a haunch, throwing its arms in up and in front to protect itself from the blow that was about to come from Jake.

"No, don't," it screamed. "We're...." The voice was cut short as Jake slammed into it.

At the last second, Jake tried to change the momentum of his swing by aiming to the side and beyond his target when he realised the person on the ground was alive, but his body continued forward. He carried on through the swing and barged into the man, knocking him over and sprawling across him as he tripped himself, but he had managed to avert his blow with the hammer.

The five of them lay in a tangle on the floor of the supermarket, grunting and panting as they raised themselves to their feet. Jake raised the hammer in his hands, aiming it at the man who was still sitting in a crouch.

The man got the message and he stayed down, close to the floor.

John heaved the other man off from on top of him and pushed him to the side, grunting with the effort. He quickly scurried back away from his attacker, jumped to his feet and raised his fist, his eyes burning with fright and fury. He lunged forward and landed a heavy blow on the side of the man's head, the vibration of the impact travelling up his forearm and jolting his shoulder.

The man dropped back to the floor with a sickening thud. John stepped in for the finish, cocking his arm back again with his fist clenched.

"Stop, that's enough, John. He's down for now!" Steve shouted from behind him as he moved down the aisle.

Everyone relaxed their postures slightly, but kept their guard up. The two men remained on the floor, choosing to adopt a passive stance, knowing that they were outnumbered against the larger group.

"What the hell is going on here?" Lee asked from behind Steve. "Looks like you've found a couple of Ninjas, John," he said, nodding to the two dark clad figures on the floor at their feet.

John's face was flushed red and his chest was inflating and deflating rapidly as he breathed heavily.

"This bastard attacked me," he said, nodding towards the man who still lay on his back beneath him.

Steve looked across at the other man who was still squatting in front of Jake and Helen. "I take it you're his pal?"

The man nodded back at him. His eyes wide with fear. "We didn't attack anyone. It was an accident."

"Yeah," the other man said from his position on the floor of the supermarket, "it was an accident. We were running to see what all the noise had been about, and I bumped into the big man here. We didn't mean it," he said as he nodded up at John.

Steve realised that they were only young men, probably no older than twenty years old.

"What's with the outfits then? You both think you're in the SAS or something?" he asked referring to the all black clothing.

"Huh?" The two of them swapped confusing glances with one another. The one below John sat up slightly. "What do you mean?"

"The black kit, hoods and all, you think you're Blade?" Steve gestured at their clothing with his hand axe.

The man squatting in front of Helen looked down at himself and then back to Steve. "We always dress like this. Even before all this started."

"Ah," Lee said in sudden realisation, "you're a pair of fucking hoodies aren't you. I bet you're the ones that smashed my mum's greenhouse too," he said with menace in his voice as he took a step closer.

John stepped back and cut the conversation short. "Steve, there's thousands of them out there. That's what I was shouting about when I bumped into your man here." He gestured toward the hoodie.

Lee looked across at him, a bemused look spreading across his face. "You mean thousands of Hoodies?"

John's eyes flashed and his voice became a mixture of annoyance, haste and alarm. "No, not fucking hoodies. Those things, they're everywhere. I don't know where they came from, but they're not the same ones that followed us across the car park."

Everybody looked to the front of the shop. The sound of the dead outside was now audible to them as they focussed their attention from the two young men and to the shop front instead. They could hear the scratching of hundreds of fingers against the glass, the thumps of fists against the windows and the moans of dozens of souls as they tried desperately to gain entry into the store.

"Shit, where did they all come from?" Jake exclaimed.

John was still looking in the direction of the entrance, slowly shaking his head. "I don't know, but we're done for. We will never get out and they will get in eventually. There's too many of them and they know we're here, too."

"Yeah, and it's your fault they're there." The man on the ground below John spoke accusingly at the five of them. "We've been trying to get them all around to the back of the building so that we could escape. We've spent the last two days shouting and banging and even throwing them rotten meat from the freezers, and then you lot turn up and invite them in through the front door. Nice going, dickheads."

"You've been stuck here?" Steve asked.

"Yeah, for nearly a week. We thought we had it made at first with everything that was in here, but more and more of them showed up by the day. Fuck knows where they were coming from or why they were coming here. We were coming to see why they were all coming back around this side when we bumped into you."

Steve, Helen, John, Lee and Jake all looked at each other, embarrassment on their faces. Lee shrugged his shoulders.

"Hey, shit happens doesn't it?"

"Well, that same shit that happens is also about to hit the fan, I reckon," John muttered. He turned back to the others. "What do we do then? Can we get out through the back?" He looked to the two hoodies.

The one by Helen raised himself to his feet with a grunt, shaking his head as he brushed himself down. He looked back at John and then to Steve.

"There's just as many back there as there are at the front."

The six of them slowly crept forward to the front of the store. They crouched down, just out of sight at the end of the nearest aisle to the bay windows and main entrance. Hundreds of gaunt faces and pale hands were pressed up against the glass, and it looked like there were hundreds more behind.

Steve looked over at the hole they had created and backed the Land Rover into and thanked their good fortune that they had decided on smashing one of the smaller sections of the window. The gap was no larger than two metres from frame to frame and the vehicle was backed up, almost flush with the breach in the integrity of the storefront, leaving a gap of no more than a few inches either side of the vehicle.

The Land Rover rocked gently from side to side as the mass of bodies pushed against it, but to Steve's relief, the wheels stayed firmly planted to the ground. He knew, though, that with so many out there, and if they realised that they only had to move the vehicle to gain entry, a concerted effort would see the Land Rover pushed aside like a flimsy inflatable toy.

"Why don't we all pile into the back of the Land Rover through the back door? We wouldn't be exposing ourselves and we could then drive out of here," Helen suggested as she peered around from the stack of shelves.

Steve shook his head, not taking his eyes away from the dead that crowded the windows. "No good. It's an old vehicle and probably not as strong as it used to be, even in four-wheel drive. If we lost traction or power, we could get stuck in the middle of them all and with all their attention then focussed on the Land Rover while we're inside it, we wouldn't stand a chance against that lot."

Jake hummed in acknowledgement. He bit down on his lower lip as he considered other options.

"What about fire?"

Steve looked across at him. "What do you mean?"

"Well, there's enough flammable stuff here to do it. Maybe we should try and burn them?"

"Yeah," John added with a sarcastic tone, "and in the process burn the whole building down, with us inside? Good one there, Jake."

Jake spun on him and hissed, "What do you suggest then?"

Steve raised his hand. "Shut up a minute you two. Now look, for the moment, they're not exactly riled up out there. If we keep out of sight, maybe they'll lose interest and their numbers will thin out. Anyway, I'm in no great rush to destroy this place. It's a goldmine and everything we need is right here. We could come back some time in the future, more organised and with more vehicles and clear the place out. We wouldn't need to leave the safety of the park for a long time after that."

"A park, what park?" one of the newcomers questioned as he raised his eyebrows.

"Yeah," Lee replied looking back over his shoulder at him, "the Safari Park. That's where we've been living."

"You got room for two more?" the second hoodie asked with pleading eyes.

Steve glanced about at the other members of his group. No one spoke and he interpreted that as either indifference or agreement. He looked back at the man wearing the hooded top.

"You help us get out of this trap we're in, and you can have your own stately room, four poster bed and all."

"You're on. You hear that, Stan, We have a new home."

"Yeah, terrific," the other hoodie said with a touch of sarcasm. He turned back to Steve. "I'm Stan by the way. That lump hammer over there is Kieran."

Steve nodded. "Charmed, I'm sure. Now come on, we had better put some distance between us and them," he said as he indicated the faces that smeared the windows with grease, blood and dead flesh.

"I told you we shouldn't have come here," Jake murmured as he followed on behind the others.

They crept back along the aisles and headed further in the store.

16

"How are we going to get through London? That place is going to be wall to wall with those things, Marcus. You know that, don't you?" Stu was sitting in the passenger seat of the Land Rover beside Marcus as he steered them along the jumbled and clogged main highway that led toward the capital.

They had managed to plough their way out of the army barracks and through the outskirts of Dover, fighting off the masses of diseased reanimated corpses that wailed and hurled themselves at the vehicle as the team fought through to the safety of the open road. In thirty-six hours, they had slowly made their way west into the heart of the country.

The amount of stalled traffic and pile-ups that created nonnegotiable tangles of twisted metal and swarms of dead that littered the roads, meant the team having to constantly detour, boxing around obstructions and roaming corpses. Sometimes, they had to travel through built up areas that were equally as infested and just as difficult to negotiate, but they had very little in the way of choice. The going was slow and it was a constant struggle to gain even a few miles before they came to another obstacle.

"I've been thinking, Stu, and I've come to the conclusion that I've no intention of going anywhere near London," Marcus replied without taking his eyes from the road ahead. "I'm hoping that we can skirt around it to the south. We could come off this road a few miles before the ring road and head deep into the rural areas, towards Salisbury. We know that area pretty well. What do you think?"

"Hey," Jim leaned forward from his position in the rear of the vehicle, "isn't that where Stonehenge is? If I am not getting to see Tower Bridge, then I want to see something. Stonehenge will do nicely."

"Jim, this is not a holiday." Sini looked back at him from over his shoulder as he watched the road behind them.

"We should've taken a boat. That's what I think," Stu grumbled as he adjusted his position in his seat.

"Stu, none of us have a clue about boats. All we did with the last one was aim it at the White Cliffs of Dover and hit the throttle. Besides, I didn't fancy hanging around down at the harbour while you went shopping for a yacht. At least this way, we have control over our own destiny. I don't know the first thing about reading the sea. We could end up sinking a mile out and then where would we be?"

Stu looked across at him, a childish smile spreading across his face. "At the bottom of the sea, Marcus," He laughed and coughed at the same time, then straightened himself. "Anyway, there are a lot of airfields in that area to the south and west of London, Marcus. Are you sure, you want to risk it? I mean, there's a chance that there could still be a large presence of army units and it could be trouble we don't need, especially as we're driving about in one of their vehicles and carrying army issue weapons."

Marcus nodded and hummed as he pondered the question for a moment, he rubbed his rough stubbly chin with one hand and continued to steer the vehicle with the other.

"Good point. I don't fancy us being shot as deserters, or worse, press-ganged into some gang fuck local militia. What do you suggest?"

"We hang a right as soon as we can once we're sure that we are clear of London and head north. There are enough minor roads to choose from and we should be able to avoid most of the heavily populated areas."

"Okay," Marcus nodded, "let's get away from London first and then we'll do a map study. As you said, that place will be infested with those things. It would be nice to find somewhere to rest up for the night, too, if possible. My back is killing me from sleeping in this bucket of bolts and my arse is numb."

Their plans to circumnavigate London were soon scuppered. Every turning they approached was completely blocked with destroyed and overturned vehicles. There had been mass pile-ups during the panic and the exit and entrance ramps were gridlocked with static vehicles where they had been abandoned by their owners, or overwhelmed by the dead.

The signs of struggle were present everywhere. Cars and trucks lay overturned. Some were burned and others looked as though they had been blown apart. Hundreds of bodies lay in the spaces between the vehicles, most of them dismembered and stripped of flesh, picked clean to the bone and unable to reanimate. Skulls and ribcages of all shapes, sizes and ages lay scattered all around like discarded waste tossed into the gutters. No one had been spared.

Marcus pictured thousands of the dead falling upon the people trapped on the roads. He imagined the confusion and the chaos that must have reigned there as people fought one another, as well as the dead, for their own survival.

He slowed the vehicle as they approached a turn off. The chaos of the slip road had spilled out onto the main carriageway and blocked their way ahead completely. An overturned heavy goods vehicle lay on its side, its large, slowly rusting hulk spanning the entire width of the three lanes of road. With no other choice, they had to stop the vehicle and search for an alternative way around.

Sini and Stu slowly approached the overturned truck, their weapons at the ready with the remainder of the team in position to give them fire support.

Stu became aware of the eerie silence that seemed to envelop them. There was no wind, not even a breeze. The heat was stifling as though the overturned truck was irradiating heat, causing the sweat to pour from his face as he edged his way closer. He noted the lack of birdsong in the area too; there was normally at least one of them chirping away somewhere at the roadside or overhead.

The only noise was the faint crunch of broken glass beneath their feet as they gently placed each foot. The air was filled with the almost warm sickening stench of rot.

Stu nervously glanced over the sight of his weapon and to the high grassy embankment to his left, almost expecting a horde of un-dead to spring forth from their ambush position and come charging down on them.

A faint thud came from the upturned container on the back of the truck. Stu snapped his head back in the direction of the noise and stopped suddenly, just a few metres short of the obstacle.

Sini noticed Stu's sudden halt and followed suit at his side, gripping his rifle even tighter in his hands and pulling it into his shoulder, ready for an attack.

Stu looked across at the tough Serb from the corner of his eye. "You hear that?" he whispered.

Sini shook his head, not taking his eyes away from the truck that lay sprawled across the road in front of them. He remained, waiting for Stu to give the signal to continue, trusting in his judgement.

"There's something, or someone in the truck."

Stu continued forward, carefully placing his feet as he walked and keeping his weapon pulled firmly against his shoulder and the muzzle pointing at the stricken vehicle. He cocked his head to the side in an attempt to zero in on the noise that he had heard.

It came again, the muffled clunk of something being dropped or knocked over inside the trailer.

This time, Sini also heard it. He removed the safety catch on his rifle and stepped out further to the side of Stu, making sure his friend was clear of his arc of fire. Both men tensed and moved to the rear of the container. The doors were sealed shut and there was no sign of anyone, or anything, on the other side of the truck. The road ahead was empty and stretched for miles in the distance towards London.

The noise must have come from inside.

Sini glanced back at the others in the Land Rover. Marcus, Hussein and Jim were all in position, their weapons raised and ready to support them or come to their rescue should they get into trouble.

"It's a case of curiosity killing the cat," Stu whispered to Sini as he reached for the handle of the container. "I just hope I have nine lives today."

Sini had no idea what Stu meant and at that moment, he did not care. He was completely focussed on the two steel doors of the trailer that would fall open the moment that Stu released the handle, revealing whatever it was that had made the noise and had the whole team coiled like springs.

Stu could feel the palms of his hands suddenly become sweaty. His heart rate had increased and he could feel the blood racing through his veins. He reached out with one hand and held the rifle firmly into his shoulder with the other, his finger already taking the first pressure of the trigger. He glanced back one more time and nodded at Sini as he raised his hand and showed three fingers.

Sini swallowed and leaned into his weapon as he took up aim at the seal of the large steel doors. He, too, took up the first pressure on the trigger, needing only to squeeze a little harder in order to release a torrent of fire into anything that poured from the truck.

"One," Stu whispered, "two...three."

He pulled the handle with one hard tug and quickly stepped back, both hands now holding his weapon as the door began to fall open. It creaked and squealed as the hinges protested against the rust that had formed around them. It seemed to take an eternity as the door gradually gained speed as gravity gripped it and it swung towards the ground. With a loud echoing clatter, the heavy steel door hit the tarmac, shattering the silence around them.

A draft of hot foul-smelling air blew in their faces like the backwash of a car exhaust. It carried along with it the reek of rotting flesh. Sini crouched and squinted into the gloom of the truck's container as he struggled to see anything past the large frame of the door.

Stu stood beside him, holding his breath.

Nothing happened.

Stu squatted beside Sini, hoping to be able to see more from a new angle.

There was a crash. Sini and Stu involuntarily jumped back, readying them for an attack. Stu thought he saw movement and squinted, scanning the dark interior. Time seemed to stand still and he could feel the tension in the air. It was as though every member of the team were holding their breath. He could feel the beads of sweat that trickled down his forehead and he was more than aware of the hairs that stood on end on the back of his neck. It seemed like a lifetime since the door had crashed open, yet he remained standing there, poised and ready to take on whatever was to come.

The outstretched hands were the first things they saw. Reaching, clutching pale hands that thrust at them from out of the gloom, dozens of them. Their bodies close behind and advancing from within the dark interior and towards the brightly lit doorway that framed the two living men drenched in the sunlight outside.

"Shit," Stu yelled, "get back, Sini. There's fucking hundreds of them in there." He began to fire into the advancing crowd.

Sini began to fire also, the bright flashes emitting from the muzzle of his rifle, instantly illuminating the dark space within the truck, allowing the two men to see glimpses of their attackers. The pale and rotten faces of the dead loomed out of the blackness towards them and it was clear that the large heavy goods truck was packed full with the victims of the plague that had ravaged the earth and the bodies of the humans that populated it.

Both men backed up, frantically firing into the truck as they moved away. Bodies crumbled to the floor, soon to be replaced by the ones following behind. The noise that the dead made, the long wailing moan, sounded more hollow and detached from within the confines of the truck as they all cried out as one. It was more haunting and poignant, as though lamenting at the men who mowed them down as they advanced on them.

Rounds began to smash into the truck from Stu's left. The holes created by the bullets of the rest of the team as they punched through the steel of the vehicle, formed shafts of light like the effect caused by a disco ball. Heads snapped back and bodies jerked as the hail of fire thumped into them. Limbs were shot away as bullets and fragments from the trailer tore through them. Soon, the floor of the truck was awash with entrails as the rounds and splinters of steel ripped through abdomens, spilling their bloated and putrid contents at the feet of the advancing corpses.

Stu and Sini ran back from the vehicle, back towards the rest of the team as they realised they were under threat of being overwhelmed from the dead that filled the trailer.

Marcus and the others continued to fire their weapons until their barrels smoked and the truck took on the appearance of Swiss cheese. The tyres were gone, exploding with a loud bang as rounds hit them. The fuel tanks were ruptured spilling diesel onto the tarmac and the superstructure began to collapse from the numerous hits that had weakened it. Within a minute of the firing starting, the sound of the dead from inside ceased.

The team remained silent, watching for any movement. One by one, they changed the magazines on their weapons for full ones, the empty ones being thrown down the fronts of their vests to be recharged later.

Stu stood staring back at the truck, smoke drifting from the muzzle of his rifle.

"What the fuck?" he asked no one in particular as a section of the framework toward the rear of the trailer suddenly buckled as the bullet-riddled steel gave way.

"Stu, what's going on?" Marcus called from his vehicle.

From their angle, Marcus and the others had seen nothing of what was in the truck. All they knew was that there was something bad enough to make Stu and Sini begin to fire and then come running back towards them. That was all the information they had needed at that time to prompt them to give fire support and begin throwing down as much cover fire as possible while the two men retreated to safety.

"The truck," Stu glanced back at him and motioned to the smouldering and bullet riddled vehicle with his rifle, "it was filled to the brim with them."

Jim stepped out from beside the Land Rover, a questioning look on his face as he approached Stu and Sini.

"Why would it be filled with dead heads?" he asked as he stood by the two men and studied the remains of the large vehicle.

Stu shrugged, not taking his eyes away from the scene in front of them. "You tell me, mate. I only work here."

They stood for a minute and watched the rear doors of the heavy goods vehicle, waiting to see if any had survived. Jim began to creep forward but kept a safe distance. After a short inspection, he looked back over at the others.

"Looks like there's still a few left, but they're in no condition to do much."

Marcus walked over to where Jim was standing. Something made him want to see things for himself. The rancid smell made his eyes water and snatched the breath from his nostrils. It was a mixture of oil, mould and most of all, rotting flesh.

"Fuck me," he cursed from between his fingers as he desperately covered his mouth and nose, "what were they doing in there?" He gagged.

Stu stepped forward and pulled his pistol from his assault vest, the hammer giving off a clicking sound as he pulled it back with his thumb. He raised the weapon, ready to dispatch the remaining dead that crawled and slithered towards them through the quagmire of their own rotting filth.

"No," Marcus ordered as he placed a hand on top of Stu's forearm. "Save your ammo. They can't do much in that state anyway."

It was clear that they had been in the truck for some time. Their bodies had become bloated and almost liquefied in the humid heat of the interior of the truck container. When the rounds of the team hit them, their bodies were so delicate that many of them had pretty much burst from the sudden change in pressure.

Hussein had moved around to the other side and peered in the trailer from a safe distance. He glanced down onto the floor at the mass of bodies that lay riddled with bullets and mutilated beyond recognition. He studied the ones that still looked relatively intact and soon realised what it was that bothered him the most about what he saw. From what he could tell, they all had something in common.

He stepped over a squirming corpse that had lost its legs and an arm. It had received a hit in the head. It was still moving but the shot had ripped away half of its jaw and cheekbone along with an eye and leaving a large flap of flesh that hung down from its face. Its lank, greasy hair lay plastered to its scalp and the pale and bloodied skin glistened in the sunlight as though coated with oil.

He looked down at the body, a pang of sympathy plucking at his heartstrings as the one remaining eye stared back at him, almost pleadingly. Hussein looked away and cleared the choked lump from his throat with a cough. He looked back down at the child and nodded, a tear forming in the lid of his right eye.

He reached to his hip, pulled his heavy machete from the scabbard, raised it above his head and took a deep breath. The blade cut through the air with a slight whistle and smashed into the side of the wretched creature's head with a loud thud and the cracking of bone. The skull caved in instantly and the child's putrid brains flowed through the large gash that the heavy steel machete had created.

"Mr Marcus," Hussein called as he walked towards them from the far side of the truck, sliding his machete back into its scabbard and rubbing a hand across his eyes and cheek, wiping away the few tears that managed to escape, "the people in the truck, they were not dead."

Stu spun on him, those very words sending a chill through his body. "Yes they fucking were," he growled.

Hussein realised his mistake and understood how Stu must have interpreted what he had said. "Sorry, I mean, they were not dead when they were first put in there." He saw Stu relax slightly. "Look, I can't see any bites."

"They all look pretty messed up to me, Hussein," Jim replied as he glanced from body to body.

"But can you see bites?"

Marcus shrugged. "He has a point, though it's a little hard to tell, what of it anyway, Hussein? Maybe they were all going somewhere and then the truck crashed?"

"Why would they leave *living* people in the back of the truck to die then?" Hussein asked. The fact perplexed him and knowing that some of them had been children too, it horrified him.

"Maybe it's because, it's a fucked up world?" Jim answered with a question of his own. "Who knows, Hussein? Maybe they meant to come back to save them or the driver got eaten and they were left trapped?"

"What a way to go, though. The heat must've been horrendous in there," Stu observed. "With no water and no air, they didn't stand a chance, poor bastards."

"Come on," Marcus announced, snapping everyone from their morbid stupor as they stared at the carnage before them. "Let's get going. We have probably attracted every one of them for miles around with all the noise. Jim, give us an ammunition state of the whole team as soon as you can and Stu, check on Sandra before we go mobile again."

Hours later, and the team had gone static on the ring road that circumnavigated the city of London. The roads headed south were completely blocked on both sides. For as far as the eye could see, destroyed burned out vehicles were crammed, bumper to bumper, on every patch of the tarmac of every slip road, leaving them channelled toward the north and the large sprawling city of London.

The mass panic that had gripped the cities had been even more devastating in the capital. There was no hope of heading south. Marcus and his men had had no choice but to turn north and run the risk of becoming an easy target on the crossing of the Thames River.

They slowly picked their way through the devastation on the road towards the large bridge that spanned the width of the river. The tollbooths were nothing but a tangled and twisted mess with vehicles having become fused in a mass pile up as they had attempted to plough their way through the barriers.

Marcus steered the vehicle through and out to the other side and brought the Land Rover to a halt. The bridge lay before them, stretching off in the distance and up over the horizon.

A number of dark figures clumsily shambled between the stalled and destroyed cars that sat motionless on the bridge. They saw Marcus and his team and began to lurch towards them, grunting and moaning as they drew closer. Marcus was not concerned; they were too far away and too few in number to pose any real threat.

Marcus hesitated as he sat behind the wheel with the engine idling in neutral. "What do you think, Stu?" he asked, not taking his eyes off the bridge.

"We're short on choices really, aren't we?" Stu replied. "Let's just try and get across as quickly as we can before we draw a crowd."

"Well, there is another option..." Marcus began.

"Bollocks to that, Marcus," Stu cut in, "there's no fucking way I'm going through the tunnel. At least here, we have the option of jumping off the bridge. Down there, we'd be screwed."

Marcus had been about to suggest the possibility of driving through the Dartford Tunnel that passes below the Thames River. Apart from the bridge, it was the only other way across as far as they knew.

"Yeah, we..."

The sound of roaring jet engines drowned out his words as a black shape passed close overhead and soared towards the city. The glow of its engines could clearly be seen as it cut through the air, away from them.

Marcus looked at Stu, an expression of excitement and surprise spreading across his face. He slammed the gear lever forward and pressed his foot to the accelerator, powering the vehicle towards the bridge. The dead that approached were brushed aside like rag dolls as the heavy truck hit them, their bodies flying in the air and hitting the ground in a tangled broken heap.

Halfway across the bridge, Marcus brought them to a stop again. They were at the highest point and the angle gave them a perfect over watch view of the entire city. Everybody dismounted from the vehicle, seemingly paying little attention to the stray bodies that staggered in their direction from the distance. By now, they automatically took note of any threat and assessed it subconsciously. The bodies on the bridge were too few in numbers and spread out to represent an immediate danger to them.

The team stood at the rail, watching the city. Those that had binoculars keenly held them to their eyes and scanned the scene before them, calling out what they saw to one another.

Plumes of smoke hung above London as fires spread and buildings became engulfed in the licking flames. The low percussion booming as gas tanks ruptured and fuel stations and even cars exploded in the heat, could be heard from every direction. Fresh balls of fire sprung in the air from every part of the city as Marcus and his men stood and watched.

"Holy shit," Jim muttered as he stuffed another spoon full of beans into his mouth, "what do you think is going on?"

Marcus' reply was interrupted by the screech of another jet as it swooped overhead and towards the city centre. The noise was deafening and the blast of hot air they felt as it passed over them was an indication of just how low the aircraft was travelling.

They watched, open-mouthed, as the city of London was slowly reduced to ash. Wave after wave of bomber jets and fighters attacked targets on the ground and, before long, the city was nothing more than a ruin. Its tall buildings were crumbling by the minute and as more bombs and missiles hit and exploded amongst them, the ancient and once beautiful landmarks were smashed and burned beyond recognition.

"It looks like the counter attack has begun," Marcus surmised as he shouted over the din.

"Yeah, but what do they expect to have left when they're done?" Jim asked as he peered through his binoculars.

"I don't think they're all that concerned about the architecture now," Marcus replied as he watched another wave of bombers drop their payload.

The plumes of smoke and dust from the explosions were followed seconds later by the thundering report of the blast as it travelled on the air towards them.

"I think they just want to cleanse the place of everyone of those walking pus bags."

"Reminds me of Kosovo, when you guys were bombing the shit out of us, Marcus," Sini said with a touch of venom in his voice.

Hussein looked across at him and nodded in approval. "I know how you feel."

"What, they're just going to carpet bomb the entire city?" Jim asked.

Marcus scanned the city with his naked eye for a moment then raised his binoculars again. "They're not carpet bombing, Jim. Look, they're hitting precise targets on their runs, one after the other."

Jim grumbled, "I don't see it, boss."

They heard the sound of more aircraft approaching from behind. Marcus turned to look for them and the approach angle that they would be flying. He spotted them in the distance. They were low and closing fast, the growl of their engines building into a scream.

"Watch, they're running on set bearings and hitting targets that are being marked for them."

The next wave of jets shot overhead with a roar, and just as Marcus had guessed, they run in together and dropped their bombs in the same area, destroying a cluster of buildings and more landmarks in the process.

Marcus turned to Stu and Jim in sudden realisation. "There are ground troops down there somewhere. Those targets must be getting laser marked for the bombers to be able to hit them so accurately. You see anything that looks like an observation post?"

They shook their heads.

"Fuck, there goes the London Eye," Stu gasped. "Looks like it just got a direct hit from a one thousand pounder."

Marcus panned his binoculars around to look in the area that he knew the large Ferris wheel would be. Chunks of masonry and steel were flung in the air in a cloud of dust and smoke. The white frame of the Millennium Eye collapsed in the swirl of debris that was thrown up from the blast, its heavy steel protesting and groaning as it was twisted and bent out of shape.

Sini stepped away from the rail along with Hussein and moved towards a number of corpses that slowly approached. Just a minute later, they were back to watching the destruction of England's capital with the others, fixated on the carnage that was being dealt out to the once thriving city, only a slight increase in their breathing as an indication of them having just dispatched four of the walking dead.

More heavy bombs landed in and around the city centre. London was being pounded into dust. The dead, obliterated.

For hours, with morbid curiosity gripping them and holding them in place, they watched as the capital city was smashed into rubble. It was both awe inspiring and gut wrenching to them to see such a grand metropolis being wiped from the face of the earth.

"There," Hussein shouted as he pulled the binoculars away from his face and handed them back to Marcus. "There are soldiers."

Marcus looked in the area where Hussein pointed. Amongst the wreckage of the city, he could make out forms moving along the streets. At first he thought that Hussein had been mistaken, but he then realised that not only could he see the flashes that emanated from the muzzles of their weapons, he could also faintly hear them. With all the thundering explosions, being dealt out by the aircraft it had been easy to miss the noise of small arms fire, but now that he could see them, he could also hear the distinct crackle of them too.

"They've been using the bombing as a screen, creeping forward behind it. Now they're just mopping up," Stu noted.

"But there is still many dead in the city, look."

Sini directed the team to look in an area so far untouched by the bombing that ran adjacent to the line of advance that the soldiers were moving on. It was hard to make out individuals and all that they could see was a dark rippling mass that moved along between the buildings. It was a swarm of the dead and they were headed straight for the soldiers.

"Shit, it'll be too late by the time the troops see them," Jim said as he spat over the railing of the bridge.

The team watched in horror as the soldiers were cut off and the dead fell upon them. At that distance, they could not hear their screams, but everyone imagined them. More soldiers pushed along other streets, attempting to clear the city of the dead as they advanced.

To Marcus, it looked like there were just too few troops to get the job done and they continued to watch as more men became cut off as hordes of the foul creatures sprang up in front, behind and to the sides out of seemingly nowhere, overwhelming the unfortunate and stranded units.

17

The fine white powder was sucked into the vacuum of the tube as he inhaled deeply through his nostril. He felt the faint sting of the fine crystals against the flesh on the inside of his nasal passages, a small price to pay for the feeling it gave him.

Instantly, he felt his blood begin to surge in his veins. He threw his head back, breathing deeply and snorting the last remnants from the outer rims of his nose and into his system as he dropped the small platinum tube on to the glass coffee table. His hearing, suddenly more acute, heard every high-pitched note that the precious metal made as it lightly clattered, then settled against the glass of the table.

A ripple of euphoria travelled through his body. The hairs on his neck stood on end and a rush of power travelled up the length of his spine, like a lightning bolt on its way to his brain. It hit him, forcing his eyes wide and as a flow of energy raced through his entire body. It was a feeling that he could not get anywhere else. Sex, gambling, danger or success in business could not give him the rush he got from cocaine.

He felt good.

He smiled and raised himself to his feet. He rolled his shoulders and shook his head, like an athlete as he steps onto the starting blocks. He moved away from the expensive handmade leather couch and began pacing the large room. He reached for the stereo and turned up the volume. *The Rolling Stones* were blasting out his favourite piece, *'Sympathy for the Devil'*. It seemed rather apt to him. For a moment, he played air guitar and sang along at the top of his voice as he rocked his head to the tune.

He placed his imaginary instrument down and moved towards the large bay windows that gave him a magnificent view of the entire city. Well, the *once* magnificent view. It was now unrecognisable.

Buildings crumbled as the impacts of the explosions rocked and destroyed their foundations. Flames engulfed entire districts and clouds of smoke hung heavy and low in the air as the city was reduced to a smouldering ruin.

Another detonation close by caused the floor to shudder and the large windows to shake and rattle in their frames. Roland stepped closer and leaned his head against the cool glass. The effects of the drugs had become drowned in the vision before him. The hairs on his neck settled and his blood became sludge in his veins. He was back to reality.

"Oh how the mighty fall," he mumbled to himself as he peered down into the streets, twenty storeys below.

He could see the crowds of dead that swarmed the corridors of the city. They were just a black sea that rippled as it moved. Thousands upon thousands of them clambered at the entrance to his apartment building. They were packed in tight against each other, all fighting to get to the door. The bombing and strafing did little to deter them. Even when the ordinance landed close by and ripped dozens of them into the air, tearing them apart then scattering them back to the ground in pieces. They paid no attention and continued to hammer away at the apartment building.

They could not get in; he had made sure of that.

One reason that he had chosen that particular building to buy a penthouse in was because of the security set up. The main doors had heavy steel shutters, both inside and outside, that could be activated at the flick of a button. Roland had done that very early on when he had realised that he was the only person left in the building and everybody else had joined the mass evacuation.

Now, he was convinced that he was the only living soul left in London and he knew that would not be for much longer.

He pulled his head back from the window and watched as another fighter jet approached. It could not have been more than a few metres above the rooftops. It was headed straight for his building. It steadily grew in size, its black silhouette appearing more like a winged demon as it seemed to zero in on him personally. He could see the rockets on the underside of its wings now and the faint grey smoke that trailed behind it as it swooped in for its bomb run.

Roland tensed his body. His muscles flexed and he gritted his teeth. "Okay," he growled to himself. "This is it, Roland old pal, this is it."

For a moment, he considered closing his eyes, but he shook the thought from his mind. He wanted to see it happen. He wanted to die with his eyes open, not shut tight with fear.

The aircraft was close now. Its engines roared and Roland was sure that he could feel the ground vibrating from it. If it came any closer, he was convinced he would be able to see the pilot's eyes.

"Come on, you fucker," he screamed out at the closing jet.

He stood with his fists clenched, his feet planted and a look of defiance on his face, as though he was ready and able to defend that patch of ground against the might of a GR4 Tornado.

The jet suddenly shot over the building in a blur, its hot afterburners leaving a trail of distorted vapour in its wake. The noise was thunderous, deafening as it roared over the building like some biblical monster come to lay waste to the city. The whole building seemed to shake and Roland could feel his innards being unsettled from the displacement of air.

He waited. Surely, the bombs or missiles would hit any second.

There was a series of low concussions, then the sound of more, higher pitched explosions in the street below. The missiles had not hit his building. Roland stepped forward to the large windows again and looked down at the horde of dead. They were being scattered and chewed up by multiple explosions. They were not particularly large detonations; more a series of dozens of small ones.

They were cluster bombs. The pilot had dropped a bomb containing dozens of smaller bombs. The mother bomb had exploded above the ground and gave birth to its children that now ripped and tore through the dead in the street, leaving them as little more than rotting chunks of flesh and bone scattered around the roadsides.

Roland let out a long sigh, his breath misting the glass in front of him. "Not this time, I guess."

He turned away from the window and the carnage below.

"I need another line I reckon," he said in resignation as he walked back to the table and picked up his platinum tube again and began preparing himself a generous helping of cocaine.

He had been well known in the higher social circles in the old days. Roland *always* had the good stuff and he was *always* happy to share. He was considered a hardcore socialite and was always invited to the trendiest of parties.

The press had referred to him as a 'Rags to Riches Playboy Gangster'. The gangster part he was not particularly fond of. After all, he had only done what he needed to do in the early days to gain his footing on the bottom rung of the ladder to success. However, the playboy accolade he embraced. It was a title that he always made sure he lived up to, though it had not always been that way.

He grew up in the East End of London and he had to fight from the gutter every inch of the way, even amongst his family. He was born into a poor family with six siblings, of whom he was the youngest, and no one held out much hope of him accomplishing much with his life as a result, but he had proved them all wrong from a very early age.

He had seized every opportunity to better himself, whether it was legitimate or not. He started out running errands for the local gang bosses and it was there that he learned to be ruthless and allow nobody to get in the way of success. At the same time, he worked hard on his education.

He saw the people that worked hard, doing long hours for small wages, and the jobless queuing up for government handouts and he vowed to himself that he would never have to do that.

By his late teens, he was running a casino and his own used car business. He laundered money and became somewhat of a loan shark. Over the years, he made more money and a bigger name for himself until he hit the million-pound mark at the age of twenty-two.

From there it was onwards and upwards. He turned away from the shadows of the underworld and invested in stocks and properties, mainly within the capital. He was an intelligent man and he could see the property market soaring. So, as the saying went, *make hay while the sun shines*, he did just that and within a few short years his investments were paying off tenfold, so much so that he threw a lot of his money into building a massive apartment complex, using and converting the old dock buildings close to the riverside.

At first, it had looked as though he had made a bad gamble. However, when a few foreign investors, football personalities, rich business men, even a member of royalty took an interest in buying his luxurious properties down by the water's edge, the rest of high class society fought and tore at each other to have an apartment that he had built.

Roland could not put a foot wrong. From there, he created his own newspaper, shortly followed by a line of magazines. It was considered as the only 'no bullshit' newspaper in the whole of the country and the public loved it.

Roland and his media company did not care whose toes they stepped on, and sometimes it seemed as though he deliberately set out to create powerful enemies. He enjoyed watching the mayhem he created because he discovered that every time he put someone in the limelight for all the wrong reasons, an army of powerful people followed that were more than eager to join his side and support him.

Roland always mused to himself that it was a cross between the old maxims of, *'keeping friends close but enemies closer'* and *'the enemy of my enemy is my friend'*.

Because of the way in which he would be splashing great stories about an individual or government or corporation one week, then the next he would be exposing their darkest secrets across the front pages of his paper and magazines, people did not know what to expect. The high and mighty feared what dirt Roland may have on them and, as a result, they all clambered for his favour.

His personal life was much the same. He discarded friends and allies as easily as he picked them up. Women came and went and he openly admitted that he had never felt anything that could be described as love for anyone or anything other than his two teenage daughters and his family.

Nevertheless, everybody loved him. He was the sort that could light up a room just by his presence and entertain even the dullest of parties with his unpredictable antics.

He had remained close to his family and he took care of them financially, though he never allowed them to look on him as a free ride for an easy life. He employed most of them in some way and he saw to it that they earned their money. In secret, he referred to his company as the family business, but he would never let his brothers and sisters hear him say that.

When the dead began to rise, Roland's newspaper was one of the first to bring the facts to the public. They printed the stories and pictures of what was happening in Africa and South America and shortly after, they ran stories of the same epidemic sweeping Europe and the United Kingdom. As a result, the government had a media injunction placed upon him. It was a bold move; a move that no previous government had ever dared to make, due to the likelihood of Roland being in possession of some of the skeletons that had fallen from their closet. For Roland, it was a testament to the scale of events unfolding around the world and the government had shown their hand.

Rather than hitting back and going all out to retaliate, Roland retreated. With such a daring move from the government, they had inadvertently given him a glimpse of the impending disaster and he saw no point in wasting his energy on bringing down a Prime Minister that was about to fall anyway, along with the rest of the world.

Instead, he began to make plans of evacuating himself, his daughters and the rest of his family to his private island in the Caribbean. Everything was set in place and ready, but his daughters and family disappeared in the chaos, and Roland was unable to find them again.

He realised that they had been swallowed up by the dying world.

The idea of being stranded on an island by himself didn't appeal to him so, as the city's inhabitants were either engulfed by the dead or evacuated, Roland retreated to his penthouse suite with a large supply of the purest cocaine that money could still buy and as much Johnny Walker Blue Label as he could find.

He knew he could not last forever up there. He did not want to. He had decided after his family disappeared that he would die in the city that had made him. It had given him life, and it would bring him death.

The thud against the door brought him back to his senses. He looked across to the far side of the room at the entrance to the master bedroom. It was still locked and it would remain that way. The thud came again, followed by a scratching noise.

He attempted to blank it from his mind but the noise persisted.

He reached to the table and swooped up the glass tumbler containing a large measure of Johnny Walker and slugged it back, gulping the glass dry. Following that, he bent over close to the glass surface and snorted a long line of the fine white powder. He sat back with a gasp, blinking at the sudden change he experienced from within him.

The noise from the bedroom continued.

"Shut the fuck up," he yelled, the veins in his neck standing out with rage. "What did you expect, you stupid bitch?"

Zoe had taken her own life a few days earlier. He had found her three weeks ago, staggering about on the fifth floor in a daze. At first, he had thought she was one of the dead that had managed to get in the building, but then he realised she was just stoned and completely unaware of anything that was going on around her.

She had been hiding in the apartment block since Roland had brought down the shutters, unaware of his existence on the top floor.

Zoe was ten years his senior, around forty nine and not completely unattractive; Roland had woken up to much worse in his younger days he reminded himself and after being on his own without any female company for so long, the little brain that was situated in his crotch had seen a silvery lining in an otherwise very dark cloud.

For the next three weeks, they indulged themselves in an orgy of drink, drugs and sex. They both agreed that the end of the world was nigh and decided to go out with a bang. That was until Roland walked into the bathroom to discover that Zoe had taken an overdose and was lying in a hot bubble bath, waiting for death. He had attempted to make her sick, to bring up the pills she had swallowed but it was no use, she was too far-gone; there was nothing he could do to stop her from dying.

In her delirium, she asked Roland to take care of her when she was gone. The thought horrified him.

How was he supposed to do it? Was he supposed to smash her head in, stab a knife through her eye and into her brain?

"Fuck you, Zoe," he spat at her. "You chose this, not me. You can stay in here and fucking rot for all I care." He locked the door and left her to die.

Now she was bouncing about in the master bedroom, knocking over furniture and struggling to break free. Roland wished to himself that he had dragged her body out of the bathroom and tossed it out of the window when he had had the chance. It was too late now, she was in there, she would stay in there and he had no desire to go opening the door to her.

He had seen people die from the bites. He had watched a number of unfortunate people suffer from the infection and fever, only to return as ravenous ghouls. He did not intend to risk that fate on himself for the sake of Zoe.

The rumbling of jet engines brought his attention away from the reanimated corpse of Zoe and back to the window. In the distance, silhouetted in the orange sky created by the slowly setting sun, he saw another aircraft headed for him. It looked much the same as the last one. It swooped low over the buildings and raced towards him with a howling screech.

Roland slowly raised himself to his feet, not taking his eyes off the approaching aircraft. His shin hit the edge of the coffee table, the pain barely registering in his clouded mind as he watched the plane draw nearer. Its engines were screaming and again, he could see the discoloured and distorted vapour trail that the jet produced in its wake.

He staggered to the window, muttering to himself as the aircraft grew in size. "Come on, you bastard. Here I am, come on, that's it."

The black shape of the Tornado banked to the left slightly and soared over the apartment that threatened to collapse in on him because of the shockwave. The building held fast and Roland found himself still standing. He was about to curse the pilot, to call him every name he could think of for missing him again.

Then, he saw them.

They glided through the air toward him. He watched them in slow motion as they majestically tumbled alongside one another, rotating in a hypnotic dance as gravity and momentum carried the two long black cylindrical shapes toward the tall apartment building.

"Oh God," Roland exclaimed with a smile and a gasp of relief, "Oh God, thank you."

He tensed his body, raised his head and thrust his arms down by his side. He kept his eyes focussed on the two hurtling bombs that fell towards him.

They were just metres away now.

He gritted his teeth. They were so close that he believed he could almost see the stencilling of numbers and letters on the side of the bombs.

He grinned through clenched teeth. "Here we go..."

18

"There'll be nothing left," Marcus sighed as he watched a tall apartment building take a direct hit, destroying the top half of it in a ball of fire.

Before it became dark, Marcus gave the order to move out. The idea of being on the bridge without being able to see anything approaching was enough to pull them from the vision before them.

They continued along the ring road, looking for somewhere to rest for the night. A maintenance road led them away into the wilderness and away from prying eyes, dead or living. It was narrow and overhung by trees that screened them from the air. Marcus was concerned that reconnaissance planes or even helicopters carrying more troops may appear in the sky above them. The high hedges and thick canopy of trees provided them with the cover they needed.

As the last rays of sunlight dipped below the horizon, the team found themselves at a junction on the outskirts of a small village and unsure of which direction they should turn. On the corner, set back from the road and nestled amongst a clump of trees, was a rustic looking old country pub. Its uneven and whitewashed walls with a low thatched roof gave the impression that it had been cut off from the technological and architectural advances of the previous one hundred years.

The sign hanging above the door read: 'The Prince of Wales'.

Stu looked across at Marcus and grinned. "Looks like the Ritz to me, mate."

Marcus bit his lip and glanced to his left and right along the country lane, unsure of whether or not he wanted to spend the night in relative comfort in the pub but blinded by the walls, or in the open where they could see any threat in advance.

Jim leaned over from the gunner's position on top. "Come on, Marcus, we're in the middle of nowhere. With everything going on in the city, I bet there isn't a single dead fuck left around here."

Marcus turned to Stu who looked back at him with puppy dog eyes. "Okay, but we have someone on sentry at all times."

"Great," Stu clapped his hands together. "I'm dying for a pint."

Marcus backed the Land Rover in the parking area at the front of the pub and close to the door. Sini and Jim joined him as he did a check around the outside of the building while Stu and Hussein remained with the vehicle and Sandra.

The public house was well shielded from prying eyes, and beyond the trees there was nothing but sprawling open fields, with the outskirts of the village to the west and south. The area was clear and the three of them wasted no time in gaining entry into the building through the unlocked back door.

Carefully, Marcus pushed the creaking door open with one hand while he raised his rifle to an aim with the other, pointing the barrel into the gloomy kitchen at the back of the building. Nothing charged at them from out of the darkness, so he slowly inched his way in over the threshold.

The mouldy smell was the first thing they noticed, but it was just the smell of stale air mixed with the damp that was to be expected in any old building made with ancient wooden beams and wattle and daub plaster. The absence of the smell of rotting flesh helped to ease their nerves as they pushed deeper in to the dark building.

Nothing moved inside. The three of them stood for a few minutes, listening for the faintest sound that would warn them that they were not alone. To their relief, the place was empty.

"They'll have to send in more ground troops at some point," Stu suggested later that night as they all sat huddled around the fireplace as the flames crackled and popped in front of them.

Its orange warming glow comforted them, putting the team at ease, and Marcus had ensured that all the curtains in the windows were pulled tight and that no light would leak out to give away their position.

"I guess so," Marcus nodded. "But I can't understand what they're hoping to achieve. Those poor bastards didn't stand a chance today."

Stu held out a mug of tea and picked up the bottle of brandy he had liberated from behind the bar and poured a generous measure into the cup.

"What do you mean?" he asked as he slurped at the hot liquid and then passed it to Marcus.

"Well, let's suppose that they manage to clear out the whole of London, what are they going to do then? Rebuilding the city isn't really an option these days and there's always the problem with the dead."

"Maybe they'll get rid of them?"

"And how are they going to do that? They may get the ones in the city, but what about the millions more outside? They are everywhere, they outnumber the living by a huge margin and I bet that margin is growing by the day. They don't seem to abide by trespass laws and have you ever seen them shy away from weapons? But okay, say they clear and secure London, I'm pretty sure that there isn't enough ordinance, manpower and aircraft to do the same to every city in the country."

"You're not exactly optimistic, are you?" Stu said with a slight smile.

Marcus slowly shook his head and looked back at him as he took a sip from his cup. The flickering glow of the fire made his face look contorted and twisted as he spoke.

"Nah, mate," he said raising the cup to his lips again and taking a long gulp. "I think we've well and truly lost this one. It's just down to the likes of us now to survive as best as we can."

"You think we will, Marcus?" Sini asked from his position beside Sandra who was tucked up in a sleeping bag, staring at the fire as she listened to the conversation.

"Survive you mean?" Marcus asked. "Good question."

Hussein sighed. "We have made it this far, we have to make it."

Stu nudged the young Iraqi at his side. "Hey, look at the honorary Brit here. One minute, he's planting bombs and firing rockets at us, now he wants a bowler hat and an umbrella to walk about with."

Hussein laughed. "Maybe you could give me an English name, like Mr. Smith or something. Do you think it would suit me?"

Everyone laughed, all except Marcus who sat quietly staring at the fire.

Stu watched him for a moment. Marcus seemed to be drifting in his thoughts, staring into nothingness as though something else was at the forefront of his mind.

"Are you thinking about the wife and kids?"

"Hmm," Marcus nodded.

"At least you have your wife and kids to go home to, Marcus," Sandra suddenly said in her thick Serbian accent. It was the first time she had spoken all evening.

"I was lucky to survive. My whole family were killed, murdered," she continued to stare into the flames, a tear trickling down her cheek. "Babies, my sisters were only babies and those monsters tore them apart." She sniffed and turned to look at Marcus, her eyes shining with tears.

"I am not speaking of the dead monsters, Marcus. I speak of the human monsters wearing uniforms that came, raped my sisters, my mother and then shot them as my father was forced to watch. You are very lucky, Marcus." She sunk her head into her shoulders and turned back to staring at the fire.

"We should try the radio again," Stu suggested, trying to break the sudden silence. "I'll go wake up Jim for his shift."

Marcus watched him as he walked away from the fire, his silhouette becoming invisible in the dark room, but he could still hear him. There was a clunk as something collided with a piece of hard furniture.

"Fuck! Christ that hurt," Stu hissed.

Marcus could hear Stu cursing under his breath as he tried to feel his way toward the slumbering Jim who could be heard from the other side of the room as he snored. He had seen and heard the exact same scene played out a million times before, from the days when he was in the army.

During the middle of the night, while on exercise or operations, someone would always walk into a tree or fall over a pack. Even accidentally stand on one of their friends while they searched for the next man on the list who was to relieve them on sentry duty, creating a ruckus even though they had tried so hard to remain quiet and tactical.

The forestry block, or patch of dead ground that they were sheltering in, would echo with the thuds, scrapes and curses of men trying, and failing miserably, to locate each other in the dark.

Marcus raised his finger to his lips to ensure that Hussein and Sini remained quiet while he listened for the next instalment of predictable events and dialogue. Then, he heard the telltale sound of a rustling sleeping bag as Stu found Jim and attempted to wake him.

"Jim, wake up. Jim, it's your stag, mate," Stu hissed in from the pitch black.

There was no answer from the thick green sleeping bag other than the loud snoring of the American.

"Jim, it's your turn on guard. Get up."

There was more rustling of the sleeping bag as Jim was finally roused from his sleep. He grunted and Marcus sat smiling as he pictured Jim rubbing his head and feeling slightly confused.

"What, what's up?" Jim asked in a sleepy voice, not even attempting to whisper as Stu had done.

"It's your stag," Stu replied, still trying to keep the noise to a minimum.

Marcus tensed himself, a broad grin spreading across his face as he anticipated what the next question would be from Jim. He had experienced both sides of it so many times, having been the man being awakened, and doing the waking. He just knew it was coming.

"What, now?"

"No, you fucking moron. In four hours time, that is why I am waking you up now, just to let you know. Get up, you stupid redneck."

Marcus could not hold it any longer and he began to laugh. The more he tried to control it, the more he laughed. It was infectious, too, because although they did not fully understand what was so funny about what was happening, Sini and Hussein were also in fits of laughter in front of the fire.

Even Sandra giggled from inside the sleeping bag.

"Is it working?" Stu asked later that night as he looked down at the radio on the table. Marcus and Stu were sitting close to the window, the antenna poking out into the night.

"Not sure," Marcus shrugged.

He was sitting beside it with a torch gripped between his teeth as he adjusted the frequency and attempted to tune it in.

"I think we got the antenna length right this time and I'm pretty sure it's tuned in okay."

"Give it a try then," Stu nodded at him.

Marcus raised the hand set to his lips. He hesitated and glanced back at Stu.

"Go on."

"Steve, it's Marcus, can you hear me?" He waited a moment. "Steve, are you there, bro?"

He leaned over and checked the dial on the side of the heavy radio casing. The needle hung in the middle of the graph, indicating that the radio was correctly tuned.

"Steve, are you there? It's Marcus."

"Maybe they don't have their radio on?" Stu suggested.

Marcus looked up, realising that Stu could be thinking the worst and trying to convince his self otherwise. It had not occurred to him that something could have happened to the park and he had just felt frustrated at his lack of skill with the radio. Now though, thoughts of the creatures rampaging through the house where his family took refuge raced through his mind. A shiver ran down his spine and he physically shuddered at the images.

He shook his head. "I'm sure they're fine. It's just us being useless with this thing."

Again, he turned his attention to the frequency dials, the tuning switch then and the antenna. All seemed in order and correct.

"Steve, Jake, anyone are you hearing me? Is there anyone there? Pick up." His voice had a note of anxiety attached to it.

A voice, faint and crackly, drifted through the earpiece of the radio. *"Marcus, is that you?"*

Marcus' eyes widened as he looked back up at Stu. "Yeah, it's me. Is that Jake?"

"No, it's Gary, it's good to hear from you, Marcus. We were starting to worry."

"No need to worry, mate. We're fine." Marcus began to relax. He could feel his shoulders settle and he realised that he had been tensing the muscles in his back and legs.

"How is everyone, where is Steve?"

There was a pause. "Steve isn't here, Marcus."

Another moment of silence as Gary was obviously trying to form the right words. Marcus could feel his muscles stiffening again and the dread knotting in his stomach.

"They've been missing since yesterday. They went to find fuel, and they never came back. Jake and a few others went with him."

Marcus ran his hand through his hair and looked up at Stu, "Shit." He raised the handset to his mouth and ear again and he took a deep breath. "Okay, Gary, there isn't a lot I can do about that. Hopefully they've just run into a spot of trouble and will be back soon." He was concentrating hard on not imagining the worst and just hoping for the best. "What about Jen and the boys? Is Sarah okay?"

"Yeah, they're fine." There was a touch of relief in Gary's voice; probably at the fact that he had told Marcus what he needed to tell him and Marcus had dealt with it.

"I'll go and get them for you."

Two minutes later and the voice of a very excited and relieved Jennifer poured out through the radio.

"Oh baby, we were so worried. Are you okay, where are you?"

Marcus could feel a lump building in his throat. Just hearing the sound of his wife's voice flooded him with an overwhelming sense of joy.

"We're okay, Jen. I'm in a pub with the lads." He could not resist the quip.

"A pub, that's typical of men. Even when the world is coming to an end, you still find time for the pub," she joked in reply.

For a few minutes, Marcus and Jennifer spoke about their sons and Steve. She did her best to sound positive but it was the not knowing and concern that came through in her voice.

"I'm sure they'll be okay, Jen," Marcus assured her.

"How is everyone, Marcus?" she asked. She sounded expectant of bad news.

Marcus sighed and glanced back up at Stu.

"France was rough going, Jen. We lost three men, including Yan and Ian. Do you remember Ian?"

"Oh, Marcus, I'm so sorry. Yes, I remember Ian, and I know how close you were."

"Yeah, he was a good man." He breathed in slowly, steadying himself from the emotion that threatened to burst out of him at the memory of losing Ian. "We took care of him, though, and brought him back to England. It's what he wanted."

They spoke for a while longer and Marcus gave them an idea of where they were. Jennifer and Gary must have been cross-referencing his explanations and directions to a map they had been looking at because

Jennifer's voice grew in excitement when she realised that her husband was just a few hours' drive away, but that was a few hours in the old days.

Now it could be weeks.

Later that night, Marcus lay in his sleeping bag, his arms folded across his chest as he stared up at the dark ceiling. He was struggling to fall sleep. Though his body craved rest and his eyes felt heavy, his mind raced. His thoughts constantly flitted from one subject to the next.

He worried about his brother. Steve was missing after going out to find more fuel, along with a number of the other survivors from the park. He knew there was nothing he could do, but he could not help but feel concerned. Steve was by no means an idiot or a weakling, but Marcus did not know the people he was with, or their abilities, and it was that that could get a person killed now.

Marcus trusted and counted on every member of his team. They had all been through the mill and he knew he could rely on them to react in the right way when it came to it, but a bunch of civilians that had been thrown together through circumstance, that was another matter. They were untrained and probably scared to death ninety percent of the time and with no natural reactions embedded into them from years of training and experience, it could cause them to freeze at the critical moment and put the rest in danger. It was that thought that Marcus could not shake from his mind. His brother could be hurt, or worse, due to someone suddenly panicking.

His family were never far from his thoughts. He longed to see his wife and children again. He yearned to hold them in his arms, to keep them close and safe. A slight smile grew on his face as he imagined the scent of Jennifer as he pulls her close and kisses her for the first time. It had been a long while since he had last been home and after everything that they had been through it now felt like years.

They still had a long way to go. He knew where they needed to go, but he did not have the first idea about which was the best way to get there. Before the dead swallowed the world, it had been a simple drive north for a few hours and then he would be home.

Now, though, no one could possibly know what kind of obstacles lay ahead, even the conditions of the roads. The most logical option would have been to take the most direct route, but times had changed. The easy route now would probably be the most dangerous and perilous. That same system of roads bypassed a number of large cities and they were probably festering and boiling over with the dead.

Everyone was aware by now of how the reanimated bodies behaved. They acted on instinct and herd behaviour. If they saw one of their own headed in a certain direction, many of them would follow. Stumbling onto a major road system would be easy for the dead that were spewing out from the city of Birmingham or Coventry. Once on the highway, then they would probably stay there as the road channelled them and fed them along in both directions. With nothing to encourage them to veer off, they would be shoulder to shoulder on both sides of the road.

As well as the dead, there was the living to consider, too. They had experienced all too well, what could happen when society breaks down. Throw a few sick minds and the means to cause mayhem into the mix, and what could go wrong had a very strong chance of doing just that.

They had experienced it first hand in Iraq, Turkey, Serbia and France, even in England at the army barracks. It would need to be the minor roads that crisscrossed the Midlands. There they could continually bypass any major built-up areas and stick to the open country.

Marcus looked over at the dark and faint silhouette of Sini as he stood watch by the window. He could see the red glowing embers of the cigarette Sini was smoking as he inhaled the fumes back into his lungs, his face being slightly illuminated by the faint light of the burning tobacco. The lounge of the public house was still and only the soft sound of people sleeping and the roar of Jim snoring indicated that there was anybody else in the room.

Marcus' eyes drooped and closed then involuntarily sprang open again. Sleep was tugging at him, but his subconscious continued to drag him back. They closed again, longer this time and his thoughts became muddled as he drifted.

There was movement in the room. The part of his brain that remained alert sensed it and forced his eyes open again. For a moment, he struggled to focus, then he saw Sini, still standing at the window as he had been just moments before but the cigarette was now gone.

Sini was crouching slightly, his shoulders hunched and the rifle he carried gripped in both hands with the butt pulled in tight. The barrel was still pointing down but it would take just a split second to raise it to aim. Sini was alert. He was bobbing his head, fighting for a better angle of view or light as he tried to identify something that he had seen on the other side of the window.

Marcus jumped to his feet, snatching up his rifle as he did so. In just a few bounds, he was standing at the side of the tough Serb, Sini, and peering through the glass and into the darkness with him.

"What is it Sini, what do you see?" he whispered from the corner of his mouth, keeping his eyes fixed on the parking area outside and his hands gripping his rifle tightly.

"I'm sure I saw something moving, Marcus." Sini craned his neck again in an attempt to locate the source of movement he had seen, but it had gone.

They stood in silence for a few minutes, watching for any further indication of anything on the outside. Nothing moved and both men began to relax.

"Sorry, boss. You should try and get some sleep," Sini whispered.

"Aye, chance would be a find thing, mate."

Marcus moved back to where he had left his sleeping bag. He placed his rifle down beside it and began to pull back the folds of the quilted material, then he stopped. He looked up at the window that was closest to him and stepped across the short distance to the glass pane. He wanted to double check. Something inside him urged him to have one final look before he settled himself to go back to trying to sleep.

He pressed his face close to the cold windowpane and stared into the darkness outside. There was nothing there; nothing moved. Satisfied, he pulled his head away...

A pale looming face sprang up in front of him on the other side of the glass. Marcus jumped with shock and sprang back a step.

"Shit...," he cried.

His rifle was with his sleeping bag behind him. Instinctively, he reached for the pistol he had tucked into the waistband at the front of his trousers. He felt the curve of the pistol grip in the 'V' shape of his hand between his thumb and forefinger. He coiled his remaining fingers around the handle and at the same time, as his hand began to pull the weapon free, his thumb clicked down on the safety catch. His right index finger was already curled around the trigger and the pistol was now free of his trousers. His wrist was twisting so that the barrel pointed in the direction of the sudden threat. He had already begun to squeeze the trigger to release the first shot.

"Don't shoot, don't shoot," the face hollered from beyond the window.

Marcus hesitated. He continued to move the pistol into the aim, but he refrained from taking up the final pressure on the trigger that would send the hammer forward, striking the firing pin against the percussion cap of the nine-millimetre brass casing that was already loaded into the chamber, and firing off the round.

Did that pus bag tell me not to shoot?

Sini arrived at his side, the weapon in his hands held at the ready. Marcus could hear the others stirring behind him.

Another person joined the face at the window and they both raised their hands. "Don't shoot, please."

Marcus stepped forward, the gun still trained on the two at the window. He eyed them with suspicion and peered into the darkness behind them. The first face glanced back over his shoulder, following the line of Marcus' eyes. The man seemed to realise that Marcus was watching for anyone else that was with them.

"It's okay, we're alone. Please, there's no one else with us, let us in."

Marcus stepped over to the main entrance and released the dead bolts at the top and bottom of the old heavy wooden frame. He ripped the door open and reached out into the cool night air for the two people that were already there waiting for the door to open. Grabbing the first of the men by the scruff of his collar and dragging him inside, he threw him into the waiting arms of Sini.

He quickly grabbed the next man and tossed him like a child's toy over to his right, sprawling him across a table and knocking chairs over in the process. The man let out a yelp and looked across to his friend as he lay with his back arched over the table.

Marcus turned his pistol on him as he sealed the door again, slamming the locks back into place.

He bounded across the short distance to the man on the table. He leaned over him, his weight pressing down on the man's chest as he thrust the barrel of his pistol in his face.

"Who are you and what are you doing here?" Marcus growled.

The man whimpered, his face contorting into a pathetic grimace like that of a child's when being chastised by its parents. He looked across to his friend, restrained by the frightful looking Serbian.

He started to cry.

Marcus had gone for the shock and awe approach with them. Knowing nothing about them, or their intentions, he did not want to give them a minute to think or catch their breath. Immediately, he set out to show his dominance over them, to make it clear about who exactly was in command of whom. Normally, the first reaction of the captives would be to acknowledge their captor's position and comply with their commands for fear of reprisals, giving them total control.

Immediately bursting into tears was a new one for Marcus.

Marcus was taken aback by the man's reaction. Instantly, he felt sorry for him but he was too long in the tooth to allow his self to lower his guard at that moment. Instead, he backed away slightly, but the pistol remained pointed straight at his face.

"Stop crying and tell me what you're doing here," Marcus demanded.

The man slid down and began to curl himself into a ball at the foot of the table, holding his head in his hands and weeping uncontrollably.

"Are they going to kill us, Pete?" he cried into his palms.

"Please, leave him alone," the other man pleaded at Marcus.

Marcus turned to him, the gloomy light revealing just the outline of the man that stood locked in Sini's grip. Marcus stepped closer, his pistol still pointed at the man on the floor.

"Okay, Pete. You can tell me instead. Are there anymore of you out there?"

Stu stepped across and stayed close to the cowering figure at the table so that Marcus could concentrate on the other.

Pete shook his head. "No just me and him." He nodded to his friend.

"Him?" Marcus asked.

The constrained man glared at Marcus, defiance in his eyes. "Yes, him. His name is Michael. He's my brother." He changed his tone when he realised that Marcus was slowly closing in on him. "Please leave him alone, he's..." he hesitated.

"He's what?" Marcus asked genuinely curious.

Pete looked down and let out a long sigh. "He's special, okay?"

Marcus looked across at Stu and then back at Pete. "You mean as in special needs, learning difficulties special?"

Pete nodded. "Yeah, that's what I mean. Please don't hurt him; it was my idea to come here. Let him go."

Stu took out his Sure Fire light and shone it in the face of the still whimpering Michael.

"Hey, mate, nothing to be afraid of. We just had to make sure you weren't dangerous is all." Stu was using his 'everybody's best friend' voice.

Michael pulled his hands away from his watery eyes and blinked in the bright light. "You...you mean like the others out there?"

"Uh, yeah, something like that," Stu nodded.

Michael smiled up at Stu, relief flooding his face. He turned his head in the direction of Pete.

"Hey, it's okay, Pete. They just wanted to make sure we weren't monsters."

They guided the two newcomers over towards the fireplace that still glowed with embers, casting a small but sufficient amount of light in the immediate area. Pete and Michael were manhandled and dumped on the floor with their backs placed against a large armchair. Even though Marcus and his men had softened their approach to the two, they were still wary, suspicious of them and ready to kill them if necessary.

Marcus handed them some water that they gratefully gulped down between them.

"I suppose I'll get a brew on then," Stu declared as he set about positioning the old-fashioned kettle on the hot embers of the fire.

Pete and Michael had relaxed a little, but their eyes were still wide as neither of them knew what their eventual fate would be.

Marcus shone his light down over the two of them as he sat down on the chair in front of them. The light travelled the length of them both and Marcus scrutinised what he saw in the beam.

"So, Pete, you're a soldier then?" he said in a casual tone.

Pete looked down at himself and then back at Marcus. "No, I'm no soldier."

"Okay, so you just like wearing the outfit?" Marcus gestured to Pete's uniform and boots with his light.

Pete shook his head. "It's what was given to me, along with a gun, but I'm not a soldier. I don't think there are any left anyway. Not on the mainland at least, except you guys."

"Except us," Marcus smiled. "There are soldiers in London. We saw them."

A look of disdain spread across Pete's face and he sneered. "They aren't soldiers. They are young boys and old men with two days training and a uniform, thrown into the thick of it as cannon fodder."

"You need to start making sense, Pete."

"They're civilians, press ganged into a militia. Everyone who made it off the mainland and to any of the islands occupied by the government and armed forces, they were set to work in one way or another, not that we were slaves or anything, but we couldn't just go our separate ways and we were still subject to state rule. That's when they brought in conscription."

"Conscription?" Marcus looked across at Stu, raising his eyebrows questioningly.

"Yeah, anyone considered of an age old enough to fight, they were forced in the new militia units. They were given a couple of days training to learn how to use the radio and rifle and that was it, they were considered ready for the great counter attack on the mainland."

"What about the regular army? Why aren't they being used?"

Pete frowned back at him, confusion spreading across his face as he looked from Marcus to Stu and then to Jim.

"The regular army? Where have you been since all this started?"

"All over and it's a long story. Go on." Marcus waved a hand.

Pete's face relaxed as he realised that Marcus genuinely did not know about certain events.

"Well, there is no regular army anymore well, not much of one, anyway. There are still a few units but they are being kept back because of their expertise and experience, or so they told us. It makes more sense to send in the expendable against the dead, the likes of us, so why waste the trained soldiers?"

"What happened to the rest?" Marcus asked as he leaned forward, eager to know.

"They're dead," Pete replied simply.

"They're dead, all of them?" Marcus exclaimed.

"Most of them, yes. Obviously, you've not been keeping up on current events, but they were wiped out in the early stages of all this." He waved his arm around him to indicate the country and its current state.

"Before anyone really understood the problem and how to deal with it, the army units still in the UK, the police force and even the fire service were thrown in to deal with the *'unrest'* and in the process, they were killed, eaten or turned into them walking dead things.

"I heard on the news that all the troops in Iran were being recalled to Britain, but apparently, many of them never made it out of the Middle East, and those that did died on the way home. There were reports of sea battles, like in the Second World War between China, North Korea, America, Britain and a whole bunch of other countries. I think Russia got involved too and they just blew the shit out of each other."

"And you got conscripted?"

Pete nodded his head vigorously. "Yeah, me and Michael. He doesn't even know how to fasten his own shoes but they still sent him. As soon as the helicopters dropped us off, I decided we should run for it. Have they cleared London out?"

"No," Jim butted in. "They just bombed the crap out of it. Pretty much flattened it and a lot of the so called soldiers were still getting attacked by those things."

Pete shook his head. "I knew it wouldn't go well for them." He looked back up at Marcus. "Honestly, we're not looking for trouble; we just want to go home. Our village is not far from here, which is why we ran. Please don't make us go back, don't turn us in?"

Stu snorted. "Why would we turn you in? We want to avoid the soldiers as much as you do. We've no desire to be cannon fodder."

Pete glanced from each man to the other expectantly. "But, but I thought you were soldiers too?"

"We are," Marcus replied. "But we don't belong to any government and we've no intention of joining in the bloodbath that the clowns in charge are conducting."

"I don't understand. I presumed you were some kind of Special Forces Unit or something, sent out to give reports on the ground and situation, and stuff."

"No, mate, we aren't Special Forces and I fucking hate paperwork. We have fought our way back from Iraq, across the Middle East and up through Europe for the past four months or so. When the news of what was happening broke, they left us in Baghdad to rot while the head shed made a run for it. We were there as private military contractors. We're all ex-soldiers, but from different countries, you see?"

"Ah," Pete now understood. "You mean mercenaries?"

Marcus chuckled. "Yeah, some people see us as that."

Pete whistled through his teeth. "Jesus, you've come all the way from Iraq? That's a long way, even when the world was normal, never mind coming through all this shit." He sounded genuinely impressed at the accomplishment.

"It was a long way," Stu added. "We've lost some good friends along the way, too, and we still have a ways to go. So you can understand our desire not to get caught up in any gang fuck like what's going on in London right now."

Pete smiled. "So does that mean we're on the same song sheet then?"

Stu nodded. "Here, get some of this brew down you," he said as he handed him a steaming cup.

19

The squawk of the birds in a sudden panic and the fluttering of their wings alerted him to their presence as he drew near. They jumped from their perches on the slowly rusting hulks of forsaken and discarded vehicles and took to the air, flying away to the open fields to the right of the highway.

At a safe distance and altitude, and together in unison, they banked back around towards him. He stopped and watched them as they approached. They twittered and whistled cheerfully, circling in the sky above. They remained out of reach as they swooped in at the swarm of insects that hung in the air around him and followed him everywhere he went.

Andy did not attempt to catch them in any way; he just watched them, mesmerised by their colours and movements. Andy liked the birds; he did not know why, he just did.

He had been travelling along the same stretch of road for days. There was no noise there, apart from the wind and the birds, and the clouds of insects that hung around him, buzzing incessantly. Andy was alone, exactly as he wanted to be.

The highway looked deserted except for the clusters of static vehicles and scattered detritus that littered the carriageway here and there. There was very little that drew his attention, other than the wildlife, and he preferred the open roads to the cities.

The cities were lifeless and dull, and swarming with the foul creatures that he feared and hated.

Andy continued to watch the birds until they had had their fill of the flies above him and they fluttered away towards the tall trees in the distance. He turned back to the road and continued his long, slow shuffle towards the horizon, his shoes scraping against the hard surface of the road and his arms swaying gently at his side.

He meandered between the cars and trucks, and now and then he would stoop to pick something up from the ground that caught his interest. He still carried in his hand the sparkling jewel-encrusted necklace that he had found lying there twinkling in the bright sunlight at the side of an abandoned car. The colours that it formed as the light bounced through it intrigued him, and for a long while he had stood holding it up to the sun, grunting and gasping as he studied the prisms that formed as its rays shone through the dazzling jewels creating and small rainbows.

Up ahead, there was movement. He could see a number of figures in the distance as they slowly moved about on the road. Andy stopped. He did not want to join them or have them follow him; he wanted to be left alone.

For a while, he hid himself behind a large overturned truck and waited for them to move away. He stood there, shuffling around in small circles and staring at his feet and when he peered out from his hiding place again, he saw that they were still there. They had not moved on as normal and they were clustered around a broken down car that sat in the middle of the road. They were not attacking it or trying to gain entry; they just stood there and stared at it.

Andy could not understand why, but he felt the urge to move forward and investigate what was happening. He could feel his curiosity grow and something inside his decayed mind encouraged him to walk towards the small group in the road. They paid him no attention as he approached and they continued to sway on the spot where they stood, or stagger and stumble around the vehicle, watching whatever it was inside that had caught their interest.

He stopped and studied the group. They were vile to look at, their emaciated bodies looked frail and their clothing hung from their bones. Their skins were a mixture of colours, browns, greens, blues and even black as some of them had baked in the sun, causing their skin to roast and blisters to form.

The air was thick with the hum of insects and Andy's very own eco system joined in with the buzzing flies as he approached, creating a dark cloud that swarmed around the vicinity of the car.

Lowering his head, he studied himself. He looked down at his shoes and followed the length of his own body, finishing off by holding his hands out in front of him. The dark, shrivelled skin that covered the bones was broken here and there, giving him a glimpse of the drying tendons beneath and the white bones of his fingers. Brown clumps of congealed and almost dry blood seeped through the open wounds in his flesh. Regardless of how much he attempted to protect himself, he still sustained minor injuries and they would never heal.

An emotion rippled through him that made him throw his hands back down to his sides. He regretted having examined himself because it did nothing but remind him that he was very much like the lurching, disgusting creatures that he saw before him staggering about around the broken down vehicle; the very same things that he avoided, even though he knew that he was one of them.

He still wanted to see what it was that was attracting them. He took a tentative step closer toward the group. They still paid him no attention and their backs remained turned towards him. He took another step, this time more boldly and deliberate; still none of them turned in his direction. He briskly moved forward and reached the first of the figures. The body was in his way and blocking his view of the car, so Andy reached for it, grabbing it by the material that hung from its shoulders. He pulled hard and the body came back towards him.

It let out a moan and attempted to turn to see what it was that had removed it from the spot where it wanted to be. As it turned, Andy forced it to the side, heaving it away from him and stepping past. Now he was close to the rear door of the vehicle, closer than the others were.

He stooped and peered in through the window.

A young child, still strapped in her seat in the back of a large family sedan, was the thing that had caught the interest of the others. She sat there, staring back at them, her misted and flattened eyes showing no sign of life. One of her arms was missing along with much of the flesh from her neck and shoulder that was now nothing more than a festering pulp of green, rotting soft tissue and discoloured bone.

In comparison, much of her long blonde hair remained. It was in stark contrast to the remainder of her face and still looked full of life as it flowed in the breeze that blew through the smashed windscreen. The long golden strands fluttered and swept around in front of her, framing her pale and lifeless face.

He watched her curiously, and she watched him in return as he stood on the other side of the door. Andy's brow suddenly raised and he felt something stir from within; grief gripped him as he stared back at the small child strapped in the seat. She was not supposed to be that way, just as he was not supposed to be the way he was. A long poignant moan rattled up from his throat, gurgling and crackling at first, before it became a steady pitched and deliberate note.

The child opened her mouth slightly, as though to join him in chorus, but no sound travelled past her crushed and torn throat. She turned away and looked down at the interior of the car around her, and then brought her lifeless eyes back to Andy, with a hint of an expression of helplessness etched across her face. She could not move and she did not attempt to break free of her bonds. She would remain the way she was, sitting there forever.

Unexplainably, Andy saw the same emotion in her as he felt at that moment. She made no communication with him, but he knew she was sad. She did not want to be there, to be that way. He turned to look at the others around him. Their unblinking black and flattened eyes remained locked on the child as though they were hypnotised by her, but she paid them no interest and stared back only at Andy.

Something registered in his mind. He suddenly knew what he had to do. He reached down for the handle of the door and pulled. With a creak it fell open, a swarm of flies suddenly taking to the air as they were disturbed by the sudden change in pressure and movement.

Andy looked down at the sparkling necklace he held in his hand and reached out toward the child, the jewels shining and twinkling in the sunlight. She stared at the piece of jewellery hanging from his hand for a brief moment and then reached out for it.

Her cold fingers touched his and she looked straight in his eyes as he handed her the gift. Andy felt something else at that moment; it could only be affection, and sympathy for the sorrowful creature that sat before him, staring back at him with its large dead eyes.

He stepped back as the child focussed its interest on the colourful row of sparkling diamonds in her hands. He moved off around to the rear of the vehicle in confusion, unable to understand the sudden multitude of different emotions that bombarded him. He stopped and looked back through the rear window at the child. Another pang of compassion hit him and he turned away.

His mind was flitting with numerous different visions, none of them clear, but he knew and understood what it was that his faltering brain was telling him to do.

He turned away and walked to the side of the road. He began scanning the overgrown tangles of weeds and long grass, and then he saw it. He reached down and hefted the heavy rusted lump of iron. It was jagged and filled with bolts. He could feel its weight and he raised it in his hand and swung it to the side, testing it. It cut through the air with a whoosh as he let it swing back to his side.

He looked back at the car, and then began to walk towards it.

The child was still watching the multitude of colours that the crystals created when he appeared back at the door. She looked back up at him and then down at the heavy object that he clutched in his hands. For a moment their eyes locked, and her cold pale face seemed to soften and flood with life.

For a long moment, Andy and the little girl stood, watching one another. He felt some kind of bond with the little creature and she felt the same towards him. They were both capable of thought and reasoning.

Again, he saw the sorrow in her eyes; the sorrow that told him that she did not want to be that way.

Andy hesitated. Something made him want to turn away, but her eyes were locked on his and he could not leave her in that way. She shifted slightly in the seat, dried encrusted blood cracked as she peeled herself away from the material, and as Andy saw the ripped and torn flesh around her shoulders and neck, an image of how things used to be flashed to the front of his mind.

He raised the heavy metal in both hands above his head. With all his strength, he brought the pointed tip of it down towards the child. He crashed it down on to the back of her head with all of his force behind it. He felt the hard bone of the skull crack and collapse as the metal forced its way through. The child jerked suddenly and then slumped forward.

She was dead.

Andy stood with his hands still clutching the shaft of iron that protruded from the poor creature's head. Blood and thick green and yellow liquids oozed out around the wound. He paused and looked at the others that stood around, all curiously watching him now.

He turned his attention back to the child. He placed one hand on her head, and then heaved the shaft of iron free. It clattered against the surface of the road as he discarded it to the side and he laid the body back in the seat, noticing that she still clutched the necklace in her small delicate hands. He paused and hung his head. He felt remorse for what he had done, and then he remembered the contrast of the little girl and the creature she had become.

With both arms, he wrenched her from her restraints, pulling her into the sunlight and holding her close to his chest. The other figures around him closed slightly, curious to see the child but keeping their distance from Andy.

He looked down at her delicate face and saw beauty. The same kind of beauty he saw in the birds and the flowers and swaying trees. She was not like him, or the others that stood or staggered about, wretched and repulsive to look at. He remembered children, their beauty and their innocence. He looked at the creatures around him and snarled, baring his teeth.

Carrying her limp body in his arms, he staggered to the roadside. He whimpered and moaned hoarsely as he walked, his body wracked with grief. He looked for a patch of grass, one that seemed the most peaceful and attractive.

Finding the spot, he placed her down, gently lowering her head so that it did not bash against the ground. He folded her arms across her stomach and wrapped the jewels that she still held, around her small fingers. He reached over and carefully closed her beautiful staring eyes, finally laying her to rest.

The others had followed him and now stood watching him as he took such gentle care of the dead child. Andy stood and turned. He watched them as they watched him. Some of them looked at him and at the body of the child alternately, as though attempting to reason with his actions. They moaned quietly and grunted as they stood and stared at him, cocking their heads as they studied him and one another.

Andy turned away and continued his slow shuffle towards the distant horizon. One by one the bodies in the road watched him as he walked away, and one by one they moved off to follow on behind him.

The low rumble of engines in the distance behind him stopped him in his tracks. He lifted his head and slowly turned to look back at the road that he had been travelling as he honed in on the direction that the noise came from.

The ones that stumbled and staggered along behind him also stopped. They stared at him, watching in expectation then they slowly turned when they, too, heard the noise. They stood there, their shoulders slumped and their hands hanging at their sides as they watched for the source of the sound.

The road was empty, except for the abandoned vehicles that littered the carriageway here and there. A few birds fluttered from one car roof to the next, screeching and twittering as they did so and scrounging whatever morsels that were available within the wrecks, but there was nothing else moving.

Andy recognised the sounds, though. They were the noises that the fast moving ones made. The others that were still the way that he had once been, beautiful and graceful and not ugly and wretched like he was now. They moved in cars and trucks, and they were fast and dangerous. He feared them just as much as he feared the ones that were like him.

In the distance, weaving between the abandoned cars and approaching fast, he saw the shape of a moving object. It was a truck. The engine was loud and it roared towards them, causing alarm to rise up inside Andy. He felt as though he was trapped and something bad was about to happen to him.

He could not get away from them and they would catch him if he tried. Desperately, he looked about at the area immediately around him. He caught sight of the tall trees across the field in the distance, but they were too far away. He looked back at the approaching truck and he saw that it was closing in fast.

An overwhelming urge for self-preservation gripped him. His instincts spoke to him and forced his faltering mind into action. The prehistoric core of his brain now took control of his decaying body.

His eyes scanned all around and his head swivelled as he searched for somewhere to hide. There was a large dip where the road met the open fields and Andy moved towards it. It was overgrown with long grass and as he stumbled down the small embankment, his feet sunk in the shallow stream that ran along at the side of the road. It squelched as the water sucked at his feet and he struggled to lift his legs free or walk as the water reached his knees, while the weight of his body caused him to sink. The water and mud bubbled and sucked at him, holding him in place and rendering him unable to move and vulnerable.

The others, not realising the danger that was headed directly for them, raised their arms and wailed excitedly when they saw the approaching vehicle. They stumbled straight for it, their clumsy steps causing them to stagger and sway as they grasped at the air between them and the soft, living flesh that they yearned. They wanted it and their cries and moans grew in tempo and volume as they watched the vehicle close the distance.

The noises that the figures on the back of the truck made only added to the atmosphere of anticipation for all. They shouted and hollered to one another and the truck turned slightly, aiming straight for the lurching figures in the road that reached out towards them.

They were close now.

Andy was in the ditch, crouching and watching the road as he saw the truck closing in on the others. The vehicle smashed into a dark shambling figure that stepped out in front of it. It hit with a loud crunch as the steel grill at the front of the truck smashed into bone and launched it through the air. The body crashed to the floor some distance away with a thud and bits of flesh being slung in all directions as the broken and jagged bones tore through the skin.

The truck stopped and those on the back began to jump down, hooting and shouting as they did so. The fast movers approached and began to attack the slow moving and lumbering creatures that approached them. They beat them to the ground with ease and smashed their skulls with clubs, scattering their brains and dark, coagulated blood across the road and cheering as they did so.

The creatures were not deterred; they continued to lurch toward the soft flesh that danced about before them, only to be pummelled to the tarmac one after the other.

Not all of them were killed. Some were grasped by the neck with long poles, guided and pushed, then thrown in the back of the truck where they were chained against the sides. They tugged at their restraints, growling and snarling at the figures that moved around them. They reached out at them, clutching with their fingers as they tried to get hold of the warm living flesh.

When they attempted to lunge forward, their heads were snapped back by their chains as they were pulled taut, dragging them back against the side of the truck. They wailed and moaned incessantly as they tried desperately to reach their tormentors who remained just beyond their grasp.

Andy was stuck. He could not move from the mud. His instincts urged him to move away and avoid them, but he was unable to. He looked down at the sludge that held him fast. A growl of frustration escaped from his throat as he attempted again to lift his feet.

There was a noise in front of him. Andy looked up and saw two of the beautiful fast movers standing at the top of the ditch in front of him. They looked down on him, and then shouted across to the truck. More came over and joined them as they stood for a moment watching him. He felt fear tugging at him. He wanted to run, but he was trapped.

Two of them carefully approached down the small embankment, a pole held out far in front of them with a noose hanging from the end. Andy cowered away from it, swatting at it with his hands in front of him as they tried, repeatedly, to loop the noose around his neck. They shouted at him and hit him on the head with the pole, laughing with each other. He did not want to get in the truck; he wanted them to leave him alone. He just wanted to walk away.

Another of them jumped across the ditch and closed in behind him. Andy crouched slightly, his hands held at his sides and the elbows bent. It was a natural instinct that forced him into that stance and he could feel the urge to throw his hands out in front of him with all his strength at anything that came near.

He gnashed his teeth and growled at the figures that shouted at him, wanting to take him away. He dodged the two in front that attempted to snare him and he continually looked back at the one that approached him from behind. He wanted to turn and face them, but his legs were planted in the mud. He twisted and thrashed as they continued in their attempt to get the rope around his neck.

Suddenly, a force from behind sent him tumbling forward. The mud squelched and threw his feet free as he was thrown to the ground. Before he could try to stand, something pinned him down. He thrashed and growled, snapping his teeth at the feet and legs that he could see moving around him. He was being shoved and pulled, and then the noose came down over his face.

He recognised it instantly as it passed his eyes. Anger flashed through him. He began to roar and thrash harder, his head jerking in all directions as he attempted to break free.

His captors shouted and laughed as they dragged him to his feet and up the embankment. They kicked him and shoved him in all directions. He was scared and angry. He knew what the fast movers did to the ones like him. He had watched them smash their heads in, set them on fire or run them down, and now they were dragging him to the truck where they had put the others.

He pulled at the cord around his neck; it cut into his soft and delicate flesh, the same flesh that he so desperately wished to preserve. His feet dragged and scuffed against the ground as he attempted to stop them from pushing him in the truck. They were too strong and they pushed him along easily.

Andy was helpless.

20

"Where are we going?" Simon whispered, a little too loudly.

Johnny was just a few steps in front of him, crouching and hugging the rough brick of the building wall as he peered around the corner and out into the open. He stepped back, his eyes still fixed on the corner of the building as he slowly moved back towards Simon. He turned his head and glared at him, a look of annoyance etched across his face as he raised a finger to his lips.

"Be quiet," he whispered as he leaned back and pointed to the corner of the building. His short stubby finger, dirt and grime embedded in the tiny creases of skin and beneath the fingernails, directed Simon's focus towards the edge of the bricks where they met the open air.

"They'll hear you."

Simon's eyes widened as he stared at the corner, expecting a grotesque and rotting corpse to stagger into view at any moment. He could feel himself wanting to step back and put as much distance as possible between him and the open ground beyond the wall. Even after being continually exposed to them since he left his bunker, he was still just as terrified of them as he was when he had come face to face with them for the very first time.

Everything about the dead frightened him; the way they looked, their smell, their movements and of course, what they were capable of doing to a person. The very concept of the dead returning to life and attacking the living was something from his worst nightmares. In fact, worse, because had never dreamed of it and it was still something he found hard to comprehend, never mind accept.

"How many of them are there?" he asked with desperation in his voice.

Johnny turned to him and blinked. The question seemed irrelevant to him. "Enough," he replied with a nod of his head.

Since leaving the house, where he had found and been saved by the eccentric little homeless man, the two of them had spent most of their time hiding in the shadows. They scurried from one building to the next, avoiding detection, or slowly and silently staggering and shuffling in the open, past hordes of the festering wandering bodies as they attempted to blend in and act as one of the dead.

Simon's nerves were shot. His mind threatened to crumble on him at any moment and he constantly battled with himself to prevent him from screaming aloud or collapsing into a blubbering wreck in the middle of the street. Since they had run from the house where he had found Johnny, they had travelled through some of the more densely packed areas of the town. Johnny insisted that he knew the perfect place for them to go, but he never told Simon where that place actually was. Every time Simon asked, Johnny just replied with, "You will see, trust me."

To Simon, it seemed as though Johnny enjoyed walking amongst the dead, as though he got some kind of kick from it. The first time they did it, Simon was horrified at just the idea of it. The fear had gripped him so powerfully he could literally feel it squeezing around his throat. Then, when Johnny smiled at him as though it was something as simple and easy as scratching his head, Simon had realised that Johnny truly was crazy and that it was not just a misconception due to his appearance.

He had watched as the scruffy little man had stepped out and casually strolled through the street without a care in the world. Simon wanted to run or to turn back the way they had come, or even to just stay where he was and cower in the corner, but he fought his fear and slowly followed the insane Johnny out into a street packed with the repulsive and horrifying things.

Simon had kept his eyes glued to the floor, refusing even to glance upward for fear that he would make eye contact with one of them. The thought of staring into a pair of those lifeless eyes, their pupils dilated into a black cavernous hole, flat through lack of blood pressure and misted over giving no hint of emotion, made him sick with fear.

He watched his own feet as he gently placed one in front of the other, concentrating on where he was placing each step and his movements. He was terrified of making the slightest sound in fear of causing one of the dead to look in his direction. Every single muscle in his body was taut and coiled like a spring. If one of them had so much as reached out for him, he would have leaped ten feet in the air and bolted for his life. It was a wonder that he did not collapse during the short, but dangerous, walk because he was not breathing for most of it. It was only later, when he reached the relative safety of the houses across the street they had crossed, he realised he was suffering with the early stages of carbon dioxide poisoning from holding his breath.

As he shuffled, he only saw the dead around him from the waist down. That scared him enough, but it was always at the front of his mind that he only needed to look up slightly and he would be face to face with the most terrifying things he had ever seen. Some of them came very close as their paths crossed, their soiled and torn clothing just inches away from his. He could even feel some of them brush against him as they shambled about in no particular direction. He heard their grunts, the sound of the numerous insects that filled the air and fed off them. Now and then, one of them would let out a long moan or sigh, sounding like someone grieving or, even bored. Their cold and lifeless bodies were so close that he would only need to reach out a little to touch them.

One body, its legs and lower torso missing, its flesh shredded and hanging from it in tatters like a grotesque skirt, pulled itself across his path as its blue and bloated innards trailed behind it leaving a path of noxious sludge in its wake. It was naked. Its skin was green with pus and maggot-filled sores that oozed up from within. He could see the bones of the shoulders working beneath the thin and putrefied skin, threatening to cut through the thin layer of flesh and expose the white tips of the blades as it reached out, alternating its arms and dragging itself along on the hard concrete of the ground.

Simon had almost bolted at that point. A gasp had threatened to escape from his throat and he hesitated before stepping over it and continuing in Johnny's footsteps.

Their smell caused his head to spin, his eyes smart and water, and his stomach churn; a stench that he could not describe. To him, there was nothing more repulsive and nauseating in the whole world. The smell itself seemed to be alive and wanted to spread itself throughout his body. It clung to his clothing, his flesh and even permeated in his hair. Most of all, it seemed to embed itself in to his nasal cavity and refused to budge. Every breath seemed to force it further into his senses, leaving him unable to get rid of it.

He was thankful that he had not eaten that day, because he would surely have vomited and given himself away to the countless creatures around him.

They had continued like that for the whole day, sometimes climbing through gardens and houses undetected, or walking amongst the dead, risking being torn apart. At one point Johnny had even turned to him as they both leaned with their backs against a wall after slowly making their way through a particularly crowded area. Simon, slouching against the bricks quivering, his knees threatening to give from under him and fighting the urge to throw up, while Johnny apathetically picked his nose, grinning back at him as he inspected the finger he had been using.

"See, it's easy, isn't it?"

"No, it fucking isn't. I have lost count of the amount of times I have almost shit myself, Johnny. Are you sure you know the best place?"

"Of course, not far now," he had replied cheerfully.

Now, according to Johnny, they were at the place that he had assured him through miles and miles of diseased filth 'was not far'. Simon felt as if they had been running, walking and crawling the gauntlet for days.

Just beyond the corner of the wall was their destination. Simon did not recognise the area and wondered where they could be and what exactly was just beyond the building behind which they sheltered. Even though he wanted to get to safety and out of the open, he dreaded looking around the corner, mainly for two reasons. The first was because he knew that there were many of the dead close by. He could hear them as well as smell them, but he could not yet see any sign of them. He knew that there must be a lot of them, because Johnny was not being his usual carefree self.

The second thing that bothered him was Johnny's idea of safety and the 'perfect place' to go. For all Simon knew, the crazy homeless man could have been leading him anywhere but safe or perfect. It could have been a football stadium full of the things.

Simon squatted down, his back scraping against the rough brick as it tugged against his clothing. Johnny moved back and crouched beside him. To their left was a rusted chain-link fence with long coils of barbed wire running along the top, and to their right, was the old brick building behind which they were hiding. Its small high windows were smashed, leaving shards of misted and discoloured glass jutting up here and there from their rotten and crumbling green wooden frames. Most of the bricks had lost their smooth flattened edges and now the raw and deteriorating clay and sand mix flaked away, slowly weakening the entire structure. Simon guessed that it had probably been derelict for years and more than likely scheduled to be pulled down at some point, but now it would remain until it finally collapsed from its own deterioration.

Out in front, beyond the corner of the wall, Simon could see a wide expanse of tarmac. It was a car parking area with dozens of abandoned cars still sitting in their line-marked parking spaces. He could see the signs that designated certain spaces for disabled people and parents with children. Shopping carts were strewn all around, their contents scattered across the floor. Simon absentmindedly wondered, *At what point during the disaster did people finally stop shopping?* At the far end of the open car parking area was a high wall, dotted with overhanging trees that looked as though it may have backed on to an industrial estate, but Simon could not be sure.

They both squatted and listened. There were no dead in sight but they could hear the distant hum of them. It was a lingering unrelenting sound and it chilled the blood of anyone that heard it and knew what it was. Simon compared it to a sound similar to that of an electric power transformer, but much more haunting and poignant because he knew they were the voices of hundreds of diseased and lost souls.

They guessed that there must be thousands of them in order to make the kind of steady uninterrupted drone that they could hear. Now and then, the sound of an individual shriek or high-pitched moan could be heard over the hum as one of the dead became excited for whatever reason.

They could also hear the endless thump as hundreds of cold, dead hands slapped and pounded against glass. It reverberated and banged, echoing around the open ground as they struck against the glass incessantly.

Simon, steeling himself, began to edge forward. He paused, taking deep breaths as he stared down at the mud and crumbled brick crumbs at his feet. He glanced back at Johnny, who returned an encouraging nod and began moving towards the corner again.

At the point where the wall stopped, Simon crouched and flattened himself against the masonry. He really did not want to look at them. His heart began to beat against the wall of his chest so hard that he could actually feel it thump his ribs. He did not want to poke his head out from around the corner and see the mass of monstrous figures that he knew he would, but he had to. He had to know where they were going before Johnny led them out there. Johnny promised him that they were almost to safety and with nothing else and no one to cling to Simon had followed along and placed his trust in the crazy old tramp.

He repeatedly reminded himself that despite the scruffy little man's appearance and eccentricities, he had been surviving on the streets since day one of the plague. Simon, on the other hand, had spent most of it either barricaded in his house, or underground. Johnny knew the dead better than he did and he knew the streets better still. His strange ways aside, Johnny was his best hope.

His cheek was flat against the brickwork of the building. He could feel the rough material rubbing against the soft skin of his face but he was determined to give the dead as little as possible of him to see.

His face cleared the brick and as his eyes quickly adjusted focus, he saw them. He could not miss them. Pressed up and packed tightly against the entire length of a long building, just fifty metres away, was a wall of grey brown figures. It was hard to tell one body from the next. All of them blended in a blur of dull shades, covered in grime and smeared with their own bodily fluids and remains.

He could see the tall windows of the buildings front; they spanned the whole length of the building and reached from the ground and up to the roof. He saw the change of light reflected from the glass as it shook and quaked against the pounding of the hundreds of bodies pressing against the large panes. Simon looked up and saw the sign above where he presumed the main entrance was.

It was a supermarket.

Either side of it were more shops, mainly clothing outlets and a tool hire shop. There was even a pet store, but at some point, from what Simon could tell, the dead had battered down the windows and rampaged through the shop, ravaging and consuming anything that was still alive in there.

A gust of wind carried the foul stench of the rotting bodies towards him. His eyes watered as his gag reflex threatened to set him off on a bout of dry retching. Quickly, he pulled his head back around the corner and to safety. He held his hand over his mouth as his body quivered, fighting back the bile that threatened to erupt from within his stomach. He crawled back to where Johnny was waiting for him.

"What do you think?" Johnny beamed.

Simon wiped the last of the fetid drool from his lips and looked at him confused. "Think of what? It's a Morrison's supermarket and swarming with those things. There's nothing to think, mate, it's a no go."

"It's our hide out," Johnny replied, as though it had been obvious. "It has everything we need and we would be safe there. To be truthful, I don't know why I never came here sooner. It's perfect."

"Are you really serious?" Simon's eyebrows were furrowed and he glared at the scruffy man. "This is your safe place that you have been leading me to? Did you notice the six billion hungry walking dead bodies standing outside the main entrance? What do you expect us to do, grab a shopping trolley and walk right by them?"

"Six billion, I've told you a million times not to exaggerate," Johnny grinned. "Anyway, yeah, we could just walk past them like we have been doing all day."

Simon almost laughed. The man was so blasé about the whole situation. "Look, I've had enough of the whole pretending to be dead thing. If we try that here, we won't be pretending for much longer, because we *will* be dead."

"But, it's…"

Simon raised his hand and cut him off. He leaned in close to his ear, grabbing him by the shoulder and pulling him towards him so that they were just inches apart.

"Johnny, it isn't perfect at all. Maybe if those things weren't all over the place, then yeah, we could consider staying, but we can't get in."

"What about that then?" Johnny asked, his eyes motioning to something in the distance that Simon had obviously missed.

"What about what?" Simon asked as he followed the line of Johnny's gaze. "I don't see what you're trying to get me to look at. You mean the cars?"

Johnny leaned in close beside him and raised his arm so that it was close to the side of Simon's head. Folding his fingers into themselves and leaving one grubby digit extended in a point.

"Over there, past the cars, on the other side is a truck."

Simon followed the line of his finger and saw the large white tanker at the far side of the car park. It was parked in a strange way, as though it had been dumped there and abandoned close to the exit to the shopping complex.

"So, I don't get it, what are you telling me?"

"Be quiet for a minute and you'll hear it. Just listen."

Johnny remained close in by the side of Simon, his arm and finger still extended and pointing toward the tanker. Simon watched for a moment, expecting to see something, then he realised, it was not what he could see, but actually what he could hear. With all the dead at the window, his own heartbeat pounding in his ears and his nerves threatening to explode out from his skin, he had not noticed it. Now, he could clearly hear it; the truck was still running. He could hear the distant but distinct and unmistakable mechanical clunk of its rumbling gurgling engine.

He turned his head slightly. "You think we should take the truck then?" he asked.

Johnny shook his head and sighed as he lowered his arm. "For a man who knows all about computers, you're not very smart are you? It means, my dear sausage, that there must be people nearby. How else would the engine still be running, and why would it be left just there?"

"Maybe they got a flat and they had to run away?"

"Nope," Johnny said looking down as he stuck out his lower lip and attempted to fold it upward over his thick moustache and toward the tip of his nose. "I reckon whoever was driving the truck is now in the supermarket and that's why all those ugly bastards are trying to get in." He reached down and picked up a piece of coloured glass then began rubbing it between his fingers. He shrugged shoulders as he studied it, "Well, that's what I think anyway."

Simon eyed him with respect. He realised that, for all his oddities and his strange appearance, Johnny was much sharper than most people gave him credit for and because his mind had been geared to much more simple matters rather than thinking about *'careers and gadgets'* as Johnny referred to them, he was able to see things more clearly.

Simon looked back at the tanker. "You're right, mate; they must be stuck in the supermarket, but why don't they just go out the back way?"

"Maybe they have," Johnny suggested.

Simon realised that he had seen something else, but his brain had not yet fully processed it. "I don't think they have."

He suddenly stood upright and edged his way back to the corner. Again, he saw the masses of reanimated corpses clambering against each other at the large windows of the supermarket, but that was not what he was looking for. Then, he saw it.

"There," he hissed back to Johnny. "There's a car parked right up against the windows. Actually, it looks more like a Land Rover shaped zebra."

Johnny took a quick look and then pulled himself back in behind Simon.

"What do you think, then? Should we try and get in there?" Simon asked turning to the short bedraggled and bearded man by his side.

"How do you think we can do that, should we try and walk by them?"

Simon spun on him, "Will you fuck off with this walking dead shit? We don't have to do that, mate. We can run for the truck and bang on the horn until those things are clear of the shop front. Then, once whoever is in the supermarket gets out and to their Land Rover, we can go with them."

"How do you know they'll let us? There are some bad people about you know, even some of the ones who are still alive." Johnny looked as though he was talking from experience.

"They'll probably be thankful that we helped them and that should be enough, I reckon," Simon offered in way of encouragement. "Come on."

Simon grabbed Johnny by the sleeve and stepped out into the open. Suddenly, he felt vulnerable. There were no walls to hide behind now or shield his vision from the hordes of rotting corpses, lingering just metres away. He broke into a trot and Johnny ran at his side. Simon noticed that his friend was unsettled and it was not due to the dead. It was the living that Johnny feared most. He had met Simon through accident and not through choice and it had been forced upon him. Deliberately going out to make new friends was not something he was entirely comfortable with, especially since the dead had begun to walk.

Simon kept his eyes fixed on the large, white tanker ahead of them. He did not want to look at the dead; hearing their moans and lament was enough for him. He could hear the sound of his own pounding heart and heavy breathing echoing in his ears. The sounds of the slapping footfalls of Johnny at his side sounded deafening, as though someone was beating on a drum. They were just metres away from the truck now, the noise of the rumbling engine growing louder in their ears as they drew near.

He had to check on what the dead were doing. The truck was almost within reach and he needed to see the position they were in before he made his next move. Quickly, he glanced to his right and then snapped his head back to the front.

The dead had spotted them as they made their dash from the cover of the building wall. Dozens of individuals had broken away from the rest of the pack and now staggered towards them. Some moved slowly, their decay and injuries hindering their movements as they headed for the two men and the tanker. Others that were less damaged and more mobile, staggered quickly, their feet taking faster steps as the weight of their bodies carried them forward. They reached out ahead of them, their withered hands grasping at the running men, moaning as they recognised the fast moving living flesh that they longed to consume.

"Come on, Johnny, we're nearly there."

Simon forced himself forward the last few metres to the cab of the truck. As Johnny vaulted up and onto the step that led into the passenger's seat, Simon sprinted past the front of the chugging engine and towards the driver's door. He reached up and pulled at the handle. The door swung open and he was met with the sight of Johnny already seated in the cab, staring back at him.

"Hit the horn, Johnny," he shouted up into the truck as he began to climb the step, gripping the steering wheel to help haul him up to the driver's seat.

Johnny leaned across and began banging his fist down in the centre of the steering wheel. The horn blazed and rang in their ears, attracting more of the dead that were still pounding against the supermarket windows.

Simon felt a sudden and heavy tug from behind. Something had latched onto his back as he was almost in the cab of the tanker. The sudden weight dragged him backward out of the vehicle. His eyes widened with terror as he let out a yelp and he tumbled back towards the floor. He desperately grasped at the widening space between him and the steering wheel of the truck as he fell. He could see Johnny still pressing down on the horn but the sound of it became distant in his ears as he tumbled in what seemed like slow motion.

The hands still clutched at his back and he felt the fingers tighten their grasp around him. He landed with a thud and he exhaled loudly as the wind was knocked from him. His head was jolted backward, causing stars to spin in front of his eyes and disorientating him.

Johnny realised what had happened as he heard the scream from Simon. He pulled away from the wheel releasing the blaring horn, and leaned over and out through the door and saw Simon, lying sprawled on the ground staring back up at him in a daze. Beneath him, Johnny saw the flailing corpse of a woman. She writhed and growled as she attempted to free herself from beneath the bulk of Simon.

"Simon, get up, get up now," Johnny bellowed as he reached his hand down to help pull him back into the truck.

Simon shook his head, coming to his senses and reached his arms behind him to help push him back up. His hands pressed down on the cold flesh of the body beneath him and the sudden realisation made him scream with fear and shock. He pushed harder, attempting to get away from the creature and force his body upward to safety.

The woman's cold claw-like hands gripped his shoulders harder, desperate to hold on to him as Simon pushed himself away from her. He could feel the nails and bones of the fingers digging into the flesh beneath his jacket. She snarled from behind him, the sound making him panic and whimper with fright. Her teeth snapped together with a clash then her mouth opened wide, revealing her blackened gums and yellowed teeth. Squirming maggots fell from the corners of her lips and her swollen dark blue tongue slithered from her gaping maw as she pulled down with all her weight.

Simon lost his balance and the weight of the body gripping him forced him back down. Suddenly, he felt the white-hot pain as the teeth bit down onto his shoulder. The agony of it flashed before his eyes like a lightning bolt as the jagged and sharp teeth broke through his skin, creating a popping crunching sound as they punctured the tissue and crushed the flesh between them. He felt the tendons rip and the muscle tear as she clenched her teeth together and pulled her head backward.

Simon screamed.

The pain shot through him and up into his brain, causing him to throw his head back and let out a long blood-curdling howl. The corpse pulled her head away, tearing the flesh from him. The air hitting the open wound forced him to scream even louder.

He attempted to roll to the side, but the thing clung to his back, refusing to be shaken off. She bit down again, tearing more flesh and muscle from him as he screamed louder and longer. Simon forced his elbow backwards in an attempt to knock her away, but the creature refused to loosen her grip.

He could feel his warm blood flooding over his neck and down his back. It pumped from the wound in his shoulder as his heart raced to maintain the flow of blood around his system. He tried again to break free, screaming and pulling away with all his strength and causing more blood to gush from his wound. Beneath him, he could hear the sound of slurping and grunting as the dead woman, still clinging on tightly to his shoulders, chewed noisily on his flesh.

Johnny jumped from the cab of the truck. He landed at the side of Simon, narrowly avoiding losing his balance and becoming entangled with the two figures on the floor. He grabbed his friend, pulling him hard and trying to break the creature's grasp on him. He yanked the screaming man to the side and away from his attacker and as he did so, he heard the sound of ripping flesh as the creature bit down on Simon's shoulder again in an attempt to prevent her prey being taken away from her.

Johnny raised his knee, holding on to Simon for support, and stamped down hard at the face of the dead woman. He felt his foot connect with the bone of the skull and the jaw gave way under the impact. The creature lost its hold and fell to the floor as its lower mandible was dislocated, cutting through the thin flesh of its face and exposing its rear teeth through the gaping hole.

He pulled Simon away, his body sagging and becoming limp in his arms.

The wailing and snarling creature tried again to reach out for the flesh of the living man as Johnny dragged him towards the truck. She lunged, narrowly missing their legs and falling forward, face first against the hard tarmac of the car park floor with a sickening thud as the bones in her face were shattered and crushed.

Quickly, Johnny hauled Simon into the cab, pushing him across to the passenger seat while he jumped behind the wheel. Simon slumped in the footwell, clutching his hand tightly over the gaping hole in his shoulder and crying through his clenched teeth. He was pale and beads of sweat poured down his face, mixing with the tears that streamed from his eyes. His body began to shudder as his stomach convulsed and forced bile up through his mouth and nose. He coughed and sputtered uncontrollably as his body was wracked with more spasms.

Johnny threw the truck into gear. He heard the loud hiss as he released the brakes and felt the engine shudder and then lurch them forward. He glanced across at Simon. Rivers of tears streamed down the cheeks of his friend, and Johnny knew they were as much from fear as they were from pain. He watched as the man sank further into the footwell, curling himself into a ball and whimpering as the reality of what had happened, and would happen, sank in.

Beyond Simon, Johnny noticed the wing mirror of the truck sticking out at an angle from the door. He craned his neck in order to see what was behind them as he pushed down on the gear lever and accelerated away. He saw the reflection of dozens of the staggering corpses headed for them. More and more were losing interest in the supermarket and joining the pursuit.

The vehicle gained speed and he aimed it for the exit, stamping down on the accelerator and forcing the heavy truck forward and away from the scene.

Simon needed help, but Johnny did not know what to do, or if there was anything he could do. He did not know where to go. He just wanted to get away and help his friend. Suddenly, he remembered the people in the supermarket. He forced the wheel around to the left, turning the large cumbersome tanker in a wide arc. The tyres screeched and the brakes groaned as he tried desperately to stop the truck from toppling over in the tight turn.

He straightened up and slammed on the brakes, bringing the truck to a shuddering halt. In front, a sea of shuffling corpses slowly made their way towards them. They filled the entire car park, their moans and cries drowning out the sound of the engine.

Johnny bit down on his lower lip as he brought a hand up to scratch at his overgrown beard. He nodded to himself, and then he began pounding on the horn again.

21

The crowd below was growing by the minute. More of the dead were arriving and joining the ocean of gaunt and rotted faces beneath the steel walkway. They snarled and cried out from within the mass and cold shrivelled hands reached upward, grasping and clutching at the air in frustration as they attempted to reach the living people above them.

The horde was swaying and bobbing like a choppy sea as they bustled and pushed against one another, some being dragged to the ground and trampled as the gap they created was quickly filled by another grey dead face. They stared upward expectantly; their blank lifeless eyes never blinking as they remained fixed on the people above them while swarms of insects circled the air above.

The incessant moans and wails of the dead and the hum and buzz of the flies, mixed in an uninterrupted din. Their sound echoed around in the tightly packed space of the unloading bay as the acoustics of the high reaching walls amplified the voices of the tightly packed dead and channelled it upward to the overhanging ledges that were attached to and jutted out from the roof. With no wind or breeze penetrating the square that was surrounded on three sides by the alcoves of the building, the stench of their rotting flesh lingered in the air, slowly drifting upward and assaulting the senses of anyone that was brave enough to peer down at them.

"Hey ugly," Lee shouted down at the mass of expectant lifeless faces.

The sound of his voice sent a ripple of excitement through the swaying corpses below. He coughed up a lump of phlegm into his throat. He carefully picked his target and took aim. He pulled his head back; holding onto the rail of the walkway to give him more thrust. He threw himself forward again to give the secreted missile more velocity and loosed it into the face of a growling corpse directly below him. The sticky mucous hit the creature on the forehead, running down into its eyes and sending it into state of fury as Lee laughed loudly and pointed.

"What you waiting for? Come and get it," he jeered at it as he leaned over the railing, reaching his hand down to just a metre above its head.

The creature below him, its face the colour of chalk and its teeth almost glowing yellow in contrast to its pale flesh, growled and shook its head as it flexed it jaw, gnashing its teeth together as it attempted to gain a metre in height to reach the warm, fleshy hand that dangled just out of reach above it. It raised its hands, the bones protruding through the tips of the fingers as small cuts and lacerations could not heal and grew in size, swiping at the air between Lee's fingers and its own.

Steve stood looking out over the tightly packed swarm of voracious rotting corpses. He made a rough mental count of their numbers and compared them to what he had last seen at the front of the store.

He leaned back and hollered in the doorway. "How are we looking at the front now?"

John's voice boomed back to him out of the dark interior of the building, "Still no change, Steve. We can't see anything except hundreds of those fuckers pressed up against the windows. You need to make more noise, I think."

Steve turned to Lee and grinned. "You heard the man, ring the dinner bell."

Lee began dancing about on the steel walkway. It echoed loudly in the bay area, shaking and rattling with each stomp of his feet. He beat the palm of his hand against his open mouth, making noises as though he was a Native American dancing around a fire. He banged against the steel railings with his iron bar, sending vibrations rippling up his arms as the high-pitched noise rang out and echoed in the confines of the loading bay at the back of the store. He was making enough noise to attract every creature for miles around, not just from the front of the supermarket.

"Come on, shit bags," he shouted. "Here I am."

He stopped and began unzipping the fly to his jeans. Steve looked across and realising what his friend was doing; he smiled and shook his head dismissively.

"They'll bite it off if you're not careful, mate."

Lee glanced across at him, a vacant look on his face as he strained and concentrated on the job in hand.

"It's okay, Steve, they can't get at it," he gasped between breaths as he forced harder. "I'll not unravel it completely. Anyway, stop watching me; you're giving me stage fright."

Lee let out a sigh and threw his head back as he relieved himself on to the heads of the dead below.

"Oh, I needed that."

Steve watched the long stream of urine as it splashed on to the heads of the bodies below. Some of them looked perplexed as the hot liquid sprayed on to their faces while others went into a frenzy as they felt the hot liquid spatter their decaying flesh, screaming and wailing, whilst shoving and pushing against each other beneath the walkway as Lee continued to hoot and laugh above them.

Lee began tucking himself back in, satisfaction etched on his face as he turned back to Steve and beamed.

"Hey, if we're here long enough, I'll need a dump eventually. That would be worth seeing."

Steve looked down at the urine-soaked faces that glared back up at them. "Nah, mate, I'll pass on that one if you don't mind."

He looked back at Lee, a serious, more solemn expression on his face. "They used to be people you know."

Lee was busy waving his arms and hollering again. He stopped mid-star jump and turned to look at Steve.

"Yeah, I know, but those people are dead now and whatever those pus bags are down there, they're not people. That's how I see it anyway."

Steve nodded in agreement, but he still viewed them with pity from time to time when he had the chance to reflect on all that had happened. He was a deep thinker and there were moments when he would look on the dead, studying them as individuals and wonder *who had they been and what had they done when they were alive?*

Often, he had to stop himself from going too far with his thoughts and dwelling on the fact that the creatures that now roamed the earth were once living individuals with their own thoughts, desires and emotions.

"I'm going to check how we're doing out front. You okay here, Lee?" he said stepping away from the railing.

Lee did not turn to answer him and he continued dancing and waving his arms as he made as much noise as possible. "Yeah, no worries, mate, all good here."

Steve turned away and headed into the gloomy interior of the storage area and administration offices at the back of the supermarket. Lee had always been unhinged so there was nothing new to worry about in that respect, but still, there was always the *'crazy idea'* factor that Lee had been prone to at times.

He remembered an incident from their childhood, when he had left Lee in charge of matters once before. A decision that proved disastrous.

During the summer holidays when they had their annual six-week break from school, there was little for the children of the neighbourhood to do and, as a result, boredom and trouble were never far away. Therefore, it was up to them to make their own fun.

Steve and Lee had their own little group during their youth. They were a close-knit bunch and to Steve, they were almost a stereotypical, *Stephen King* style gang that always seemed to be a template for the child characters in his books. They had the gang leader, Steve, and the unpredictable and unstable character in the form of Lee. The 'nerd' and the 'fat kid' were also accounted for.

One day, they had built themselves a base camp in the garden of one of their friend's houses. The friend happened to be Lee's cousin and the token *'fat kid'* of the gang, Chris. They spent the whole morning clearing out the junk and motorbike engine parts from the disused shed they would use as their lair and by midday, they had a cosy little clubhouse. They had even gone to the extent of fitting old discarded rugs and furniture, even nailing up wallpaper because Chris' father would not allow them to use paste.

The four of them stood back and admired their efforts with pride, safe in the knowledge that they had somewhere to hang out during the long summer evenings and maybe, parents' permission allowing, even sleep from time to time with sleeping bags and a campfire, and of course, ghost stories.

"Right, Lee," Steve had said as he turned to his old and trusted friend before he left to go and get his lunch, "look after the place while I'm gone. I'll only be half an hour."

Lee waved him off. "Yup, no worries, Steve, I'll look after it."

Thirty minutes later, Steve noticed black clouds of smoke billowing from the garden of Chris' house as he approached. Sprinting through the gateway, he was met with a sight that beggared belief.

The wooden den that they had worked so hard on now had gaping holes in its walls and roof. A fire raged in the corner as the wallpaper and furniture fed the blaze, allowing the licking flames to spread and travel up the walls, reaching to the ceiling and igniting the wooden roof.

Chris lay in the mud in front of the clubhouse, clutching his abdomen and screaming like a stuck pig with a screwdriver protruding from his stomach while Lee and Dave, the *'nerd'*, stood on the roof waving their arms and shouting for help.

The story unfolded that, once Steve was gone, there was no one to keep Lee in check. As he rummaged around in a toolbox that they had found amongst the junk, Lee had produced a screwdriver and decided it would be a good idea to thrust it into the large, soft belly of his cousin, Chris.

As Chris shrieked and dropped to the floor in agony, Lee panicked and in his attempt to avert any attention from the screams of his bleeding cousin, he decided to conduct a fire drill to ensure that the clubhouse was safe. Realism was the key in his mind, so he struck a match and held it to one of the dried out rugs, and within seconds the fire engulfed a whole portion of the clubhouse while Lee ran around, kicking the wooden slats from the walls, creating makeshift fire escapes.

Afterward, and true to form, Lee denied any involvement in the incident and blamed everyone else.

Steve smiled to himself at the memory, shaking his head as he walked along the dimly lit corridor. He could hear Lee, still outside on the steel balcony, taunting the wailing and frustrated dead below him.

John stood in the doorway at the far end, ready to relay messages from the other members of the group in the front of the supermarket, keeping Steve and Lee updated on the movements and size of the crowd outside pressing against the windows.

"Keep an eye on him, will you?" Steve nodded to John as he passed. "Don't let him do anything stupid."

John chuckled. "Lee, do anything stupid? You have him all wrong, Steve. No worries, mate, but if he decides to jump down there, don't expect me to follow him. He's a crazy bastard, that friend of yours."

Steve stopped. His eyes suddenly widened as he held on to the doorframe, staring back at John and cocking his head to one side.

John was about to apologise, thinking that he had offended Steve with the remarks about his friend. Steve held up a hand, silencing him before he had the chance to speak.

"Do you hear that?" he asked, turning his head and angling his ear towards the open doorway where Lee continued to make a racket.

John shook his head, "I don't hear anything. What is it?"

Steve changed the angle of his head, focussing as he tried to identify and pinpoint the noise he had heard. He was sure he had heard something other than Lee banging about and screaming out the lyrics to the song, *'Yellow Submarine'*, accompanied by the moans of the dead outside.

"I thought I heard..." He took a couple of steps back towards the door that led out on to the steel walkway.

"Lee," he hollered, "shut up a minute will you?"

The noise and the singing stopped abruptly and Lee shoved his head back through the door and peered into the gloom. "What's up, Steve, you don't like my singing?"

"Shut up and listen," Steve snapped. He stared at the floor, a look of deep concentration spread across his face as John and Lee looked at one another, perplexed.

Steve snapped his head back up, his eyes like saucers. "Shit, the tanker," he exclaimed. "Someone is in the tanker. Lee, stay here," he ordered and bolted through the door and deeper into the supermarket.

He bounded down the steps in the dark stairwell that led to the shop floor, his feet slapped against the linoleum flooring and his breathing echoed around him in the tight space. He took the stairs five at a time, his palms sliding along the handrail to guide him and prevent him from falling in the darkness. He burst through the double doors at the foot of the staircase and out into the brightly lit supermarket interior, illuminated by the sun beaming through the tall glass panes that ran the length of the building's front and the wide expanse of skylights above. The doors slammed shut behind him with a bang as he took off down the aisles to where the others waited and watched the dead outside.

"The truck," he shouted. "Where's the truck?"

Helen was standing at the far end, her arms folded across her chest as she turned to see Steve sprinting down the aisle and screaming something about the truck. She suddenly felt unnerved at the sight of him in a panic.

"Steve, what's up, what's happened?"

Steve skidded to a halt as Jake and the two young newcomers, Kieran and Stan, appeared from around the corner. Gasping for breath, he struggled to form his words.

"The tanker...someone is in it." He sucked in a deep breath. "Can't you hear it?"

The four of them paused and stared at the hundreds of dead figures that stood and stared back at them from beyond the tall windows. They craned their necks to see above the bobbing heads of the wall of gaunt and lifeless faces, trying to catch a glimpse of the large tanker that they had positioned at the entrance to the shopping complex the previous day.

Helen suddenly spun and grabbed Steve by the arm. The others also turned to him as they, too, heard the sound of the tanker's horn.

"Shit," Jake muttered, "someone's stealing our truck."

Steve ran forward and vaulted himself up on to one of the checkout counters, standing on his tiptoes to get a better view. He was just a couple of metres away from the glass barrier that separated him from the horrific figures outside. He saw the numerous bodies that turned away from the rest of the group at the window as they staggered towards the far end of the car park. They had been so tightly packed in at the windows, that no one had been able to notice the crowd starting to thin out from the rear, and their continuous wailing and hammering at the glass had drowned out the noise of the truck's horn blasting away.

"There it is," Steve shouted as Stan jumped up beside him. "It's just sitting there."

Stan saw the dozens of bodies that now surrounded the tanker and watched as they began to beat at its doors and steel bodywork.

"What's he doing?"

"I'm not sure, but I think whoever it is, they're trying to help us out," Steve replied, not taking his eyes away from the large fuel truck.

Steve knew they needed to act quickly before the tanker was swamped and overrun by the dead. He spun and jumped down from the checkout counter.

"Jake, go and bring Lee and John back in and tell them we're leaving out through the front. Be quick about it, too, because we don't have much time."

Jake nodded and turned into the aisle, breaking into a sprint as he headed to the rear of the supermarket and towards the staircase.

Helen stepped in close by Steve's side. She touched him lightly on the arm, gaining his attention. "You think this will work?" she asked.

Steve could see the apprehension in her eyes. He knew exactly how she was feeling because, at that moment, he had the very same fear running through his veins. But they had to move.

He nodded and motioned to the faces at the window. "I think it will. Look, you can see them thinning out. A few more minutes and we can pile into the Land Rover from the back and make a run for it to the tanker."

Kieran glanced across at Stan, raising his eyebrows, questioning the plan.

Stan shrugged back at him. "Sounds good to me, no time like the present and all that."

Steve heard their exchange and saw the doubt in Kieran's eyes.

"Look, it's the same plan we were going to use anyway. Only they're scattered out around the front rather than them all being around the back. We planned on moving when they were thinned out anyway, not when they were all completely gone."

"I don't know, Steve," Helen interrupted. "If we get stuck out front between here and the tanker, we'll be surrounded with nowhere to go."

Steve stared at the windows and bit down on his lip. "We'll be fine. As long as no one loses his or her head, we will do okay. Once we get to the tanker, whoever it is inside can just follow on behind us. They can come with us if they like, but that tanker is ours. That's the only reason we came here in the first place and I don't want to be leaving empty handed." He finished the sentence with a tone of determination and defiance in his voice.

A crash from deep within the supermarket, followed by the sound of pounding footsteps approaching from behind them, alerted Steve that Lee and John were on their way along with Jake.

Lee came to a halt in front of Steve, slightly out of breath. He peered past him and out into the car park.

"You're right, Jake, their leaving."

Steve turned to see that there were much fewer of the dead now than there had been just a minute before. He tossed the keys to the Land Rover across at Jake.

"Right, we need to move now. Jake, you're driving, mate. Everyone else, get in the back."

They turned and ran towards the broken window that was blocked by the rear door of their vehicle. Jake led the way, as he had to climb over and into the driver's seat from the rear compartment. He kept his attention focussed on the rear door ahead of him as he moved, avoiding any eye contact with the dozens of corpses that now pounded harder against the windows while their excitement grew as they watched the living human flesh dancing about just inches away from them beyond the glass barrier.

Jake leapt the last couple of metres to the rear door, fear and nerves gripping him from within. He wrenched the door open and began to scramble inside.

"Come on, hurry up," he screamed back at the others as he felt the Land Rover begin to rock and judder as the crowd swarmed and started to push against it, beating their fists at the outside in an attempt to gain entry.

Lee followed and vaulted through the rear compartment, landing in the passenger seat next to Jake who was fumbling with the keys, trying to insert them in the ignition. His hands shook and sweat poured in his eyes as fear clawed at his nerves, hindering his attempts to get the vehicle started.

"Come on, Jake. Get this bucket of bolts started, will you," Lee growled as he flinched from the dead that hammered against the window at the side of him. He turned his head and called back to the rear compartment and out to the people that were still in the supermarket.

"Come on, let's fucking go."

Jakes hands were trembling more by the second as he struggled to line the key up with the small slit in the steering column.

"Fuck, fuck," he murmured to himself from fear and frustration.

The rear of the Land Rover dipped slightly as Stan and Kieran climbed in and scurried up close behind the driver's seat. The key slid into the ignition and Jake let out a gasp of relief as he turned it. At first, the engine coughed and sputtered, then rumbled as the motor turned and the pistons began to pound down onto the cylinders, igniting the fuel and creating a chain reaction.

Jake dipped the clutch and threw the vehicle in gear, holding the clutch just below the bite in anticipation of a speedy get away once that everyone was aboard. He looked back over his shoulder and saw John, both hands holding on to the rear doorframe and hauling him up to the rear compartment.

"Come on, John, come on," he chanted to himself through gritted teeth.

A bloodied figure suddenly slammed itself into the window beside him. The skin from the lower half of its face was gone with blood and mucous dripping from its jaw as the pale dead eyes stared back at him. It hit the glass with a thud, causing Jake to flinch and squirm away with shock.

His foot slipped from the clutch and the Land Rover suddenly juddered and lurched forward a metre, and then stalled.

He looked across at Lee, his eyes wide with panic as he realised the possible consequences of his mistake. He reached down and fumbled with the keys again, trying desperately to get the engine started.

In the sudden movement of the Land Rover, John lost his balance. His foot slipped from the rear step of the vehicle, and while his hands remained gripping the frame, his body fell forward. His forehead hit the steel bumper with a thud, sending a white flash of pain that emanated from his eyes and shot into his brain. He lost his grasp on the doorframe and landed on the ground in a heap. He sprang back to his feet and attempted to reach the frame of the door again as Stan and Kieran thrust their arms out to him.

"John, come on, grab my hand!" Stan screamed as he reached out from the rear of the vehicle, willing the man forward and to safety.

The dead closed in all around him. John felt the terror rising within him and began swinging his fists and pummelling the heads that were closest as he fought his way toward the Land Rover. The dead toppled to the ground as blow after blow sent them flying with broken skulls from the impact of the powerful man's shovel-like fists. Their hands grasped and clutched at him as he powered his way through. He could feel numerous clutching fingers tugging at his clothing, trying to drag him back into the crowd, but they could not stop him; he was too strong for the dead.

John reached out, his fingers just inches away from Stan. A dark figure, its skin charred and burned leaving its features unrecognisable, lunged out from around the side of the Land Rover. It wrapped both hands around John's forearm, the bony fingers digging into his skin as it latched onto him tightly. It pulled its blackened, grinning face closer, gnashing its teeth in anticipation as it moaned loudly. Its mouth opened wide, bearing its rotting and broken teeth.

John screamed with fear, his eyes bulging from his head as he stared down into the black festering cavern of its mouth. He yanked his arm hard, trying to break the creature's hold, but it held him in a vice-like grip as it pulled itself closer, leaning its head and gaping mouth towards the thick fleshy forearm of the struggling man.

The thing moved to bite down on the soft flesh as John threw a punch at the creature's head in an attempt to pull himself away in time, but it was too late. His fist hit hard against the eye socket, crushing it beneath the blow and causing a large portion of its face to cave inward. The force of John's punch sent it sprawling, but not before it had bit down, its teeth piercing the skin.

As its head snapped backward, it tore a large portion of flesh from John's arm. He felt the skin tear and the muscle beneath being ripped from the bone as the corpse was launched away by the blow. A gush of blood shot through the air, splattering himself and the dead closest to him. He began to scream. For a second he stood there, staring at the oozing and throbbing bright red wound as he howled with pain fear and anger.

More of the dead closed in around him.

Stan and Kieran jumped from the vehicle and began kicking and punching their way through in an attempt to save John.

The dead pulled the burly man to the floor, swarming him and tearing at his flesh. John was on the ground, the dead piling in on top of him, screaming as he curled himself into a ball with dozens of wounds to his shoulders and upper arms as their teeth and clawing hands set upon him.

Kieran reached him first and gripped him under his arms as he pushed and kicked the frenzied dead aside.

"Stan," he screamed. "Grab him, Stan. Help me."

The pair of them hauled John back and bundled him into the rear of the Land Rover. The dead moved in and slammed themselves against the door as Stan managed to pull it shut, trapping and severing one of their putrid arms in the process. It dropped to the floor of the vehicle and Stan kicked it to the corner as he spat at it in disgust.

Lee was screaming and shouting with anger from the front while John, wailed and howled with pain as he bled from the numerous wounds to his body. Kieran quickly removed his jacket and began tearing the sleeves from it to use as makeshift bandages to cover John's injuries. All the time, the dead battered at the vehicle.

"Jake, get this fucking thing back to the window, Steve is still in there!" Lee shouted.

Jake began to back the vehicle up. Its engine roared as it struggled against the weight of the dead that surrounded it. A mass of gaunt and grotesque faces pressed in from all sides and their hands slapped against the glass and steel panels of the vehicle, rocking and jolting it under their blows. There were so many that Jake could no longer see the building behind them.

John continued to scream from the rear compartment as Stan and Kieran did what they could to stop the bleeding. He rolled around on the floor, pulling away in pain from anyone that tried to touch him. The floor of the Land Rover slowly began to turn red with the flow of John's blood.

"It's no use," Jake shouted. "There's too many of them."

Lee began punching the dashboard in front of him in a state of fury. He rained down his heavy blows into the hard plastic and before long, it began to dent and cave inward beneath his overwhelming assault.

"You fucking wanker, Jake. You fucking wanker!" he screamed repeatedly.

Jake slammed the vehicle into first gear and pressed down hard on the accelerator as tears streamed down his cheeks. "I'm sorry. I'm sorry, my foot slipped..."

The veins in Lee's neck threatened to burst through the skin as his rage grew. He wanted to smash his fist into Jake's face and pummel him to a bloody pulp for his mistake.

"You're a fucking wanker, Jake. You fucking useless faggot. If Steve and Helen are hurt, I will feed you to the fucking things myself," he spat with venom. "Get us over to the tanker now, you dick, then *you* can go back for them."

The Land Rover thrust itself free of the mass of bodies that had entombed it and picked up speed as it raced towards the far side of the car park, and the tanker. Jake pulled the steering wheel left and right, weaving the vehicle between the bodies that lunged for them. Some were too close to avoid and they were smashed to the ground by the impact of the steel bumper on the front and crushed beneath the heavy wheels, their ragged and broken bodies being spat out to the rear as the vehicle ploughed forward.

Steve and Helen backed away from the gaping hole in the window frame that the Land Rover had left in its sudden forward movement. They had seen John fall and become engulfed by the dead before the crowd closed in around the window frame, blocking their view. Now, the dead poured into the supermarket, barging their way past the metal frame that had once contained the large window. They staggered and lurched into the store and began to spread out as they moved in their own directions along the walkway beyond the row of checkouts close to the windows.

Steve and Helen gripped each other's hands tightly as they edged their way back towards the aisles, hoping to avoid detection as they silently made their escape. They both held their breath, placing each foot carefully and silently as they backtracked to safety. Steve fought against the urge to turn and run. His instincts screamed at him to grab Helen and charge along the aisle for the rear of the supermarket.

They were cut off, trapped.

There was probably still a large crowd of the things at the rear of the building and dozens, hundreds more poured in through the front. Stealth was their best chance of survival now. As long as the dead did not notice them, they could get through to the storage area at the rear of the building and plan their next move carefully and without making any rash decisions.

They were almost in the aisle and out of sight of the creatures that spewed into the supermarket.

The material of Steve's jacket suddenly snagged one of the shelves that jutted out from a display unit, stacked with cans of beer. The rack swayed and lurched to the side, threatening to spill its contents to the shop floor. Steve quickly reached out, holding his hand against it and correcting its movement.

Two cans, perched at the top of the pyramid shaped stack, swayed as the last of the vibrations rippled upward through the display. Steve held his breath, his eyes willing the tin cans to right themselves.

They toppled, clattering to the floor, the noise echoing throughout the supermarket like a church bell.

The dead stopped still and instantly fell silent as the last remaining resonance of the falling cans dissipated into the walls of the building. Every one of them slowly turned in the direction of the sudden commotion. Their dead eyes locked on to the two terrified living people standing just metres away from them in the aisle way.

For a moment, Steve and Helen stared back, rooted to the spot.

The closest of the dead, its grey and wrinkled flesh sagging from its face as its deep sunken eyes studied the two figures before it, sluggishly raised a withered pale hand out in front of it. Its fingers gently caressing the air between them as its mouth slowly opened and a long, low haunting moan seeped from deep within its throat.

The rest joined it in its mournful chorus, the supermarket suddenly erupting with the lament of the dead.

"Shit," Steve gasped as he began to turn, dragging Helen with him. "Run."

22

Johnny watched the events unfold in front of the large building ahead of him. He sat clutching the wheel of the tanker, staring out through the windshield and urging the people that were fleeing from within the supermarket to move faster.

The dead that had been attracted away from the main swarm around the supermarket entrance by his continuous horn blasts pounded at the body of the large heavy truck. Their dull thumps echoed around in the cab, sounding like a bass drum in the distance as they surrounded and assaulted the tanker. There was no way they could get in, he knew that, but it would not be long before there were so many of them that he would not be able to move the vehicle.

"Come on, hurry," he murmured to himself as he watched the zebra-painted Land Rover begin smashing its way out through the crowd that swamped it.

It lurched and rocked as the dead threw themselves against it, desperate to get at the people inside as they clawed at the hard exterior and windows.

Slowly, it fought its way through, its engine powering the wheels forward and roaring with the strain as it began to plough over the walking corpses that littered the car park of the supermarket.

Beyond them, he could see hundreds of the grotesque lifeless figures pouring into the building through the open window and into the dark interior. They fought and jostled against each other, their arms flailing and clawing at the bodies closest to them in an attempt to climb through the empty frame and into the store.

The escaping vehicle was approaching fast now. It swayed between the reaching, lurching creatures that turned to meet it as it came closer, throwing them into the air and to the side like discarded trash as they were hit by the hard exterior and tossed to the side.

He witnessed as one body stepped directly into the path of the oncoming vehicle. The bumper smashed into its lower limbs, snapping the bones into a million fragments as its body folded forward. Its face smashed down on the hood of the Land Rover, its skull shattering and splattering the windshield with rotted grey matter and congealed, almost black, blood. The remainder of it was dragged beneath the wheels, its body being mangled and crushed, and spat out behind in a bloody minced pulp of flesh and bone.

Johnny could now see the driver of the vehicle. His eyes were wide with terror behind the wheel as the passenger thrashed and screamed in the seat next to him. He looked across to the footwell of the passenger seat of the tanker. Simon sat slouched with his back against the door, his head thrown back and his eyes shut tight as he clutched at his bloodied and swollen shoulder and neck. He sucked in deep breaths through his gritted teeth and he winced with each intake of air.

"Simon," Johnny spoke. "Simon, can you hear me?"

Simon said nothing, his eyes remaining screwed tightly shut as he sucked in another breath, his face grimacing. He nodded.

"The people from the supermarket are on their way," Johnny said as he glanced back out the window to check on the progress of the Land Rover. He looked back down at the dying man whom he had only met two days earlier, but already, considered him as his only friend.

"We will go with them and get you some help, okay?"

Simon banged the back of his head against the passenger door, adding to the dull thumps of the dead outside.

"You know there's no help for me, Johnny," he gasped. "I've been bitten and you know what happens to people who get bitten. You've seen it happen, you said so yourself," he said between clenched teeth.

Johnny felt helpless. He wanted to believe that his friend could be helped, that maybe he could survive.

"Don't say that, Simon. Don't give up."

Simon's head slouched forward, his eyes staring down at the floor between his feet. He slowly raised his head again and looked back up at the scruffy little man sitting behind the wheel. The tears filled his swollen red eyes again as he spoke.

"I'm fucked, Johnny. I won't make it," he said with a shake of his head.

Johnny turned away, his heartstrings tugging at him as he realised that Simon was right and had already given up.

The vehicle from the supermarket raced up and came to a screeching halt beside them. The dead around the tanker turned and staggered toward the new commotion and began to slam their hands and their bodies against the Land Rover. The black and white zebra-striped paintwork was smeared with the dark brown and red handprints of the hundreds of rotting bodies that had been pounding against it. Anything that protruded from the vehicle, such as wing mirror frames and wheel arches, were coated and caked in clumps of clothing and flesh that had been torn from the countless dead that had clambered against it.

Johnny reached down, gripping the lever to the window and began turning it, the glass slowly lowering in jerky movements. He leaned in close to the small gap at the top of the window and shouted out to the occupants of the other vehicle.

"We have to go. We will follow you."

The terrified face of the man sitting behind the wheel just stared back at him with bulging eyes as the dead continued to press their faces against the glass beside him. He was frozen, his eyes clearly showing that he was traumatised and in complete shock.

Johnny saw the passenger lean across and grab hold of him by the scruff of the collar, shaking him violently in his seat. The passenger's hands waved animatedly as he screamed something to the petrified driver. Suddenly, they began to clamber over one another as they changed seats, the angry man now sitting behind the wheel. He glanced back up at Johnny through the blood and filth smeared window, anger and rage burning in his eyes as he put the vehicle into gear.

Both vehicles were surrounded and close to being engulfed. They rocked and shook as the horde of reanimated dead slammed their bodies against them, wailing and moaning as they tore at each other for position closest to the living people trapped inside. Their cold grey and rotting hands reached up, grasping at the windows, their nails grating against the glass as they attempted to claw their way inside.

Johnny heard the rumbling engine of the Land Rover change gear and the revolutions rise as the driver pressed down hard on the accelerator. It suddenly bounded forward, dragging some of the closest bodies beneath its wheels and undercarriage as it churned them like meat in a grinder, crushing and mixing blood and bone into a pulp.

The wheels of the Land Rover spun against the soft tissue of the dead, struggling for traction as the suspension rocked beneath the weight of the crowd. The tyres suddenly gripped against the hard tarmac of the road and shot the vehicle forward with a cloud of black smoke billowing from its exhaust.

Gripping the wheel and releasing the brake with a loud hiss, Johnny powered the tanker forward, ploughing the dead into the ground and turning the heavy truck in a wide arc to follow on behind the Land Rover.

They headed for the exit, the dead staggering after them, reaching out and wailing loudly in frustration as they lurched after the living that fled from their grasp.

The Land Rover and tanker raced away, turning onto the main road that fed from the slipway to the entrance of the supermarket. They bobbed and weaved between the abandoned vehicles that littered the slip road and the lumbering creatures that stepped out in front of them as they attempted to reach out and grab hold of the speeding vehicles.

A short distance later, on an empty stretch of road, the zebra-painted vehicle stopped. Johnny brought the tanker to a halt behind it with a screech of tyres and a loud hiss of hydraulic brakes. He moved the gears to neutral and remained seated behind the wheel as he watched the driver of the Land Rover climb out, and turn to look at him.

The man stormed towards the tanker, his face contorted and red with rage. Johnny felt fear crawling up the length of his back as he stared back into the wild eyes of the approaching figure.

He wanted to climb out and run away. He feared what this man was about to do to him as he was clearly overcome with emotion. He glanced across at Simon, slumped in the footwell and still clenching his teeth with pain as he gripped the gaping wound in his shoulder, the blood seeping from between his fingers.

The man approached the tanker; his eyes glaring up at Johnny and making him want to look anywhere but straight at him as he attempted to sink himself deeper into his seat. The door was wrenched open and the raging man stood there, his face glowing red and foam forming at the corners of his mouth. His wild eyes glowered at Johnny as he scowled with the veins in his forehead threatening to leap from his flesh.

"Who the fuck are you?" he spat.

Johnny felt his throat tighten, his words becoming lodged in his chest and unable to escape as an all-consuming fear raced through him.

The man gripped the door, pulling himself up towards him, his teeth shining in the sunlight as he peeled his lips back over them.

"I said, who the fuck are you?"

"I...I am, Johnny," he stammered.

The cab of the tanker dipped to the side slightly as the man heaved his self upward and onto the step of the door so that his face was just inches away from him. Johnny could feel his hot breath against the side of his face. The man craned his neck, his eyes narrowing as he inspected the interior of the driver's compartment. His gaze fell on the body of Simon, slumped in the corner.

He looked back at Johnny and growled, "The pair of you out, now."

"But...but, my friend..., he is hurt. One of those things bit him," Johnny tried to explain, gesturing toward Simon. "Please, we only wanted to help you. We don't want any trouble. We saw that you were trapped and we came to help."

"Out, now," the man demanded again, his eyes speaking volumes and telling them that there was no room for negotiation.

Johnny climbed down from the tanker. His knees trembled as he stepped onto the tarmac below. His throat was dry and he glanced about at the area around him. They were in the middle of an overpass, overlooking the slip road that filtered onto the supermarket car park area. He could see the large building of the store at the far end and the countless figures that continued to swarm the hole in the window and pour inside. Hundreds more were headed for the exit ramp, slowly making their way towards them.

Three more men climbed out from the Land Rover and approached with quick and determined bounds. Johnny felt his heart skip a beat and his knees threatened to give as he watched them draw nearer. He wanted to run, to get away from them and go back to hiding in his house or walking amongst the dead as he continued about his business, as he had always done, but he could not leave his friend to whatever fate these men decided to deal out to him. Johnny would stay by Simon's side. He had already decided that to himself.

The first to reach them, a slim built man in his mid twenties, called out. "Lee, calm down. He helped us out of that place, remember?"

"Shut up, Jake," the angry man named Lee snapped back. "It's your fault that Steve is stuck back there and John is hurt."

The two younger men, both wearing black hooded jackets and a look of malice on their faces, stood to the side of Jake. They glanced from Johnny and back to Lee and they looked unsure of what to do.

"Come on, Lee, it wasn't his fault, it could have been any one of us that was driving the truck. Jake did okay. It was an accident, Lee," one of them said as he reached out and rested his hand on Jake's shoulder in a show of support for him.

Lee turned on him, his teeth bared. "And who are you, Stan, Jake's new fuck chicken?"

He turned back to Johnny who stood in silence, watching the exchange between the men.

"You, get your friend out of there and go. You're not coming with us," he looked around at the others. "We're going back for Steve and Helen."

"Come on, Lee, you can't just leave him here. He helped us and…" Jake began to protest against Lee's decision.

Lee whirled and bounded towards him.

Jake began backtracking, raising his hands up in front of him, ready to defend him against an assault. Lee cocked his elbow backward and clenched his fist as he closed in, aiming his blow at Jake's face.

The two hooded men suddenly jumped forward before he could launch the punch, enveloping Lee in a two-man bear hug. The three of them crashed to the floor as Lee thrashed and struggled between them. He flailed his arms and kicked his feet, clawing at the eyes of Stan and headbutting him as they rolled and tussled in a heap.

One of the hooded men jumped up, stepped back and began launching a series of heavy blows aimed at Lee's head. They struck with sickening thuds as they rained down on him mercilessly. Lee's head bounced from the tarmac, a stream of blood shooting from his nose and mouth then. His body was suddenly still.

Stan unravelled his arms from around Lee and climbed to his feet, wiping at the blood that gushed from his own nose. The three of them stood for a moment, staring down at the limp form on the ground.

"Sorry, Jake, but we had to do it. He was out of control, mate. He would've killed you, you know that," Stan spoke.

Jake nodded as he stared at Lee's face. It was smeared in blood with a large gash on his forehead.

"Is he okay, Kieran?" he asked, turning to the young man that had punched Lee unconscious.

"He'll be okay," Kieran replied as he squatted down and inspected Lee. "He'll have a headache when he wakes up and probably, he'll want to kill me but at least he's under control, for now."

Stan turned to Jake, "Look, I know that Helen and Steve are your friends, but we can't go back in there after them."

Jake nodded, his eyes remaining fixed on the unconscious Lee at his feet. "Okay," he announced, looking back up and focussing his attention on Johnny. "Your friend is hurt, did you say?"

Johnny nodded.

Jake walked to the edge of the road towards the concrete barrier of the overpass. He peered out at the supermarket and saw the hundreds of bodies that shuffled around the car park and the hundreds more that spewed into the buildings and onto the exit road. There was no sign of Steve or Helen.

His heart felt heavy. He felt responsible for what had happened. It was his fault. Steve and Helen were missing, probably dead, and John was bitten. Everyone knew what happened to the people that were bitten by the infected dead, and it was all his fault.

"Okay," he said turning to the others. "We need to leave. Maybe Steve and Helen will be all right but we cannot stay here. Those things are headed this way and we need to take care of John and Lee," he turned to Johnny, "and your friend."

23

"What we got here then, Robbie?" Tobias shouted up to the driver.

The flatbed truck pulled up as the soldier at the gates slammed the heavy steel barrier back into place with a loud reverberating clang. Its large wheels crunched against the gravel of the parking bay beneath them as the four tonne truck came to a halt directly in front of him. The driver threw his door open and jumped out whistling cheerfully, his high pitched notes drifting through the air as he strolled toward Tobias.

"A truckload of these dead heads for you, boss," Robbie replied as he came to a halt in front of his friend and commander.

He removed the magazine from his rifle, pulled back on the cocking lever, clearing the chamber and catching the ejected round in mid-air with a lightning speed swipe of his hand as he continued to whistle.

"No survivors?" Tobias asked as he lit a cigarette, the blue-grey plumes of smoke billowing around him.

Robbie snorted and spat a wad of phlegm onto the gravel below his feet. "Didn't see any, boss, but to be honest we weren't exactly going door to door."

Tobias nodded as he eyed the man to his right. He had known Robbie a long time. Though he was lean and always looked a little underweight, Tobias knew how fierce and strong the man was when the time called for it. He had a natural core strength that Tobias had never seen in any other man, punching and lifting much more than was expected from a man of his slight build. In his younger days, Robbie had been the Welter Weight boxing champion for the army and in thirty-seven bouts, he had never lost, and twenty-eight of them were by knock out.

The pair of them had joined the army on the same recruit intake, and though they were originally from different ends of the British Isles, they had struck up a strong friendship and had been close ever since. In the fourteen years that they had known each other, they had been inseparable. They climbed the ranks and attended most of their courses together, always trying to outdo one another as they competed for dominance in their friendship, but Tobias had always had the edge on Robbie, something that the other bitterly refused to accept.

Every operation the battalion had been on, Tobias and Robbie had ended up in the same platoon or company together. They fought side by side during the invasions of Afghanistan and Iraq early on at the turn of the millennium, and they were both Platoon Sergeants in the same company when their battalion was sent in as part of the coalition during the invasion of Iran.

When the plague hit, their battalion had been decimated in the battles for the Midlands in the opening stages of the outbreak. At the time, no one really understood the problem and those that did never passed the information all the way to the bottom. As a result, soldiers were sent in to fight an enemy that could not be beaten. The dead would never retreat or cower away from any amount of devastating gunfire and they would never throw their hands up in surrender.

The pair of them had fought side by side, watching their friends fall all around them and being torn to shreds as the dead overwhelmed their positions. When they were finally pulled back, what remained of the battalion was able to fit in just one of the sixteen Chinook helicopters that were sent in to rescue them.

Subsequently, Tobias found himself being left in charge of a platoon of men that had been thrown together from the battered remnants of other companies. They were quickly and half-heartedly resupplied and sent to a small Territorial Army barracks on the outskirts of a large town. There, they joined a handful of mechanics and radio specialists and were told to defend the perimeter and await further orders.

Those orders never arrived, until a week ago.

For months, they listened as the army and government lost control of the country against the onslaught of the dead. They heard the dying transmissions of whole regiments that were overrun and consumed by the hordes of rotting corpses that attacked any living thing they saw. With despair, they bore witness to the death of their country and their once proud armed forces.

They looked on, helpless as the number of the dead grew in the town beyond their walls. They opened their gates to the flocks of civilians that fled the chaos, giving them shelter and a degree of safety behind the high, reinforced fortifications of the barracks. Eventually, there was no one left to rescue. From a population of around eighty thousand, less than a hundred had made it to the protection of the base.

Tobias and his men were forgotten about in the mayhem. Whenever they managed to gain communications with another unit, or the recently formed Mainland Joint Operation's Command, nobody could give them any information or suggest when they were likely to be resupplied or reinforced.

The MJOC had been set up to command and control the evacuation of the military units of the country to the islands that had been set up as Forward Operating Bases. Eventually, it would be the main Operations Room for the counter offensive. That was the concept at least.

The chaos was spreading too fast and the control element was nonexistent as units either disappeared from the map board, or deserted to save their own lives after being given insane orders to recapture this town or that city. Tobias and his men looked on in disbelief as the high command and their staff panicked and ordered units, some real and some completely imagined or no longer in existence, into battle. It was almost like witnessing the stupidity of the First World War over again. The brass ordered assault after assault until eventually there were no more troops to send into the fray.

The Prime Minister was said to have crumbled and collapsed into tears over the large map board in the Operations Room, as he was given a tactical briefing of the military situation, position and capabilities by the high command at MJOC headquarters, stationed on the Isle of Man. He had been carried away never to be seen again, and rumour had it he had suffered a nervous breakdown. More rumours circled that a rogue Major General had ordered him to be executed for cowardice.

When the MJOC lost control of the mainland and retreated to the safety of the islands, Tobias and his men were left to rot. Their calls went unanswered as the radio operators sat for hours, days and weeks, signalling for help and information. The air was dead and all they received in reply was the hiss of static. Eventually, they gave up trying to contact anyone and the radio operators fell in to a listening watch, working in shifts around the clock, listening for any stray transmissions.

The ad-hoc unit was close to falling apart. Some men jumped the walls while others drank and fought each other. Tobias saw what needed to be done. The men had lost hope and leaving them to their own devices was out of the question. At the end of the world, with no one to control them, a bunch of armed soldiers was a dangerous thing. They needed to carry on as an army unit, with a command structure and focus, discipline and orders.

He instilled a new sense of pride in them, pointing out the fact that where other units had succumbed to the dead and perished, they had held out. They took on the duty not only to protect the civilians within their walls, but to live side by side with them. They became a community with the survivors of the town bringing their own skills and expertise to the table. The soldiers, of course, provided the security and carried out the hazardous tasks of searching for supplies, or keeping the hordes of dead away from the walls.

More, personal, relationships had flourished between the soldiers and the refugees. Many found comfort in each other as they came to terms with the losses they had suffered and the harsh realities of the new world. Friendships had arisen as they all worked together and toiled to make the best of what they had and inevitably, deeper, more physical relationships had blossomed. Even Tobias looked forward to his evenings when he and Katie, the long legged raven-haired barrister, could be alone together.

The troops and refugees soon realised that they were on their own, and their future was up to them. A garrison town mentality arose, centred on their continued independent coexistence and survival and the relationship between military and civilian. They had all but forgotten about the government and the planned counter offensive and its build up that they had seen so many news reports about before the transmissions stopped.

That was until a week ago, when one of the radio operators from the night shift had come banging on Tobias' door in the early hours of the morning. He was flustered and struggled with his words as he attempted to gain control of his composure. He waved a piece of paper in front of him excitedly as he stammered.

"Okay, just take a breath and tell me what the problem is," Tobias had said as he ruffled his hair and rubbed the sleep from his eyes.

"It's a message, we got a message."

Tobias' eyes had shot open, suddenly shaking the swirling fog from his still sleeping brain as he snatched the piece of paper from the young radio operator. He read the message and raced back to his room, banging into furniture as he jumped into his clothes and hitting the intercom at the same time to alert Robbie and the other section commanders, telling them to meet him in the radio room.

The message had been sent in Morse code and read:
Sierra one three, this is MJOC.
Counter Offensive H-hour: 0600 28th August 2015.
Collect six specimens of reanimated from your Area of Operation ready for collection.
Standby for air resupply and reinforcement,
Wait Out.

"Why Morse code, Tobias?" Robbie asked, reading the piece of paper as they gathered around the radios in their Operations Room.

"No idea, maybe the brass has gotten paranoid and thinks the dead have learned to read and write?"

Dozens of messages streamed in as the radio operators scribbled them down on pieces of paper, handing each one back to Tobias and Robbie. Only one had arrived with their call sign at the top, *Sierra One Three*. The remainder was the same message repeated over again, but for different units.

"Jesus, I didn't realise there were so many of us left on the mainland," Tobias remarked as he looked down at the ever-growing stack of messages piled at the side of the radio operators. More were being added by the minute.

One of the radio operators leaned back from his chair and looked over at Tobias.

"To be honest, I think most of those call signs don't exist anymore. Only two have replied so far, three including us." He looked back down at the logbook in front of him and read, "Whisky One Two in the south east, and Romeo Five in the north."

"And we're slap bang in the middle," Robbie muttered. "We haven't exactly got a good forward operating base network to launch a counter attack from, have we?" he said as he worked out their dispositions in his head.

"Has anything come through about the operation, where they intend to start the break in, or a mission statement or warning order?" Tobias asked.

The radio operator shook his head, "Nothing as yet. Just that Morse code message telling us to stand by is all we've received."

Since the coded message, nothing had been sent addressed directly to Tobias and his men but a steady stream of radio traffic grew in the earphones of the radio operators. They studied their maps and plotted what they heard over the airwaves, giving them an estimate of what was happening around the country. From what they could surmise, London, Nottingham, Leeds and Edinburgh were the break in points. They would be the first places that the task force would attack.

It made sense to Tobias, because those four large cities were linked with the same major highway running the length of the country. Once they were cleared and secured, they would act as Forward Operating Bases and the main highway that linked them would be a solid linier supply route, making it easier for troop movements as they broke out to begin the clear up and reoccupation of the mainland, one town and city at a time.

At least, in Tobias' mind, that was the plan. With the top brass and their behaviour and strategy in the closing days of the mainland evacuations, anything was possible and it may have just been a fluke that the MJOC had chosen those four cities.

They listened and waited, expecting to hear the sound of helicopters and bombers in the sky above them, but none came. In the meantime, the men of the base began preparations for the break out. They checked their equipment, their weapons and vehicles and settled in to the age old *'Hurry up and Wait'* maxim of the British Army.

Tobias looked up at the truck. He could see the filth encrusted bobbing heads of the dead that were on-board and watched as their rotting hands reached over the side, trying to climb the steel walls to which they were chained. They thrashed and moaned as they struggled against their bonds, watching the living people that moved about, just out of reach beyond the tailgate at the back of the truck.

"Okay, Robbie, let's get them in the cage." He sighed as he exhaled a cloud of smoke from his lungs.

They had cleared out one of the caged mechanics tool stores to house the reanimated bodies of the six specimens that they had been ordered to capture. No one cherished the idea of keeping them anywhere near where they ate or slept in the main part of the barracks, so the mechanics cleared out their equipment from one of the large stores in the garages to keep them secured.

Tobias had inspected the makeshift cell beforehand while the mechanics reinforced it and added welded steel plates around any potential weak points. He checked and ensured that the steel cage would hold and arranged for a two man guard to be present at all times, throughout the day and night. The last thing any of them wanted was six of the dead on the loose within the walls of the barracks.

The truck slowly backed up to the entrance of the cage, its rear nudging the steel frame with an echoing bang as the driver made sure that there was no gap for the dead to escape through. The men standing on top of the cab began herding the dead towards the tailgate, pushing and shoving them with their long poles.

The creatures twisted and whirled, thrashing their arms and grasping at the long staffs that prodded them. A couple of the men almost lost their balance as their pole was jerked and wrenched in the hands of the dead and they came close to tumbling into the back of the truck amongst the hungry ghouls.

As they were pushed to the end, towards the cage, the dead slipped and tumbled from the bed of the truck, hitting the concrete floor with wet sounding slaps, their joints dislocating and bones breaking as they made contact with the hard floor. They writhed and floundered as they attempted to stand up, becoming entangled with each other as the next body fell from the truck, landing on top of them as it was shoved from the tailgate.

Tobias watched the progress and eyed the soldier that stood by, ready to slide the heavy gate shut once the last of the creatures were secure inside. He could see the fear in his eyes. The beads of sweat poured down his forehead as he gripped the heavy steel door. He glanced back up at Tobias, his pale moist skin reflecting in the beams of sunlight that poured through the large shutter doors of the garage. Tobias nodded to him and the man returned the gesture, assuring him that regardless of his fear, he was steadfast in his duty.

The walking corpses lunged back at the opening from within the cage, attempting to climb the tailgate of the truck. They beat their hands against the cage in frustration and rage as they realised that they were trapped, unable to climb the obstacle and get at the living people they could see before them.

They moaned and wailed loudly, their voices echoing around in the long open-plan building of the mechanics workshop. Tobias felt a shiver run down his spine. He did not envy the job of the men that were to stand guard over the dead, listening to their ghostly poignant moans bouncing from the walls and high ceiling all day and night.

There was just one of them left in the truck, and then they could slam the heavy steel-barred door shut and feel secure again. Tobias stood on top of the cage and watched as Robbie hefted his long pole and aimed it at the emaciated corpse. It did not get agitated or flail its arms like the others. It did not even wail or moan. It just stood there, looking back at Tobias, its eyes fixed on him and studying him.

Robbie's pole poked it in the back. It spun, sidestepping the second thrust and glaring back at the man on top of the cab of the truck. Robbie lunged again, this time making contact with the creature's midriff and knocking it backward towards the tailgate. It growled back at Robbie, a low hoarse grumble rattling from its throat, but still it did not try to attack or even approach the living it saw all around it.

"This is the one that wanted to fight us when we found it hiding in a ditch, Toby," Robbie called down with a grin.

Tobias looked back at him, his brow furrowed. "Hiding in a ditch?"

"Yeah," Robbie nodded. "It was stuck in the mud and was hiding from us, as though it was scared. When we tried to capture it, it stood its ground and tried to fight back. It took three of us to get the noose around its neck and into the truck."

He swung the pole again, aiming it to whack the figure on the side of its head. The dead man swayed and ducked his head, the pole sailing harmlessly above him.

"Fuck, did you see that?" Robbie exclaimed.

Tobias nodded slowly, his eyes fixed on the defiant corpse standing on the bed of the truck. "Yeah, I saw it," he replied slowly with a nod.

He had never seen one of the reanimated bodies behave in such a way. For one of them to be in such close proximity to the living without being excited to the point of smashing itself to pieces to get at them, was completely unheard of. He had seen thousands, millions of them and they all reacted in the same way when they saw warm living flesh. But the one that stood on the back of the truck, eyeing them with what he could only describe as a degree of intelligence, was an exception to the rule.

"Come on, dickhead," Robbie taunted as he began jabbing the creature again. "Get in the cage with the rest of your friends. There's a good lad."

"Hang on, Robbie. Leave him be a moment," Tobias ordered, raising his hand as he stared down at the body that stood its ground. He squatted down on top of the cage, lowering his profile to a less threatening stance. The creature followed him with its unblinking eyes, its body turning slightly so that it remained facing him, but angled ready to defend itself.

Tobias was at the very edge of the cage, the toes of his boots just inches away from the frame and easily within reach if the reanimated corpse was to lunge at him. Their eyes remained locked as they scrutinized one another. There was nothing in the dead man's mannerisms that indicated to Tobias that he wanted to attack, or hurt him in any way.

"Careful, boss," Robbie called from the roof of the cab.

The corpse turned to glance back at the man wielding the pole. He eyed the long staff that he held in his hand then looked to the sides of the truck, as though contemplating making a run for it.

"It's okay, Robbie. If it wanted me, it would've tried it by now. Look at it; have you ever seen one like this?"

Robbie raised the pole and grunted, "They all look the frigging same to me, Toby. You're not after making it your pet are you?"

The head of the creature slowly rotated as it examined the frame of the cage and the five other clambering corpses that hammered against the tailgate and rattled at the steel bars of the enclosure. It looked back up at the man crouching above him.

Tobias felt a cold hand run down between his shoulders and along his spine. What he saw in the creature's eyes was hatred and revulsion. He clearly saw that unmistakable emotion etched across its face and it was not aimed at him. It was revulsion for the other corpses that were clambering at the cage below.

It glanced back at Robbie and then back to Tobias. It remained defiant but it realised that it had no way of escape. It took a small step closer to the cage, its eyes narrowing as it peered into the darkness of the enclosure. It glanced back up at Tobias, and then taking another careful step towards the makeshift cell, it reached out and gripped the frame of the door. It kept its eyes locked on Tobias as it moved and began to lower itself to a crouch, holding on to the sides of the truck and gently easing itself into the enclosure.

The soldier at the side of the cage forced the door shut, its frame rattled and banged loudly in the garage as it sealed the entrance, trapping the six dead inside.

Tobias stepped down on to the truck and squatted, peering into the gloomy cage and watching the corpses as they hurled themselves at him, thrusting their hands through the bars and clutching their fingers in an effort to grab hold of him.

He looked past them; the dead that clambered at the front of the cage held no interest for him, but the dark figure at the rear of the cell, standing alone in the corner and staring back at him, did.

24

"They left us," Helen screamed as she was dragged through the aisles by Steve.

She could feel his hand wrapped tightly around her wrist, his grip almost cutting off the circulation of her blood to her fingers.

Steve's feet pounded on the linoleum floor as he raced towards the double doors that led to the storage area of the supermarket. The dead moaned in unison behind them as they staggered after them. Their lament echoed throughout the store, bouncing along the narrow aisles. Their footsteps skidded and scraped along the ground, shelving and displays being toppled as they crashed into them in their haste as they saw the energetic movements of the escaping couple.

"They had to, they had to leave us."

Steve gripped Helen's hand tighter as he dragged her along behind him. He was just metres away from the large double doors at the end of the aisle now, his stride already shortening as he braced himself, ready to launch his shoulder against them.

The doors flew open with a crash as they rebounded off the wall of the dark staircase. The noise bounced from one wall to the next as it travelled upwards into the gloom. Steve paused for just a moment, creeping forward as he peered up the steps, squinting through the darkness and double-checking that there was nothing waiting for them at the top before they began their ascent.

"Okay, we're clear," he said as he turned to Helen.

She was standing on her tiptoes, peering through the small glass windows set two thirds of the way up in the large heavy double doors. The supermarket was already overflowing with the dead. Hundreds of them poured in through the gaping hole in the window. They slowly made their way along the aisles, reaching out and groaning as they headed towards the doors that they had watched their prey escape through.

Helen turned to Steve as she felt him tug on her arm again. "Where are we going? There are still hundreds of them out back, isn't there?"

Steve was climbing the stairs, two at a time, as he led her by the hand, keeping her behind him in case anything sprang up in front of them.

"We have no choice. We can't stay here and that's the only other way out that I know of," he gasped between breaths.

His heart was pounding and his chest heaved with the sudden strain and exertion. He poured with sweat and the adrenalin and fear coursed through his veins like fire.

"Hopefully, the ones at the back of the building will have heard the commotion at the front and followed it."

They rounded the first flight of stairs and began to climb the next. They could see the sunlit doorway above them that led to the corridor containing the offices and then out onto the steel walkway above the loading bay.

There was a sudden crash below them. Steve stopped just long enough to lean over the handrail and see the dead that spilled into the stairwell. Their moans and footsteps crept up towards them, sending shivers down the spines of Steve and Helen as they felt the icy cold hand of terror grip them. They were packed in, shoulder to shoulder, and Steve watched as countless heads, some almost bare skull and others, their hair matted and filled with filth and grime, began to clamber up the steps.

"Come on, faster Helen, they're in," he gasped.

They cleared the last step and sprinted through the doorway of the office corridor as the haunting sound of the dead chased them up the stairwell, snapping at their heels. The pair of them raced towards the bright sunlight at the far end.

Steve skidded to a halt as he reached the exit at the end that led on to the steel balcony. He quickly glanced back, checking that they were still alone in the corridor and that none of the creatures chasing them had yet made it up the two flights of stairs. He could hear them, tramping on the stairs as their heavy clumsy feet powered them upwards, but there was still no sign of them.

Helen gingerly stepped forward, creeping towards the railing of the walkway, her light steps making an almost inaudible clunk on the steel grate, but it was loud enough for the sea of dead faces below to hear.

Their heads shot upward, their flat lifeless eyes locking on Helen and Steve and their wails rising as they saw the two people at the doorway above them. The crowd surged and swayed, tussling and pushing at one another as they struggled for position, their arms flailing in the air above them.

"Shit," Steve growled. "We're stuck. There's too many of them."

Helen looked back along the corridor then stepped forward onto the balcony, leaning over to get a view of the entire loading bay, searching for somewhere they could climb down and remain out of reach from the hungry pack.

The dead below her screamed and wailed, anticipating tearing into her flesh as she leaned out, just out of reach above them. She pulled back and began eyeing the roof and the ledge, then ran along the edge of it as it formed an overhanging sheltered outcrop above the loading area.

Steve had taken a few steps back into the dimly lit corridor. He pulled at one of the handles of the office doors, checking to see whether it was locked. The handle turned and the door swung open with a creak. The air rushed in and mixed with the stale atmosphere within the room, causing particles of dust to fly up to the shaft of light pouring in through the open doorway and loose papers blow from the desk. The sunlight from outside in the loading bay penetrated the room, revealing a small cubicle enclosure containing just a computer desk and a couple of office chairs.

"We could hide in here," he whispered back to Helen as though he did not want the dead to hear his plan.

Helen turned to look back in the corridor, seeing Steve standing by the open door to the small room staring back at her. She shook her head dismissively. The very thought of hiding and waiting to be discovered terrified her more than running in the open with the things chasing her.

"No, Steve, they'll find us and we will have nowhere to go."

Steve stepped away from the small office and out onto the steel walkway. The echoing sound of footsteps at the top of the stairs marked the arrival of the dead in the corridor. In the gloom, the dark bobbing mass of silhouetted, growling creatures slowly advanced on the brightly lit doorway, towards them.

Helen reached out, grasping the thick steel vertical beams that supported the balcony and stretched all the way up to the rooftop.

"Come on, Steve, we're going up."

Reaching her hands high and gripping the support beam, she heaved herself up and climbed onto the rail of the steel walkway, her hands tightly clutched around the girder. She bent her legs slightly and pushed off the railing with her feet, shimmying up the thick steel shaft. With all the strength she could muster, she pulled herself upward, thrusting one hand over the other as she quickly gained height away from the walkway and Steve.

"Come on then, what are you waiting for?" she grunted with the effort.

Steve watched her as she began her ascent. Regardless of the situation they were in, he was impressed. Though he was no male chauvinist, he had seldom seen a woman with such upper body strength and able to power up an obstacle with such ease on the first attempt. He doubted that most men could even do it and he wondered if he could manage it himself. Helen was only a slight woman. Her body, though perfectly formed and toned, did not appear to have that kind of power, but the headway that she was making up the support beam told him that Helen was far from being a weakling.

He hurled himself forward at the railing, reaching out at the same time and grasping the beam, just below Helen's feet. He glanced back down at the faces that stared up at him as they swarmed around the loading area directly below him. He looked back along the corridor, into the gloom. Dozens of figures loomed out from the darkness, their grey faces devoid of all life and their thrashing arms closing on him fast. They bounced from wall to wall, their rotting bodies leaving long black smears on the white paint.

As Helen had done, he pushed himself upward from the railing, giving himself a metre's start on the beam. He grunted and gasped with each heave as he thrust hand over hand, pulling himself upward.

Helen was already at the lip to the roof of the building. She threw her arms over on to the asphalt, gripping the ledge between her elbows and chest and forcing her shoulders upward. She took in a deep breath and rocked her legs from side to side as she built up the momentum for the final leap. With a cry, she threw her legs out to the side of her, the toes of her right foot making contact with the ledge of the roof and gripping it as she began to heave herself up to safety. She pushed herself onto the rooftop, rolling away from the edge and gasping with relief as she lay staring up to the cloudy sky.

Steve was half of the way up, the dead now hammering against the beam below him as they spilled out from the corridor and onto the steel walkway. Their clumsy footsteps clattered against the grating of the balcony and echoed around in the loading bay, joining the crescendo of cries and moans from the dead below.

More of them spewed out from the building and onto the rickety balcony that shook and trembled beneath their combined weight. Steve felt the vibrations travelling up the beam and into his arms. He could hear the creaks and groans of the fixtures as they strained to bear the mass of bodies that threatened to collapse the entire structure. Brackets began to separate from the wall as the rusted bolts became loose in the crumbling cement that held them in place. Steve watched in horror as the support beam that he climbed suddenly jutted out from the wall of the building.

He felt the steel support that his body was wrapped around judder and rock as the dead that were just below him pulled and heaved at it, pushing it away from the wall just a little further with each thrust. He reached another hand upwards, wrapping it around the beam and heaving himself a little further as he attempted to escape the gaping maws of the creatures that lingered just inches below the soles of his feet.

More bodies piled out from the door and onto the walkway. The balcony was now so packed that the weight of the dead that were still in the corridor, pushing forward as they attempted to reach the open doorway, caused some of the creatures to topple over the railing. They landed on the heads of the others below in the loading bay. They were carried off like rock stars that were stage diving, as grasping hands pushed and pulled them aside.

The material of Steve's jacket slipped against the smooth metal of the column to which he clung. His hands grasped tighter around the beam as his body began to slide downwards. He kicked and thrashed with his legs in desperation, hoping they would grip the slippery steel beam. He felt his shin hit the hard metal, the pain shooting up along his nervous system and screaming inside his brain.

His fingers were losing their grip. Their knuckles and tips were white where they pressed against the support beam and the blood was forced out from them as his grasp slowly weakened. His eyes were shut tight as he grimaced and groaned in an attempt to muster the strength to lunge upward and gain a better hold.

His grip was weakening and his body was slowly beginning to slide downwards, towards the waiting corpses below him.

Helen reached over from the roof, leaning as far forward as she dared, she stretched out to Steve, her fingertips brushing against the collar of his jacket. She leaned further, glancing back and checking the position of her feet as she grunted from the strain. She felt the material curl under the joints of her fingers as she closed them tightly together. With all her strength, she began to heave.

Steve felt the sudden lift as Helen clutched at his jacket. It was enough for Steve to risk a fresh leap at the beam above him. With a huge effort, he shot upward, his hands clapping against the cold metal of the strut. With Helen's help, he shimmied upward and towards the ledge.

As Steve reached the top, Helen gripped him by the shoulders while he threw his legs up on-to the lip of the roof. She yanked him backward, a loud grunt escaping from her throat with the strain as Steve tumbled forward on to the roof, collapsing on top of her. They both lay there, entangled with each other, panting for breath as the frustrated reanimated bodies below them continued to pound against the steel column.

"Fucking hell," Steve gasped. "Thanks, Helen."

The sound of crunching metal emitting from the loading bay below them forced Steve and Helen to their feet. They crept towards the edge of the roof, fearful of getting too close, and peered over just as the crowded walkway began to collapse.

The steel hinges were ripped from the wall as they became weakened from the weight of the dead on the balcony. Slowly, it tilted outward over the loading bay; the creatures that packed it toppling over the railing as the entire structure crashed onto the heads of the dead below, crushing countless skulls in the process.

More were scattered backwards as they were hit by the heavy steel grates and beams. Bones were smashed, limbs were torn from their sockets and flesh was ripped open, spilling strings of intestines and internal organs at their feet. The crippled bodies sloshed about in the quagmire while the remainder of the crowd surged forward again, trampling them into the foul grotesque swamp of human remains and bodily fluids beneath their feet.

"Bollocks to this," Steve growled as he began tearing at the jacket that he wore. "This fucking thing has done nothing but cause me dramas. First the beer cans, then the fireman's pole routine with those things snapping at my arse."

He pulled the jacket from his shoulders and began waving it around his head like a lasso.

"Here you are. You can have it," he shouted as he let go. It sailed in the air and fluttered down to land on the heads of the dead.

"What do we do now?" Helen asked as she watched the carnage in the loading bay.

"Find a way off this roof for a start," Steve replied as he began looking around him for a possible way down.

"And then?"

Steve turned to her and shrugged. He leaned forward and peered back down at the dead in the loading bay.

"We find a car that still works and get back to the park. I know it sounds a lot easier said than done, but that's what we *need* to do."

"Well," Helen glanced to the far side of the rooftop, "the cars out front are out of the question, there are a thousand of those things down there."

They both began to walk the length of the roof, searching for an escape route. At the far left hand side of the building, a drainage pipe ran down from the roof and into the grid at the base of the wall. The area below was clear of the dead. A couple of large, steel bins were all that was in the small alleyway that ran along the side of the building. It was quiet and would allow them to be able to climb down, undetected.

Steve climbed out first, sliding down the pipe as his feet scuffed against the rough brick. On the ground, he checked the immediate surroundings again, ensuring that they were still unnoticed. Helen began her descent and quickly reached the ground. They paused for a moment, listening for any sign of the dead.

"This way," Steve whispered as he moved towards the corner of the rear of the building. "We'll try and get back on to the road, find a car that we can get started and follow the link way back towards the park."

They reached the corner and paused, their backs leaning against the wall as they steeled themselves.

Steve glanced back at Helen. "You ready?"

She nodded in reply; her eyes were wide and her body tense as she prepared herself for more running and climbing, with the dead close on their heels.

Steve stepped out from the corner.

"Shit," he cried.

A wall of the walking dead was just metres away, making their way towards them along the rear wall of the building. Shoulder to shoulder, they staggered and lurched along as they followed the length of the supermarket. They saw him. Hundreds of pairs of eyes locked on Steve as his sudden animated movements alerted the dead to his presence. They wailed in chorus as they quickened their pace towards him.

"Back, get back, Helen," he shouted as he jumped around the corner, almost colliding with her. "We can't go that way. It's wall to wall with them."

The pair sprinted back towards the front of the supermarket. Without bothering to stop, or even slow down, they raced into the open and onto the car park, unsure of what the situation was like out at the front store. It did not matter; it was their only other option.

Hundreds of figures shuffled around aimlessly on the tarmac between the static cars. A tightly packed crowd continued to push and shove one another at the entrance to the building as they piled into the interior. Some of the dead in the open spotted them as they ran out from the alleyway and began to stagger towards them. More of the walking, rotting corpses turned and followed as their moans alerted others that were close by.

Steve and Helen headed for the area of the dilapidated and crumbling building situated at the lower end of the car park. Helen chanced a glance back over her shoulder. The pursuing corpses that Steve had come face to face with at the rear of the supermarket appeared from around the corner of the building. A few that were more agile staggered out in front, groaning and reaching out with their arms, forcing their unsteady legs forward as they followed the living people.

They reached the derelict building and threw themselves around the corner, their feet crunching on the broken glass and rubble below them in the mud. Steve was breathing hard, his legs shaking from the adrenalin as his blood coursed through his veins. Helen ran at his side, her arms pumping as she ran at full pelt.

At the far end of the building, they saw a narrow dirt path that led between a clump of unkempt trees and high bushes, obscuring their view beyond. They raced towards it as the first of the dead appeared from around the corner behind them. Steve felt the long, thin reaching branches and rustling leaves swipe at his face as he ploughed through them, Helen close on his heels as she followed.

The path led them to a street that ran parallel to the supermarket. To the right was the city, and to the left it would eventually lead them back on to the link road that they had travelled along when they first arrived at the shopping complex.

Steve turned to his left without slowing, his sense of direction guiding him the way they needed to go. They could hear the moans and cries of the dead as they slogged their way through the trees behind them. The branches above shook and swayed as the pursuing creatures bounced from tree to tree in their haste to catch up with Steve and Helen, and the nesting birds squawked and flew from their perches in droves, flocking in the sky and circling above.

The street was empty and quiet and Helen could hear the deafening sound of their footsteps as their echo bounced from building to building. The sound of the dead behind them filled her with terror, spurring her on as she stepped into the lead, ahead of Steve.

As they approached the junction at the end of the street, Steve motioned for her to turn left towards the link road. She was just a few metres ahead of him and she began to angle her run towards the turn. Suddenly, she jumped to the right and sprinted away in the opposite direction as she neared the corner of the last building.

"Right, turn right, Steve," she shouted back over her shoulder without slowing her pace. "There are more of them coming."

Steve changed direction and followed in her wake, glancing back to his left to the street they had originally intended to turn into for their escape. Lurching figures were moving towards them, the bright sun casting the creeping shadows of the bodies towards the junction. There were not as many as there were behind them, but enough to stop them from considering that particular street as an escape.

Helen turned right at the junction and into the next avenue. They were headed in the opposite direction from where they had wanted to go, but they had little choice. They pounded along the road, keeping to the centre of the street and away from the houses that lined it. More of the dead appeared from the gardens and buildings to their left and right and joined in on the chase as they saw the living people sprinting by.

Steve's lungs burned as he tried hard to keep up with Helen who ran along in front of him, seemingly taking the exertion in her stride. She was much fitter than he was and he worried that he would eventually hold her back as he tired.

They approached another junction up ahead, the streets to the left and right, packed with the shambling bodies of the dead. Steve glanced back and saw the road behind him filling with them. They were cut off with only one direction to go.

They had to keep going.

They raced across the junction, deeper into the suburbs of the city.

25

Sophie sat staring out towards the northern part of the park from her vantage point on the roof of the mansion. The day had turned into a blustery one with white and grey clouds racing across the sky as the high winds swept them along, leaving just short intervals of sunshine as it peered through the gaps in the billowing cloud.

She hated days like this. It was as though the weather could not make up its mind. The sun never seemed to appear for long enough to warm the air around her, leaving her sitting there dressed in a thick parka as though it were winter.

She swept back the long strands of blonde hair from her face and turned to see Carl as he appeared at the door to the roof, carrying two steaming mugs in front of him. He slowly made his way across the gravelled rooftop, a look of concentration fixed on his face as he carefully avoided spilling any of the hot coffee.

"Ah, you must have read my mind," she smiled.

"I couldn't leave you up here without a brew, could I? Besides, it's my shift soon so I thought I would come and have a natter with you first."

Sophie frowned at him as he passed her a cup. She wrapped both her hands around it, feeling the warmth radiate through the china mug as she blew at the steaming liquid.

"Why, is there something wrong?"

"You mean apart from the fact that the dead have decided to get up and walk and eat us, and half of us are missing and we have no idea where they could be? No, everything is just fine mate, couldn't be better," Carl snorted and rolled his eyes in mock annoyance.

"Sarcasm is the lowest form of wit, Carl," she informed him in a tone of voice that reminded Carl of his grandmother.

"Bollocks," he huffed. "It actually takes more intelligence and fast thinking than shitty 'knock knock' jokes."

She smiled up at him, shaking her head in resignation and then glanced back over the wall towards the north.

"Where do you think they could be? Do you think they're okay? I mean, do you think anything has happened to them?"

Carl sat down heavily on the chair next to her, the wooden legs creaking under his weight. He sighed as he looked out across the open grassy plane and took a loud slurp from his cup.

"I really don't know, Sophie. They have been gone a long time now and they should have only been a few hours, but it's been two days."

Sophie looked down thoughtfully at the dark liquid in the mug between her hands. "What's your honest opinion though, Carl, do you think they're dead?"

He shot her a hard look as if she had just spoken a sentence of forbidden words, as though it was a sin even to whisper such a statement. His features softened when he saw the expression on her face. She was not prepared to mince her words or to avoid the reality or the possibility of Steve and the others having fallen victim to the millions of dead that roamed the land outside the walls of the Safari Park.

"I don't want to think of that to be honest, Sophie. I know it's a possibility, but I am just hoping that they have run into a little trouble and it's held them up."

"Me too," she replied. "I just can't help but think the worst though."

"You shouldn't. We need to stay positive."

"But you're forgetting one thing though, Carl," she watched him expectantly, waiting for him to ask her to explain.

"And that is...?"

She smiled slightly, her unwavering ability to lighten the mood of a gloomy conversation radiating through to the surface.

"You're forgetting that I am an unflinching pessimist, Carl, and a pessimist is never disappointed."

Carl threw his head back, his coffee spilling over the sides of his cup and splashing onto his lap as he laughed. He had grown a great fondness for Sophie. Even though she was young and extremely pretty, they were not the reasons that drew him to her. It was the fact that she never failed to make him laugh. He could always count on her to lighten his mood and that is why he always insisted on joining her on the roof half an hour earlier than he was due to begin his shift. Just a few minutes of conversation with her would enable him to face the next four hours of boredom and frustration as he stood watch on the rooftop.

"Gary, we're coming back. Can you hear me, Gary?"

Sophie glanced up at Carl, excitement glowing in her eyes as the radio suddenly came to life in front of them. Carl snatched it up in his hand.

"Jake, is that you?"

"Yeah, it's me. We're nearly there. We are at the rear gate, we..." his voice trailed off in a hiss of static.

"Jake, say that again mate, you're breaking up."

Sophie stepped in closer and looked out from the rooftop in the direction of the rear of the park, expecting to catch a glimpse of the returning members of their group.

"I said, we are at the rear gate and we have a couple of injured people." There was a pause. "They've been bitten."

Carl's eyes grew wide as he took a step closer towards the wall that surrounded the roof of the mansion. He joined Sophie in scanning the horizon, searching for any sign of the others. His mind raced as he struggled to absorb the information he had just heard. He looked across at Sophie; the expression on her face betrayed her growing fear.

"Did he just say, 'they've been bitten'?" she asked.

Carl nodded, looking back down at the radio in his hand. "Yeah, he did. Sophie, go and warn Gary."

She turned and headed for the door. She could feel the sweat begin to seep from her palms and her mouth and throat turn dry. Just those few words, informing them that a member of their group had received a bite from the dead, were enough to make her tremble.

Carl raised the handset to his mouth again, "Jake, who…who has been bitten?"

There was no reply and Carl could feel his anxiety growing with every second that he remained without information.

"Jake?" he shook the radio in his hand.

The rumble of an engine drew his attention away from the static hissing radio and towards the north. He saw a thin glimmer of brilliant white as the sun peered through a break in the clouds and reflected from the cabin of a large vehicle. Slowly, the remainder of the vehicle climbed over the summit of the small rise that dipped towards the rear gate.

"Jesus," Carl mumbled to himself. "They've brought a whole tanker."

The zebra-painted Land Rover appeared over the crest of the hill and overtook the slow lumbering truck. It raced towards the mansion, bouncing in the air as it hit the small dips and folds of the undulating grassy plain. Carl could see the figure behind the wheel, Jake, struggling to stay in his seat as he was rocked and jolted with every bump. He was not slowing. In fact, from where Carl stood, it looked as though he was trying to speed up.

"Shit…"

The Land Rover screeched to a halt on the gravelled car park at the front of the house. Its wheels locked, but the momentum and weight of the vehicle caused it to travel a few metres further, flinging small stones and dust up all around it. Before the vehicle had come to a halt, the passenger, a tall and powerfully built young man dressed from head to toe in black, was already out and running to the rear of the Land Rover.

Gary and Sophie paused in confusion as they watched the newcomer dart from the blood and grime encrusted vehicle. They shared a look of uncertainty and dread.

"For fuck sake," the young man cried to them." Help me."

Sophie and Gary sprinted to the rear of the vehicle as Jake jumped from the driver's seat. He was pouring with sweat and looked as though he was about to collapse.

"What happened, Jake?" Gary asked as he joined the black clad figure at the back of the Land Rover.

The young man wrenched the door open as another stranger, smaller in build but dressed very much the same, sprang from the interior.

Gary gasped and jumped back with shock. The young man fixed him a menacing stare for a moment, and then turned back to the vehicle, reaching inside.

"Here, help us with them," he snarled.

Sophie let out a gasp when she saw the three limp bodies in the rear compartment. Involuntarily, she raised her hands to her mouth as she watched the two newcomers begin dragging them out by their legs. She recognised John, his deep red stained shirt torn and oozing blood from the numerous wounds beneath. He groaned as he was carried from the vehicle, his face pale and soaked with sweat.

The second body, she did not know. He was unconscious and a large dark tear in the skin between his shoulder and neck indicated the area where he had been hurt. From his appearance and stillness, she suspected that he was already dead.

Then, she saw Lee. His face bruised and battered, and covered in blood. He, too, was none responsive. Sophie felt herself fill with despair. She liked Lee, more than she allowed herself to admit, and seeing him now, injured and close to death, a flood of emotion that she found impossible to hide suddenly swept over her.

Jake pushed past them and began helping Gary lift out the second man.

"His name is Simon," he grunted with the effort of carrying the unconscious man. "He helped save us from the supermarket where we were trapped."

Gary did not reply. He stared down at the man as he helped Jake to carry him towards the main entrance. Simon was heavy in his arms and Gary could feel the muscles in his shoulders and back struggling with the strain.

Jake looked back and saw Sophie still standing at the rear of the Land Rover, staring at the body of Lee.

"Don't worry about him," he shouted over his shoulder. "He hasn't been bitten, just beaten up. Help us with the others."

Sophie took a careful step closer to the rear compartment of the vehicle and peered over the body of Lee. Though his face was covered in blood, she could not see any bites. The rest of his body seemed undamaged. Without realising it, she let out a sigh of relief. She reached over and checked his breathing. He seemed fine. Bloodied and battered, but nothing serious as far as she could tell. She turned towards the house and followed the others.

A heavy rumbling to her right stopped her in her tracks. She turned just in time to see a large white truck appear from around the corner of the house. A small scruffy man sat behind the wheel high up in the cabin, staring down at her as he manoeuvred the vehicle into the car park. She stepped back tentatively, shielding her eyes from the glint of the sun as it reflected from the windshield.

"It's okay," shouted one of the new arrivals as he reached the door of the house. "He's with us."

Jennifer and Karen appeared at the large double doors, holding them open as the four men struggled up the few steps toward the foyer. Sophie followed them as she glanced back at the truck and the little bearded man as he climbed down. She recognised him from somewhere, but she could not remember where exactly.

People ran back and forth within the large entrance room of the mansion. Nervous voices bombarded one another with anxious questions as the four men laid John and Simon on the floor of the foyer.

The children were terrified. Jake caught sight of David and Liam, clinging to their mother as they stared in horror at the two wounded men on the floor. Their eyes flicked from one man to the other and the pools of blood that steadily grew beneath them.

"Jennifer," Jake called. "Can you take the kids out of here, please? I don't think they should see this."

"What's happened to John, Mummy?" David asked.

Jennifer turned her sons away from the carnage and steered them towards the kitchen.

"Shhh, it's okay, don't worry about them just now. Come on; let's see if there is any ice cream left. I'm sure Karen has some hidden away."

Jake watched them as they left. "Okay, help me get them to the store room at the back." He groaned and nodded his head towards the far end of the foyer as he began to scoop up the legs of Simon.

"Stop," Gary ordered as he held a hand out at Jake. "Why are you taking them to the store room?"

Jake straightened, a questioning look etched on to his face as he stared back at Gary.

"They've been bit, that's why."

"So you just want to dump them in that room and be done with them?" Gary's tone was filled with anger as he questioned Jake's morality.

"Gary," Jake sighed, "they've been bitten. We cannot leave them in here. It's not safe for any of us."

Gary clenched his fists and took a step forward. He felt the heat radiating from his own body as his blood pressure increased. A shiver ran up along his spine, and he felt the hairs on his neck and forearms stand on end.

Through gritted teeth, he snarled, "Jake, what in God's name is wrong with you? That's John laying there, a friend of ours. Do you want to discard him like a bag of rubbish? Get a grip on yourself, they are not dead yet. We have to help them and do whatever we can for them"

He leaned over the two unconscious men and began to check their pulse and breathing while examining their wounds.

Jake's shoulders slumped. "Sorry, Gary, you're right. I'm just scared, is all."

Gary kept his eyes on John and Simon as he nodded. "I know, Jake. We all are. Help me carry them over to the sofas."

He turned to the two young men that had arrived with Jake. "You two, if you're going to be staying here, you may as well help out. What are your names?"

"I'm Stan," the first introduced his self and nodded at his friend, "and this is Kieran."

"Good, I'm Gary. Give us a hand, will you?"

The four of them hefted Simon and John and carried them the short distance to the sitting area of the foyer. Karen arrived from the kitchen with a bowl of hot water, towels and dressings for the wounded men and placed them down beside Gary as Claire and Sophie began helping to care for the injured.

Gary stepped back and approached Jake.

"What happened out there, lad? Where are Steve and Helen?"

Jake stepped back and leaned against the heavy antique table, shaking his head and unable to look Gary in the eye.

"I don't know where they are. We were split up. It was awful, Gary, and it was my fault. If my foot hadn't slipped off the pedal, John would be okay and Steve and Helen would be here with us." He began to shake his head more vigorously.

"It's my fucking fault," he stated again as he looked up. His eyes were wet with tears and his bottom lip quivered.

"Jake, you're not making sense. How is it your fault? What happened?"

"It's not his fault." Kieran stepped up to them and placed a hand on Jake's shoulder as he turned to Gary.

"He was driving when we were making our escape from the supermarket and the clutch slipped under his foot. John fell and Steve and Helen were surrounded by those things. It could've happened to anyone."

He looked back down at the sobbing Jake. "It could've happened to anyone, mate. It isn't your fault."

"He's right, Jake. It could have been anyone of us that was driving." Gary nodded, trying to console his friend.

The heavy doors to the front of the house crashed open and Gary spun to see Lee stumble into the foyer. He was unsteady on his feet and he placed a hand against the wall to balance himself while the other was held firmly against the side of his head. The little scruffy bearded man was at the side of him, his arm around his waist and helping him to walk.

Lee paused, his palm still pressed against the side of his blooded and swollen face. With fire and pain in his eyes, he glared at Kieran and Jake.

"Cunts," he mumbled to himself before collapsing back onto a large armchair.

Gary continued staring at Lee for a moment, then looked to Jake and then to Kieran, perplexed. "What was all that about?"

Kieran shrugged. "He was out of control, so we had to put him out."

"You mean, you put him down," Gary spoke his words in a tone that indicated he was aiming the question directly at Kieran. "You beat Lee up?"

Kieran looked down at Gary, "Yeah, me and Stan."

"You fucking jumped me, more like," Lee growled as he sat forward, inspecting the blood on his palm from the wound in his head.

"These bastards filled me in when I wanted to go back to rescue Steve and Helen."

"We couldn't have gone back," Stan said in a raised and angered voice. "There were too many of them and we would all be dead now."

Lee did not reply. He leaned back in the chair and grumbled something unintelligible. He winced and groaned with pain as Sophie knelt down in front of him with a wet towel and began cleaning up the gash in the side of his head.

"Oh don't be such a big baby, Lee," she smiled at him. "You'll live."

Gary nodded at the skulking, bearded man that remained close to the door. He looked scared and vulnerable, and unsure of where to go or what to do.

"Who is this, then?"

"That's Johnny," Stan replied.

"Yeah, Johnny Boots," Kieran added.

Gary and Stan looked at him curiously.

"Johnny Boots," Kieran stated again to his friend Stan in an attempt to jog his memory. "Surely, you know him? He's the local celebrity homeless bloke. Everybody knows who Johnny Boots is."

A moment of realisation flashed across the face of Stan. "Ah yeah, I know him. There's even a Facebook page for him. I've seen him all over the place, walking about and laughing at people. I heard a rumour that they were making a film about him."

Kieran looked disapprovingly at his friend. "You're as dumb as a bag of hammers, aren't you, Stan. You believe everything they put on that stupid site, don't you."

"Just what I heard," Stan shrugged.

"Okay, Ant and Dec," Gary interrupted, "well you'll be part of our gang now, I suppose. For now, go get that tanker and drive it round to the back."

"We don't know how to drive one of them," Stan admitted.

Gary shook his head. "Take Johnny with you then. He brought it here so you can help him." He looked over at Johnny. "That okay with you?"

The shy bearded man nodded in reply.

"We need to go back for Steve," Lee grumbled from the armchair.

Gary turned and looked down at him. "You're in no condition to go anywhere, Lee. Once we have patched you up and done what we can for John and Simon, we will see what the best course of action is."

"We can't go back to the supermarket, Lee," Kieran added. "There's thousands of them there and I bet Steve and Helen wouldn't be there anyway. If they have any sense, they would be long gone. If we go back, those dead shits will be all over us like a tramp on chips." Kieran glanced up at Johnny who remained in the corner, watching everyone. "No offence, mate."

"None taken," Johnny shook his head. "I'm not a tramp. I have a home." He paused a moment in thought. "Well, I did have."

"Lee," Kieran stepped forward towards the bloodied and bruised man sitting in the large armchair. "You need to understand mate, I know Steve is your friend but we can't go back there. Steve wouldn't want us to either. He knows how risky it would be, and besides, like I said, he won't be there."

Lee let out a long sigh, finally giving into reason and slumping back in the large cushions of the armchair.

"You're right," he agreed. "But that doesn't mean I'm your fucking mate now." He turned his gaze towards Stan. "Or you. You two wankers jumped me. You couldn't have done it on your own."

Kieran nodded, understanding that it was now a matter of pride and that eventually, the strong proud lion that was inside of Lee, would need to put matters back into their natural order. For his own self-respect, Lee needed to reclaim his position of dominance over the two young men.

"Okay, Lee. When you're healed, we'll settle it."

Lee went to stand but Sophie pushed him back, her hand pressed in the centre of his chest and her eyes locked on his.

"No, Lee. Leave it."

Kieran nodded to him, a nod that was almost a bow of respect before a pending dual. "Give it time, mate. We'll have our day."

Lee glowered, and then watched Kieran and Stan leave the room, headed towards the tanker with Johnny in tow. Kieran walked with his head up, his shoulders back and an overwhelming air of confidence. Stan was less imposing. He avoided looking into Lee's eyes.

Lee knew that he could easily take Stan in a stand up fight, maybe even Kieran, but he also knew that at that moment, in the condition he was in, he would not stand a chance. His pride had almost gotten the better of him, willing his damaged and exhausted body into a second battle with Kieran while he was at a disadvantage. He suspected, though, that the powerful young man, through his own sense of fair play and his principles, would have backed down knowing that it would not be a fair contest.

Lee sighed and smiled to himself.

"What you grinning at?" Sophie questioned him as she rinsed off the bloodstained towel in the fresh bowl of hot water.

"Nothing," Lee shook his head. "Just, well, they aren't bad lads really."

A shriek from the couch shocked them as Simon suddenly sat bolt upright, knocking the dressings from Claire's hands. His eyes were red and his face as pale as marble. The top layer of his skin looked almost transparent and the multitude of veins beneath the surface was visible, looking black as they contrasted with his pallor. He looked about the room, his burning eyes fixing on each individual in turn. He turned his head to the attention of the wound in his shoulder, the torn flesh turning black around the edges and the muscle and sinew shining bright red beneath.

He let out a whimper and looked back at Claire.

"I'm going to die, aren't I?" His eyes were pleading with her, begging her to contradict him.

Claire felt lost. She did not know what to say to the man.

"We don't know that, Simon," Gary said as he knelt down beside the couch. "You're in good hands here and we will do all we can for you." He did not know what else to say to him.

Everybody had seen people bitten by the dead, and no one had been known to survive the infection that would ravage the body afterwards.

"Johnny," Simon said in a quivering voice. "Is Johnny okay? Where is he?"

"Johnny is fine, Simon," Claire replied. "You need to rest. Don't worry about Johnny. He is here with us. He's safe."

Simon's eyes began to glaze over and roll upwards. His body seemed to lose all the strength to remain upright and he slowly sank back down again, drifting into unconsciousness.

"I...I only...wanted a tent...," he murmured.

Gary placed a hand on Claire's shoulder. "I'll take over here. You had better go and see to Sarah. She will want to know where her dad is."

Claire nodded and passed the dressings over to Gary as Carl came bounding down the stairs, an anxious look on his face.

"Lisa came to relieve me." He looked down at John, who was still unconscious on the couch. "Shit...," he groaned.

He and John had become close and Carl already knew that he had lost his friend.

Gary looked up at him with sympathetic eyes. "We'll do what we can for him, Carl. Here," he handed him a pile of dressings and towels, "help him."

Jake had remained quiet and inactive throughout. He slumped against the table and his head drooped so that his chin rested on his chest. Lee watched him from the large armchair. He could feel his anger abating and being replaced with empathy and compassion. He knew that it was not Jake's fault and that it could have happened to anyone.

Slowly, and in agony, Lee leaned forward and began to climb out of the chair, grimacing with the pain that throbbed in his head. Sophie tried to stop him as he raised himself.

"It's okay; I'm not going to do anything stupid, Sophie."

He smiled at her, reopening the cuts to his face as he did so. He leaned forward and kissed her hard on the lips. His skin flushed and he felt the heat glow from within her as she kissed him in return.

"I've been dying to do that for ages," he whispered into her ear.

Without opening her eyes, and savouring the moment, Sophie groaned, "Me too."

Lee staggered across to Jake. His legs were unsure of themselves, but he fought hard to keep his composure and dignity. He reached the table and placed a hand onto it to balance himself as he turned and leaned his back against the hard antique wood. He was now side by side with Jake and, for a moment, he watched the young man at his side, unsure of what to say. Eventually, he followed his instincts, placing an arm over Jake's shoulder and pulling him in close. Jake began to sob on Lee's shoulder.

"Shhh, it's okay, mate. I'm sorry for losing my rag with you back there." He rubbed Jake's back. "Honestly, I'm sorry, Jake. It wasn't your fault. Do you hear me?"

He lowered his head and lifted Jake's chin so that they could see each other. "I mean it, it wasn't your fault. I was just upset and worried about Steve and Helen is all. I would be the same way if it was you that was left behind."

Jake leaned back and blew out a long loud sigh in an attempt to gather himself. He wiped his eyes on the back of his sleeve and turned to look at Lee.

"I just wish that my foot hadn't slipped. Steve and Helen would be here now, and John would be okay." His voice threatened to break again.

Lee nodded in thought. "Well you know what they say about wishes don't you; you can wish in one hand and shit in the other and see which one fills up first."

Jake snorted a laugh that was halfway between a whimper and a snigger. For some unknown reason, Jake had always found it very important that he be accepted as a friend by Lee, even more important than Steve and Gary. He was drawn to the uncompromising, hard hitting and sometimes, completely wild, almost feral man. He was not sure what it was. He had considered that he could be attracted to Lee, but he soon realised that he was not. It was something else, an intense respect he had developed for the man and his attributes, however Neolithic they seemed. Jake realised that, in the old days, a man like Lee would have been considered socially retarded, maybe even inept but in the new world, Lee was a warrior and a leader.

"Thanks, Lee," he smiled. "It means a lot."

"Don't be daft, you big poof." Lee slapped him across the back as he felt that the atmosphere had grown a little too tender for his liking.

"Come on, let's help Gary. We can't sit around here sulking all fucking day."

Jake smiled and nodded at him. He felt his heart soar and swell now that he had been given the tough love man talk from Lee as he followed him over to where Gary and Carl helped the two wounded men.

Sophie glanced over at Jake as they crossed the room. She smiled slightly and Jake returned the gesture. Her smile grew broader and then she followed it by sticking out her tongue and giving him a wink.

26

"Okay boys, it's time we got moving."

Marcus looked across at Stu standing by the door, checking the area immediately in front of the building. He turned to Marcus and held up a thumb, nodding at the same time.

Jim finished packing up the heavy High Frequency radio after they had checked in with Gary for the morning. He stood up, throwing the pack over his shoulder and nodding to Marcus, indicating that he was ready to move.

"You sure you don't want to come with us, Pete?" Marcus asked.

Pete remained standing by the fireplace; his brother, Michael, still curled up on one of the benches beside it, snoring and giggling in his sleep.

"No," he replied, shaking his head. "As I told you, we live close by, and besides we would only slow you down."

Marcus shrugged. He was not going to argue with the man. If he chose to stay behind, it was entirely his choice.

"Okay, here," Marcus held out his hand and Pete saw the dull sheen of the black metal. "Take it. I'm sorry we can't offer you more, but it's the best we can do I'm afraid."

Pete took the pistol in his hand. The weight and cold of the metal was strangely reassuring to him. "Thanks, Marcus, and good luck to you all."

"You too, mate." Marcus reached out and shook Pete's hand. They shared a moment of eye contact that spoke volumes. They both knew that very soon, either one of them could be dead, maybe even both of them, but their eyes willed one another to make it and survive.

Marcus turned away. Quickly, he checked his weapons and bounced up and down on the spot to settle his heavy assault vest that was loaded down with ammunition. It had always been his habit. He compared it to a boxer waiting for the bell of the first round as he loosens up, ready for action. He headed for the door as the rest of his men began to exit.

"So long Pete. Look after that brother of yours," Jim called over his shoulder as he stepped outside.

"Yeah Pete, add me on Facebook when you get the chance," Stu added.

Pete watched through the window as the team of battle-hardened veterans mounted up on to their vehicle. "God speed, lads."

Jim put the vehicle in gear and began to head towards the main road. "What do you think, Marcus? Will they make it?"

Marcus looked back over his shoulder at the old country pub as it slowly disappeared out of sight around the bend in the lane. "I hope so, Jim."

That morning, Marcus and his team had conducted a map study. The best that they could find had been an old, out of date A to Z road atlas in one of the drawers along with an old Ordinance Survey map behind the bar. They decided that they would use the main artery roads only to get them away from London and to put some distance between them and the capital. After that, they would stick to the minor roads, avoiding densely populated areas and most importantly, likely highways that the military could be using as main supply routes.

They still feared the idea of being caught up in the counter offensive that they could hear in the distance as the assault on London continued. The faint screech of the jets as they flew in on their bomb runs and the dull thuds and booms of their ordinance as they hit their targets echoed across the miles of ground that separated the large city from Marcus and his men.

By late morning, they had reached what they considered a safe distance from London and they turned onto the maze of minor country roads that crisscrossed the Midlands. The small towns and villages had given way to vast expanses of rolling countryside, but the roads there still held their own dangers. Stalled or crashed vehicles littered the country lanes, forcing them to slow down to a crawl as they negotiated the obstacles. It was at these times that the team were at their most vulnerable; being caught in a bottleneck that forced them to reduce their speed made them an easy target for both the living and the dead.

"Hold it, Jim. Slow down."

Without any questions, Jim eased off on the accelerator and gently applied the brake, bringing the speed of the vehicle down to a crawl.

They were travelling along a narrow lane that was barely wide enough to fit two saloon cars, side by side. Their British Army Land Rover was much wider than the average civilian vehicle and it would be difficult for them to manoeuvre if they ran into trouble.

Trees lined the roadside to their left and a low hedge with an open field, gently rising up to a wooded area on the high ground, to their right. Up ahead, and obscured by the overhanging trees that drooped down towards the road, Marcus could see something. He could not make it out, but he could also smell smoke, acrid smoke that burned his throat.

"What is it, boss?" Jim asked as he craned his neck in an attempt to see further along the road.

"I'm not sure. You smell that?"

"Smells like a mix between aviation fuel and burning rubber to me," Stu offered from behind them.

Marcus nodded as he made a hand gesture, signalling for Jim to reduce their speed even further. He scanned the land to his left and right, then twisted in his seat to get a view of the road behind them.

"What's going on, Mr. Marcus?" Hussein asked as he looked down from the gun position and saw the troubled expression on the team leader's face.

Marcus shook his head, "I'm not sure but I don't like this."

"You don't like what?" Sini asked.

"I think the road may be blocked up ahead," Marcus replied as he raised himself in the passenger seat to get a better view. "We'll have a hard time of turning around if it is."

Sini looked at the roadside to his left and right. Deep drainage ditches run parallel to the road and up close to the tarmac. The Land Rover took up nearly the entire width of the narrow country lane.

"Shit," Sini hissed.

Marcus turned to Jim, "Okay mate, push on, slowly. If we can chuck in a one-eighty up ahead, then do so and we'll head back the way we came."

Jim pushed the vehicle in gear and began to creep forward again. To their horror, the road became narrower, to the point where the hedgerow was almost brushing the paintwork of the Land Rover.

Marcus fidgeted in his seat. He knew they were trapped. All he could do was hope that the blockage up ahead was negotiable with no crowds of dead waiting for them. The smell of the smoke became stronger. It drifted in thin wisps through the trees above and became thicker as they drew closer.

With nowhere in sight that offered the possibility of turning around, Marcus called a halt again. Jim brought the vehicle to a stop and slipped it into reverse, keeping his foot pressed down on the clutch, ready to back up at speed if needed.

"Stu, Hussein, you two come with me," Marcus ordered twisting his neck so that he was facing the people in the rear. "Sini, Jim and Sandra, you stay with the vehicle while we have a look." He turned to look at Jim. "At the first sign of trouble, get out of here. If we get split up, the emergency RV will be that little cottage we saw two kilometres back on the right of the road, okay?"

Jim nodded, "Roger that, boss."

The three of them dismounted from the vehicle. Marcus gently pulled back on the cocking lever of his rifle to check that it was ready to fire. He knew that it was, but he always liked to be sure. He eased it back just enough so that he could see the brass casing of the chambered round, then he gently pushed the lever forward again until he heard the click.

Stu leapt across the ditch to the right of the road and began pushing his way through a small gap in the hedgerow. Marcus followed and Hussein brought up the rear of the small recognisance patrol.

"Up to the high ground, Stu," Marcus said in a low voice from behind him.

Stu nodded and began to pace across the field. It had been a long time since there had been anyone to harvest the crops that grew there. It was now overgrown and tangles of long grass and roots threatened to snare their feet as they made their way up the hill.

Close to the top, Marcus paused and turned to look back at the road. It was hard to see with the hedgerow and trees obscuring much of it. He could feel the trickles of sweat running down along his spine as he breathed deeply from the effort of the hill. He could just make out the upper part of the Land Rover. It seemed so far away. They were out in the open and vulnerable, and Marcus could feel his blood chill at the thought.

"Sini," Marcus spoke over his radio, "radio check."

"Loud and clear, boss."

"Good to me. We're near the tree line, about to turn north."

"Roger that, got you visual."

Stu reached the tree line and turned left, following it along and paralleling the road. He glanced to his right in the trees, the thick foliage and gloom blocked his view after a few metres. The woods looked dark and ominous and the sounds of cracking branches and rustling leaves sent a wave of unease through him.

Stu raised his hand, signalling for Marcus and Hussein to stop. They obeyed the command, crouching down on their haunches and remaining silent. Stu, without speaking, looked back and called for Marcus and Hussein to close up to him. Again, they obeyed and keeping their profile as low to the ground as possible, they made their way forward.

"What we got, Stu?" Marcus whispered as he arrived at Stu's shoulder.

"Not sure. There's too much smoke to tell, but whatever it is, it's just a hundred metres or so away," he said looking down to his left where the hill dropped into the shallow valley.

Marcus raised his binoculars to his face and scanned the dark billowing clouds of smoke that rolled upwards in the air from a wide area in the low ground.

"I can't make anything out," he stated.

Waiting for a gap in the black veils that curled and swirled across the fields and road, the three of them crouched and watched. As the wind shifted direction slightly, the clouds of smoke, for a few seconds, parted.

"Wait," Hussein hissed. "I can see something. Looks like a crashed plane."

Marcus and Stu scanned to the area where Hussein pointed. He was right. Through their binoculars, they were able to make out the twisted and scorched remains of what appeared to be a C130 Hercules. Multiple fires burned all around it from spilled aviation fuel and the wings appeared to have been ripped off in the crash, leaving the long, cylindrical hull sprawled across the width of the road. A long wide trench of disturbed earth running down the hill to the north betrayed the plane's final moments as it had crashed onto the ground. Wreckage and equipment were strewn everywhere with numerous fires smouldering all around.

"Looks like they were carrying supplies for the offensive, what do you think happened, Stu?" Marcus asked as he passed his binoculars to Hussein to have a look.

"No idea, mate, but have a look at that." Stu pointed past the dark smoke and into the distance, towards the north.

Before Hussein had had the chance to raise the binoculars to his eyes, Marcus snatched them back. In the distance, and obscured by the plumes of smoke and shimmering heat of the burning aviation fuel, Marcus could see white and green patches scattered across the open fields. He struggled to make them out at first, but then his eyes focussed and he felt an icy hand grip his throat. Strewn across a wide expanse of open ground and hanging from the trees a few hundred metres away, Marcus recognised parachutes, dozens of them.

Marcus had served in the Parachute Regiment, and he recognised a Drop Zone when he saw one. The vast open ground was ideal for a mass drop. Away from the immediate surroundings of built-up areas and with the low rolling fields, it was a perfect choice for a DZ. However, something had gone terribly wrong.

"Looks like they gave the green light when the pilot realised the aircraft was going down and the troops bailed out."

"Where are they then?" Hussein asked from behind.

Marcus looked down at the ground below his feet. Even after all these years since leaving the army, he still felt an overwhelming sense of loss when he saw or learned of the deaths of fellow paratroopers.

"They're still there, Hussein," he said in a quiet and solemn voice as he passed the binoculars back to him.

As he focussed, Hussein clearly saw the bodies of the men that hung limply from the cords and straps of their parachutes, still secure in their harnesses. Looking closer, he saw the flinching and struggling movements of the reanimated troops as they fought against their bonds. He looked into the low ground, at the wide-open fields where many more deflated parachutes lay. Dozens of figures thrashed and clutched at the webbing that was still attached to the large sheets of parachute silk enveloping them. Some lay entangled on the floor in their rigging lines, while others staggered to their feet, attempting to walk but being dragged back down by the weight of their equipment.

"Shit, Marcus, look!" Stu exclaimed in a hushed voice. He pointed down to their left, to the smoke that surrounded the crash site.

Through the breaks in the rising black and grey columns, Marcus could see movement on a vast scale. A sea of shambling figures closed in towards the downed aircraft. Marcus scanned along the road towards the south, in the direction they had come from. Through the trees on the far side of the narrow country lane, he could see hundreds more of the dead, headed towards them.

Marcus felt his heart begin to pound. He spun around and looked in the fields to their south. More flesh hungry ghouls stumbled across the open ground, the smoke from the crash site attracting them from the villages and towns for miles around.

Their vehicle was in a blind spot, Sini and Jim unable to see and oblivious to the approaching danger.

"Sini, get out of there," Marcus ordered over the radio. "You've got dead closing in from the west and south."

"Where, Marcus?" Jim replied. "I can't see anything."

"Fifty metres to your left," Marcus' voice took on a tone of urgency. "Get the fuck out of there, now. We'll meet you at the ERV."

From their vantage point, Marcus, Stu and Hussein saw the Land Rover begin to back up along the road. The dead to the west saw them too and began to crash through the row of trees and spill onto the narrow road. The vehicle began to turn a bend and then they were lost from sight to Marcus and the others.

"Okay, Stu, we need to get in the woods and head back to the RV."

The three of them stood just as they heard the crackle of distant gunfire.

"They're behind us," Sini's voice screamed through their earpieces, his voice loaded with panic, "hundreds of them, blocking the road."

More gunfire followed as Sini opened up with his rifle into the mass of dead.

Marcus watched as the Land Rover came into view again, racing back to the area where they had dismounted. The road was now teeming with the reanimated corpses of the dead in both directions, completely cutting off any chance of escape.

Stu took aim through the site of his rifle. The loud resounding crack as he began to fire echoed down from the high ground and to the shallow valley below. Marcus and Hussein followed suit and began picking off the dead that closed in on all sides of the beleaguered vehicle and its occupants.

Bodies fell as the rounds smashed through their heads and into their brains. Others jerked and shuddered as the shots missed their targets and hit other parts of their body. Stu had already fired a full magazine in them without making a difference to their numbers.

"Magazine," he cried, informing the others that his weapon was empty and he needed to reload.

Marcus and Hussein continued to fire. More shots, quicker in succession, rang out from the road as Jim, Sini and Sandra fought to stem the flow. To their right, Marcus caught a glimpse of more figures headed in their direction, up the hill and through the smoke from the direction of the crash site. Attracted by the noise of the weapons and the flashes from their muzzles, the mass of bodies that had been obscured from the smoke, now began to emerge from the billowing oily clouds like a living nightmare.

"Bug out, Jim. Head for the high ground," Marcus ordered.

There was no reply, but the fire from the low ground continued.

"Sini," Marcus tried again. "Debus and head for the high ground," he screamed into his radio.

Suddenly, through the sight of his rifle, Marcus saw figures crashing their way through the hedgerow away from the road and towards their position on the hilltop. He took aim at the first, and then released the pressure on the trigger.

"It's them," he called to Stu and Hussein. "They're bugging out and moving towards us. Check your targets."

"Roger that," Stu replied, without letting up on his rate of fire.

More of the dead appeared in the fields to the south and the mass of bodies to the north drew closer by the second as they staggered up the hill. Marcus conducted a quick battle appreciation in his head. Their only option was to head east, through the woods to their rear. All other directions were teeming with the shambling bodies of the dead.

Jim was out in front with Sini at the rear, helping Sandra as they crossed the field and ascended the hill as fast as they could. Through his weapon sight, Marcus could see that she was struggling. She clutched at her abdomen, the pain from the emergency appendix operation hindering her as Sini continued to drag her along towards them. They were just a hundred metres away, but Marcus knew that they could not afford to allow Sandra time to rest. The moment they arrived, they had to move to the trees and try to put as much distance between them and the pursuing dead as quickly as possible.

The first of the bodies from the right were now just twenty metres away. Stu turned and began to take out the lead creatures in an attempt to spare them just a few seconds more before Jim, Sini and Sandra reached them.

Panting hard and pouring with sweat, Jim stumbled the last few metres of the hill and dropped to the side of Marcus. Sini and Sandra were just seconds behind him. Marcus saw the agony in Sandra's face. Her features were twisted and she whimpered and groaned with the pain. He could see that it was a struggle for her just to remain upright.

"We need to move," he informed them with a sympathetic nod towards Sandra. "We can't stay here, we got to keep going."

Raising her head and groaning, Sandra nodded to him, understanding the need for them to get out of there as quickly as possible.

Marcus turned to Jim. "Did you salvage anything?"

Jim continued to battle to catch his breath.

"Just ammunition," he gasped as he dropped the heavy pack from his shoulder, filled with the loose magazines and rounds that they had taken from the barracks. "I couldn't get the radio, boss."

Marcus nodded. He understood that the three of them were lucky to have made it out with their lives, let alone lugging a heavy radio with them.

Stu led the team into the woods, his rifle held hard into his shoulder and his finger running along the side of the trigger guard, ready to fire on anything that sprang up in front of them.

Marcus took one final look in the fields and valley below. It swarmed with the approaching dead, all of them with their eyes locked on Marcus and his team as they made their escape. He knew they would follow.

"Okay, Stu, take us in. As quickly as you can, but not so quick that we can't react to any threat that pops up."

"No worries, mate," Stu replied in a whisper.

They were just a hundred metres in the trees when they heard the first of the dead behind them begin crashing their way through the wooded area. They moaned in frustration, their wails echoing through the trees. The sounds of the branches and rustling leaves crackling under their feet seemed to come from all around in the densely packed wood. Marcus resisted the urge to rush and increase the pace. Sandra was in pain, close to collapsing, and the prospect that there could be more of the dead in front of them filled him with trepidation.

It was a natural wood, so there were no lines or channels that they could follow between the trees. Within a few hundred metres, it became hard to tell if they were headed in a straight line. The dim light that the small breaks in the canopy allowed was insufficient for them to see more than twenty metres ahead of them. The few narrow beams of sunlight that penetrated through the high branches and leaves created mirages, which played on their nerves.

Repeatedly, Stu spun, his finger gently squeezing the trigger as he saw a figure or movement, only to realise that it was the discolouration on the bark of a tree from the sunbeams or the swaying branches high above casting moving shadows on the ground. They had slowed to a crawl; all the time, the sounds of the pursuing dead resonated all around them, stalking them through the wood.

The trees around them creaked and groaned as they swayed in the breeze that rushed through the woods. Mixed with the moans and wails of the dead, it was an eerie and terrifying atmosphere for the six people that were unsure of their bearings as they pushed deeper.

A sudden crash to their right and a dark figure, its features shaded in the gloom, stumbled towards them. Hussein raised his weapon and quickly fired two shots in the creature, the first hitting it in the chest and the second in the head. The flash from the muzzle of his rifle illuminated the immediate area, drowning it in a moment of brilliant white light. For just that brief second, Marcus saw more figures close by, stumbling through the trees and turning in their direction.

"Go, Stu. They're all around us. Go, go," Marcus screamed from the rear.

A chorus of cries and wails erupted from the darkness in all directions as the dead saw them and gave chase. They bounced from tree to tree, stumbling over roots and crashing through branches as they attempted to close the gap between themselves and the fast moving living people that fled from them.

Stu sprinted forward; another figure loomed at them from the murky darkness. It was so close that he squeezed the trigger without having to aim. In the flash of light as the round exploded from the barrel, he saw the face cave inward and a spray of bone and brains erupt from the back of the creatures head. Before the thing hit the floor, Stu had passed it. He could hear the rest of the group close on his heels, their heavy footfalls, grunts and gasps of breath echoing through his ears.

More shots rang out as other team members identified targets and engaged them. The moans of the dead had become a constant hum throughout the woods, an indication of just how many there were surrounding them.

"I can see light," Stu called back over his shoulder as a thin silvery sliver appeared in the distance between the tightly packed trees.

He raised his weapon and fired again at two more lumbering bodies that crossed his path. The stock of the weapon bucked hard against his shoulder, but it did not slow him; he was used to having to fire accurately on the move.

"About three hundred metres," he called back again.

The area around them began to clear. The trees were less dense and more sunlight managed to penetrate the foliage. The dead closed in on all sides. They were everywhere. The rate of fire intensified as every member of the team began to pick off the closest reanimated corpses, but it did not seem to affect their numbers. It seemed that from behind every tree, a walking corpse waited for them.

They were close now, just a hundred metres from the open ground and they would be clear of the dark and claustrophobic wood. Marcus spurred the team on from the rear, growling at them to keep up the pace, regardless of their exhaustion. He could see Sandra ahead of him, being dragged by Sini as she stumbled and cried, tripping over roots and being whipped by the low branches that swiped at her body.

Marcus felt for her. She must have been in agony, having had an operation with minimum care and pain relief since, and having to run for her life while the dead closed in all around. She must have felt completely vulnerable and reliant on the team to pull her through. He made a note to himself that if they got through and could find somewhere safe, they would go firm for the night, allowing her some rest and attention from Stu's medical skills.

Stu burst out through the last remaining trees and into brilliant sunlight. His eyes had become so accustomed to the dark gloom of the woods that he squinted from the sudden assault on his retinas. More of the dead were headed in their direction from the open ground to the east. Though they were spread out, they seemed to be everywhere and as far as his eyes could see. The downed aircraft and their gunfire must have attracted every creature within ten miles.

Off to the left, and at the top of a small rise, Stu could see what looked like a sprawling farm complex. The sunlight glinted from the bare metal of the corrugated iron rooftops of the large, rectangular sheds. He turned and headed towards them. The remainder of the team, without slowing, following him as they cleared the tree line.

"We need a vehicle, Stu!" Marcus yelled from the rear. "Any will do at this fucking moment," he added as he sucked the air deep into his lungs.

The sweat ran in rivers along the length of his spine. Between the exertions as he ran for his life, warmth of the summer's day and weight of the equipment and ammunition he carried on his body, Marcus could feel it all beginning to take its toll. His heart, lungs and legs screamed at him for a halt and his head pounded, threatening to fracture his skull from inside, but he knew they could not stop. They had to push on, regardless of their extreme fatigue.

The trundling figures in the fields all around them turned and began to follow. They were spread out and scattered over a vast area, but Marcus knew that it would not take long for them to converge and become a seething tightly packed mass of dead faces and clutching hands surrounding them.

Stu reached the gate and wall that spanned the width of the cattle grid leading to the farm. A quick cursory check informed him that there were no dead in sight within the complex. He scaled the aluminium gate and landed heavily on the other side, his feet sinking up to his ankles in a thick quagmire of mud and cow droppings.

Jim crashed down beside him, sending streaks of filth through the air that then splashed back over his lower legs.

"Nice," he exclaimed as he looked down.

Stu and Jim pushed forward to the corner of the first of the long rectangular sheds and covered the area as the others scaled the gate and wall.

"No sign of any vehicles," Stu whispered over his shoulder as Marcus crouched down beside him, scanning the area for himself.

"We'll just have to push on through to the far end; hopefully there might be a car around the front of the farmhouse." He nodded to the old brick building to their front and on the left of the farm complex.

Stu stood and stepped out from the corner.

A noise to his front made him freeze on the spot. Fifty metres away, at the far end of the shed, the body of a man stumbled out from around the corner of the farmhouse. It tripped over a piece of machinery that lay half buried in the mud, falling forward and sprawling in the filth as more staggering corpses appeared from around the house.

"Shit," Stu hissed. "Back, back."

He began to edge his way towards the corner, retracing his steps.

"We've got dead in front of us," he whispered as he joined the rest of the team squatting in the mud.

"Coming up behind us too," Jim informed them in a low voice as he peered over the wall and gate leading back out in the fields.

Marcus, in a crouch, began to make his way along the wall and towards a door at the gable end of the long shed. He reached up, twisting the handle and aiming his rifle into the gloomy interior of the building.

"Looks clear, everyone inside, quick."

In the shed, they paused for a moment, letting their eyes adjust to the low light. The floors were covered with the remains of the farm animals.

The carcasses of pigs and cows lay strewn all over the place, mixed in together and stripped to the bone. The building reeked of rotting meat and the clouds of black and swollen flies that swarmed all around them harassed the six new arrivals continuously.

Stu began to walk along the length of the building, carefully placing each step and keeping to the central walkway as he picked his way around the dismembered remains that littered the floor. The heat inside the building was stifling, making him nauseous as the warm sickly scent of the putrid dead animals assaulted his senses.

The door behind them suddenly rattled and shuddered under the impact of something on the outside. The noise echoed through the building all around them, magnified by the cavernous space and dislodging small chunks of masonry and dust that drifted down on to them from the high rafters above.

"Shit," Jim cursed. "They know we're here."

More thumps and thuds jolted and rocked the door as dozens of the dead crashed against it. Marcus could see that the hinges were already starting to give under the pressure as they shifted in their positions.

"Move, Stu, get to the far end. That door won't hold them."

The six of them began to run. A final crunch and the door behind them caved inwards and a wave of the sickening creatures began to pour into the building. Marcus turned and began to fire. Bodies tumbled as their brains were blown from their heads, but more came and replaced them as they scrambled through the doorway.

Sandra suddenly let out a scream and Sini turned just in time to strike the attacking creature that jumped at them from the darkness inside one of the animal pens. Its bony fingers reached out for her and its blood-encrusted mouth opened wide as it lunged forward.

The butt of Sini's rifle caught it in the side of the neck, but it did not slow the momentum of the thing. It continued forward, grasping Sandra by the arm and pulling itself in close to her. Sini fired, his rounds smashing into its face and sending it reeling backwards and down to the ground as he pulled Sandra back towards him and turned to run.

She screamed again. The body that had attacked them was not dead; its hand clutched around her ankle, pulling her away from Sini and down towards it. It thrust itself upwards, its mouth agape, and sunk its teeth into the soft flesh of Sandra's calf muscle.

She howled with the pain as the flesh was ripped away from her. She stumbled and fell to the ground, smashing her head on the hard surface with a resounding crack. Sini stepped across her and fired a burst in the head of their attacker. Its skull exploded in a cloud of blood and bone as the rounds thumped through it.

Grabbing Sandra by the arm, he began to pull with all of his strength. He glanced back and saw the cold and grotesque dead faces converging on them from the smashed doorway. He turned the other way and looked up at Marcus as he approached to help him.

Another loud crash indicated that the door at the far end of the shed had given way to the assault of the dead. The light from the outside streamed in through the open doorway, silhouetting the bodies that stumbled inside and towards them. They moaned ravenously when they saw the six people before them. Their hands reached out and they began to stagger forward, their pace quickening in anticipation.

"There's another door. To the right, to the right," Hussein cried out as he stepped up beside Stu and began pumping rounds into the advancing crowd.

Marcus began to lean forward, to help Sini carry Sandra.

"No, Marcus," Sini said calmly. "She won't make it."

Marcus looked down in Sini's eyes as he knelt beside the unconscious Sandra. He looked at the wound in her leg. Bright red blood oozed from the gaping hole and onto the floor. More blood poured from her ears, indicating to Marcus that she had probably fractured her skull when she fell.

"We can try to..." Marcus began.

"No, Marcus. She will not make it. You know that." Sini's face held the expression of a man that had already accepted that the woman he loved was gone. There was no way he would leave her for the dead to devour, or allow her to go through the pain of the infection only to turn into one of the things he despised so much.

"Come on, Sini, we have to go," Marcus pleaded.

"I'm going nowhere, Marcus," Sini replied with a gasp, almost laughing. "Get out of here." He reached in his vest and pulled out the claymore mine that Stu had given him.

"Go, I'll take care of these fuckers," he snarled, indicating the swarm of dead that were just metres away now.

Marcus saw in his eyes that Sini's mind was made up. He would stay with Sandra. Raising his weapon, Marcus aimed and fired into the crowd one last time as Sini prepared the claymore.

"Here," Sini said, holding out the rifle in his hand. "Take it, I don't need it anymore."

Marcus did not know what to say to his friend but he knew that there was no way he could change his mind. He reached down and took the weapon from Sini and, with a final moment of eye contact, Marcus nodded to him and turned to follow the others.

"Good luck, Marcus!" Sini shouted calmly and matter-of-factly without taking his eyes away from the detonator and claymore mine in his hands.

Cold hands reached out for Marcus as he ploughed his way towards the open door through which the remaining members of his team had escaped. He ducked his head, shoulder-barging his way clear of the staggering and lunging bodies that attempted to block his path. He burst through the doorway and back out in the light. Stu, Hussein and Jim were to his left, moving along the outside wall of the building.

"Where's Sini?" Stu asked as Marcus came parallel to him at a sprint.

"He's not coming," Marcus screamed as the rest followed suit and increased their pace. "Run."

A moment later and the air around them seemed to evaporate. The pressure threatened to suck their lungs out of their chests and their ears to explode. A deafening boom followed by the shockwave threw them forward and down to the ground. Marcus felt his internal organs jolt within his ribcage as the force of the blast rippled through his body.

Entire sections of the shed walls blew outwards, carrying with it dozens of dismembered bodies of the dead that had filled the inside of the building.

The hundreds of tiny steel balls that were packed into the explosives of the claymore shot out in all directions, smashing through the rotting flesh of the creatures and punching holes through the remaining metal walls of the shed. The frames of the building smashed and, weakened by the shockwave and shrapnel, began to cave inwards as Marcus and the others managed to pick themselves up and sprinted away from the building.

Marcus' head spun and a deafening ringing sound reverberated around inside his head. It felt like he was running through water and his legs disobeyed his commands to speed up. Everything seemed to slow down and become distant as the effects of the shockwave continued to disorientate him.

Bits of debris and flesh that had been caught in the blast and sent high in the air rained down over a wide area, littering the ground with a grotesque mixture of mangled body parts and twisted metal. They thumped to the ground with large clunks and wet slaps.

In the confusion, and while the reverberations of the blast continued to echo around the complex and beyond, Marcus and the remains of his team were able to cross the courtyard of the farm, headed towards the main house and out on to the road on the far side.

"Car," Stu exclaimed, pointing at the parked saloon on the driveway.

Quickly grabbing the handle, he realised it was open and piled himself inside. Marcus, Jim and Hussein followed him.

Panicked and in shock, Marcus turned to Stu. "Can you start it?"

"No worries, I'm already on it," Stu replied as he began fiddling with the steering column and the wiring inside.

A moment later and the engine began trying to turn over. The starter motor whined and clicked as Stu tried repeatedly to get the car started.

"Fuck it, take the hand brake off," Marcus ordered as he threw the door open and climbed out.

"Turn right off the driveway, it's downhill, we'll bump start it," he shouted from outside as he began to push at the doorframe, forcing the car forward and towards the road. He groaned and grunted as he threw his weight into the push.

The first of the dead appeared behind them from around the corner. It saw Marcus and began to stagger towards him, moaning and grunting loudly as more joined it from the side of the farmhouse.

Marcus heard it but did not turn to look. He pushed hard against the frame, feeling the heavy vehicle building speed as it rolled down the driveway.

"Okay, Marcus, get in. Get in," Stu yelled from the driver's seat.

In one swift movement, Marcus gripped the roof of the car and threw his legs in the footwell of the passenger seat.

"Go, Stu, go," he screamed as he slammed the door shut and saw the bodies that converged on them.

Stu threw the wheel across to the right and felt the gentle jolt as the wheels dropped from the curb and onto the tarmac. He kept his foot pressed down on the clutch and his eyes glued to the dashboard read outs, watching the speedometer. As the needle hit fifteen miles per hour, he pulled his left foot from the clutch pedal and stepped down on the accelerator.

With a jerk and a growl, the engine caught and grumbled as it began to turn over. He quickly changed up a gear and raced away, leaving the dead at the farm complex behind as they staggered after them and into the road.

"Shit, shit," Marcus growled to himself repeatedly as he smashed his fist down hard on the dashboard in front of him.

"Sini wouldn't leave her," he said, turning to Stu. "He wouldn't leave her."

Stu kept his eyes on the road ahead of them. He swallowed the hard lump that began to form in his throat and nodded solemnly.

"I know, mate. I know," he said quietly.

27

Steve hugged the wall of the building, his back pressed up against it as he slowly made his way along towards the corner. He looked back at Helen; her eyes bulged with terror, like that of a rabbit caught in the headlights of an oncoming vehicle. With each step, his heart skipped a beat. He dreaded standing on something that would make a noise and give them away.

They had managed to outrun the hordes of dead that pursued them into the city, but they were not far behind. The sounds of their moans could be heard in the street where they had just come from. The haunting, poignant wails of the hundreds of walking dead glided through the narrow streets, channelled by the high walls and buildings, assaulting the already threadbare nerves of Helen and Steve.

It was getting dark. The sun had dipped behind the buildings of the city and the streets were cast in an eerie orange glow as the dying rays reflected from the hundreds of windows set in the tall apartment and office blocks around them. Long shadows reached out in the road, throwing the street into near darkness at ground level. The city was a graveyard of a dead civilisation. Everywhere reminders of what once was stood as testaments to the drastic and catastrophic changes that had happened to the world around them.

Cars, dozens of them, lay abandoned in the streets. Some parked by the roadside and others, left in the middle of the roads as their occupants had fled. In some places, the static vehicles were nothing more than a tangled and twisted jumble of steel, burned and scorched out of recognition. Shops, their doors caved inwards and their windows broken, stood in silence, their dark interiors cavernous and foreboding as they looked out onto the street.

Steve clutched at Helen's hand and froze to the spot. Slowly, he slid down the wall and into a crouch. Twenty metres away two figures appeared. They sauntered through the shadows, moving slowly and studying the vehicles that they passed. They moved from one to the next, stopping each time and pressing their faces up close to the glass, then moving on to the next one.

In the low light and dark shadow, only their silhouettes were visible. Steve could not distinguish their features or even the clothing they wore, but what they were was unmistakable. They shuffled as they walked, their bodies leaning forward at their waist and their hands hanging by their sides, swinging slightly, like a pendulum as they walked.

Steve and Helen remained silent and still as the two ghostly figures slowly passed them, just metres away from where they were hiding. They were close enough for Steve to be able to hear the scrape of their shoes on the tarmac and the low grunts they made as they shuffled along the street.

The closest one suddenly stopped. It let out a long moan, as though frustrated that their search had wielded nothing of interest. It turned and scanned the street once more then continued around the corner and to the next avenue.

Steve and Helen traded glances. Even with little light, the whites of their eyes stood out in the darkness. They were both terrified and they knew that they were trapped in the city for the night. It was too dangerous to try to find their way out. The dead never slept and roamed the streets endlessly. To try to make their way out of the built up area in the darkness would be suicide. They needed to find a place to hide until the morning, when they could see the dangers better.

They continued along the street, away from the mass of bodies behind them that seemed to be getting closer by the second.

Steve turned to Helen and leaned in close to her ear. "We need to move faster. They'll catch up with us if we stay at this pace," he whispered. "Just stay close and do what I do."

"What are you going to do?" she asked, fear making her voice tremble.

"Make like dead fucks," he replied. "Just walk slowly and watch where you put your feet. Hopefully, we won't draw any attention that way but at this rate, we'll never find a safe place for the night."

Helen looked him in the eye. "I don't think that anywhere in this city is safe, Steve," she whispered hoarsely.

He nodded in agreement. "Just do what I do. We'll make it."

They both stepped out into the street, pausing for a moment as they checked to see if any of the dead were close by. There were none in sight, but their echoing moans could be heard throughout the city, bouncing from the buildings that channelled their miserable lament along the streets.

Steve turned and slowly made his way along the pavement that ran along the side of the road. He stayed in the shadows as much as possible, their gloom helping to mask their appearance. They shuffled slowly, always listening for any telltale signs of the dead up ahead of them.

In the far distance, deep within the city, they heard the faint clang of metal against metal, followed by the crash of breaking glass. It could have been anything Steve told himself; a survivor being chased or a swarm of the dead discovering an animal hiding in the darkness. The one thing that the sound did tell him was that the dead were relentless.

They never rested or gave up. If anyone were careless enough to be seen, a mass of staggering bodies would soon converge on them. No matter where they hid, or how well fortified their position, the voracious creatures would pound and hammer at any barricade until they had fought their way inside.

At the corner of the street, Steve and Helen paused for a moment. They checked in all directions, careful not to walk out into a seething mass of bodies. The streets to the left and right were very much a mirror image of the one they had just travelled.

The signs of chaos and panic were strewn everywhere. Buildings burned to their frames and cars blocking the roads, their doors left hanging open. Bodies, stripped to the bone and dismembered littered the streets, the tatters of their clothing still clinging to the carcasses that had been consumed entirely, rendering them unable to reanimate. Swarms of flies swirled in dark clouds over the remains as the rats scurried around in the gutters, picking the bones clean of any remaining flesh.

They turned onto the street. The dark buildings loomed above them. Steve shuddered. It felt like the street was becoming narrow with the walls slowly edging their way inwards. Menacing, dark doorways stared out at them like the eye sockets of lost souls, beckoning them to enter and be lost forever.

Steve desperately wanted off the streets. He felt Helen's hand gripping his even tighter, her palms sweating in his. The smell was almost unbearable. The rotting corpses mixed with the stench of untreated waste and abandoned garbage, blending into a noxious mix that seemed too heavy to rise above the buildings and instead, hugged the ground and added to the decaying filth of the city.

They continued to move slowly, their bearings completely confused. Steve no longer knew in which direction the Safari Park was. With the darkness, fear and confusion, he had become completely disorientated. His only hope was that daylight would enable him to recognise their surroundings. Now, the street was just a dark corridor with grey and black monolithic buildings and unrecognisable features reaching high above them.

In the street ahead of them, darker that the shadows in which they moved, Steve could see black figures wandering aimlessly in the road. They headed in no particular direction and randomly staggered in and out from between the stalled cars, bumping into objects in their paths and even each other. They were spread out, but Steve did not want to risk trying to walk by them undetected.

He turned to his right; a gaping doorway looked out onto the street at them. He had little choice.

"Here," he hissed and pulled Helen along behind him.

Close to the door, a loud crunch, ear splitting in the stillness of the night, rang out from below his foot. The sound of breaking glass echoed all around them as his weight pressed down on the broken bottle. For a moment he paused, cringing and waiting for the noise to subside.

Helen glanced down the street. The dark staggering figures had also stopped. They had heard the noise and now began to lurch towards them. She could hear their questioning moans and scuffling feet as they headed in their direction, towards the source of the noise.

Steve stepped forward to the shadow of the doorway. The interior was in complete blackness and a low lingering whine came from within as the wind wisped about inside the building from the open door.

He stepped closer, desperately trying to force his eyes to adjust to the darkness so that they could escape the approaching dead.

A pale and gaunt face, its teeth bared and hands stretched outward, its fingers clutching the air, lunged at him from within the building. Steve yelped and threw himself backwards, crashing into Helen and knocking her to the floor.

The creatures in the street heard the commotion and quickened their pace.

Steve was unprepared for the assault and he was taken completely by surprise. He thrust the flat head of the hand axe upward, catching his attacker under the chin and sending it reeling back in the dark doorway. He reached down and grabbed Helen by the scruff of her collar as he turned to run, not waiting for her to climb completely to her feet.

The figure at the doorway regained its balance and staggered out after them. It moaned and growled angrily as it shuffled from the doorway and onto the street. Steve saw more dark figures emerging from the shadows all around them.

They were surrounded.

Helen raised her bat high above her head and crashed it down on to the skull of the corpse that had attacked them from inside the building as it came in for a second attempt at ensnaring one of them. The small baseball bat hit with a crunch as the heavy wood fractured its skull, caving it inwards. For a moment, the creature stood there looking at Helen, an expression of astonishment on its face. Its eyes rolled back, its knees buckled beneath it and its body slumped to the ground.

The dead continued to multiply and close in.

"What the fuck are we going to do, Steve?" Helen asked with anger as she turned in tight circles, watching the lumbering grotesque forms as they encircled them.

The first to reach them appeared from behind a car. It bolted out from the dark and launched itself at them. Steve turned just in time to sidestep the thing and brought his axe across his body in a wide arc, smashing it into the back of its head. The blade stuck in the bone, the remnants of its brains creating suction like wet sand around his feet. Steve, still gripping the short helve of the axe, was dragged to the floor as the body collapsed.

Helen stepped forward and took a swing at another that approached. She missed. As she followed through with the force of her attack, the creature lunged at her, grabbing her by the waist and tackling her to the ground. She landed hard, the wind being knocked out of her for a moment and stars flitting through her vision. She could feel the cold, bony fingers digging into her flesh and saw the gaping maw, its fetid teeth and blackened tongue glistening in the dark, as it bowed its head towards her.

She thrust the bat upwards, jamming it into its mouth. She shoved harder, hearing the teeth break and the jaw dislocate. It continued to push its weight down onto her, its hands grasping and clutching at the skin on her neck as it attempted to get a firm hold on the writhing Helen below it.

Steve freed the axe, the suction making a wet slurping sound as he pulled it from the head of the dead body at his feet. Taking aim, and with every ounce of force he could muster, he stepped across and threw a kick into the face of the creature that had Helen pinned to the floor. Its head shot back with the impact, the bones in its neck snapping audibly as they were forced beyond their breaking point.

The body went limp and rolled to the side, allowing Helen to gain her feet again.

More and more were appearing out of the blackness and the ring around the two stranded people grew tighter by the second. The sea of ungainly and menacing silhouettes wailed and moaned, their cries growing in intensity and attracting more dead from neighbouring streets.

"This way, Steve," Helen shouted and took off towards the other side of the street.

She headed for a set of steps that led into what she thought looked like an apartment block. The main difference that she noticed was that no dead had appeared from the door of that particular building, and she hoped that fact meant that the building was empty.

Steve followed her. He flew up the steps and in through the large wooden doors into complete darkness. He paused for a moment. There was no sign of Helen and he could hear nothing from within the building. His nerves screamed at him. At least in the street he could see something. Here in the darkness, he could not even see his hand in front of his face.

"Helen," he whispered hoarsely in the pitch black. She did not reply. "Helen, where the fuck, are you?"

He trembled as he gripped his axe in one hand and held the other out in front of him, trying to feel for her in the dark. The hairs on his neck were standing upright and a shiver ran up through his spine, assaulting his brain like a bolt of lightning.

With a resounding boom, the large heavy doors behind him slammed shut, trapping him inside. He sprang backwards, away from the door as his throat emitted an involuntary cry. A hand reached out and grasped his arm. He pulled back and slammed into something hard against his hip.

"Shit," he cried as he stumbled and raised his axe to defend himself.

"Steve, you dick," a voice hissed at him from the darkness. "It's me."

For a second, he felt like crying as the tension of the moment was released. "Jesus, Helen. You scared the shit out of me. Where are you?" He still could not see anything.

"I'm here," she replied and he felt her hand touch his own. He grasped it tightly, the contact with another living person being the only comfort he could find at that moment.

"Can you see anything?" he whispered.

"A little, I think we're at the stairs."

The doors to the entrance suddenly shook and jolted as something crashed against them, the bangs sounding like gunshots as they echoed around in the spacious hallway. The dead had caught up with them.

"Up," Helen ordered, "up the stairs, Steve."

They began to climb, taking two steps at a time as they ascended the staircase. The clatter of the doors continued to follow them as they were assaulted incessantly from outside. The moans of the dead snapped at their heels, staying with them even when they had climbed up to what they believed to be the fourth floor.

The moon had made an appearance and shone through the windows of the building's corridors, illuminating the interior of the upper floors to a small degree. The place seemed untouched by the ravages of the dead and the chaos that engulfed the city. The hallways were empty and many of the doors to the individual apartments were still intact and locked.

"Where are we going?" Steve whispered from behind.

Helen stopped and turned to him, her face glistening palely in the dim moonlight. "I haven't a clue. I was hoping you had a plan."

Steve shook his head and sighed with an audible touch of a laugh. "My head is still in the hallway, Helen. I'm still shaking like a shitting dog and my brain is mush."

"Some use you are," she huffed. "I should've just brought my frigging vibrator along."

Steve had to stifle his laugh in the palm of his hand. The throwaway remark from Helen had caught him completely off guard.

"Even at times like this, your mind is still in the gutter, Helen."

A loud, crunching noise resounded up and along the staircase. Steve leaned over and glanced down through the narrow gap in the banisters, all the way to the ground floor. A shaft of faint glimmering light illuminated the hallway from the moon outside. It flickered and faded as the shadows from dozens of the dead disrupted the gentle glow that managed to shine through into the building.

Steve turned to Helen, his eyes wide with fear. "They're in," he said, stating the obvious.

They stood for a moment, unable to think clearly on what their next course of action needed to be. They listened to the echoing footsteps of the creatures as they began to pile into the building. Their moans lingered in the air as the acoustics of the staircase carried them up through the floors and back down again. It was enough to rattle the nerves of even the most strongly resolved person.

"Come on," Steve whispered. "Up, we have to keep going up." He turned and began to move towards the next flight of stairs.

Helen pulled back on his arm. "And then what?" she asked. "We don't know what's up there or if we can find a way out."

"We can't stay here, Helen. We have to move."

The sounds of the dead got louder in their ears as they staggered upwards along the stairs. Moans, footsteps, crashes and thuds were all mixed in a terrifying chorus as the horde of creatures clumsily ascended.

Steve turned and headed up the next flight. He was unsure of how many floors there were to the building, but at that moment he wished that they were endless. He wanted to put as much distance between them and the dead as possible.

"Once we get to the top floor," he whispered back as he reached the next level, "we'll see if we can get to the roof. There's bound to be a fire escape up there."

Helen followed. She understood his reasoning and the need to continue climbing. She just dreaded the unknown and the possibility of being trapped on the top floor, listening to the unseen walking corpses slowly making their way up to them.

Another seven floors up, and panting hard for breath, Steve turned onto yet another landing. The hallway was much the same as all the others that they had passed through during their ascent but there were fewer doors along the corridor. He headed towards the window, illuminated by the moonlight and expecting to find another flight of steps leading them to another floor.

There was nothing, just a dead end.

"Shit," he huffed, "we've run out of road. Look for a fire escape."

The noises from below were more distant now as Steve and Helen had been able to move much quicker than the ungainly and uncoordinated dead, but they were still coming. They would carry on upwards for as long as their misfiring brains or instincts told them to and with the weight of hundreds more of them spilling into the building, the creatures at the front would be forced upwards.

The fire escape was in the opposite direction from the window. Steve launched himself at it, hitting the bar with his palm and expecting it to swing open. It did not budge. Instead, as his weight landed against it, the door just rattled in its frame, the noise alerting the creatures below and causing a ripple of excitement to travel through the mass of rotting corpses as they attempted to quicken their pace.

Something else clattered from the door as Steve's weight had thrust against it. In the dim light, he could see the glint of dozens of steel links. Someone had chained the door shut and then secured it with a padlock.

"Fuck," he exclaimed. "We're trapped, Helen. The door is chained and locked."

Without feeling the need to inspect the impenetrable barrier herself, Helen turned and began to move back along the hallway, pushing against each door as she passed and attempting to turn the handles.

Steve watched her in the low light. He could only see her silhouette as she moved further along the corridor. He silently begged her for forgiveness for getting them into the mess that they were in now. He blamed himself; they should have just taken the fuel and left, but instead he had decided to take them shopping.

"You fucking arsehole," he cursed himself under his breath.

He stepped towards the top of the stairs and, straining his eyes, attempted to peer into the darkness to check on the progress of their impending doom. Moans and wails assaulted his ears and the stench of their decaying bodies forced their way into his nostrils. They were close now, maybe just two floors below and gaining ground by the second.

"Here," Helen called to him in a whisper from the darkness. "In here, Steve."

He followed her voice and found her standing at the far end of the hallway by the door leading to an apartment. He looked at her and then at the door.

"What?"

She nodded at the handle, "It's open."

Steve reached down and twisted the brass lever in his palm. It turned all the way down and the door budged slightly with a faint click. A small black crack appeared between the door and the frame in which it sat and a gust of stale air wafted in his face. Though it was far from fresh, the air was free from the foul odour of the dead. He pushed it further, the hinges whining slightly in their brackets. The room within was as dark as a tomb and nothing stirred.

Raising his axe, Steve stepped forward into the narrow passageway, Helen following closely behind him. They both paused, cocking their heads to the side, listening for any sign of movement within the apartment.

Fearing that there could still be a body inside, Steve took up a fighting stance. One hand and foot placed out in front of him, his knees bent slightly and the axe held up at shoulder level, the blade pointed towards the interior.

"Hello," he whispered warily into the blackness. "Is anybody in here?"

There was no reply. They paused again, concentrating and focussing for even the slightest telltale sign that they were not alone.

"I think it's empty," he said turning back to Helen.

The noise from the dead in the stairwell grew in intensity. They were close. Helen gently closed the door to the apartment and began to shove the bolts across in the top and bottom, sealing them inside. She did it as quietly as possible, not wanting to alert their pursuers to the apartment in which they were hiding.

Gingerly, they both stepped forward together. Their eyes flitted from one shadow to the next, trying desperately to penetrate the inky blackness that could hold any number of terrors awaiting them.

The hallway opened up to a large expanse. At the far end, and running the entire width of the apartment, floor to ceiling windows stared out over the city. The moonlight flooded in through the huge glass panes and bathed the room in a pale blue light. It was bright enough for Steve and Helen to be able to see and identify objects inside the room without having to scrutinise or look too closely.

"Now this is luxury, wouldn't you say?" Steve grinned at Helen.

The room was filled with the finest furniture and fittings that money could afford. Ornaments and paintings that looked as though they belonged in a gallery were placed on display on expensive looking contemporary tables or hung from the walls. A television, the largest that Steve had ever seen, sat fitted in its alcove on the far wall, a huge and comfortable looking leather couch sprawled in front of it.

To the right was the kitchen, sleek and elegant, and filled with the most modern of appliances and gadgets; Steve imagined some of the finest chefs in the world being more than happy to cook a meal there.

Helen began to walk through the room, craning her neck and checking every corner for anything that could be lying in wait for them.

Steve was in awe and rooted to the spot. The penthouse apartment was the sort of home he had always dreamed of and it was clear to him that a rich man had lived there, not a woman. In his eyes, it had that man signature to it. Although the owner had obviously wanted to show off his wealth and live in comfort there was nothing that was too overly sentimental about the place. To a degree, it was minimalistic without the usual clutter you would find from a woman's touch. There were no vases of wilting flowers or rows upon rows of family photos along the large sprawling fireplace, and spying the drinks cabinet and home entertainment system, including numerous games consoles, confirmed it for him. It was a real man's hang out.

"Are you going to stand there all night with a hard on, or are you going to help me check this place and barricade that door?" Helen asked in a reprimanding tone.

Steve snapped out of his wonderment and turned to her. "Sorry," he said. "This is really something, though, don't you think?"

Helen growled. "It won't be if those stinking corpses come barging through the door because you were too busy drooling over your new home."

Together, they searched each room. It was bigger than they had first thought.

"Christ, there's more rooms here than the whole building put together," Steve whispered in awe as they approached the last door. "No wonder there's only a couple of them on the top floor."

Helen ignored him. He was starting to get on her nerves with his excitement over an expensive and luxurious penthouse that had no place or use in the new world. She reached down for the handle and twisted, pushing the door open.

A set of steps led upwards and to where she presumed was the roof. They edged their way forward and climbed the short staircase. The door at the top was unlocked and led out onto a rooftop patio, complete with barbeque, garden furniture and a chest freezer. They quickly scanned the open roof around them, ensuring that they were alone, and then retreated back inside the apartment.

Steve began hauling the large, heavy drink cabinet into the hallway and placed it up against the front door. Next, they began dragging a long table to place behind the cabinet and wedged it so that it was pressing against the wall at the end of the hallway, rendering it impossible for the door to be forced open.

Satisfied that they were as safe and secure as they were going to be, they both set to searching the apartment a second time for anything that could be of use. Food and water were at the top of their list and they had to make do with soft drinks and stale biscuits. Neither of them had eaten all day and they wolfed down the meagre meal as though it would be their last.

As the morning sun crept into view over the tall buildings of the city, its bright rays poured in through the large bay windows, piercing through the thin skin of Steve's eyelids and waking him with a start.

Realising what the light was, he sat upright rubbing his face, the leather of the sofa creaking below him.

Helen was already up. She stood by the entrance to the hallway, staring towards the front door of the apartment. Steve's mind was in a fog and as the mist slowly lifted, his senses began to retune themselves to their surroundings. He became aware of a steady thumping noise, like a bass drum being beaten in the distance. He looked around confused; then he remembered.

He jumped up from the couch and sprinted across to join Helen at the barricade. He stared at the door. It shook in its frame with each bang as the dead hammered away at it from the other side.

"You think they'll get in?" Helen asked without looking at him.

"I doubt it. That door is too thick and it will be reinforced with steel inside it, and the hinges, too. They won't be able to get enough of them between the banister and the door to be able to force their way in, I shouldn't imagine."

He stepped forward and began to climb over the table and cabinet they had wedged against the door, carefully placing each foot and hand so as not to make a noise or hurt his self. He reached the door and looked back at Helen as she stood watching him. He gently lifted the cover to the peephole and pressed his eye against the lens. The distorted image that he saw on the other side was enough to make his blood freeze in his veins.

The hallway was packed, shoulder to shoulder, with hundreds of the dead. They all struggled to fight their way to the door of the apartment, growling and snarling at one another as they pushed and shoved their way through the crowd.

Steve climbed back over the barricade and jumped down at the side of Helen.

"We aren't going to be getting out that way. It's wall to wall with them out there," he said looking back at the door.

"The roof then," Helen replied. "It's the only option."

Steve nodded at her as he looked in her eyes. He was impressed with her calmness and composure. His nerves were screaming at him from inside, but he was determined not to show it.

On the rooftop, they had a clear view of the city and the streets below. The area around the base of the building was packed with the dead. It was impossible to make out individuals due to the altitude they were at and the volume of reanimated bodies that crowded the street.

"I think every pus brain in the city has come looking for us," Steve remarked as he stepped away from the edge.

"The good news is," he said with a slight smile, "I know where we are now. If my bearings are correct, then I would say that the main filter road that links the city to the ring road is about four streets in that direction." He pointed off towards the west.

"How will we get there?"

Steve looked at her and grinned. "Easy, we go across the rooftops."

For the better part of the day, Steve and Helen negotiated the roofs of the buildings that lined the street. They used the fire escape ladders to descend, stealthily creeping across at ground level in the alleyways that ran between the buildings, then scaling the steps that led up the sides of adjacent apartment and office blocks. They played a deadly game of cat and mouse with the hordes of dead that were never more than a few metres away.

They poured with sweat due to the effort and their nerves, which were beyond breaking point. They reached the far end of the street and paused for breath before they began their descent to the ground again.

"They're more spread out at this end," Helen noted as she looked down over the lip of the roof.

"What do you reckon?" Steve asked as he raised himself upright and joined her at the edge. He glanced down to the road below and watched the dark swaying figures that slowly edged their way to join the mass crowd at the far end.

"It will take forever going from rooftop to rooftop, Steve." She looked up at him. "Two or three streets to the slipway, would you say?"

He nodded, dreading the suggestion that he knew she was about to put to him. "Yeah, about that, I think."

Helen paused a moment in thought as she eyed the ground far below them. She then turned to him, a look of determination on her face.

"I say we make a run for it then. Down through there."

She pointed at an alleyway that ran between the buildings on the other side of the street. It looked as though it headed in the direction that they wanted to go.

Steve sighed, shaking his head. "Fucking hell," he said. "Come on then, let's do it if we're going to do it."

They made their way down the fire escape stairs of the final building in the street. At the bottom, they began to creep their way towards the corner that looked out on the road.

Dozens of corpses meandered their way towards the apartment block where they had stayed the previous night. They shuffled along, oblivious to the two living human beings that hid in the shadows just mere feet from where they were.

Helen was right, they were more spread out and Steve believed that they would be able to sprint through them and away along the alley before most of them had even realised that they were there.

Steve looked at Helen, and for a moment they stared into each other's eyes.

"Okay then, darling. This was your idea and there's no backing out now."

Helen nodded. "You ready? On three," she whispered.

She took a series of deep breaths, building up the oxygen levels in her lungs to feed her muscles for the coming sprint. She looked back at Steve.

"Okay, okay one, two…three."

They jumped to their feet and ran.

28

Ten miles short of where they wanted to be, the car finally gave up its battle. The engine cut out and regardless of how hard Stu tried, it failed to spring back to life.

"That's it, Marcus, we're dead in the water."

Marcus eyed their surroundings and shrugged. "Well, looks like we'll have to tab," he said using the army term for an extremely fast paced walk whilst carrying full kit.

"We'll have to get a move on, though, because I don't fancy spending a night under the stars. Camping isn't what it used to be."

The four remaining members of Marcus' team climbed out of the broken down vehicle and began adjusting their equipment for the hard walk ahead.

"Do you know how to get there?" Stu asked as he checked that all of the pouches on his assault vest were securely fastened.

"I grew up here, Stu. Of course I know," Marcus replied then turned to Jim. "You okay with this, old man? We Brits tend to move quicker than you guys and there's no singing while we do it."

"Fuck you, boss," Jim retorted with a grin. "I'll manage."

Marcus pulled out the map and began to study it. Now and then he would look up and glance about at the country around him, checking that the features matched up with what he was looking at on the piece of paper in his hands. After a short while, he folded it away and stuffed it in his inside pocket, satisfied that his bearings were correct.

They were still in the country, surrounded on all sides by low hills and fields. In the distance, they could see the hazy blue silhouette of the city. Marcus knew that they would need to skirt around in a wide arc to the west in order to avoid the heavily populated areas, adding to their journey. He looked up at the sky. The sun was starting to dip towards the horizon, casting its orange and pink rays through the atmosphere. He checked his watch.

"Okay, it's roughly seventeen kilometres to the Safari Park and about three hours of daylight left, shouldn't be a problem."

Everyone began taking large gulps from their water supplies, ensuring that their bodies were hydrated enough for the hard slog ahead. No one could afford to become a burden to the others due to dehydration.

Marcus led the way.

They took off at a quick pace and thrust their way along the narrow road. They were shielded on both sides by high hedgerows and they made a point of keeping to the centre of the road as much as possible. They moved rapidly, but every member of the team kept their vigilance, scanning every bush or dip in the hedge for possible threats.

Within just a few kilometres, everyone was soaked in sweat. It ran from their heads and down their faces, stinging their eyes. More sweat poured down their backs, causing their clothing to become saturated as their close-fitting assault vests did little to allow for any airflow between their skin and the material of their shirts.

Their legs burned, screaming at them as the lactic acid built up in the muscles. Their lungs gulped in each breath as though it was their last as their bodies fought hard to keep them moving at the fast pace that Marcus had set.

Jim was finding it a struggle. It had been a long time since his military days and running around, carrying full kit, was not the sort of thing he was used to anymore. When Marcus raised his hand from up ahead, signalling for them to halt as they approached a junction, Jim was silently happy to give his body the few minutes' rest that it so desperately needed. He stopped and leaned forward, resting his hands on his thighs, feeling the pain in his legs and back begin to subside.

They closed up and crouched at the side of the road, eyeing the junction and listening for any sign of the dead. The only noise they could hear was the whistles and tweets of the birds that lived in the hedgerows and fluttered overhead.

Marcus stepped forward and glanced along the road to his left and right. There was no sign of the creatures that had ravaged the world. There was no sign of anything, not even broken down vehicles. It was peaceful and he could have been forgiven for regarding the scene as being pleasant. The thought of the millions of dead that must be crowding the city was never far from his mind though.

They moved off again, the tempo just as swift as when they had started. Marcus could feel the heels of his feet starting to rub. He knew that blisters would form, but he cherished the idea that within a couple of hours he would be wrapped up safe, his feet immersed in a bowl of cold water with his wife and children sitting beside him. It was those thoughts that spurred him on. He refused to slacken the pace.

At another junction, they paused again. The city was off to their right. They could see the sprawling suburbs in the low ground stretching off in the distance and then blending with the tall buildings of the metropolis. Marcus recognised many of the landmarks as he looked at the skyline through his binoculars. Although he knew that the city was dead, and things were very different now, it warmed his heart to see the familiar sites and know that they were so close to their final destination.

"You see that?" Marcus said, pointing to the signpost on the far side of the road.

A jumble of plaques pointed them in all directions towards numbered roads and even the city centre. Another sign below, brown in colour, pointed them towards the Safari Park.

"We're almost there, boys." He looked back with a grin at the others.

The strain showed on their faces, but Marcus could also see the relief, knowing that their long and hard journey that had brought them all the way from Iraq was almost over.

Marcus stood and groaned. He arched his back and shrugged his shoulders to settle his equipment.

"The road straight ahead will link on to the ring road, about a mile further on." He pointed in the distance with the muzzle of his rifle. "We follow that for another mile or so, and then head northwest."

"You think we will get there before dark?" Hussein asked.

Marcus looked at each of them. "Well, that's where the problem lies. The ring road could be a drama. We don't know what it will be like, but short of traipsing cross-country, through the fields, we've not much choice."

"Fuck sake," Stu grumbled. "I'm already breathing through my arse as it is. I don't fancy us having to run from those fucking things."

They pushed on. It was not long before they came to the slipway that led them onto the ring road. More buildings, houses and shops, had begun to spring up around them as they drew nearer to the city and the signs of chaos and the dead littered the streets.

The country lane had opened out to a wide double width road as it began to enter the suburbs. They saw the carnage that the dead had left in their wake as they multiplied and seized control of the cities. Cars and personal belongings lay scattered all along the ring road. Puddles of dried and rotting blood were everywhere, mixed in with the skeletal remains of animals and people alike. Flocks of birds and swarms of insects circled the skies above as they kept an eye on the ground below, waiting for the four men to pass before they could resume feeding on the morsels that the dead had left behind.

Marcus slowed the pace slightly. There were far too many obstructions and blind spots for them to continue to race along safely. They had to scan their eyes along the ground, between the vehicles and into the distance continually. They moved silently, every man listening intently for any indication that they had been seen.

Jim watched over the barrier wall of the ring road as it rose up to an overpass. Far below, he had a bird's eye view of the destruction that had befallen human civilisation. Every building was in ruins. Their doors smashed inwards, the remains of inadequate barricades discarded to the side. Nearly every window that he saw was shattered.

Upturned cars and trucks littered the street. Newspapers and other waste drifted through the streets on the currents of air that flowed between the houses and buildings, while burnt out vehicles sat in silence as monuments to the anarchy that had reigned in the dying days of humanity's dominance over the planet.

Jim also saw the bodies, hundreds of them. Lying in the streets and left to rot, they slowly wasted away and began their long journey towards becoming dust. It was a pitiful and terrifying sight.

Jim also noticed something else.

"Marcus," he whispered loudly as he pushed his way forward. "Marcus, have you seen any?"

They all stopped and crouched down, turning to look at Jim. "Have we seen any what?" Stu asked.

"Have you seen any of the dead, I mean the walking kind?"

It dawned on them that they had not. They had seen hundreds of bodies, but none that were moving. Marcus glanced around him, studying the lay of the land and making his own appreciation of the situation.

"Maybe they're all in the city? Something could've attracted them away from the suburbs," Marcus suggested.

"I doubt it," Jim shook his head. "Not all of them. There's always a few that stick around, you've seen enough of them to know that."

Stu nodded. "He's right. Something is up."

"Well we can't turn back now. We'll push on but keep an eye out," Marcus said impatiently.

Home was so close that he could almost taste it and his heart skipped at the thought of anything standing in the way of getting there.

They turned off the ring road. The sun had already dipped beneath the western horizon and the sky to the east had already begun to grow dark. At the bottom of the slipway, Marcus stopped. He raised his weapon up to his shoulder and began scanning in all directions. Stu, not sure why Marcus had stopped but knowing that there must be an anticipated danger up ahead, stepped out to the side and began to scrutinize the area for himself.

"What is it, Marcus?" he hissed from behind.

Marcus said nothing but began to slowly edge his way forward, headed towards something in the road that was unseen to the others.

Stu moved up closer from behind. He smelled the stench of decaying flesh and heard the hum of flies. Marcus stopped and studied a bulky form on the ground in front of him. Moving closer, Stu recognised the stripped carcass of what he thought was a cow. It had been picked completely clean. Its legs were missing and the head, nothing more than a skull, lay discarded a few metres away. It was nothing new to them; they had seen hundreds of consumed animals along their journey. The dead ate everything they could get their rotting hands on.

As he moved closer, Stu soon realised what had grabbed Marcus' interest so much. He saw the chain and ropes that had secured the animal to the barrier of the road. Someone had deliberately left it there for the dead.

"Jesus," Jim mumbled. "Why would anyone want to feed them?"

Marcus shrugged. "Maybe whoever did it thought they could satisfy their appetite and the dead would leave them alone? Fucked if I know, but I don't want to hang around to meet them. We could be next on the menu."

Just a few hundred metres further on, they found the remains of another animal. Again, it had been incapacitated and chained to prevent it from escaping.

"What the fuck," Jim exclaimed.

Marcus looked up and turned in the direction they had come. He then turned in the direction they were headed and an icy finger ran along the length of his spine. The trussed animals had been planted in the same direction that they were going.

Marcus suddenly remembered Gary telling him over the radio that they believed there was a saboteur in their midst. Now, seeing the devoured animals deliberately planted for the dead, he was sure that someone was trying to lead the creatures to the park, the same park where his family were.

"Come on," he ordered, suddenly jumping to his feet and beginning to run.

They were just a few kilometres away and the thought that they could already be too late filled him with panic. Fear drove him forward, his legs pumping as fast as they could as he raced towards the Safari Park.

Stu, Jim and Hussein had also realised the same and followed Marcus. They sprinted for all their worth, their hearts pounding in their chests as they pushed their bodies to the limit. It was growing darker by the minute and the stars were already beginning to show in the dark sky to the east as the last rays of sunlight cast its dazzling colours over the western sky.

They sprinted by more dead animals, stripped of flesh and chained. Marcus increased his pace. From somewhere deep inside, he pulled out his reserves and powered forward. Suddenly, he stopped. The rest came to a halt behind him.

They were just metres away from the junction that led on to the access road of the Safari Park.

Jim's eyes bulged and his jaw almost dislocated when it dropped open as he stared at the sight before them. The street was packed with the staggering corpses of the dead. The snared animals had done their job and it looked as if all the dead in the area had converged towards the park.

Individuals began to detach themselves from the mass of bodies as they saw the four living men behind them. They staggered towards them, moaning loudly and reaching out to them. Their wails and movements attracted more of them to follow, and soon hundreds of the dead were headed straight for Marcus and his men.

Stu raised his weapon and began to fire. He poured round after round into the crowd without making the slightest difference to their numbers.

"What do we do, Marcus?" he screamed over the sound of the gunfire.

Jim and Hussein had also begun to shoot into the mass. Bodies dropped by their dozens, but more followed and continued to congregate towards them.

Marcus was shouting something to Stu, but his words were lost in the crescendo of the firing rifles. Stu stepped to his left, closer to Marcus and continuing to pick off his targets.

"What?" he screamed over the din.

Marcus moved in close to him and screamed in his ear. "The claymore, clear us a path," he shouted pointing to the bulging pouch on Stu's vest.

Stu suddenly realised what Marcus had been trying to tell him. He began to fumble with his vest, releasing the fastening clip to the pocket that contained the deadly mine. At the same time, he began screaming across to Jim and Hussein to follow him to cover.

Marcus was down beside a wall, covering the rest of the team as they jumped in next to him and into the protection that the thick bricks provided.

Stu was fumbling with the claymore. His hands shook uncontrollably and refused to obey his commands as tried to prepare the mine as quickly as possible.

"Come on, Stu," Marcus screamed as he pumped more rounds into the approaching sea of decaying flesh. "They'll be all over us like a cheap suit in a minute."

More of the dead tumbled to the floor as the five point five six millimetre rounds smashed their way through their brains. The road became a writhing mass of flailing arms and wailing voices as the creatures trampled over the fallen and staggered towards the four men.

"Okay," Stu shouted. "Good to go."

He raised himself up and grunting with the effort, he hurled the claymore as far as he could into the mass bodies.

"Down, get fucking down," he screamed.

All four of them flattened themselves to the ground, covering their ears and opening their mouths to prevent the impending shockwave from shattering their teeth. Stu slammed his palm down on the clacker in his hand.

A split second later, the ground seemed to erupt all around them. A flash of light and a geyser of debris shot in to the air, sending dozens of the dead with it and scattering them over a wide area. The steel balls packed tightly into the explosives shot out in all directions, ripping their way through flesh and bone and shattering the top layer of bricks from the wall that Marcus and his team used for cover. The shockwave erupted out from the centre of the crowd as the mine was detonated, flattening everything for a hundred metres.

With ringing ears and blurred vision, Marcus jumped to his feet.

"Fuck me," he mumbled as Stu, Jim and Hussein raised themselves up beside him.

The claymore had done its job. The steel balls had ripped through the swarm, tearing them apart. The shockwave had done the rest. It had tore through the mass of dead and shattered their bones, leaving them as nothing more than sacks of rotting flesh.

Bodies lay strewn and twisted all around them. Those that were not dead were incapable of walking and lay in pools of their own filth as their remaining bodily fluids seeped out onto the ground all around them. Legs, heads and other body parts that were no longer recognisable as being human, littered the street like grotesque displays of art.

"Go, go," Marcus screamed, jolting the rest of his team into action.

He took off along the road, trying his best to step over the bodies as he ran. It was almost impossible to do, and on more than a few occasions his boots sank deep into the smouldering, dismembered remains of corpses.

They reached the junction. Only a few of the dead had managed to regain their feet and staggered towards them. They quickly dispatched them as they began moving through the crossroads.

Marcus paused a moment and looked to his left. A barrier of felled trees spanned the width of the access road leading down to the park. Through the branches, he saw more of the dead making their way towards them, the shooting and explosion obviously being what had attracted their attention.

"They're on the right," Jim shouted as he turned and fired wildly into the dark figures that made their way along the adjoining road. The shots were high and smashed into the buildings behind them.

Stu stepped in and raised his rifle.

"Don't shoot," a voice cried out from the darkness as two shadowy forms began to run towards them.

They did not move like the dead; even the runners that they sometimes encountered were not so articulate. More to the point, the dead did not speak.

In the gloom behind the two approaching people, Stu could see a dark wall of bodies following them. He took aim and began to fire past the two running people and into the mass. Tracer rounds shot out along the street, glowing red in the darkness and looking like the laser beams from a science fiction movie. They thumped into the crowd, burning brightly as they pierced the flesh while other tracer rounds ricocheted upwards in the darkening sky.

"Don't shoot," the voice, screamed at them again, "stop fucking shooting at us."

"Run, you two, run!" Stu cried back at them.

The two figures flinched and cowered with every shot that whizzed by them, but they carried on forwards, sprinting towards the junction.

Ten metres out and Marcus' eyes grew wide. "Steve," he gasped. "What the fuck are you doing out here?"

Steve came to a halt in front of him. His face was bright red and his chest wheezed as he fought for air. His upper body fell forward and he braced his hands on his thighs, coughing and spluttering as he did so. A moment later and he threw his body upright and his head back, looking into the eyes of his brother.

"Good to see you too, Marcus," he said as he reached out and hugged him.

Marcus looked at the woman his brother had arrived with; she was beautiful, despite the strain and fear in her face and she held her composure much better than Steve did.

"I take it you must be Helen?" he said with a smile.

She nodded, placing her hands on her hips and breathing deeply as she regained her breath.

"We need to move, boss," Jim called as he watched the crowd of corpses from the street and beyond the barrier approaching.

Steve, still gulping for air, turned towards the road that ran along the outer wall of the Safari Park on its eastern side.

"This way," he croaked. "We've been using the rear gate to get in and out." He set off at a steady jog, Helen close on his heels with Marcus and the rest following.

Marcus caught up with his brother and ran at his side. "Someone has been leaving breadcrumbs, Steve."

"You mean the animals?" Steve replied without taking his eyes off the road ahead. "I know. They lead all the way to the city. There's a fucking millions of those things following us."

They reached the gate that led on to the track at the rear entrance of the park. Marcus put his hand out to his right and across Steve's chest, stopping him in his tracks.

"Hang on," he whispered.

Tethered to the fence and chewing away on the grass that grew beside it, a goat stood, completely oblivious to the danger that it was in. It looked up at them and bleated.

Marcus turned to the others and held a finger to his lips. He moved in closer and peered into the darkness of the trees that overhung the narrow track as Jim began attempting to free the animal.

"I think whoever did this, they're still here," Marcus whispered as he leaned in close to Steve. "Follow me and keep quiet." He turned to look back at the others and almost laughed.

Jim, clutching the chain in his hand like a dog leash, stood watching them expectantly with the goat standing at his side, a far from intelligent look on its face.

"Jim," Marcus whispered, "why you bringing the goat?"

Jim looked down at his new friend and then back up at Marcus as though the question was a stupid one.

"Well," he leaned forward and whispered in reply, "we can't leave him here, and besides, I like goat's milk."

"There's a problem there, Jim," Stu said with a smile. "You said it was a *'him'*. How do expect to milk it? I want front row seats to that event."

Jim looked back at the goat then shrugged. "Fuck it, he's still coming with us."

Marcus and Stu led them forward along the track with Steve and Helen close behind. Jim, Hussein and the new edition to the team, the goat, covered the rear.

With the fading light and the thick overhanging trees, it was hard to see the track. Marcus and Stu stepped carefully, unsure of what to expect up ahead of them. They crept along with their rifles aimed straight ahead of them, ready for anything that appeared out of the darkness.

Marcus could hear something. He looked at Stu and raised his hand to his ear, nodding his head to their front, in the direction he suspected the sound to be coming from.

Stu cocked his head, focussing his hearing and squinted into the gloom. It sounded like the telltale clinks of metal against metal, as though someone was hammering away at something.

A few metres further on and Marcus stopped and moved into a crouch. Everyone followed suit. Just ahead of them and silhouetted by the faint light that cast down into the park on the other side of the fence, two figures squatted by the gate. They spoke to one another in hushed voices and Marcus was sure that one of them sounded feminine.

It was hard to tell what they were doing or whether they were armed, but regardless, Marcus and the other survivors needed to pass through the gate and in the process, stop whatever it was that the two people ahead of them were doing. He looked to his right and nodded at Stu. Together, they sprang to the feet and bounded forward.

The sudden movement and noise of their footsteps alerted the two figures at the gate to their presence. The first turned, wielding something in its hand and raising it above its head. Marcus did not hesitate. He squeezed the trigger and sent four shots racing towards the dark shape that he judged to be a threat.

In the bright muzzle flash, he saw the figure of a man jerk as the rounds punched through his chest. The man screamed and tumbled backwards, hitting the fence and slumping to the side.

The other figure was too slow to react. Stu had already closed the distance and launched himself in the air, landing heavily on to the person's back. He began pounding away at its head and neck with the butt of his rifle, raining down heavy blows and forcing them to the ground.

She began to scream.

29

Simon's pale white skin was soaked with sweat. His eyes were sunken and his cheekbones protruded more prominently, giving the impression that his skin seemed to be stretched taut over his face. His eyelids fluttered continuously and his breath came in hoarse gasps as the infection raged through his body.

Johnny stood by him, watching over him and doing what he could to comfort his friend; there was nothing else that he could do. He knew that Simon was going to die and Johnny wished that he had the strength and character to speed up the process, to relieve him of the suffering that he was going through.

For the past two days, since he was bitten, Simon had existed in a realm that was neither living nor dead. As the virus ravaged his body he became more delirious, sinking in and out of consciousness and completely unaware of his surroundings. The fever burned stronger in him by the hour. Sometimes, he would flail his arms, screaming and crying out unintelligible sentences, and other times he would burst into laughter for no reason. Simon was beyond help and Johnny felt completely helpless.

John lay on the bed placed beside Simon. He, too, was in a similar state. The veins in his neck stood out black against his deathly pale skin as his blood raced around his body, carrying the ever-multiplying infection as it slowly destroyed him from within.

Carl also stood vigil over the two dying men. He and John had been close, as Johnny and Simon had, and they felt that it was only right that they be the ones to help them pass over. He looked across to the far corner of the room. On the table lay the instrument that he and Johnny had agreed was best to take care of the two unfortunate men once they died.

A knot formed in his throat as he pictured himself carrying out his duty. His stomach churned and he felt a wave of nausea flood over him. He did not relish the task ahead, but he was determined to see it through, his last act as a friend to John.

The windows in the room suddenly rattled in their frames, closely followed by a low muffled booming sound in the distance and the floor beneath their feet vibrated, as though the house was being shifted by some gigantic machine. Carl looked at Johnny in confusion. The scruffy little bearded man looked back at him calmly, shrugging his shoulders.

"What the fuck was that?" Carl asked, knowing that Johnny had as little idea of what it could have been as he did.

Carl turned and headed for the door. "Stay here, Johnny, I'll be back soon."

In the foyer, the people of the house had begun to gather. Everyone had heard the sound and felt the vibrations, and their curiosity compelled them to investigate. Excited and concerned voices echoed through the house and questions bounced around in the large space of the main reception room to the mansion, but there were no answers.

"Whatever it was, it was big enough to rattle every window in this place," Lee stated as he looked around the room, studying the windows and ceiling.

"Could it be the gas mains, maybe a ruptured pipe?" Karen offered.

"No," Gary shook his head as he peered out through the windows and into the darkness. "It was something much bigger than a pipe bursting, darling."

"What about the army, could it be the counter offensive?"

"I don't think so," Gary replied, still squinting into the gloom on the other side of the window.

At that moment, heavy footsteps echoed from along the corridor that led from the top of the stairs. Stan appeared at the balcony, his face full of alarm and his chest heaving. He raced down the stairs and into the foyer as everyone turned to him, anxiously waiting for what he obviously had to tell them.

"What's going on, Stan?" Gary asked calmly.

"Something just blew up," he gasped.

"Fuck me, brains as well as good looks," Lee mumbled.

Stan ignored the remark and continued to try to focus on his words. "Something exploded up by the barricade at the junction."

"At the junction," Gary looked at Karen. "Maybe it *was* the gas mains then."

"No, it wasn't gas," Stan shook his head. Clearly, there was more to tell.

"Well, what was is then, Stan?" Sophie asked impatiently.

Stan shrugged, "I don't know what the explosion was but someone is shooting, too. We could see the bullets flying in the air from the roof. Sounds like there's a few of them," he added.

Gary's face took on an expression of dread. The idea of having armed people running around so close to where they were made him think the worst: *marauding gangs,* he thought, but he refrained from saying it out loud for fear of starting a panic.

Claire appeared at the top of the staircase. "He's right, I've just been up there but the shooting has stopped now."

"Where have they gone, Claire?" Jake asked up at her.

She shrugged. "I don't know, the shooting just stopped and it all went quiet."

Carl had already stepped out through the main doors to see and hear for himself. Gary followed him and joined him on the steps.

"We've no weapons here, Gary. If it is someone that wants in, we're defenceless to stop them."

"We need to lock this place down," Gary replied.

Carl shook his head. "It won't do any good. Like I said; what will we defend with, sticks and stones? I think we should look at evacuating the park, Gary."

A few minutes later, four more shots echoed across the open fields of the park. It was hard to tell for sure, but Gary thought that they had come from the rear gate area. He turned and ran back inside.

"Okay," he shouted to the people in the foyer, "we need to get everyone together." He was doing his best to sound like he was in control but fear gripped him and it showed in his face and his trembling voice.

"Get all the children and be ready to leave."

Everybody began to bombard him with questions, all at once. They were frightened and the thought of leaving the safety of the park filled them with terror. He stepped over to Karen, his wife. She wringed her hands incessantly, which she always did when annoyed or upset. Her eyes were wide and they darted about the room, looking from one person to the next as the panic began to spread.

"Karen," Gary said in merely more than a whisper, "I think whoever it is, they're at the back gate. They will be here soon. I think we should go, but I will not leave without you. If you stay, then I stay too."

The sounds of the children, being dragged from their beds and asking all manner of questions, drew his attention away for a moment. They were being ushered down the stairs by their parents and Kieran, having come from the roof, closely followed.

He made eye contact with Gary.

"Someone's coming." He tried to say it without drawing the attention of the rest of the survivors, but they all heard.

Gary turned and looked at the people assembled in front of him. They were out of time. The main door suddenly clanged as it was slammed shut by Carl and he began to lever the bolts into place.

"No," Gary spoke, raising his hand up in front of him. "Don't lock it."

Carl turned to him, a look of exasperation on his face.

Gary nodded calmly. "Don't lock it, Carl. Like you said, if they want in, they'll get in and they may take it as a hostile move if we barricade ourselves in here."

Carl understood and nodded as he stepped back from the large doors. He moved across to where his wife and son stood, placing his hands protectively around their shoulders as they stared back at the heavy wooden doors of the house.

The whole room fell silent as everybody waited. They stared nervously and expectantly at the entrance to the old mansion. The fear and anxiety in the room seemed to sit in the air like a thick and invisible fog as the seconds slipped by, bringing everyone close to breaking point as their nerves threatened to snap.

Jake looked across at Lee. For the first time, he could see that the tough man was unsure and afraid. Sweat dripped from his forehead as he waited along with the others. Lee turned and looked him straight in the eye and nodded. Jake could see that, despite his obvious trepidation, Lee was ready to fight anyone that walked through the door.

They heard voices approaching from outside, then the large wooden doors suddenly flew open, banging from the wall and shuddering as the impact reverberated through it.

Two large and bulky figures stepped forward from the gloom, throwing a dark bundle ahead of them. It landed on the floor in front of Gary, yelping and crying as it hit the hard surface and curling itself into a ball.

The two men stepped forward into the light of the foyer. They were terrifying in appearance. Their eyes shone wildly and their expressions were as hard as stone. They stared at the people before them, their eyes burning into the faces of each individual as they scanned the room, all the time, remaining silent and motionless in the doorway.

Gary looked straight back at them. He saw the rifles in their hands and the ammunition they had strapped to their bodies, but he stood his ground. He was not challenging them, but he did not want to appear subservient neither.

"Fuck me," Lee said hoarsely as he gaped at the new arrivals.

The man in the front turned in his direction. He locked eyes with Lee and gave a slight nod of his head towards him.

A commotion behind the two men heralded the arrival of more people. Excited and strained voices could be heard drawing nearer as they made their way up the steps to the house.

A gasp from behind made Gary turn and he was just in time to see Jennifer crumple to the floor as she collapsed. One of the men at the doorway watched as Jennifer fell. He stepped forward and began to push his way through the assembled crowd and towards her. More people suddenly burst into the room from the doorway.

Gary stepped back slightly, and then he recognised Steve and Helen.

He, too, almost collapsed. "Steve," his voice was little more than a whimper as the tension was suddenly released. "Steve," he repeated, not knowing what else to say as he saw his friend, alive and well.

"Daddy," Sarah squealed as she let go of her mother's hand and ran towards him.

Steve dropped to his knees and caught her as she leapt into his arms. He hugged her tightly, not wanting to let go as the tears began to pour down his cheeks.

Helen realised that most of the people gathered in the foyer were still holding their breath. They were in shock and unsure of what exactly was happening.

She smiled at Gary as she stepped forward.

"Well," she said cheerfully. "I suppose I had better be the one to make the introductions then." She swept her hand behind her, indicating the four strange men.

"That's Marcus," she said nodding towards the man that crouched over Jennifer with Liam and David hanging from his arms, "and these are his friends; Stu, Jim and Hussein."

The three men still standing by the door nodded at the people that stood rooted to the floor of the house, slack-jawed and staring at them.

"It's a pleasure," Jim said in his Texas drawl, still clutching in his hand the chain that was attached to the goat. "We haven't named him yet," he said looking down at the animal, "but I was thinking something along the lines of, *'Lucky'*."

"How about calling him, *'Barbeque'*?" Stu suggested with a grin.

"No way," Jim shook his head adamantly. "He's mine and no one is eating him."

Jake looked down at the bulky form on the floor, still whimpering and curled into the foetal position.

"And who's this?" he asked.

Helen nodded at him as she stepped forward. "See for yourself," she said reaching down, gripping the quivering figure by the hair and dragging it upright. She twisted her hand and snapped her wrist back, exposing the woman's face to the people of the house.

A chorus of gasps echoed around the room.

"Stephanie," Gary exclaimed.

She looked up at him, her large face easily recognisable through the blood, grime and tears. Her eyes darted from Gary's to the people that stood around her, glaring back at her.

"We caught her and that rat of a husband of hers at the rear gate," Steve said as he raised himself to his feet.

"Jason, where is he?" Jake asked.

"Marcus killed him and Stu managed to batter this lump of shit into submission."

"They've been leading the dead to the park," Helen added. "They've been tying animals to buildings and fences, leaving a trail that led right to us."

Gary was lost for words. He just stood there, staring at Stephanie in complete shock.

"People are dying because of this fat bitch," Lee growled as he stepped forward.

"It was you wasn't it, Stephanie?" Gary said down at her. "It was you that sabotaged the fuel and opened the rear gate to let the dead in. John is dying because of you," he spat with venom.

People had begun to edge their way forwards, towards her. Angry eyes glared at her as rage engulfed them.

"Tie her up," Steve ordered as he saw people on the verge of losing control and tearing her limb from limb. "We'll deal with her later."

Carl and Jake dragged her away and into one of the storage rooms, wrapping cords around her hands and feet and locking the door shut.

It was late and most of the people had finally retired to their rooms, including Marcus and his family. He had wasted no time in getting away from the bombardment of questions that he knew were coming. He helped put his children to bed, and then locked himself and his wife, Jennifer, in their room and away from prying eyes.

Stu sat on one of the large sofas in the foyer, his head thrown back as he relished the comfort of the large couch. Jim and Hussein were doing the same, smiling to one another as the realisation struck home that their long and arduous journey had finally ended. They could now relax, but none of them had taken the step towards removing their equipment, or even letting go of their weapons. Their assault vests and rifles had been a part of them for so long; they would feel completely naked and vulnerable without them.

Jim grinned across at Stu and nodded towards the ceiling.

"He's like a dog with five dicks," he said referring to Marcus. "After all these months, I'm surprised he didn't need a wheelbarrow to carry his balls in."

Stu laughed and nodded, understanding exactly to what Jim was referring. Hussein still had not come to full grips with the western humour and looked at them quizzically.

"We thought you were marauders," Gary said with a smile.

Stu chuckled. "That's exactly what we are and have been for the past four or five months. How do you think we survived?"

Gary nodded, understanding that the men before him had had to do whatever it took to make it through, all the way from Iraq.

"We thought there would be more of you," Jake added.

Stu opened his eyes and brought his head forward from the headrest of the couch. He fixed Jake with an unflinching stare and slowly shook his head.

"They didn't make it," he replied in a low voice.

Gary stood. "Would you like some tea or coffee?" he offered.

Jim looked up at him and smiled broadly. "You got anything stronger?"

With a whisky bottle slowly depleting on the table in front of them, Gary, Jake, Lee and Helen sat talking with the survivors of Marcus' team until late into the night.

"What about the counter offensive?" Jake asked. "We've been watching the news reports and they say it won't be long before all the major cities are back in our hands."

"Don't believe a fucking word of that bullshit, my friend," Jim snorted as he drained his glass.

"We've seen it first hand," Stu added. "It has been a disaster from the moment it started. Those troops are nothing more than cannon fodder. The dead are firmly in control now and the armed forces are in full retreat."

Gary looked down and shrugged. "Then I guess that we really are on our own then."

"Better that way, mate," Stu replied. "Believe me."

Carl and Johnny suddenly joined them from the room where Simon and John lay dying. The expressions on their faces were as hard as granite and their eyes stared straight ahead of them as they approached the others seated in the foyer.

Steve looked down at Carl's hand. He clutched a long screwdriver in his palm, the steel shaft smeared with blood that ran down to the handle and dripped from his fingers.

"It's over," Carl announced hoarsely. "John and Simon are dead. We've taken care of them, they won't come back."

Carl and Johnny both collapsed heavily onto the large sofa. Carl let out a long sigh and rubbed his face, sniffing back the tears that threatened to burst from his eyes as he struggled to keep his composure. His friend, John, was dead and he had taken it upon himself to be the one that drove the screwdriver through his ear and into his brain. It had been hard for him to do but he had reminded himself of the alternative.

He knew that John did not want to walk around after he was dead.

"Pour us one of those will you, Gary?" Carl asked, nodding at the bottle of whisky that was placed on the table in front of them.

"A large one, please, if you don't mind."

30

Robbie lay on his bed, smoking a cigarette and listening to the sound of the rain hammering against his window. The storm had been raging for the last couple of hours and rivers of water trickled down the glass panes and cascaded onto the window ledge. He always enjoyed listening to the rain, especially when he was warm and dry, indoors.

There was a knock at the door.

"Who is it?" Robbie groaned, not wanting to be disturbed.

The handle twisted and the door opened with a creak. He recognised the silhouette in the doorway immediately.

"Ah, Toby, what's happening, buddy?" he asked as he sat upright with a sigh, swinging his legs over on to the floor and reaching for his boots.

Tobias stepped forward and closed the door behind him. He had a grim look on his face and he clutched a piece of paper in his hand. It looked as though the weight of the world was resting upon his shoulders.

Robbie sat staring back at him expectantly. "Well, what's up?"

Tobias sat down across from him, sinking deep into the armchair, which was the only other piece of furniture in the room apart from the bed. He let out a sigh and passed the paper over to Robbie.

"It's the offensive; it has ground to a halt." He paused a moment then added, "Looks like it will fail altogether, Rob."

Robbie sat in silence for a moment and read the messages that the radio operators had intercepted and written down. There was no good news on that scrap of paper.

Messages to and from MJOC showed that the simultaneous assaults on London and Edinburgh had failed. Worse still, all communications with the ground forces of the London units had been lost. Once again, it looked as though the high command had greatly underestimated the enemy, believing that firepower and numbers alone could defeat them and they had learned nothing since the opening days of the plague.

"What do you think happened?" Robbie asked looking up.

Tobias shrugged. "Can't be sure, can we? And we're not likely to find out. Personally, I think it was a mixture of overconfidence, bad planning and the lack of experienced troops spearheading the offensive."

He sat forward in the chair, placing his fingers together. "You know as well as I do that most of the regular army were wiped out in the early days of this shit storm."

Robbie nodded. "Yeah, and since then they've had to fall back on boys and old men."

"Well, you can bet your arse that there will be no reinforcements or support arriving for us now. We're on our own, Robbie."

"What do we do, stay here or try to find somewhere else?"

Tobias thought for a moment.

"The first thing we do," he replied, "is get rid of the specimens from the garages. I don't want those bags of shit living next door to where we sleep."

Robbie nodded. "I'll get a few of the lads to take care of it."

"No," Tobias stated, rising to his feet. "We'll do it, now."

Tobias and Robbie made their way through the long cavernous garages. Their footsteps echoed through the darkness as the rain beat down on the steel roof above them, sounding like thousands of tiny pebbles being dropped from a great height. They could see the cage and the dim light that surrounded it at the far end. The grunts and low sorrowful moans of the dead drifted to their ears as they approached.

The two soldiers standing guard turned to them and nodded. There was no need for any formalities like standing to attention for the higher ranks in the unit anymore. Tobias did not see it as necessary, even to the point where everyone was on a first name basis.

"How's things, boys?" Robbie asked as he came to a halt.

"Same shit," one of the soldiers replied indifferently, "different fucking night, Robbie. You know how it is. Standing here watching these pus bags isn't the best duty I ever pulled."

Tobias smiled. He knew all too well some of the dull and soul-destroying tasks that soldiers have to carry out from time to time. He had done more than his fair share of them.

"Well, after tonight, you won't need to worry about it anymore," Robbie replied.

Tobias stepped closer and peered in the cage. The dead inside threw themselves at the bars, thrusting their hands through the small openings and clutching at him as he remained a safe distance away.

"You had any dramas from them?" Tobias asked, indicating the dead.

The soldier shrugged. "Just the usual, really; sometimes they bang away at the cage, and others, they just stand their drooling at us."

Robbie turned and grinned at him. "You mean like the time that Taff took us all to that gay bar in Soho, in uniform, when we were providing security at the Olympics?"

The soldier laughed and nodded as he remembered the night that Robbie referred to. "Yeah, a bit like that."

"Well, we're getting rid of them. The offensive has failed and it's pointless and dangerous to keep them here," Tobias said as he interrupted the reminiscing.

He pulled his pistol from his holster and took a step closer. The first of the creatures continued to snarl at him, swiping its arms at the space between it and the living beyond the bars of the cage.

Tobias took aim carefully, slowly squeezing the trigger. A flash of light exploded from the barrel, the sound of the bullet echoing thunderously around the large garage. The round smashed into the creature's forehead and erupted outwards from the back of its skull. It dropped instantly, slumping down the steel railings of the cage with its hand still sticking out through the bars.

Robbie joined him and they shot three more in quick succession, leaving just two still standing.

"Stop," Tobias ordered.

He peered in the cage and at the far side. There, stood the figure of the defiant corpse he had watched and reasoned with the day they had been put in the enclosure. It remained in the shadows, watching the men outside as they killed the other dead around it. It had not attempted to attack the bars of the cage, as the others had done, but instead seemed to want to preserve its existence and keep out of the line of fire.

Keeping his eyes focussed on the figure in the shadows, Tobias raised his pistol again, pointing it at the head of the growling, lifeless face that pressed itself up close to the bars of the cage.

He fired again, the crack of the round booming in their ears. The body tumbled backwards and hit the floor with a thump. Still, the figure on the far side did not move or even acknowledge the demise of its fellow dead.

"Okay," Tobias said turning to Robbie. "Open the cage."

Robbie blinked back at him in confusion. "But, there's still one in there, Tobias."

"I know that, Robbie. Now, open it."

Robbie nodded and did as Tobias demanded. He released the locks and slid back the bolts, allowing the door to slide open. Robbie and the two soldiers stepped backwards, their hands gripping their weapons tightly as they waited for the one remaining creature to come bursting out of the dark interior of the cage.

Only Tobias stood his ground. He stood in front of the entrance, staring into the blackness. His pistol was back in its holster and his hands were resting unthreateningly by his sides. He could sense the thing watching him, but he felt that he was being weighed up, studied more than looked on with ravenous eyes.

Robbie and the two soldiers looked at one another with concern, but remained silent as they watched their commander at the door to the cage.

"It's okay," Tobias' voice called out in the darkness. "You can come out. No one will hurt you."

The figure did not budge or show any indication that it was willing to move, or understood anything that Tobias had said.

Tobias stepped back and away from the entrance, giving the creature the opportunity of freedom from the narrow confines of the cell. A few moments later, he heard the shifting of feet and from out of the gloom, the one remaining dead slowly stepped forward.

It moved cautiously, suspicious of the four living people carrying weapons that could easily end its existence. Nervously, it stepped into the low light of the entrance. It stopped and looked at the bodies of the dead around it. They lay motionless, congealed blood and rotting brains oozing from the gaping wounds in their heads. It looked back at Tobias, staring straight into his eyes.

Tobias understood. He turned to the others. "Lower your weapons, it's scared."

"*It's* scared? I have shit my pants twice already, Tobias. What the fuck are we doing?" Robbie remarked from behind.

"Just do it, Robbie. I don't think it wants to hurt us."

The figure in the doorway watched as the weapons were slung over the shoulders of the soldiers. It looked back at Tobias again, and then stepped forward, out from the cage and into the open.

It stopped, waiting for whatever was to come next.

Tobias walked towards it. It cowered slightly, as though it was about to retreat into the darkness of the cage behind it again.

"No," Tobias said in a soothing voice and holding his hands out in front of him, "it's okay. No one is going to hurt you."

"Fucking hell," Robbie exclaimed, stepping forward and around to the side. "I've never seen one look scared before, let alone try to run away."

Tobias and the figure were close now. Just an arm's length separated them as they both stood silently, watching one another. Tobias fought to keep his composure as the smell of the creature drifted into his nostrils.

A sudden flurry of movement from the side caused the body of the man to reel as Robbie lunged. As quickly as he had stepped in, Robbie jumped back, clutching something in the palm of his hand.

"What's this then?" he asked as he opened the wallet.

Tobias held out his hand, indicating to Robbie to hand it to him. The wallet was mouldy and damp. It had been in the man's pocket since the day he had died and Tobias cringed at the thought of the untold amount of filth he was holding in his hand. However, the curiosity was too great. Tobias was intrigued by the thing that stood before him, unflinching and defiant, staring back at him with eyes that told him there was still a spark of intelligence behind them.

He pulled out a driving license and read the name aloud, "Andrew Moorcroft."

The creature's eyes widened and a low hoarse gasp escaped its lips as it clearly recognised the words that Tobias spoke.

"Your name, it is Andrew Moorcroft?" Tobias asked in an attempt to communicate with the dead man in front of him. The dead eyes looked back at him, unblinking.

"Andrew, that is you, isn't it?" Tobias spoke, pointing the license at him.

Andy looked at the license and then back at Tobias. His expression changed, raising his brow as his mouth opened, releasing a long sorrowful groan. He brought his fingers up towards Tobias' hand and touched the plastic of the identification card. His brow furrowed then raised again as he was clearly bombarded with distant memories. He moaned gently and affectionately as he took the card from Tobias, studying it and stroking the face of the man in the picture.

"Jesus, it knows its own name," Robbie whispered.

"That's why we're letting him go," Tobias replied as he watched Andy and handed him back his wallet.

Andy took the wallet in his bony hands and stared down at it. He gently ran his fingers over the leather, caressing it, and grunted as he felt familiarity surge through him.

"Letting it go? Are you serious?"

"Look at him," Tobias replied. "If he was like the others, he would've attacked us. I don't think this poor soul is interested in the living. I get the impression he is more afraid of us that we are of him and he just wants to be left alone."

Andy looked up at him and then back at Robbie. There was no malice or aggression in his face as he studied the men before him.

Robbie realised that Tobias was right. The thing in front of them was unlike the others. It made no aggressive moves towards them, even now, in the open and with no restraints, it stood its ground and did not make any indication that it wanted to harm them.

Tobias stepped back and moved towards the door. He threw it open and motioned for Andy to follow. Andy hesitated. He looked around at the three other men in the spacious garage and then at the open door.

The rain had stopped and the twilight gloom of the evening caused the wet surfaces to sparkle as the light slowly began to fade into darkness.

"They won't hurt you, Andrew. You're free," Tobias called back from the doorway.

Andy nervously staggered towards him, still clutching the wallet and driver's license in his hand. A wave of emotion flowed over him as he realised that he would not be destroyed and that they were offering to let him go. He longed to be free again, to be left alone and allowed to walk away.

Out in the open, Tobias walked alongside of Andy as they moved towards the gate and the barricade. Andy moved slowly, his feet scuffing along the ground as his eyes remained fixed upon the gate ahead of them.

Tobias watched him intently. It was hard to believe that here he was, walking alongside one of the un-dead. He had never imagined such a thing. He could see that the body of Andrew Moorcroft was much the same as the others. It was withered and slowly decomposing with all manner of creatures infesting it, but his brain was different.

There was still a spark of life in the dead man, and Tobias could see it.

Robbie and the two soldiers followed close behind, still in awe of the courage, or stupidity, that their leader was showing and the fact that the dead man seemed to understand everything that was happening.

Tobias opened the large heavy gate and with an open palm, gestured to the outside world.

Andy looked at him, then at his hand that indicated his freedom. He turned and looked back at Robbie, and then back to Tobias.

"Go on," Tobias nodded. "You can go."

Andy took a tentative step towards the opening, and then stopped. He turned back to the man that was setting him free and reached his hand out.

Tobias looked down and saw that Andy was reaching towards his chest. The cold bony palm of his hand lightly touched the material of Tobias' shirt, remaining there for a moment as they both stared at one another.

Tobias looked down at the dead hand that rested on his torso, close to where his heart was. He looked back up at Andrew and saw a glimpse of something behind his dead eyes. He realised that, the lifeless man before him was trying to say, *'Thank you'*.

Andy nodded slightly, then turned and walked away.

END

ICE STATION ZOMBIE
JE GURLEY

For most of the long, cold winter, Antarctica is a frozen wasteland. Now, the ice is melting and the zombies are thawing. Arctic explorers Val Marino and Elliot Anson race against time and death to reach Australia, but the Demise has preceded them and zombies stalk the streets of Adelaide and Coober Pedy.

www.severedpress.com

The Coalition

When the dead rose to destroy the living, Ron Cutter learned to survive. While so many others died, he thrived. His life is a constant battle against the living dead. As he casts his own bullets and packs his shotgun shells, his humanity slowly melts away.

Then he encounters a lost boy and a woman searching for a place of refuge. Can they help him recover the emotions he set aside to live? And if he does recover them, will those feelings be an asset in his struggles, or a danger to him?

THE STATE OF EXTINCTION: the first installment in the **COALITON OF THE LIVING** trilogy of Mankind's battle against the plague of the Living Dead. As recounted by author **Robert Mathis Kurtz**.

www.severedpress.com

MACHINES OF THE DEAD

The dead are rising. The island of Manhattan is quarantined. Helicopters guard the airways while gunships patrol the waters. Bridges and tunnels are closed off. Anyone trying to leave is shot on sight.

For Jack Warren, survival is out of his hands when a group of armed military men kidnap him and his infected wife from their apartment and bring them to a bunker five stories below the city.

There, Jack learns a terrible truth and the reason why the dead have risen. With the help of a few others, he must find a way to escape the bunker and make it out of the city alive.

www.severedpress.com

JUDGMENT DAY

Dr. Jebediah Stone never believed in zombies until he had to shoot one. Now they're mutating into a new species, capable of reproducing, and the only defence is 'Blue Juice', a vaccine distilled from the blood of rare individuals immune to the zombie plague. Dr. Stone's missing wife is one of these unwilling 'munies', snatched by the military under the Judgment Day Protocol.It's a new, dangerous world filled with zombies, street gangs, and merciless Hunters desperate for a shot of blue juice. Has the world turned on mankind? Is Mortuus Venator the new ruler of earth?

www.severedpress.com

TIMOTHY
MARK TUFO

Timothy was not a good man in life and being undead did little to improve his disposition. Find out what a man trapped in his own mind will do to survive when he wakes up to find himself a zombie controlled by a self-aware virus.

www.severedpress.com

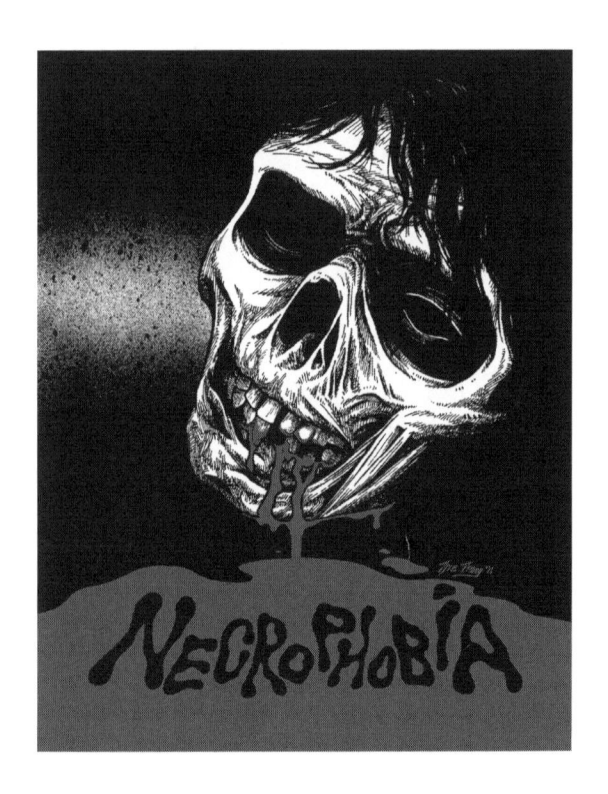

NECROPHOBIA

An ordinary summer's day.
The grass is green, the flowers are blooming. All is right with the world. Then the dead start rising. From cemetery and mortuary, funeral home and morgue, they flood into the streets until every town and city is infested with walking corpses, blank-eyed eating machines that exist to take down the living.
The world is a graveyard.
And when you have a family to protect, it's more than survival.
It's war.

www.severedpress.com

Printed in Great Britain
by Amazon.co.uk, Ltd.,
Marston Gate.